Gallow Falls

Alex Nye

GALLOW FALLS
Alex Nye
© Alex Nye 2023

Published by:
Fledgling Press Ltd,
1 Milton Road West,
Edinburgh,
EH15 1LA

Cover design by Graeme Clarke
www.graemeclarke.com

www.fledglingpress.co.uk

ISBN: 9781912280605

Printed and bound by:

Ashford Colour Press

For Joe, Micah and Martha

Gallows Hill

A clear high moon hangs like a lantern in the sky.

If you were an owl, or any other bird of prey, or simply an astronaut enjoying the view from a space station, you might hone in with your telescopic eye and see an area of dark forest below, the pointed tops of trees stretching for miles. And you might, in that carpet of dark green, eventually see a small clearing, where the trees make way for one tree in particular, an ancient oak, and beneath that oak, a square of turf, where a man is digging in his shirt sleeves.

He bends and grunts, shovelling the dark earth, one spadeful after the next, onto the bank accumulating above him.

It's an eerie scene, although there is no one nearby to witness it.

When an owl cries out, he pauses, stands, and takes note of the silent trees crowding close. The sigh of the wind stirs the branches, enough to freeze his blood.

Time stands still in that forest.

If we believed in curses, we might be inclined to believe that a curse has been brought to this place tonight. But the locals will tell you that the curse which hangs over Kilbroch is centuries old.

Kells Wood, and the scattered hamlet of farmsteads and houses around it, has borne this curse since the time when women were drowned in the pond at the bottom of the gorge – under the supervising eye of the laird of the castle – while crowds watched on with glee.

The night wears on, and the digging eventually stops, and at some point during the early hours the man places a body in the grave and shovels the earth back over as if he is planting a tree. One which will never bear fruit or life.

On a branch high above him an owl sits, twists its feathered head, and holds the image in its amber eye, focusing.

Its eyelids click like a camera shutter on the image, as if recording, taking note. Once. Twice.

The man works.

The owl watches.

And the moon has nothing to say.

Twelve Years Later

Laura has marked out the area for inspection. She's excited to see what will reveal itself. She has metal pegs pinned into the ground, and string stretched taut. She knows what she is looking for. At least, she thinks she does.

Around her the trees gather silently like ghostly witnesses. She has to kneel, and it makes her neck and shoulders ache with the effort. She is completely concentrated on the few inches of dust in front of her nose, as she scrapes away with her trowel. Very delicately, so as not to disturb too much of the soil, she probes away, millimetre by careful millimetre.

The light is fading and she knows she ought to give up for the evening, repair to her camper van, light the stove, make some tea. Maybe a pot noodle. But she can't help herself. She has to keep digging. Even without the support of her colleagues, she loves this task, and she focuses everything on what is in front of her, hoping for the big find.

Dusk creeps steadily closer, crawling from between the trees like a dark animal. She ignores it, because she has a job to do and doesn't have time to waste on fanciful notions. She's never allowed an isolated location to put her off before.

The name of the hill alone is enough to spook even the hardiest of archaeologists, amateur or otherwise.

Gallows Hill.

A gnarled old oak hangs just above her. Its branches stretch in a great twisting canopy; its spreading roots are beneath her feet, beneath the moss, beneath the area of her dig.

Scrape, scrape is the only sound, as not even a faint breeze stirs the trees tonight.

7

Something, she doesn't know what, makes the hairs prickle on the back of her neck, a creeping, tingling sensation that draws her attention. A faint breath, as of the earth itself exhaling. She looks up.

She's surrounded by trees. Kells Wood is not large, but large enough, isolating her from anyone else. There's no through road here. Anyone passing is heading for one of the converted cottages, or the castle. Or Broch Farm in the distance.

She feels watched. Deer maybe, lurking in the undergrowth. Silent watchers, keeping still for minutes at a time. She frowns slightly, peers deeper into the trees.

Gamekeepers inhabit these woods. There is at least one that she is aware of. Lives in the gamekeeper's cottage with his daughter, on the tree-lined avenue that heads up to the castle. They're a silent bunch, if her reading of *Lady Chatterley's Lover* is anything to go by. Not given to conversation. In all the books she's read, they creep about, watching people. She gets too much of her knowledge and experience from books rather than real life.

She tries to keep her thoughts light. No sense in spooking herself. After all, she's got to come back to this spot every day for the next three or four weeks. She can't afford to start imagining an unwanted intruder lurking about in the trees.

She was so excited when she got the funding for this project. She had studied aerial photographs of the area which hinted at the possibility of a Bronze Age broch. She pinpointed this particular hill as a likely spot, and is convinced she will find what she is looking for, despite the lack of encouragement from her colleagues at the university. The success of her funding application was a small victory, affirmation, if she needed it, that her work is meaningful. When you're relying on the renewal of six month contracts for your academic livelihood, that matters.

Laura's mind expands as she travels across the centuries,

those thousands of years and millennia, into deep time which isn't even deep time at all, really, but shallow time, if you weigh it up in the balance against the birth of the planet. This is the part of her job she loves, delving into the dark mists of the human imagination, accompanied by the verification of science.

Human time is so shallow, she thinks, so surface-deep, and buried under this earth are the ghostly remnants of skeletal structures that once stood tall, when this hill was bare rather than cloaked in trees as it is now. The building she is looking for is shaped like a cooling tower, where families lived protected within its circular walls, although of course only the base of those walls remain, buried by centuries of accumulated earth deposit.

This is what drives her, the way that the search can expand the mind, release the imagination into a time before, which inevitably makes you aware of the time after, and the time yet to come. Particularly poignant at the moment, she thinks, with the new rules we are living with, not to mention the current state of the world reminding us how fragile we all are.

She thinks, briefly, how people long ago thought of the trees and rocks as spirits, before they began to build permanent shelters and cultivate the land. What must it have been like to see the world through those ancient eyes, knowing so little about what things were really made of, and yet, perhaps, knowing so much more.

Rolling her shoulders to ease some of the tension from hours of stooping, she returns to her task.

It's then she hears the crack. A twig trodden on, breaking the silence, snapping the thread of her thoughts so she's back in the present, staring into the trees. They're so tightly packed in places that she can't make out anything clearly.

Then a shape, the outline of someone who seems to slip back behind the trunk of a tall pine.

9

She shouts across at them, 'Hey?' Partly to show she isn't afraid.

But whoever is there decides to run. Too fast for her to glimpse them in the dusk. They are merely a blur between the trees, disappearing into the depths.

She stands up, takes a few steps, but they're already too far away to see.

She doesn't know it but above her an owl watches, hidden by foliage, waiting for its hour of dusk to arrive.

She downs tools for the day and heads back to her camper van, taking the same narrow path through the bracken that she has taken every day since she got here.

Her sky-blue camper van sits in the lay-by below, where the road bends to the right. It's a single-track road with no markings. Tarmacked, but too narrow for more than one vehicle. She chose a spot in a wide passing-place, with enough space to park and set up camp. It's surrounded by trees, thick pine, and behind it, a double-rutted track made by tractor tyres cuts through into an unappealing stretch of woodland where no one goes.

She feels a little uneasy, and is annoyed with whoever disturbed her. If they had anything to say, they should have made their presence known and she'd have shown them what she was working on.

The sight of her van brings a smile to her face. Laura loves her van. It's home for now, containing all she needs to keep body and soul together. Seeing its sky-blue exterior and metal trim is like catching a glimpse of home lurking down there, waiting to embrace her with its warmth.

But as she draws nearer she can see there's something lopsided about the way it sits, something not quite right. Before unlocking it, she takes a look around. One of her tyres is flat. She stands back to look properly.

'Shit,' she murmurs.

She has a spare, but it's still a nuisance, and she's tired.

She just wants to relax. She bends to inspect it. Was it like that earlier? A slow puncture perhaps.

She goes to the back of the van where she keeps her jack, and the spare. She wants to get this fixed before the light fades.

As she works, her head bent to the wheel, her sense of unease grows. She looks around her nervously. What she doesn't want is for a pair of boots, male boots, to suddenly appear within her line of vision out of the surrounding forest.

She works on, trying to ignore a mounting sense of dread.

Should she trust her instincts and get the hell out of there?

But first she needs to fix this tyre.

When at last it's done, she flings her tools down and takes a long look about her. Shadows are gathering between the dark corridors of pine.

Scooping everything up and replacing it in the boot, she climbs into her camper van and locks the doors with a huge sense of relief.

She tries to settle down for the night, lights her gas-burner, places the small camping kettle on it, filled with water.

The night stretches ahead of her. The idea of being parked up here on the edge of Kells Wood seems suddenly a little disconcerting. She has good locks though, and a car alarm. She's sure she'll be fine.

Glenwhilk

Dawn breaks over Kells Wood. Its luminous glow spreads over the scattered homesteads of Kilbroch, and the early risers stir from their beds and make a start on the day.

The summer months are a good time for these residents. The winters are long and bleak, with darkness falling early and daylight hours short, so when the season changes, they revel in the length of the days.

Callum MacGarvey is splitting timber inside the open barn where he keeps his tools. He spends a lot of his time doing this. The whine of the buzz saw as it slices through the logs is satisfying. He knows his trees. Beech burns well, pine not so good: it sparks and crackles like an exploding firework so he never gathers pine. Birch is a slow burner. A bit like me really, he thinks. He spends a lot of his time exploring the conifer plantations on the land around here. He knows all about them, how they were planted in the 1780s, how European Larch, Scots Pine and Norway Spruce arrived in the 1830s and 40s. But now it's mostly Sitka spruce, native to the west coast of North America, and useless for burning as far as he is concerned.

He's lived at Glenwhilk for five years now, since his life collapsed. He doesn't look back often. It's not a good idea to dwell on the past. Everyone knows that, especially a man like him.

His work shed and hangar sits just below the farm, not far from his cottage. He has a van and a trailer, and an agreement with Strabane up at the castle. He clears bits of neglected woodland that lie far from the main roads, with the blessing of the local estate, fills his hangar, splits it, and sells it by the ton, giving Strabane a third of all the profits from whatever he sells. He mainly clears birch and larch, but is happier with beech or any other hardwood because he gets more money for it, although it takes longer to season.

Ear defenders clamped to his ears, he is lost in his own world as the splitter cuts through each log, dividing it in half and then in half again. It's almost a dance in his mind, a balletic movement that requires his complete concentration.

When he was out gathering timber earlier, he glimpsed Ruthie again. Silent Ruthie, who never speaks, just staring at him through the trees. He nodded, but she didn't acknowledge him. She never does. He doesn't know what that's all about. People are odd, especially around here, but as long as he keeps his head down, he doesn't mind.

He just wants a quiet life, that's all. To forget about the past, and nurse his grievances. Of those, he has many.

When a red Mini turns up in his front yard, Callum is completely unaware. He works on, cocooned by the noise of the machinery.

Joan Metcalfe climbs out of the driver's seat, takes her stick out of the boot and heads purposefully past his cottage and towards the hangar, drawn by the deafening whine of the saw.

He is forced to work with his back to the entrance, which he doesn't like, so he's not aware of her until she moves into his line of vision.

He silences the machine, startled.

'Joan? Don't creep up on me like that.'

'Sorry. I'm interrupting.'

'It's okay. I could do with a break anyway. What can I do for you?'

'I was just passing.'

'What would I do without you keeping an eye on me, eh?'

'I'm just an old woman, looking for company.'

He laughs as he walks with her towards the door of his cottage.

'What kind of a state will I find this place in today?' she asks him.

'No worse than usual. Tea?'

'Please.'

Joan has become an old friend of his since he took up the lease at Glenwhilk. They had an inauspicious start to their friendship, beginning when he ran into her dog on the way back from Dunbrochan late one summer's evening. It was dusk at the time and the dog was loose on the road. He caught it side-on and felt the impact. When he got out to investigate, it lay on the roadside, blood trickling from its jaw, panting up at him. He lifted the poor thing into his van, and drove it to Joan's villa, the house with all the tumbling plants in the front garden.

He had knocked on her door and held up the dog in his arms, watched Joan bend and cry. It broke her heart, but oddly enough, she forgave him. When he asked her why, her answer was simple.

'You could have driven on, left the dog at the side of the road,' Joan told him. 'But you didn't. Instead, you decided to tell the truth.'

'And for that, you reward me with your friendship?'

'It's not everyone who tells the truth,' she told him.

Callum had sighed. 'Much good it does me.'

And that was the sore truth of it.

So, they'd become good friends since then, despite Joan's sorrow and grief at losing her canine companion. She'd recognised Callum's guilt, his need for forgiveness and she'd opened her door to him.

God knows, he'd needed a friend at the time.

That was five years ago. Now they are still friends, better with each passing year.

He leads her into the cottage now, and they sit at the

kitchen table, Joan tutting at the mess as she lifts yesterday's newspaper from the only spare chair.

'Sorry,' he begins to fuss.

'Oh, don't fuss, man. You know it makes no difference. You can't hide anything from me.'

He looks at her and smiles. There is something unnerving about Joan's brusqueness, her direct attitude which never pulls any punches. He likes her for it.

She watches him while he fills the kettle at the tap. 'You heard about what happened to Laura?' she asks suddenly.

'Laura?'

'Young archaeologist lassie, digging up on Gallows Hill,' Joan says.

'Jesus, woman, you know everyone. Even when they've only been here five minutes.'

She nods and winks. 'I make it my mission in life.'

'Anyway, what happened to her?' He looks alarmed now, wondering if it's bad news. Joan has always maintained this place is cursed and he sometimes wonders if she's not far wrong. He came here to hide, but bad news seems to follow him around.

'Her vehicle was attacked up in the woods.' She waits for a reaction and then adds, 'She was sleeping in it at the time.'

'Jesus!'

'She's fine,' Joan adds quickly. 'Someone tried to frighten her, that's all, but she's pretty shaken up.'

'What happened?'

'They smashed a side window. Ran away before she could catch sight of them, but gave her a bad fright, I can tell you.'

Not much in the way of crime ever happens in Kilbroch – the odd bit of poaching – so anything like this is noteworthy.

'Unusual,' he says, as he brings two steaming mugs to the table. People even leave their barns and garages

15

unlocked around here. 'Kids, d'you think, messing about, trying to frighten her?'

Joan shrugs. 'Your guess is as good as… Odd, though, don't you think?'

'Has she cancelled the dig?' he asks.

'Cancelled it?' Joan shakes her head. 'Seems to be made of sterner stuff than that.'

She sips her tea thoughtfully. 'Anyway, she's moved her camper van up to the castle, parked it in the courtyard.'

'Perhaps she feels safer there.'

'Perhaps.'

Joan studies him for a moment. 'I came here with a proposition actually.'

He raises his eyebrows comically. 'Oh yes?'

Ignoring him, she continues. He senses it's difficult for her to talk about the next bit. She takes her time, builds up her courage to speak.

'I want to know what happened to my grandson.'

Callum freezes for a moment, his cup halfway to his lips. He never met Joan's grandson but he'd heard rumours that he ran away from home twelve years ago, before Callum took up the lease at Glenwhilk. It was reported to the police at the time and there was some kind of investigation, so he'd heard, but no one could trace the missing teenager. And from what Joan has said to him over the years, they hadn't tried very hard.

He lowers his eyes out of respect, a sympathetic nod to her grief.

'I'm sorry, Joan,' he begins.

'Oh, save your platitudes. They're no use to me. That's not what I'm after.'

He doesn't say, but he's heard people talk about it in hushed voices, malicious mutterings laced with a hint of accusation. The boy who disappeared, who ran away from home. Why did he run? What was so awful about his home

16

life that he chose to pack a rucksack one day, walk out of Kilbroch and never come back? That's what people hinted at.

Callum listened with half an ear, but preferred to say nothing. Anything could have happened to the boy since, a sixteen-year-old out in the world by himself. He could have wound up homeless on the streets of any city in the UK. In any event, Robbie MacBride became just one more missing person. Posters showing his face from his last school portrait had been taped to the doors of the local supermarkets in Dunbrochan, and throughout Scotland, but people go missing all the time, and they don't always want to be found.

He waits for her to continue.

'I want you to find my grandson. I want you to tell me what happened to him.'

Callum stares at her. 'How can I do that?'

'I know it's a big ask.'

'I thought the police told you what happened to him? He ran away.'

She scoffs. 'Oh, the police. Don't get me started. You, of all people, ought to know…'

'Okay, okay,' he nods, not wanting her to continue.

'So?' she holds his gaze for a moment.

'It's not so easy.'

'I realise that.'

He contemplates the scars on the table, flaws that run through the wood. 'Why now?'

'Because.' She pauses for a moment, and he can feel the stubborn set of her shoulders and the look in her eye. He knows Joan well enough to predict that she won't take no for an answer. 'I'm fed up with the lies people tell.'

She doesn't explain who she means by 'people'.

'It was before my time.'

'Yes, before you moved to the area which will give you a fresh perspective.'

'I'm not a detective.'

'You used to be.'

'I left the force nearly ten years ago.'

'And I'm not a biology teacher anymore, but... once a teacher, always a teacher.'

He smiles. 'That's not quite the same thing, Joan, and you know it isn't.'

'Isn't it? I'll pay you, if money's your concern.'

'It's not that,' he replies.

'What is it then?'

Joan is so persistent. He can imagine her being ruthless with her own pupils twenty or thirty years ago. Formidable, even.

'Fear?' she says now, trying to catch his eye. 'Because I know what that's like. I know about fear. Fear of failure, of loss. I've lost so much I've nothing left to lose.'

He looks at her quickly. They have so much in common, he and Joan. Perhaps that's why they get on so well. Life's experiences have left them raw.

'It's been twelve years,' Callum says. 'How do you expect me to find anything after all that time?'

'I trust you.'

'It'll take more than trust to find out what happened to your grandson. What about the police? Didn't they question people at the time, search the area?'

Joan looks scathing. 'They were useless,' she says dismissively. 'Didn't take it seriously. When they found out he was gay, their attitude changed remarkably.'

Callum stares at her. 'What difference...?'

'What difference did that make? To the investigation? It made all the difference in the world. They said he'd gone off with someone, that lots of young boys like him run away. By choice.'

He thinks for a moment. 'Did his father know he was gay?'

Callum knows Owen, and can't imagine him dealing with his son's sexuality in a calm and reasonable manner.

Joan laughs. 'It was obvious. To me and his mother at least. Owen never accepted it. Not sure it even occurred to him. Fathers can be like that, you know. And things were different back then. It wasn't so easy to admit you were gay. I mean, now people are more open and accepting, but then? Forget it!'

'You think the police didn't take his disappearance seriously for that reason?'

'Well it wouldn't be a first, would it?'

He acknowledges this quietly. He can feel her bitterness and he understands it, having his own burdens to carry about police incompetence and the damage it can cause.

'They kept looking for a couple of years, but when nothing turned up, no clues, they gave up.'

They sit in silence for a moment.

'He's still here, Callum. I know it.'

Callum looks at Joan across the table and senses the landscape breathing outside, exhaling like a living being, the pine-scented hills and the endless miles of forest and plantation beyond.

'And if I find nothing?' Callum says.

'Then at least you and I will have tried.'

He thinks about it for a moment, without committing himself.

'There's always been something malign hanging over this place. Don't you feel it sometimes? A curse.'

'Why don't you leave, then?' Callum asks.

'God knows. Ruthie is still here. And Robbie.'

'But I thought?'

She cuts him off. 'Robbie is still here.'

Callum shakes his head. He can't digest all of this right

now. He can't do this. He's been out of the force for more than ten years, and he has no intention of going back.

'I'm sorry.'

She glares at him and he feels her disappointment. Nothing new there. He's used to disappointing people.

But Joan hasn't finished with him yet.

'Why *did* you leave the force?' she asks now. 'What happened?'

'D'you really want to know?'

'Yes, I really want to know.'

'I didn't leave voluntarily. I was hounded out.'

The expression on his face makes it clear he is not yet ready to talk about it, so she nods and smiles.

'Well, seems we've all got things to hide.'

He gives her a quick double-take. 'So our visiting archaeologist will carry on with the dig then?' he asks.

'Laura? Yes, she'll carry on. Not sure I'd fancy camping up there myself though. It's called Gallows Hill for a reason.'

'Aye?'

'There's an atmosphere. There have been stories about it over the years.'

'What kind of stories?'

'Well,' she smiles to herself. 'Two boys camping up there reckoned they saw a body hanging from one of the branches one night. Terrified the wits out of them. Left their tent and ran home, back to Dunbrochan. Came back the next morning to collect their tent, no sign of a body.'

Callum laughs. 'Too much of the old whacky baccy, perhaps?'

'Perhaps,' she laughs. 'But it's not those kinds of ghosts I'm looking for. I want to find my grandson.'

'I wish I could help, Joan.'

She nods, and gets up to leave.

As he watches her cross to her Mini, he feels the

unspoken words 'you owe me' drifting like smoke across the yard towards him.

Ruthie

Back in her own house Joan empties the shopping from her boot, stacks it in her kitchen cupboards and moves through to her conservatory. She sits down at the table. It's the warmest room in the house. The sun pours through the long glass windows on a day like this, and she likes to sit here and paint, surrounded by plants.

A jug full of used paint brushes sits in front of her. She pushes it aside and props her chin in the palm of her hand, stares out at the softly retreating fields beyond. She remembers when two small grandchildren sat at this table with her, drawing. She smiles at the memory.

But even then there were dark clouds building on the horizon, threatening their happiness. She never quite knew what it was, but things were out of kilter. Something was always wrong between her daughter and... that man. Her son-in-law, Owen.

And now look at what has happened to us all, she thinks.

She can't afford to grow melancholy. She hauls herself up, walks through into the kitchen to make something to eat. Life must go on, as it has done all these years.

Callum stands at the window of his cottage, staring out at the yard where his battered red van sits, covered in dust. Off to the right, the sun glints off the corrugated roof of his work shed where he keeps his tools and where piles of logs lie heaped high and steaming in the cool shadows, ready for delivery.

He's chosen an odd life and he knows it. He's chosen a life of retreat and seclusion, hiding away from his past, trying to lay his own ghosts. He likes Joan, he's close to her, but he doesn't want to become entangled in someone else's tragedy. He's intrigued, yes, but he pulls away at the thought of getting involved. Joan has her sorrows, but he has his own to contend with.

'Why me?' he had asked her, 'And why now?'

'Because you're here,' she replied. 'And you were a good detective.'

'Was.'

'And I think someone's trying to hide something.'

He hadn't asked who. He hadn't pursued it any further than that, or encouraged her to talk more. As she had so rightly guessed, he was afraid, and fear dampens curiosity. He has no desire to know, no desire to probe, and certainly no desire to become a private investigator. He just wants a quiet life, away from the media circus of the past, atoning for his sins, seeking forgiveness in his own way.

He wonders for a moment why that young woman – Laura, Joan said her name was – wants to carry out that dig, all on her own, without the support of her colleagues. He can't help being curious. He shakes the thought away. All he wants is to exist here in his quiet secluded cottage, watch TV in the evenings, unscrew the cap of the whisky bottle and seek solace on his sofa without thinking – especially about the past.

As he crosses the yard on his way to the work shed he notices a figure on the brow of the hill, outlined by the light behind her. A young woman, walking quietly through the fields, solitary as usual. He raises his hand in a wave, but she doesn't wave back. Probably too far away.

Ruthie.

What must it have been like to lose her brother all those years ago?

Callum prefers to mind his own business, but Ruthie is a mystery, for sure. She never speaks. She just wanders the fields and woods hereabouts, avoiding people, something she is uncannily good at. Right now, it looks as if she is heading towards the chapel and the gorge just beyond it.

Dark-haired, dark-eyed, kind of sad-looking. And what's particularly sad is that a distance has grown between Joan and her granddaughter. Joan never visits the house where Ruthie lives. And likewise, Ruthie never visits her grandmother. Relatives who live within two miles of each other and yet never care to darken one another's doors. What was all that about? Joan is angry with her son-in-law, Owen, that much is obvious. But why?

He walks into the shadow of his work shed, the entrance open to the fields and the sky. He likes the height of this space, almost cathedral-like. Birds live in the rafters, and the corrugated roof creaks as the sun hits it. He puts on his ear defenders, throws the switch and loses himself in the act of dividing the logs, surrounded by his circle of noise as it radiates outwards. His arms and wrists ache with the effort, but he's used to it, and he enjoys taking his anger out on the wood. Better than venting it on human beings at any rate, those closest to him, those he loved and left.

He tries very hard to lose himself in his work, dismissing all thoughts of Joan and her strange request. She's a tough old character, that's for sure, but she's not going to get him involved. The past is the past, he told her, and that's where it should belong.

'This isn't the past, Callum,' she'd insisted. 'It isn't over yet. It hasn't even begun.'

In his experience, people should always look forward. There's no sense in looking back, even for him. Regrets follow everyone but if you give them too much licence, too much room in your head, they become a disease. Walk with your eyes on the horizon all the time, never glancing back over your shoulder. Despite himself, he knows how hollow and empty those intentions are. So easy to say, so much harder to put into practice.

As he works, his thoughts inevitably lead back to Joan, running their conversation through his head. Surely the police would have explored all avenues at the time, he thinks, investigated every possibility? As Callum knows, when a young person chooses to disappear, they can stay that way forever if they want, and more often than not, the mystery is never solved. Families go on hoping and grieving for years, and often die not knowing the truth. That's the sad reality of it. He doesn't know which is worse. God knows, he was glad to give all that up, watching other people's pain and suffering and failing to help, and if Joan thinks she can persuade him otherwise, she has another think coming.

Kells Chapel

She heads down the slope towards Kells Chapel. For some, the loneliness of the woods would be overwhelming, but not for Ruthie. It's all she's ever known. Birds flit and call to one another and a wind sets up a stir in the highest branches as last year's leaves crunch underfoot.

She stands still for a moment, and listens. If she peers between a gap in the trees, she can see Ben Ledi rising above the sweep of forest and green hills in the distance, its peak no longer dusted with snow. And behind her is the sound of water flowing through the gorge. It roars after winter rains, but is quieter during the summer months, always there, a constant in her life. At the moment the land is dotted with clouds of yellow broom and gorse with sheep grazing in between.

Ruthie saw her grandmother earlier, visiting that man in his cottage, up at Glenwhilk. She misses nothing. They think she keeps herself apart and separate, which she does, but she still knows exactly what is going on, who leaves their house at what time.

She knows they're good friends, Callum and Joan.

She never visits her grandmother, although she's seen the older woman watching her from time to time across the fields, and she knows where she lives of course. Joan will stop her car, wind down the window and wait, hopefully, but Ruthie is like a wild animal. She never draws near. She keeps her distance from everyone.

She was thirteen when her brother disappeared. She had always been a strange one, but after he went missing she lost her voice completely. She cut herself off, lived in a closed-down universe where she didn't need to communicate and didn't have to confront the possibilities and complexities of life, walked alone in the only landscape she has ever known, the one she once shared with her brother.

She's close to nature. She watches the birds, spends whole days outside, unobserved by human eyes, sitting in strange places, little invisible hideouts she has built for herself where no one intrudes because no one knows they are there. Her father is the gamekeeper so why should she have any fear of discovery? He's the only one who knows this forest as well as she does. The family up at the castle, who own Kells Wood, have no kind of intimacy with the land. The land doesn't really belong to them despite their ancestry, Ruthie knows that. If these woods belong to anyone, they belong to Ruthie and Owen. Just as they once belonged to Robbie. Before he went away.

When Ruthie was a teenager, she somehow managed to avoid the scrutiny of social workers. She kept her head down, did her work when she was asked and avoided school the rest of the time. She'd always hated the big modern building with its echoing corridors and clanging bells and her parents had assisted her in the game of truancy and avoidance, especially after Robbie went missing. They didn't force her to attend when they saw how unhappy it made her. Besides, they had other more pressing matters on their mind at the time.

She remembers the old days, being bullied in the school corridors, back when Robbie was still around to stick up for her. He'd be twenty-eight now. If he appeared along the path up ahead of her, would she recognise him?

She'd recognise him alright. She'd know him anywhere. Her almost-twin despite the three years between them.

Robbie.

Her mind rolls back the years.

Remembering the school bus dropping them at the end of the road, and she and Robbie walking home together, up the lane, seeing the grey smoke above the roof of the cottage. Laughing. She can smell the smoke drifting in the air towards them. She stops at that point. The memory goes no further. It's a soft, hazy vision. And that's the way it must remain.

People think she must be lonely, spending all of her time alone in Kells Wood, but she loves it here. She's never lonely as long as there are no people to remind her of what she might be missing. She is a silent presence in Kells Wood, on Gallows Hill. Along the glen and in the gorge she picks her way silently, seeing things others miss, listening, taking it in, absorbing nature.

She keeps ferrets and stoats in her back garden, and up until recently had a dog who followed her everywhere. The loss of Buddy was massive, but she lives close enough to nature to know that's the way it works. Life begins and it ends. And there is a bit in between which we call our life, and that is a journey we must try to enjoy because it won't last forever. Ruthie understands this, though she never expresses it in words anymore. Words have long since fled, to be replaced by a silence that asks nothing of her.

She just has to avoid thinking too much.

Outside, she lives for the moment, but once enclosed by walls, echoes of the past can float up from the depths without warning. She closes her eyes now and the voices come. The memories. The flashbacks. The shouting.

She remembers being a child in the cottage where they grew up, where she still lives with her father. She remembers standing in the hallway, and seeing her parents fight.

'Our own son!' Her mother's pained voice, shrieking.

'Keep your voice down. She'll hear you.'

'He was my son and I loved him.'

'I loved him too.'

Then Ruthie appearing silently in the doorway.

'Alright Ruthie?'

The anger exploding from both her parents. The anger, the pain and the rage.

Then a blank. Nothing after that. She remembers nothing.

Except that Robbie isn't with them anymore. And she can't even remember his face, even when she looks at the old photos. Her dad put them all away, eventually, didn't want to look at them.

Up ahead she can see the old chapel between the trees in the distance. It tops the ridge of the gorge, its graveyard perched above the drop where you can hear the tumble of the burn below.

When a tall figure she hadn't noticed before stands upright on the other side of the crumbling stone wall, Ruthie stops. It looks as if he was bending to one of the graves. She recognises him as George Strabane from the castle, her father's employer, and wonders at seeing him here. He never strolls about Kilbroch and Kells Wood, despite owning most of it. He's mainly to be seen in the driver's seat of a Land Rover, passing through. She wonders what he's doing here.

She expects him to turn, but he doesn't. Instead of heading for the main gate, he disappears behind the chapel.

Ruthie advances cautiously. She likes to wander here, between the moss-covered graves. It's a peaceful place, the way it merges with the moor beyond, its walls crumbling into soft mossy decay. When she reaches the old chapel, she wanders past the porch and turns the corner to see if George Strabane is still there. There's no sign of him. There's a steep path down to the gorge from here, but he'd have had to scramble over the wall to access it.

Strange man, she thinks. They think I'm strange, but he's stranger still.

She finds a spot on a flat tombstone shaped like a coffee

table, in the shelter of the building, and sits herself down. Takes stock.

A gnarled old oak guards the edge of the graveyard, next to the tumbling wall, which barely keeps the hillside at bay. At her back the chapel sits in its perpetual silence, forever closed to the public. The family at the castle prefer to keep it that way. They will open it up for weddings, to raise cash, and they will bury the one or two locals who live in Kilbroch, if a family insist upon it and have no other plans for cremation over at Falkirk, but other than that, the place remains largely obsolete, a closed book, with wire mesh guarding the top half of the doors enclosing the front porch. Pigeons roost on its apex and in the rafters if they can find their way in. Soft grey feathers float to the ground.

Ruthie sits quietly, and listens. Because she is largely silent these days, sounds have become more important to her over the years, the melancholy cry of curlews, the fat burble of pigeons, a rook. The water talking in the gorge, communicating to her its love of life.

Her own mother's grave lies in this burial ground, below the oak, next to the crumbling wall. Mosses cover most of the headstones, but Lydia MacBride's stone remains bare.

Ruthie doesn't think of her mother when she sits here, though. She thinks of other things. She thinks of her estranged grandmother turning up in her red Mini at that man's cottage, Glenwhilk. Callum, she thinks his name is. And she thinks of her clambering out of the car, leaning on her stick, and walking with him to his cottage. She wonders what they have in common, and what they have to talk about.

There is too much talking in the world, as far as Ruthie is concerned. Too many words. What does anyone have to say that can possibly be important or relevant?

There is nothing to say. She realised that a long time ago.

Standing to leave, she notices a speckle of blue and white at the foot of her mother's headstone. She steps between the graves, bends down to look. A few gathered wildflowers, tied with a bit of gardening twine. She touches the delicate flower heads with one finger. Other people lay flowers for her mother then, even after all these years, and it occurs to her now that she might have caught George Strabane in the act of putting them there, absurd as that might seem.

Her gaze remains impassive, inscrutable. Whatever she thinks, she rarely shares.

She walks on until she reaches the gamekeeper's cottage where she was born, and where she still lives, despite the terrible things that have happened and the grief that has visited their door. Sturdy brick house with crow-stepped gables, a homemade lean-to conservatory at the back, attached to the kitchen, which catches the sun. Her father put it together from the remains of a metal-framed greenhouse he salvaged. There's smoke coming from the chimney and Owen is standing out in the yard.

'Where've you been, Ruthie?' he tries, smiling as she passes him.

When she makes no reply, he sighs, giving up, as he gives up every day.

The Gamekeeper's Cottage

Late afternoon sunlight finds its way into the entrance of his work shed. His pile of split logs has grown. He's only got a few orders at the moment, but in Scotland people still want their log burners, even during the summer months. A fire at night, until the weather gets really hot, is what most people like around here.

He's trying not to think about Joan and what she asked of him, but he doesn't quite succeed.

Her son-in-law, Owen, is a friend of Callum's, up to a point. They pass the time of day together, chat, share news, but rarely about their own personal lives. Owen never mentions his son or his wife, or the fact his daughter is mostly silent. He likes Callum because he gives Owen space, and doesn't pry. He accepts people for what they are without asking questions. Not bad for an ex-detective. And certainly not typical.

Callum drives the van along the lane, past Joan's house, intending to scope out another bit of woodland in need of a tidy up, but stops when he catches sight of the gamekeeper's cottage, its chimneys appearing through the trees.

It sits at the bottom of a tree-lined private road that sweeps on up to the castle, the turrets and central tower of which you can't quite see from this angle. Too many trees.

Owen is in the front yard, so he winds the window down and gives his old friend a thumbs up.

'Owen!'

'Callum,' the gamekeeper replies. Their usual terse greeting.

'How you doing?'

'Not bad. You?'

'Same. What you up to?' Callum asks him.

'What does it look like?' He throws down his tools and gives Callum a grin. 'Drink?'

'Thought you'd never ask.'

As he follows his friend into the hallway, he admires its solidity as usual. An old grandfather clock stands against one wall, immovable, as if it was there before the house was built. Callum sometimes imagines the grandfather clock came first and the house was built around it afterwards, the way a house might be built around an old tree. He glances at it and thinks it's a shame that Owen never bothers to wind it anymore. What use is a grandfather clock if it no longer speaks, if it no longer marks and measures time? It's like robbing an old man of his voice.

There's no sign of Ruthie. She's disappeared inside, upstairs somewhere, making herself scarce as usual.

'Ruthie?' Owen calls up the stairs hopefully. 'We've got company.'

No response.

Callum makes no comment, because he knows how it is.

They've been friends since Callum moved here five years ago. Owen is taciturn, quiet, but then so is Callum, and neither of them ask too many questions. At least Callum doesn't, usually.

Thinking of Joan's visit earlier, he feels a shadow of guilt edging his discomfort, and makes an effort to hide his thoughts.

Owen is a very private man. They live within a two mile radius of each other, but they respect one another's privacy.

He watches his friend open a kitchen cupboard, take out a bottle of whisky, pour his friend a shot, but abstain himself.

'Go on, Owen,' Callum says. 'You can't be bartender all the time.'

Owen shakes his head.

'You make me feel bad,' Callum says, but he lifts the glass to his lips all the same, knowing he can't resist.

'Don't worry about it, man. We all have our vices,' Owen smirks as he levers off the top of a non-alcoholic beer, takes a sip.

Callum knows that his friend doesn't drink much, but always keeps a bottle handy for when his pal turns up. It's a little routine that has crept into their lives over recent years.

'Tell me, Owen, why don't you ever partake of the amber nectar?'

Owen shrugs. 'Fear of losing control, I suppose.'

'And what would happen if you did?'

Owen laughs, but doesn't reply.

Both men are quiet for a while, as they often are.

'It's a good life, this, isn't it?' Callum murmurs, sipping his whisky.

'The woods, you mean?'

'Aye, the woods and the countryside.'

Owen stares ahead of him where he can make out the trees at the bottom of his garden. 'D'you ever miss Glasgow?'

Callum laughs and shakes his head. 'Never.'

'I could never hack it in a city,' Owen adds. 'Wouldn't last five minutes in an office.'

Callum doesn't doubt it. He likes Owen. He went to school with boys like him, boys who couldn't bear to be inside and always wanted to be outdoors, fishing or hiking. But there weren't too many gamekeeper jobs available in Glasgow. Some of them went into the Parks Department, ended up working for the Council, tending municipal garden spaces, places like the Botanics if they were lucky. It helped if you were a Protestant, of course, not that anyone was supposed to mention that. One or two ended up in prison. It was that kind of school.

He can see that Owen wouldn't have been happy in Pollok, where Callum grew up.

'You heard about Laura?'

'Laura?'

'Young archaeologist lassie, digging up at Gallows Hill?'

'No. What?'

'Her camper van was broken into, in the night. Terrified the life out of her. Opted to sleep up at the castle instead.'

'And Strabane's alright with that?' Owen says.

Callum shrugs. 'Appears to be.'

There is a slight pause.

'She's alright, by the way. Laura. It was just a scare. Whoever did it, didn't follow through.'

'Well, that's a relief.'

Callum lifts his whisky and watches it swirl in his glass, leaving an oily bead up the side.

Owen is thoughtful for a moment, shaking his head.

'Youngsters, d'you think?'

'Hope so. Hope it's nothing more sinister than that. Even so.'

Callum finds himself watching his old friend curiously. 'Joan came to see me earlier.'

'Oh yeah. How is the old bird?'

'She's okay. Still wants some answers though.'

'Answers?' A look of pain crosses his friend's face, as he struggles with his emotions. There is a long silence, then Owen's expression changes as a wave of realisation washes through him. 'Don't open that door, Callum,' he warns.

'I'm sorry, mate. It's just…'

'D'you think I haven't wondered what happened to him? D'you think I haven't lived with it every day of my life?'

Callum begins to apologise, and hates himself for stirring up the past. God knows, he'd hate it if his own past was raked through.

35

'It's been twelve years,' Owen tells him. 'And in all that time, I've had to learn to live with it. With what it did to my family.'

'I know it's hard.'

'You don't know,' Owen mutters, then glances towards the hallway. 'He was my son.'

Callum follows his gaze, into the darkness, but there's no one there. If Ruthie is lurking on the stairs, listening, she doesn't make herself known.

'We all need to be forgiven for something, Owen.'

Owen stares at him, uncomprehending. 'Why d'you say that?'

Callum holds his breath, doesn't answer, and Owen doesn't pursue it. Instead he asks, 'And what have you ever done that you need to be forgiven for?'

He thinks of his wife and son, now estranged. He thinks of how his career ended, punished for telling the truth.

'Plenty,' Callum says. 'Plenty.'

'What has that old witch been saying?'

'Nothing.'

'Oh, come on. I know the two of you are thick as thieves.'

He sips his whisky, playing for time, wishing he'd kept his mouth shut. He can feel Owen's eyes on him, watching.

'You're just like the rest of them, then. Nosy bastards down in the village, always suspecting the worst, trying to get off on someone else's tragedy and suffering. Ambulance-chasers, every last one of 'em.'

'Hey, take it easy,' Callum urges him.

'I lost my son. What d'you expect me to say?'

'I'm sorry. I didn't mean...'

Callum looks up to see Ruthie standing in the doorway, the darkened hall behind her, wearing a faint look of bewilderment. Wide-eyed, haunted.

'Ruthie.' He greets her with a nod and a smile, but she's

as non-communicative as ever. Nods in return, with the barest acknowledgement.

Callum gets up to leave. He knows he's gone too far.

Owen doesn't usually say this much. He's largely reticent and reserved. Tight-lipped. Guarded, even. He hopes he hasn't messed things up.

'I'll leave you to it,' he says now.

'Aye, do that.' Owen remains seated. 'Tell Joan I was asking after her,' he says sarcastically from his chair.

Callum pauses, but doesn't turn around. He's aware that Owen and Joan haven't spoken to one another in years.

As he drives away from the gamekeeper's cottage, he feels the shadow of their past trauma trailing him. He doesn't understand what the conflict is all about, between Joan and her son-in-law, but he's pretty sure he's going to find out.

As he turns left at the bottom of the drive and takes the narrow road between the tall hedgerows, he hopes he hasn't just lost a friend. He curses himself for his lack of sensitivity, blundering in, opening his mouth before thinking. He ought to have learned his lesson by now. Steer clear of people, don't get involved, and certainly don't be drawn into Joan's quest for closure. There can be no mileage in that route, despite his own curiosity about the case. If there are any answers to be found, he is not the one to find them, and he can imagine his friend Owen wouldn't thank him for trying.

Glentye

It's another quiet night in Kilbroch.

The single-track road winds its way between Kells Wood on one side and sloping farmland on the other, broken by the occasional line of crumbling stone wall. A soft grey dusk paints the trees with lilac shades that edge towards gold and violet. The pencil-thin trunks of the birches stripe the carpet of moss-green with their shadows. A more tranquil scene would be hard to imagine. The scattered inhabitants appreciate that tranquillity and only some of them are cognisant of the stories of menace that pervade the history of this glen. Joan is one of them. As a teacher, she makes it her business to continually learn. Every day is a school day, her daughter used to joke.

She's a sensible, level-headed woman, but grief can do strange things to a person's sanity. For instance, she's noticed things moving about the house lately, objects misplaced.

'You're an old woman,' a friend warned her. 'You'll forget where you left things.'

'I'm not that old!' she retorted.

'Oh, come on, Joan. I walk into a room these days and I can't even remember what I'm doing there. I'm not unique. You'll be the same.'

Joan didn't pursue the matter.

She lies now, in the dark, listening. The carpets on her stairs are thick, the windows insulated and warm, the house unbearably comfortable at times, but she hears it. One creaking stair, and the sigh of a breath.

She lies there, paralysed, unable to move as the door creaks open. There is a smell, a strange sickly-sweet odour as of something softly rotting. She holds her breath, doesn't move her head. She wants to move, she wants to cry out, but she can't. Something pins her in place, so that she can't even turn her head sideways on the pillow.

Then there's a sound, soft footsteps crossing the room, a shadow near the bed where she lies, unable to move. There is someone there, watching her. She can feel their eyes upon her. And then they move away, towards the dressing-table. She hears the clank of metal against glass, something being laid to rest, moved. Soft footsteps retreating at last to the open door, back out onto the landing. And still Joan is unable to move, as if some terrible force paralyses her, robbing her of the ability to stir a muscle.

Then a sudden crash, or a door slamming, something like it, and Joan is instantly awake. She sits on the edge of the bed for a minute, gathering her thoughts. Her breathing is shallow and she gasps for air. Sweat stands out on her forehead. She begins to understand that she has just woken from a lucid dream, so powerfully life-like, it's as if she was awake.

She thinks again of that sound, like a distant door slamming. Did she imagine it, was it part of her nightmare? She struggles across to the door, leans over the bannister at the top of the landing, and calls out a name. 'Robbie?'

There's a world of fearful hope and longing in that cry.

There's no movement below, but she proceeds cautiously down the carpeted stairs, leaning heavily on the wooden rail.

'Robbie?' she tries again, searching the shadows. Moonlight reaches into the hallway from the front door, which has been left wide open. She stands on the threshold, looking out.

She shouts his name out into the darkness, but only silence laps towards her.

Turning back into the house, she can see the hall table beside the door, the bowl with her keys in it.

'Not the best place to keep them,' Callum has always warned her, but she never listens.

Softly closing the door behind her, she stands still now, listening to the silence in the house, wondering. A silence so complete she hears one tiny drip from the kitchen tap landing in the stainless steel sink. If she strains her ears any further she feels as if she'd hear the granules shifting in a bag of sugar in the cupboard. Layers of domestic silence, a click from a radiator that sounds like the claw of a rodent.

And once again she calls out hopefully, 'Robbie?'

She's still half-asleep, but even in her waking moments she knows this is madness. Grief drives her to the edge of surreal imaginings which she never shares with others. Callum thinks she is a sensible old woman, but she doesn't tell him what she thinks she hears at night. She doesn't want to lose credibility in that way.

Best he doesn't know.

After all, she has her reputation to think of. Her reputation as an acerbic, feisty woman of a certain age who is completely unafraid of life because she has nothing else precious left to lose.

But this is different. Her front door left open? She can't help wondering – and hoping – who her intruder might be.

It's only when she returns to her room that she remembers the clanking sound from her dream, and turns to the dressing-table. The framed photograph of her daughter lies face down on the glass top, as if placed like that deliberately. When she touches it, it feels ice-cold against her fingertips. She puts it back in its upright position, climbs back into bed.

Outside the night rolls on towards dawn, and deep time and shallow time meet somewhere in the middle, in forgotten layers which bed themselves down gradually in

40

the soil. Some people choose to disturb that soil and search for what is lost, for what is hidden, questing and reaching for the past.

That must be what Laura's business is about, Joan thinks, sifting through the soil to find the little fragments, physical evidence of a life once lived.

Joan does not believe in ghosts, but sometimes, she admits to her friend who she meets for coffee every fortnight, it's as if they believe in her.

Kilbroch Castle

Laura Pettigrew sits on a stool outside her camper van, gazing down at the gorge below. It's a beautiful spot, this. Miraculous that she has the privilege of spending the next three weeks on this dig, all alone. Miraculous she got the funding, although none of her colleagues were quick to support her.

But that scare the night before last has left her feeling pretty wobbly. She's not one to be easily alarmed. She lurks about in all sorts of lonely places. It's the job of an archaeologist. But the incident of the broken window has left her shaken.

She wonders if she ought to consider postponing the dig, but she can't bear the thought of that. She's waited so long to get stuck in and the season is perfect for it. On reflection, she's pretty sure it was a prankster. Teenage boys maybe, having a laugh? Smashing her window while she's sleeping to see if they can frighten her. Well, they succeeded. But it's probably nothing more sinister than that. An opportunist hoping to break into the van, not expecting there to be anyone sleeping inside.

She feels safer up here at night anyway, parked beside the castle, on the terrace, the sunken gardens and the beautiful sloping grounds spread beneath her. Doesn't know why she didn't think of asking before. Strabane had quickly agreed to let her stay up here, although he hadn't been all that keen on the dig going ahead in the first place. He took some persuading.

'So, what brings you to excavate my land?' he had asked her, with more than a trace of sarcasm, when she approached him initially about the project.

She had explained to him that she'd been studying aerial photographs of the land and suspected the spot the locals have always known as Gallows Hill, hidden in the woods, surrounded by trees, could very well be the site of a Bronze Age broch.

'And what makes you think that?'

'The shape of the earth backs up my theory,' she told him. 'And either way, I intend to find out the truth.'

'Do you?' he said, in a dead-pan voice that seemed to throw doubt on every word she spoke. 'And if it is the site of a Bronze Age broch?'

'Then we'll know more about the history of this place. And more about our ancestors.'

'And then you'll cover it up again, and go away?'

She'd laughed at his friendly tone as he spoke. 'I suppose so.'

'I'll give you three weeks,' Strabane had said. 'Three weeks on my land, and then you'll have to leave, whether you find your broch or not.'

'Agreed.'

And then he'd left her to it. Lord of the Manor. Except he wasn't a lord. He owned a castle, Kilbroch Castle, in the middle of a vast woodland, on the edge of a glen. How he came to own it, she did not know. Nor did she care to pry. Her business was with the past, and with whatever remains of a skeletal structure lay under the layers of accumulated moss and soil.

She's still sitting there, nursing a morning cup of tea, when a dusty red van eats up the gravel of the long drive. She watches the driver step down and walk towards her. He's a small, well-set man, dark hair and eyes, a shadow of stubble across his jaw.

'I heard about the scare you had the other night,' he begins. 'I'm Callum MacGarvey, by the way,' he offers. 'I live over at Glenwhilk.'

43

'News travels fast.'

'So you're not packing up and going home then?'

She regards him suspiciously. 'Does it look like it?'

He smiles and nods, realising too late he has wrong-footed her and not knowing how to rectify it.

'Sorry. A friend of mine was telling me about the incident. Joan Metcalfe?'

Laura looks blank. 'I haven't been here that long. Haven't really got to know many people.'

'Glentye. First house on the right before you get to the chapel?'

Laura doesn't answer at first, still reticent, but her brow clears as she remembers the woman in the red Mini who spoke to her once or twice, and she can't stop her natural friendliness from taking over.

'Oh, yes. I think I've spoken to her before. Nice woman. Mad about plants.'

He smiles. 'That's her. So you'll go ahead with the dig anyway? That's good news.'

'It would take more than that to put me off. I've only got three weeks but I intend to stick at it.'

'I hope you succeed. Will we have Neil Oliver and Alice Roberts crawling about the place?'

She laughs. 'I don't think so, no. It's not that big.'

'Big enough for someone to try to scare you though.'

'Maybe they were just playing a prank.'

'Maybe. What happened?'

Laura gazes down at the sunken gardens, the sweeping treeline, hears the murmur of the burn in the gorge below. This is such an enchanting place it's hard to imagine any crime ever being committed here.

She pauses before answering him, trying to make light of her ordeal.

'I was in the van, trying to get to sleep as usual. And someone smashed a side window. Simple as that.'

'Did you see anyone?'

She squints up at him for a second. 'Why d'you ask?'

He is immediately aware of how that sounds. 'I'm just trying to help Joan with some enquiries, that's all.'

'Enquiries?'

'It doesn't matter. I'll leave you to it.'

He begins to retreat to his van, but she calls him back.

'No, wait. What enquiries?'

He pauses, wondering how much to tell. 'Her grandson went missing twelve years ago. Joan wants to know what happened to him.'

She looks at him, frowning. 'You're some kind of detective then?'

He laughs and shakes his head.

'Then why is she asking you to help?'

He gives a comical, self-deprecating shrug. 'Good question! I have no idea. Listen,' he adds, 'I appreciate you feeling suspicious. It's perfectly understandable.'

She studies him for a moment. 'So you live near here?'

'I do.'

'Tea?' She holds up her flask.

He hesitates, surprised at the invitation. 'Don't mind if I do.'

He watches as she climbs into her camper van and reappears moments later with a blue pottery mug.

'Thanks,' he smiles, as she pours from her flask.

'Looks like a real home from home you have here,' he adds, nodding towards the van.

'It is,' she says. 'I love it.'

Even as she speaks, however, she can't help cautioning herself. This Callum MacGarvey could be anyone, as far as she's concerned. She feels her twin brother, Simon, and her mother, muttering their usual grim warnings and advice. They sit in her head like a couple of affectionate watch

45

dogs, ever present, but on this occasion she decides to pay them no heed.

Callum, for his part, is aware of how he might be coming across, some scruffy itinerant van driver turning up to ask lots of questions.

He sips his tea. 'You've picked a perfect spot here anyway.'

Laura nods, and turns her head to regard the view. 'I think I'll feel safer up here, rather than staying overnight in the woods.'

'Have you reported it to the police?'

She nods. 'They said they'd send someone over at some point. Hasn't happened yet though.'

'Hope they don't take too long about it.'

She pauses. 'They said they were pretty busy,'

Callum makes a sarcastic sound, and takes a sip of tea.

'They also said they were sure it was teenagers mucking about.'

'And they'd know that, would they?'

She puts her head on one side. 'You don't seem to be a fan of the police?'

'I have my reasons. So they smashed a side window when you were sleeping. What did you do then?' he asks.

She gives a nervous half-laugh. 'I climbed into the driver's seat and drove up here. Pronto.'

She remembers the terrifying drive through the darkness, her headlights swarming up the narrow road, aware of the drop on her right. She'd been worried she'd misjudge the verge and plunge the van headlong into the trees. She'd kept driving to the junction at the corner, turned left, up the steep incline past the gamekeeper's cottage and over the cattle grid into the grounds of the castle.

Didn't stop till she got to the building, where a security light flashed on above the baronial-looking doorway. Then she pulled up, turned off the ignition. Kept the doors

46

locked, and tried to sleep. She stayed awake until the dawn chorus began, and a grey light edged its way through her curtains. And that was how George Strabane had found her early the next morning, when he went out with his dogs. He tapped on the window which wasn't broken, and she peered through, half-asleep, full of apologies.

George Strabane had been okay with her staying up here, but she couldn't shift the idea that he seemed mildly amused rather than concerned for her welfare, which she found deeply irritating.

She doesn't tell Callum all of this.

But sitting here on her camping stool, while Callum sits on the terrace wall, sipping tea and enjoying the view, she can't help feeling this is a superior camping spot to the dank lay-by she'd chosen beneath Gallows Hill.

Kilbroch Castle is not as grand as it looks. For all its turrets and battlements it's a touch dilapidated inside. As George Strabane frequently complains, it's hard to maintain a house and grounds this size without employing a vast army of servants, which he cannot afford to do. Estates this large require staff, and Nathan the gardener can only achieve so much on his own. Strabane doesn't do too badly though, and he knows it.

He stands at the drawing-room window on the first floor and stares down at the gravelled terrace. Something is arresting his attention below.

Around him are stuffed animals in glass cases, caught in the rictus of death. The family are used to living with hunting trophies scattered about the place, part of the furniture. Above the fireplace, it looks as if a giant stag has stuck its head through from the library next door. It's a room that, despite its marvellous view and long sash windows, speaks of death. It can be a draughty old place in the winter, difficult to heat, as his daughters are constantly reminding him.

'Put another jumper on,' his wife used to say, years ago, before she became so gravely ill.

Beautiful wild gardens shelve beneath the terrace in soft undulations, bushes and trees softening the aspect down to the gorge. He practically has his own woodland in the garden, divided by Gothic archways, salvaged or stolen from the ruins of a cathedral two hundred and fifty years ago. He has an orangery, a walled garden, extensive greenhouses, a burn which tumbles over stepped rocks, all completely natural, wild, in keeping with Kells Wood.

But Strabane isn't standing here to admire his own gardens. He's concentrating on the two people below, one perched on a camping stool, the other on his low terrace wall beside the sky-blue camper van, mugs of tea in their hands while they chat.

He mutters something under his breath about the place turning into a bloody campsite.

When he'd found her parked on the drive just before dawn the day before last, he'd made no comment at first. He'd not been a fan of the project in the early days, even when Laura Pettigrew suggested there was reason to believe that Gallows Hill was actually the site of a Bronze Age broch.

'Don't you like archaeology?' she had asked him, in her direct manner.

'Yes, I like archaeology,' he replied. 'But I also like my privacy.'

Which she'd accepted, readily enough, but had still managed to prevail upon him to let her go ahead with the dig. In all honesty, he had no choice. Right to roam and all that. It wasn't as if the site was in his back garden. It lay deep in the woods, where public access was freely available, even though hardly anyone ventured that deep.

So he walked the dogs as usual that morning, then, on his return, he gently rapped the window of her van. There was a pause, before Laura's head popped between the flimsy curtains, her chestnut hair pulled back into a messy pony-tail.

He could hardly refuse the girl, knowing she'd had such a fright. She claimed she felt safer camping up at the castle, but he still wasn't a fan.

He looks down now, and studies the pair below, his eyes narrowed.

'Daddy?'

He spins rounds.

Sophie stands in the doorway, her jogging gear on.

She comes to stand beside him at the window, and looks down. 'Is that the archaeologist?'

Her father nods quietly.

'D'you think she'll find anything?' she asks.

Strabane glances at her.

'At the site, I mean?' she adds quickly. 'A real Stone Age broch?'

'Bronze Age,' he corrects her quietly.

'It's so exciting. Imagine if she finds any bones. We might become the centre of the universe.'

'I hope not.'

'Nothing ever happens here,' says a third voice.

Strabane's youngest daughter has come into the room, bringing with her an air of sullen resentment. She is more guarded than her sister, watchful.

Her father ignores her comment.

All three stand at the window, watching the scene below unfold, although there is nothing really to observe.

'Who's that with her?' Sophie asks now, still excited about the prospect of an archaeological dig on their land.

Strabane speaks sideways, not tearing his gaze away from the couple below.

'Callum MacGarvey,' he replies. 'You know, the chap who lives at Glenwhilk?'

'Oh, Callum,' Sophie says.

She sees him a lot when she's out jogging; he always gives her a nod and a wave. Sophie is the friendly member of her little family, depleted in numbers by the death of their mother from cancer several years ago, when Lottie and Sophie were little.

It seems that much sorrow has visited Kilbroch over recent years. Some maintain it's part of the old curse of Kilbroch, stealing the first-born of every family, except the statistics don't really match that theory. It's true though, as some say, that Strabane's wife was an eldest child. And then there's Robbie, people whispered.

'But he's not dead,' they whispered back. 'He ran away, remember?'

'Aye, so they say.'

Lottie leaves her father to his vigil at the window and retreats into the shadows of the house. She hates the way her father just stands there, spying, as if he has anything to worry about. She doesn't say so, though. Let Sophie maintain the illusion that everything is fine. Lottie won't pretend.

At the window Strabane flinches as he hears a door slam. The castle is so huge it's hard to make a door slam effectively – sounds become deadened by the space and distance, the many rooms and walls dividing them – but Lottie manages it somehow.

He notes this, but says nothing.

'You off jogging again?' he remarks to his eldest.

She nods, lifting one foot behind her and holding it by the ankle in a stretch.

'I might chat to our new resident on the way out,' she adds.

'She won't be here for long,' Strabane says.

'How do you know?' Sophie asks.

He turns and smiles.

'Trust me.'

'Hi there!' A young voice takes her by surprise.

Laura has just parted with the newcomer, Callum MacGarvey, and is still gazing thoughtfully at the view, contemplating the day's work ahead of her. She spins round to see Sophie in jogging gear, smiling.

'Hi,' she replies. 'you must be...?'

'Sophie.'

'Pleased to meet you, Sophie. My name's Laura.'

'I know who you are,' Sophie says quickly. 'Daddy says you're digging on Gallows Hill?'

'That's right.'

'What do you hope to find?'

'Well, I suppose evidence of the people who once lived there, what their lives might have been like.'

'Your Bronze Age broch. Daddy said.'

Laura nods, wondering what else they talk about, what impression he gives to his daughter about the whole thing.

'That's right.' She hesitates, wondering if the girl really wants to know or is simply being polite, but she can't help herself. 'It's a kind of fortified dwelling where a family – maybe a couple of families – would have lived long ago. About three thousand years ago, give or take. They weren't poor by any means.'

'You know all that?'

Laura nods.

'But how, if you can't see the walls or the building?'

'It's to do with the soil, and I'm finding the remains of walls, the first few inches.'

'And you have to imagine the rest?'

'I suppose so, yes.'

'Weird,' Sophie says.

Then she smiles briskly. 'Well, it's nice to meet you Laura.'

Laura watches as the girl heads towards a gap in the courtyard wall, and jogs down a steep flight of stone steps to the gorge below. She wonders how the girl manages not to trip or fall, the steps being so uneven and slick with moss as they are, but she supposes she must be pretty familiar with the area.

She shakes out her cup and replaces the lid on the flask.

The girl was an odd mix of naivety and forthrightness, Laura decides, oddly overprotected for her age. She makes an educated guess that she must be about eighteen.

She makes a mental note to describe all of this to her twin, Simon.

She likes to run things past him, keep him informed. It's part of their long-distance relationship. They might be removed by distance, but technology keeps them connected.

She gazes around her at the terrace, the stone parapets, the ivy-covered central tower, the tops of the trees in the gorge below, massing across the horizon, the sloping gardens and woodlands and tall boundary walls. All of this, she sighs. Simon would love it.

Digging up the Past

As Callum drives back to Glenwhilk that morning he thinks about his conversation with Laura. She's an attractive young woman. There's something natural and vibrant about her. Since he and his wife split up, he's preferred to isolate himself, which hasn't exactly been difficult in recent months with repeated lockdowns and guidelines.

Everyone has been so restless these days, that the normally quiet road to Kilbroch has become busier than usual, whole families trooping out from Dunbrochan to clock up their daily ration of exercise. What did they do in the old days, he wonders, before lockdown? Probably piled into their people carriers and jeeps and headed off elsewhere. But then the thought occurs to him, why bother to live in a place, if you spend the majority of your time wanting to escape from it? That has always puzzled him about the affluent residents of Dunbrochan, for that had become the modern norm when his own son was growing up. Get in your car. Go elsewhere. Never stay home and just kick a football about in the garden or meet up with your pals. Those days are gone now, a ship that sailed a long time ago, without him on it.

His old red van clatters over the cattle grid. As he drives past the gamekeeper's cottage on the right, he looks out for Owen but there's no sign of him this morning. He still feels guilty about the way their conversation ended last night, verging on the hostile. He feels he handled it badly, and blames himself.

Then his thoughts shift to Laura and what happened to her up in the woods. Who would want to frighten her, and

53

why? Was it a random attack, teenagers messing about, as the police suggested? It's just, as anyone could confirm, there aren't that many teenagers around here.

Callum checks his thoughts, reminding himself that he is not inclined to follow up on Joan's inquiries. He has no intention of getting involved. He'll leave all that policing business to the local constabulary, thank you very much, and get on with quietly living his own life.

He feels deeply sorry for his friends. One lost a son, the other a grandson, but it was all a long time ago now, and maybe the police were right and Robbie will simply turn up one day, return to his family and his childhood home and explain where he has been all these years, and what took him away. Callum doesn't think there is any mileage at all in digging up past events, despite Joan's stubborn insistence that her grandson is still here.

He sees a flash of movement in the trees to his left, a large stag careering through the woods, its red coat appearing and disappearing through the thick greenery, galloping like a horse, powerful, wild. It comes to a halt, turns and stares at him with a regal gaze, affronted at the intrusion.

Callum gazes back at it, mesmerised by its beauty. He has lived out here for nearly five years now, and he still enjoys the apparent wildness of the landscape, a boy from Glasgow, buried away, deep in the countryside.

His wife was shocked that he was prepared to give up everything, to walk away from his past life, a career he'd built up over the years and one he was good at. He and Theresa had got out of Glasgow when they were young, moved to the suburbs and tried to carve out careers for themselves, a nice house, a nice garden, two cars, a good postcode. Then he gave up everything they'd worked so hard for.

Defeatist, she called him.

Bitch, he called her, when he was drunk, which was

quite often nowadays. He managed to keep dry and sober during the day, but it was that six o' clock fix that always got him, the itch in his stomach, an itch of boredom, of hunger that nothing else would fulfil.

He gave it all up, to come and live here in relative seclusion, picking up joinery work, delivering firewood by the van load to a narrow range of customers, firewood he'd already gathered, seasoned and chopped himself. That, and his pension, was enough to get by on, for what little he needed.

He glances through the trees on his right, where Gallows Hill lies. Then he pulls up in the lay-by where Laura's camper van had been parked the night it was vandalised. Cranks the door of his van open, jumps down, takes a look around. The ground is dry, old wheel ruts marking the dust.

A red kite lets out a prolonged cry, a purity of sound he never tires of hearing. He watches it circling the air above the treeline. A thing of beauty, floating up there above Kells Wood, until others join it in graceful wheeling movements. Their cry is poignant, haunting, and unbearably beautiful. There's a real atmosphere here. You can't help but feel it.

He can see the path through the bracken, trodden by Laura on her way to the dig site. It leads up into the forest, to the brow of that hill, hidden by greenery, where one large oak stands out as distinct from the birch and pine around it. Was that the actual tree that had acted as a gallows for the locals of Kilbroch once upon a time? Joan would be the person to ask about that.

Laura will have to come back here, to carry on with her dig. He can't help but admire her. It would take some courage, or bloody-mindedness, to return here on her own to kneel for hour upon hour in those woods, scraping away with her trowel at the roots of that gnarled old oak. After a scare like that, he's not sure he'd want to do it.

It's a lonely spot, even during the day. And although

he doesn't hold any truck with ghost stories, and he's certainly not superstitious in any shape or form, still he can't help thinking about that story Joan told him, of the boys camping under that tree, who scarpered pretty quick when they thought they saw a corpse dangling from one of its branches.

As Callum had said, too much of the old whacky baccy probably, but even so. Makes you think, he murmurs to himself. He listens to the wind moving in the trees, watches where the red kites circle, and then, when he drops his gaze, realises he is under observation himself.

Ruthie, Owen's daughter. She walks this way regularly, of course. No one knows these woods like Ruthie. A real recluse. But seeing her there takes him by surprise. He nods at her and is almost sure she nods back, before she goes on her way.

Is it normal to be so silent, he wonders? Can she be happy, functioning like that? A retard, some unkind locals have remarked in the local pub down in the village, but Callum ignores that kind of comment. He can't bear the judgements people make, the narrow-mindedness. If Ruthie is silent, that's her business.

She's only twenty-five, which would make her thirteen when her brother went missing.

Can of worms, Callum thinks quietly to himself. And he does not intend to open it.

What is it with her, though, he can't help thinking, as he watches Ruthie's slim figure vanish between the trees.

He makes his own way up to Gallows Hill, parting the bracken and wafting away the clegs until he gets to a ridge with a buckled wire fence, which he steps over. Then he ducks beneath a heavy branch of spruce, and stands upright to see the land shelving away above him, that infamous oak on its crest, cradled by dark forest and trees. There's a circle of stones to one side of the oak, where old fires have been

56

set. Few know of this spot, but the odd camper has been known. He can see the area where Laura has been working, metal pegs and twine marking out the soil, and now he can see that there are ridges here, evidence perhaps of some ancient structure that once stood here, thousands of years ago.

He doesn't really get archaeology, doesn't get how it works. So you dig up the soil and earth to discover a series of small walls, but unless you find examples of pottery or treasures of some kind, the rest is all hearsay. You have to imagine what has long since vanished, re-build it in your imagination which seems a bit of a disappointment to him.

Still, he admires Laura's passion and enthusiasm for the subject. He can see where she has slowly and painstakingly scraped away at some of the soil, a blanket of emerald green moss and earth peeled back to reveal the bare bones of what might just be... could possibly be... evidence of some ancient structure. It looks as if she has a long way to go yet.

He stands upright and takes a look around. Thick dense pine planted too close to let the daylight through, on two sides, so that anyone could watch you from the darkness of those shadows. Made you feel a bit exposed, hunted even. If he was digging here all day, bent over the brown earth with a trowel in his hand, he'd feel the need to keep checking, a quick 360 degree glance to make sure no one was standing in the trees, watching. As Ruthie was just doing.

On the other side of the hill is natural woodland. Birch, ash, oak and chestnut, all growing together in a delicate tumble of an ecosystem, not planted by hand, but gradually evolved over the centuries. It is this part of Kells Wood that he loves, with its soft tussocky ground, its reedy bogs to catch you unawares. Any trees which have fallen in high winds over the years expose their roots to the sky, and creatures make their homes here, among the twisting snake-like roots.

He pauses for a moment, then decides to make his way back to the road.

The dig is completely hidden from any passing traffic, high above the track, screened by trees and undergrowth. The road itself is single-track, with no destination at its end except Broch Farm, and a couple of cottages belonging to a lawyer and an artist. Wind turbines gently spin in the far distance on the high moor, like Space Age paraphernalia.

Vehicles are rare on this road, unless it's the gamekeeper, Owen, or one of the residents of Kilbroch. Not even locals from nearby Dunbrochan come up this far, maybe the occasional dog-walker, the more adventurous type, but other than that, Callum generally knows who is passing through. Since lockdown, people will make it as far as the gamekeeper's cottage sometimes, but generally they turn back before the chapel, and never make it as far as Gallows Hill.

He hears the sound of a motor now, a soft growl on the road beneath, invisible.

The growl disappears into the distance, leaving behind pristine silence, broken only by the cry of the red kites still circling above.

Running Away

Callum pulls into Glenwhilk to find Joan's red Mini parked in his yard. She's sitting in the front seat, with the door wide open, waiting for him.

'You again?' he jokes, as he watches her struggle out of the driver's seat with her stick. He'd offer to help, but knows she would bat him away.

'Can't get rid of you these days, can I?'

She nods her consent. 'So?'

'So what?'

'Have you made up your mind yet?'

'Jesus, woman. You're persistent. I told you. I'm not a detective.'

'You said that before. I'm not asking you to be a detective.'

'What then?'

'I'm just asking for a little help. To find my grandson.'

'It was more than ten years ago, Joan.'

'Twelve,' she corrects him. 'Historical crimes can be solved.'

'You're certain it was a crime then?'

'The police said not, at the time, but I think otherwise.'

He feels a wave of pity. She must have spent the past twelve years tormented by the thought of what might have happened to Robbie.

'The not-knowing is almost worse than the knowing.' He'd heard that phrase used before in a missing person's. He'd only dealt with a few cases like this, but Joan was right, he did have a good nose for this sort of thing. He had life's experience and his harsh upbringing in Pollok to stand him in good stead. If anyone could suss out the darker motives of people, then he could – it's just…

'I've left all that behind, Joan.'

'So you said.'

'Why don't you try the police again, ask them to reopen the case?'

She shakes her head and gives a derisive half-laugh. 'If they were useless the first time, what makes you think they'll be any different now? They were adamant he left of his own free will.'

'Why?'

Her eyes light up with a glimmer of victory, aware she has him hooked at last. 'He took his passport with him for a start.'

'Oh,' Callum thinks for a moment.

'And he had such a poor relationship with his father, so they thought he'd a good reason to leave.'

'Owen?'

'Aye, Owen,' Joan nods. 'They thought he ran away to escape from a bad atmosphere at home, a bad home life. But Robbie would never do that. He was sixteen, you see. Maybe if he'd been a girl it might have been different. They might have taken it more seriously. I don't know.'

Callum is quiet. The two of them are still standing in his yard, the fields sloping away on either side, sheep nibbling the long grass. He can glimpse the familiar roofline of Kells Chapel over the next hill.

Maybe he didn't go far enough to escape, he thinks now. Perhaps he should have headed off to an even deeper wilderness to avoid the responsibilities of his past life dragging him back out into the open.

'What did you do, Callum?' Joan says now, her eyes twinkling. 'Was it something bad?'

'It wasn't me who did anything.'

'Then what are you so afraid of?'

60

'I don't want to be a private investigator, I told you.'

She eyes him quizzically. 'Have you got anything else lined up? Well then. Like I said, I'll pay your expenses. And for your time.'

When he doesn't reply, she barks 'Fine. Go back to chopping your logs then.'

She turns back to her car, but he stops her.

'Wait. Look, there's a reason I don't want to touch police business again. I don't trust them. They hounded me out of the force, I told you that. Even when I was the only one telling the truth. I stood on the witness stand, in front of a public gallery, and...'

She doesn't let him finish. 'So everyone else is a hypocrite. So what's new in the world? Tell me something I don't know.'

Joan is a harsh woman; maybe her own personal losses and suffering have hardened her, but he still can't help admiring her straight way of talking. Truth is, she is a great mentor and friend to him, and they have an immaculate rapport. He's often thought that.

'Okay.' He says the word before she can climb back into her vehicle. He gives his assent, reluctantly. 'I'll help you.'

Her eyes light up, and her lined old face relaxes into a smile of relief. 'I knew I'd get you in the end,' she says, not bothering to hide her sense of glee.

'I'll do my best. I'll see what I can find out.'

'Thank you.'

'I can't promise anything.'

She acknowledges this silently. 'At least we will have tried.'

'I'll need your help and co-operation.'

'Anything you need...' she adds.

It is at this point he realises he has just taken on his first case as a private investigator.

'You should get yourself a business card,' Joan jokes, but he shakes his head.

This will be his first and last case, of that he is sure, and if he finds out anything that will help put his old friend's mind at rest, then perhaps that will go some way towards appeasing his own conscience.

When his phone rings, he reaches inside his hip pocket to retrieve it. He glances at the screen and realises it's his ex-wife calling. Odd, because he hasn't heard from her in more than a year. Frowning, he swipes to accept the call, mumbling, 'Don't go yet, Joan. I just need to take this.'

She nods quietly, and sits in the driver's seat with the window down.

He holds the phone to his ear, speaks his wife's name. 'Theresa.'

'Hi, Callum. How are you?'

'I'm fine but…'

'But what?' she snaps back, quick as a flash.

He wants to ask her why she is ringing him now, when he hasn't heard from her in months, when she wouldn't take his calls or reply to any of his texts.

'I was beginning to wonder if you'd changed numbers.'

'Cut the sarcasm, Callum.'

'I wasn't being sarc…'

'I'm ringing because I need to tell you something.'

'Okay.'

'Andy and I are getting married.'

He frowns, suddenly aware of the sheep on the hillside, their comical bleats, and of Joan listening from a distance, or trying not to, at least.

'But how is that…?'

'We need a divorce, Callum. It's time.'

He sighs heavily. 'You don't pull any punches. Couldn't we discuss any of this first?'

'I tried, Callum, a long time ago. Remember?'

He didn't actually. It was all a blur. After he left his job – or was pushed out, more like – the stress of those intervening years meant that a lot of the normal stuff, family stuff, had suffered, and he didn't honestly remember a lot of what happened, only that it hurt. Hurt like hell.

'While you've been hiding away in the countryside, Callum, some of us have moved on.'

Bitch, he thinks, but doesn't say it out loud. Hearing the way she speaks, the vindictive tone, he wonders why he still mourns the loss of his marriage, of their relationship. Perhaps because it was the only one he had, and it was about family loyalty. Sticking together. Except they have failed spectacularly at that.

The hurt and the betrayal, the breakdown of his marriage makes him feel like a failure. Truth be told, it might be why he drinks. Although can he really pin his weakness on that?

'And when will you be seeing our son, Callum?'

He opens his mouth to protest. He has tried, God knows he has tried.

At the mention of his son, his heart clenches painfully.

'It was you who took him to live in Somerset, if I recall?'

'There you go again. Back-stabbing. Casting blame. What did you expect me to do? And Somerset is not that far away.'

'It's not that near, either.' He could curse himself. He hasn't heard from her in months, and here they are sparring again, as if all the bitterness of betrayal has never gone away.

'How is Mattie?' he asks now, quietly.

'He's fine. Not that you care.'

He goes to open his mouth again, but she snaps, 'We need to finalise things. I take it you won't contest?'

She waits mere seconds for a non-existent response, and finishes, 'I'll be in touch,' before hanging up.

He stares at his phone for a moment, slips it into his pocket, and feels Joan's eyes on him.

He nods and smiles. 'Just the ex,' he mumbles, but he feels no judgement from Joan. That's one of the things he really likes about her.

'We all have our troubles, Callum,' she murmurs, resting her elbow on the open window.

'You can say that again.'

The Broch

Ruthie crosses the garden to the hutch where she keeps her ferrets. She smiles in affection as she opens the cage, picks one of them up and allows it to curl around her shoulders. It sits there, attached in a way you wouldn't expect of such a creature, its small eyes blinking in the sunlight.

She feeds it a titbit from breakfast, strokes its golden fur, then returns to the house with it curled inside her denim jacket. She performs a few household tasks with the creature still attached, washes a few cups and bowls, and stands them on the draining board to dry.

Her father is off somewhere, attending to the pheasants maybe. The gamekeeper's cottage is quiet and oddly domestic, but Ruthie is keen to escape outside.

She could take the ferret with her, but is unwilling to risk losing her in the woods, so after finishing what she needs to do in the house, she places her gently back inside the cage.

Ruthie's world is largely about avoidance. But she likes it that way. She went to college for a short while, after leaving school, but it didn't last. She gave up after six months, came back to the gamekeeper's cottage to stay with her dad where she grew up. With all its secrets, its pain, it was better than elsewhere. The trauma of losing her brother was so huge that the only place she could deal with it was at the very place where it happened. A trauma envelope, they call it. If she stays close to the scene of the tragedy, then she can control it. Life cannot explode in her face too painfully.

She knows that others perceive her self-imposed silence as weird, but it protects her to some extent, and those closest to her accept it for what it is, allowing her to continue as she is. She had a short stint in the local charity shop for a while, as a volunteer worker, and people said it was good for her, forcing her to speak with customers across the counter, and with the other volunteers, but Ruthie couldn't agree with them.

What is good for Ruthie are the woods.

She is in love with the woods.

Her parents lived in the gamekeeper's cottage before either she or Robbie were born. It is the only home she has ever known.

Her world is small, circumscribed, but safe.

She knows the heavy pieces of furniture that stand in the shadows of the hallway, the great clock, which Owen forgets to wind so that it too is as silent as Ruthie, as if they share this thing in common – the need for hush. There is a reverence at the heart of the house, in the hallway, as if those who remain are still waiting.

Ruthie leaves the cottage now, and follows the familiar track through the natural woodland. No one treads these invisible tracks apart from Ruthie, and her father of course, when he feeds the pheasants, keeping the feed bins full. Strabane likes to keep the land maintained with a good stock of pheasants for the shoots in the autumn. He hires the castle out sometimes, to visitors, as a way of raising extra cash. They'll often take a pot shot at a deer.

Twigs crack underfoot, moss squelches. The branches of ash, birch and oak drape the air with their soft greenery.

She is intimately familiar with every season here.

She can access the gorge beneath the castle too, with its torrent of water flowing full in the winter months, reducing down to a murmur in the summer.

She's surrounded by soft silver birches, but through the branches she can glimpse the rolling farm landscape beneath, marked out by a drystone wall, and a scattering

66

of cattle. Beyond that, deep natural woodland that no one enters, too wild and inaccessible for the public to bother with. They stick to the single-track road instead.

Where the woods become less natural is where the plantations begin, too densely packed with a depressing monoculture to be good for the soil, as her dad is always reminding her, but no one listens to him, least of all the people who own the land. A belt of pine trees so dense and dark that when Ruthie enters here, no one can see her. She is invisible, as she creeps nearer towards the spot they call Gallows Hill.

She gets so far, then stands still. She can see her through the fronds of pine and spruce, that girl, Laura Pettigrew, the archaeologist, on her knees again at the site, scraping with her trowel.

Ruthie watches her, but doesn't reveal her own presence.

When a twig cracks under her heel, she sees Laura stop working and glance up, a frown on her face.

Ruthie holds her breath, keeps so still that she almost melts into the trees, like a wood sprite. That's what her dad used to call her, when she was about eleven years old. 'Our little wood sprite.'

Memories from the time before. When they were still happy.

She watches Laura hesitate, then return to her work, determined as ever.

She is either very brave, or very stupid, Ruthie concludes, although she can't decide which. If she'd been mock-attacked in the middle of the night, the window of her camper van smashed in, she wouldn't be coming back here to dig, even during daylight hours. She'd heard them talking, Callum and her dad. Being so quiet means that people often say things in front of you, assuming you are deaf as well as partially mute. Eavesdropping leads to all kinds of knowledge, Ruthie finds. So as she watches the

67

young woman, she thinks she must be mad to keep digging here.

Taking a risk, she walks closer, steps out from between the trees, drawn by... she doesn't know what, really.

Laura jumps when she sees Ruthie step into the clearing. Startled, she holds a hand to her chest. 'You scared me.'

Ruthie says nothing.

'D'you want to come see what I'm doing?'

Ruthie hesitates for a moment, then nods and walks closer.

Laura points with her trowel to the earth.

'You can't really see much from this angle. You have to use your imagination a little, but see that line of soil there, a slightly different colour from the rest?'

Ruthie looks closely at the spot Laura indicates.

'We think that's the outer wall of a broch.'

When Ruthie looks blank she adds, 'A kind of stone structure, shaped like a beehive, where a couple of families might have lived. It was good for protection. Prime site, on top of a hill. No trees then, probably. They'd have been rich folk. Not poor. Hey, d'you want coffee?' she adds, turning to grab her flask.

'I always have a flask of strong black coffee on the go. Keeps me awake. Helps me concentrate.'

Ruthie accepts the cup, and takes a sip.

Laura, for her part, studies Ruthie, wondering – as everyone does – why she is a woman of so few words, longing to be the one to draw her out.

'I hope you like it black. I haven't got any milk.'

Ruthie doesn't answer.

'You live near here?' she asks.

Ruthie nods.

'You're Owen's daughter?"

She's heard about the family briefly from Callum, but it's clear Laura has gone too far. Ruthie doesn't like questions.

She doesn't like people prying. All she wants is to see what it's like, to watch this educated young woman who camps by herself in the middle of the woods – her woods – and decides to dig up the earth to find some physical evidence of a historic building. What must it be like to be so confident, so sure of yourself, so able to make your own positive choices and decisions in life? Ruthie cannot imagine that. She is fascinated, appalled, intrigued.

Handing the cup back, she silently takes her leave with a wordless nod.

Laura watches the young woman retreat, utterly perplexed.

A part of her can't help wondering – were you the one? Who tried to frighten me the other night?

What's your story? Laura thinks.

Whatever it is, Ruthie is telling no one.

Joan

Callum is sitting inside Joan's conservatory. There is a flourishing of plants all around him. Joan has green fingers. He marvels that despite her sorrows – of which there are many – she's still able to tend her plants and grow a garden. Tomato vines, wildflowers, peonies, hollyhocks, night-scented stock: you name it, she grows it.

It's a modern, 1960s build, tucked away off the road to Kilbroch, screened from prying eyes by high hedgerows. Few people pass this way. At the back, the house enjoys a view of rolling fields, grazing cattle, the tip of Kells Chapel just visible in the distance. It's harsh and lonely during the long Scottish winters, glorious during the short summer months.

Joan comes through from the kitchen now, bearing a photograph album in her arms.

'I don't often look at these,' she says, taking her seat beside him. 'But… it's important you get a full picture.'

'Tell me everything you know, Joan.'

She looks at him and shakes her head. 'Everything? I wish I could. There are so many unanswered questions.'

He waits, while she opens the album, and displays snapshot after snapshot of her two young grandchildren. Happy smiling infants, playing together in a sandpit, standing side by side on a beach, posing, grinning, birthday parties, opening presents on Christmas Day amid a chaos of ripped wrapping paper, the usual family moments captured on film. It looks perfectly ordinary.

'Is that Robbie?' Callum asks.

She nods. 'That's him, and his sister when they were little.'

A look of deep pain crosses Joan's face now, but she contains herself and carries on. She knows how to be strong. God knows, she's had years of practice.

As he looks at the pictures, Callum hesitates, feeling a tremor inside him. He's not sure he can do this, after all. It reminds him too much of the past. But Joan is his friend, and she is placing her trust in him. She's turned to him because no one else will believe her.

'Owen and Lydia were good parents,' Joan says, although he can sense a trace of doubt in that statement.

'Lydia?'

'My daughter.'

He's about to ask more when Joan stops him, leads the conversation in a different direction, and he allows her to lead, knowing this is much more difficult for her than it is for him.

'Robbie and his little sister were very close, you know. When Ruthie was bullied at school, Robbie stood up for her. They were like peas in a pod. Three years between them, but it made no difference – the gap, I mean. People say that siblings can't be close if there's more than a two year gap, but I think that's nonsense, don't you?'

Callum nods, silently acknowledging the idyllic picture she is painting.

'Then,' Joan struggles a little. 'When Robbie became a teenager, Lydia seemed to have problems.'

'Problems?'

'I'm not sure what they were, but she was not quite herself.'

The sorrow on Joan's face is unmistakable. 'I think they were struggling, but she wouldn't turn to me, even though I kept offering to help. Something was wrong, but I don't know what it was.'

She takes a deep breath. 'He went missing one night in October. I'll never forget it,' she adds grimly. '8th of

October 2010. Hard to believe it's so long ago now. Feels like yesterday…'

'Did the police find anything… to indicate what might have happened to him?'

Joan sighs. 'A few of his things were missing. His rucksack, and, like I said, his passport. That's why they decided he ran away. They put up posters, did all the usual things, but they drew a blank.'

'And what makes you think I won't draw a blank too?'

She shrugs. 'I don't know that. But I'm willing to try – if you are.'

He lifts his gaze to the window, and his eyes rest on the rolling expanse of farmland outside. 'I don't know, Joan,' Callum says. 'Stirring up the past…'

'As far as I'm concerned, it's with me every day. I give the impression of carrying on, same as normal. Tough as old bricks. And I am. But no one knows what it feels like.'

Callum lowers his eyes, thinking of how Owen had said much the same thing the other night, although that conversation had ended on a more hostile note.

'I just need to know, Callum. Owen is my son-in-law, but he has nothing to do with me.'

'And Ruthie?'

'She barely speaks to anyone. I try, but…'

'What came between you all?'

Joan's brow darkens, but instead of answering she says, 'There's something bothering my son-in-law's conscience, Callum. And I want to know what it is.'

He decides to be honest. 'It's going to be difficult. I don't want to make enemies.'

'Have enough of those already, do you?' she laughs.

He can't help admiring her. She's spot on, as usual.

'Owen is my friend.'

'Aye, so you think.'

'I'll do my best, Joan. We'll see where it takes us. But I

72

can't promise anything. Can I take this?' he adds, pointing to a snapshot of two young teenagers, brother and sister, standing side by side in front of a fence, a field with grazing ponies behind them. In other pictures they are laughing, joking, messing about, revealing a depth of sibling love. In this one, you can see their faces more clearly.

Joan nods. 'You can take it. Here,' she hands him another, of her daughter Lydia holding a toddler.

He glances down at it, and again, he wants to ask more, but something in Joan's manner makes him hesitate.

'What about Lydia?' he asks now.

'What about her?' Joan says.

He's not clear in his mind what happened to Lydia, and Joan doesn't seem able to talk about it, or expand.

He sighs, and Joan adds quietly. 'She died. That's all you need to know.'

This doesn't satisfy him in the least, but he turns away. He has plenty of time.

After all, this case has waited twelve years to be solved. It can wait a little longer.

Slippage

Back at his own place, he opens the fridge to a jangle of glass bottles, and struggles with his demons, the six o' clock fix being one of them.

Every day he tells himself he'll not rely on drink tonight. He'll stay sober, keep a clear head for the morning, and every evening the ritual of the fridge draws him back. The satisfying crack as he levers the top off an ice-cold beer, the first glug as it hits his stomach, unwinding the tension in all of his muscles.

Will there ever be a night when he doesn't drink?

Outside his window one blackbird sings. The same one, changing its note and its musical tune every time. It sits proudly on a fence post, inspecting its kingdom. He wishes he could find solace in these small things.

Sitting down at the kitchen table, he takes out the snapshots Joan gave him and looks again at their happy smiling faces. Ruthie looks almost unrecognisable, incandescent with happiness, her mouth expanding in a wide smile.

Brother and sister. They stare into their own future, unknowing.

For years he's observed Ruthie wandering Kilbroch in silence, a mysterious figure. He likes her father, Owen, enough to pass the time of day with him. He knew there'd been a son once, but that was all he knew – until Joan issued her challenge. Running the pad of his thumb over the first snapshot, he gazes into their eyes.

'What is your secret?' he whispers. 'What is your past?'

In his experience, everyone has a past. No one is a blank page, even faces as young as these.

As he sips his cold beer and watches the sun set in a blaze of colour across the fields, he wonders what his first approach might be.

A missing teenager, a father who no longer speaks to his mother-in-law, a silent sibling. A historic case, but one with ramifications for the present, the mother of the boy also deceased, but Joan reluctant to talk about it. Then he thinks about Laura's archaeological dig up on Gallows Hill and the attack on her vehicle during the night. Were the two linked? That would be the obvious conclusion to jump to, Callum thinks, as he stares at the endless sky from his window, the tip of Kells Chapel just showing above the crest of the hill, touched by the fire of the setting sun.

Or would it?

Was someone trying to scare Laura, and if so, why?

He doesn't want to suspect his friend Owen. It seems like the ultimate betrayal. Anyway, he's not even sure if that's what Joan is meaning to imply. But why now? he thinks. Joan has explained to him what she thinks – that if anyone is capable of finding her grandson, then it's Callum, but is there more to it than that?

His thoughts then turn to his estranged wife, Theresa, who moved down to Somerset four years ago, taking their only son with her. It hurts to think about that. Now she wants a divorce, which in all honesty is probably the only sensible course after a split this long.

Leaning back in his chair, he finishes his first beer and resists the impulse to reach for another. If only one were enough, but it never is.

On second thoughts, he decides that what he really needs is a sociable drink, a visit to the Kilbroch Arms on the edge of the village. Pick up some local gossip, kill two birds with one stone.

Before he leaves, he pins the two snapshots on the door of his fridge, keeping them in place with a couple of fridge magnets his son bought.

Locking the door behind him, his figure retreats into the yard.

Inside the kitchen, one of the magnets slips, and the snapshot of Lydia with her toddler son in her arms slides to the floor. It lies amid the stains and crumbs, a captured moment lost in the past, reduced to mere litter.

Callum will pick it up off the tiles the next morning, when he notices, and pin it back in place.

The Kilbroch Arms

When his old red van pulls into the front courtyard, he can already see the face of his quarry at the window, sitting in a corner seat, on his own.

He orders a pint at the bar, telling himself he'll walk back if need be, leave the van here for the night, then walks across to join his friend.

'Owen?'

'Callum.'

He slides into a seat, observed by several locals. The head of a dead stag stares above them, its glassy gaze fixed on the wall opposite. Sharp antlers obtrude from the walls and light-fittings, fighting with the tartan décor but not quite winning. It's a décor to impress tourists, but whether it succeeds or not is another matter.

Callum can't help noticing the awkwardness of the other drinkers in the bar, the way they avert their gaze from Owen's direction. If they do look at him, it is with frank curiosity. He wonders how many of them know about Owen's missing teenage son, how many were here twelve years ago?

'I've just been to see Joan,' Callum says.

Owen looks up. 'Oh yeah? You two are quite pally nowadays.'

'She spoke about your son.'

Owen's face darkens. 'I've told you. I don't want to talk about that.'

'I understand, it's just… it must have been hard.'

'It was.'

'I wanted to ask you about Lydia.'

His face changes, and an expression of anger twists his features for a second. 'What about her?'

'How did she die?' Callum asks softly.

Owen glances around nervously, not wanting others to eavesdrop, but a sudden burst of laughter at the bar changes the atmosphere.

'What's Joan been saying?' he adds now, more quietly.

Not enough as it happens, Callum thinks. 'She misses her granddaughter.'

'Her choice.'

'She wants to see Ruth, and she wants to know what happened to Robbie.'

Owen shakes his head and Callum can feel the pent-up rage and frustration in the man.

'What's the point?' he mutters under his breath. 'Nothing will bring Robbie back.'

'He's still missing, Owen. Perhaps there's some chance that he's still…'

'He's not coming back,' Owen says.

'How can you be so sure?'

Owen suddenly fixes Callum with an agonised stare. 'You're just like the rest of them then!' he says.

'Sorry?'

Owen nods his head in the direction of the other drinkers, those staring and pretending not to stare. 'Suspecting the worst, digging up rumours. Is that what Joan's up to?'

'Owen, I never meant…'

'D'you have any idea what I've been through?'

'No, I don't.' Callum thinks of his own estranged son, down in Somerset, for the briefest of moments.

'He was my son,' Owen raises his voice now.

'I know, I know. Calm down, man,' Callum says gently, aware of a gathering silence in the bar.

Owen glares across at the other customers. Two men at

the table opposite lean their heads together and whisper. He pushes his chair away and walks out, leaving Callum alone.

Callum nods at the two men opposite and gives a nervous smile.

Leaving his beer on the table, he follows Owen out into the courtyard, where tables and chairs sit, with blankets folded over the back of them, and cars are parked in front of the lawn

'Owen, wait!' he calls.

Owen pauses at the door to his Land Rover. 'I've got nothing to say to you.'

Callum stands still, desperately thinking on his feet, hoping there's a way he can backtrack and remedy the situation, repairing Owen's broken trust in him.

Owen is about to climb into the driver's seat when he stops and adds, 'You're welcome to do Joan's bidding, Callum, but if she finds out the truth she'll end up regretting it.'

Callum stares at him. 'So you know the truth?'

'I didn't say that.'

Callum steps back as Owen climbs into the driver's seat of the mud-splattered Land Rover and drives off. He watches as the tyres spit gravel and the lights of Owen's vehicle retreat onto the main road. 'Well, that went well,' he mutters under his breath.

He wonders, not for the first time, why Joan has entrusted her case to him. And what did Owen mean, that if Joan found out the truth she'd end up regretting it. Why? What truth? What else does Owen know, but is not saying? For a man who doesn't want to be seen as guilty, he's making himself seem remarkably suspicious.

Ghosts

Driving back to the gamekeeper's cottage, Owen can feel the rage and the shame fizzing through him all over again. Those looks in the bar, the hostile stares, the muttering. He'd thought it would pass, that he could face it down, but the ghosts of the past will always be with him. He'll carry them to his grave.

Why did he think he was entitled to a quick half pint in a sociable setting to while away an evening, after all these months of lockdown, to remind him he wasn't alone in the world? He should have known it wouldn't be possible. Perhaps he should have cut his losses a long time ago, moved him and Ruthie away from here, and attempted to begin a new life elsewhere.

He thinks of Callum and his questions. Opening up old wounds, stirring up the past, the pain and the hurt. How easy did Callum think it was to live with such a loss? A double loss. His wife and his son. And then to be blamed, or suspected while his neighbours murmured of abuse and exchanged dark rumours to satisfy their lust for gossip.

Passing Joan's lit windows, he stops the Land Rover for a moment. Tall hedgerows screen the house from the road, but he can see someone moving in an upstairs window. His mother-in-law. What has she been saying?

Joan stretches up to close the curtains, sees the lights of the Land Rover on the road below, hesitates. Stares down at her son-in-law, who stares back.

It's the most eye contact they've had in years.

Owen shakes his head, starts up the engine and drives on.

Joan's upstairs window is the only light in all that

fathomless black where deep time and shallow time nudge against each other insistently. On his right he can make out the shape of the chapel, abandoned but not ruined, locked against the public, peeping above the brow of the next hill, hugging its history to itself.

The single-track road unspools before him. He takes the bends too fast, running the risk of a head-on collision with something coming the other way. But not only does he not care, he's also pretty sure there'll be no one else about tonight. Who goes to the shops this late, if you live out in Kilbroch? No one has a reason to leave at this hour.

So when he rounds the next bend and sees a black BMW in his path, he slams on his breaks, and winces as the two bonnets nearly touch.

Pat, the lawyer who lives way past the castle, nearer to Broch Farm.

'What the...?'

Pat leans out apologetically, all smiles. 'Sorry!'

'One of these days...' Owen shouts.

Everyone knows Pat drives too fast. He lives up here to hide from his enemies, of which there are many. Used to be a lawyer in Glasgow, before he retired, represented so many dangerous criminals over the years, getting them off the hook for violent crimes, that there are plenty who would like a piece of revenge. But Pat was only doing his job, and making a mint at the same time. Right and wrong, justice, didn't come into it. Everyone is entitled to a defence, he would insist, if quizzed about it.

Owen can remember telling Callum about it. 'You know he keeps a plane in his shed?'

'What? An actual plane?'

Owen had laughed. 'A means of escape. In case anyone traces him and finds out where he lives.'

They had sniggered together with good-humoured laughter at the idea. Before tonight, Owen had actually thought of Callum as his friend, someone he could trust, pass the time of day with.

Owen pulls onto the grass verge to let the other vehicle pass. It stops when they draw level.

'Just picking my daughter up from the airport,' Pat calls, before winding his window back up and hurtling onwards along the narrow lanes towards the M8.

Owen turns right at the signpost, bumps over the first cattle grid, and pulls up beneath the beech trees.

The gamekeeper's cottage squats there in the darkness, with all its memories and its history. It used to be a happy place. He wonders again why he never left after Lydia died, but seeing his daughter Ruthie standing in the garden, looking up at the owls (or so she says) he knows why. They're both trapped by the tragedies that took place here. They can't move forward or back. Trauma holds you a prisoner in one place. Owen knows this.

He sits in the driver's seat for a minute or two, before mustering the courage to go inside. He wipes a hand across his face. If he could wipe away the memories as easily, he would. But you do what you do. You make a decision in life and you live with it, and he has to live with his now.

Why was Joan probing at old wounds after all this time? Why not leave it alone? It wouldn't bring either of them back.

He's furious. With Joan. With Callum. With everybody. But mostly with himself.

He watches his daughter for a moment. She reminds him of her mother, Lydia. Absent ghosts are everywhere in his life, in this cottage, in Kilbroch itself. With her long dark hair, she looks almost the same as she did when she was a child, fifteen years ago. It's only in the daylight, if you draw close, that you realise she's a young woman now. Twenty-five. She ought to be embarking on an independent life elsewhere – that would be the normal thing to do – but that won't happen now. It can't happen. Secrets and lies tie them to this place, and to each other. And he'll be damned if Joan will ever prise them apart.

He closes the door of the Land Rover quietly. Ruthie doesn't like loud noises.

'Alright Ruthie?' he murmurs.

She doesn't reply.

He knows she won't.

He walks past her into the house. Above them an owl hoots.

You can't see it from here, but on the rise of this driveway, beyond the next bend, lies the castle, in its beautiful show-case gardens, open to the public every May.

The same breeze moves through those gardens too, and in the greenery above the gorge, stirring the mass of leaves, moving along the silent pathways where no one treads. Privacy, ownership is a wonderful thing. A lonely thing.

Ruthie stands there, listening, after her father has gone inside.

Joan sits on the edge of her bed, manoeuvres her legs up under the covers, drags her book from the bedside cabinet. She tries to concentrate on reading, but it's difficult. Her thoughts jigger about in a manner that's quite unlike herself. She's a tough cookie usually. Everyone says so.

But they don't know the half of it.

She saw her son-in-law earlier, stopping outside her house on his way home, staring up at her window. They're in one another's thoughts. She wonders if Callum has spoken to him. Asked him any difficult questions? He looked angry. But then her son-in-law always looks angry, surly at the best of times. Some people said it was the grief, others said it was a tell-tale sign of guilt. The gossips, the rumour-mongers liked to point the finger at Owen when her grandson went missing. 'It's always the husband,' they whispered. Some people love to suspect the worst, to dig down into a darker place than most would normally venture. People love it, the bones of someone else's tragedy to pick over.

Joan doesn't know what to think. She just knows that her son-in-law and her granddaughter have not been entirely honest with her, that they are hiding something.

'I don't know what it is,' she told Callum earlier, 'but I intend to find out.'

'With my help, you mean?'

'With your help. Or without it.'

She's still not sure if she has convinced him to help her. Callum is a law unto himself, but he was once a gifted detective, she is sure of that. If anyone can help her get to the bottom of this, lay the ghosts to rest, then Callum can. Besides, who else can she ask? No one else is stepping forward to assist an old woman in her fruitless search.

He didn't place any trust in himself, but she did. The school teacher in her will always recognise a pupil that – with only a bit of encouragement – could out-shine themselves.

'When will I stop thinking of grown adults as my students?'

Never, is the answer. If she hasn't dropped the habit by now, at seventy, then it is unlikely she ever will. She can't help it. When she encounters a group of adults, she can always tell which type of pupil they would be in a classroom setting, how they would operate, where they would stand in the pecking order. Group dynamics play out in both the classroom and the 'real world', and some people – as Joan knows – just never grow up.

There is a ragged gaping hole in Joan's life that will never be filled. She has buried her daughter, and she has stared into the worst pit of hell that life has to offer. She has no fear anymore. When you've lost everything, you have nothing left to lose.

Leaning over, she switches off the bedside lamp, silencing any further thoughts. She hopes her ghosts won't visit her tonight.

Above her house, stars gleam in the gathering dark, while the land stretches for miles in every direction.

Strabane

The next morning Callum wakes with a sore head as usual. Every morning is the same. Takes him a while to become almost human.

As he drinks his morning coffee he realises he's got a different task ahead of him, something to occupy his thoughts other than his own past.

When he's driving up to the castle later, he sees Owen outside the gamekeeper's cottage and stops his van.

Owen looks at him sarcastically and shakes his head. 'You again?'

Callum smiles. 'Listen, Owen, about last night. I'm sorry.'

He remembers Owen's reaction the night before, his anger at having his privacy invaded, at the probing of old wounds, his fury with the other drinkers, their stares, their whispers.

'Tell me, Owen,' he adds now. 'Why do you bother to go to the Kilbroch Arms at all, if the other drinkers give you such a hard time?'

'I've asked myself that,' Owen says.

'And?' Callum pauses. 'Have you come up with an answer?'

Owen narrows his eyes. Callum understands that Owen would be within his rights to walk away, to turn his back, but he doesn't.

'Maybe I go to remind myself I'm still human. Am I supposed to change my habits, just because other people have a problem?'

Good point, Callum concedes. He can understand that.

'I thought you were a teetotaller?'

'I'm a man of moderation,' he replies. 'Is that a crime?'

Callum laughs. 'That's true. And no, the odd drink is not a crime.'

'You'd know, I suppose,' Owen adds sarcastically.

Callum accepts the criticism as deserved, and as he drives on, he finds himself hoping, really hoping that Joan is wrong about her son-in-law. He doesn't want to suspect the worst of him. Who does?

George Strabane notices Callum's old red van approaching up the drive, and frowns as he folds his newspaper.

He hears the bell as it shrills right through the hallway, up the sweeping wooden staircase to the spacious drawing-room on the first floor where Strabane likes to sit with its view of the gardens below.

'Daddy,' Lottie's voice calling from elsewhere.

Strabane throws his newspaper down on the table. When he opens the front door, Callum is standing there, as he knew he would be, scratching his stubble, and regarding Strabane with a quiet smile.

'What can I do for you Callum?'

'I wanted to ask a few questions.'

'About?'

Callum appears to hesitate. 'I'm just trying to get a handle on a few things. Joan's asked me for some help, some advice really, and I thought you might be able to supply me with a bit of background.'

There is a long pause before Strabane offers sarcastically, 'A bit of background?'

'That's right.'

'To what, exactly?'

'To a historic disappearance that took place here twelve years ago.'

There is a long pause.

'Owen and Lydia's son, you mean?'

Callum nods.

Strabane gives a half-laugh, but there is a hint of irritation on his face as he glances past Callum's shoulder at the driveway beyond.

'Shouldn't you be gathering wood?'

Callum smiles. 'I'm self-employed. It's up to me when I work.'

Strabane narrows his eyes and sighs.

'Do you remember when he went missing?' Callum persists.

Strabane takes a second to answer. 'I understood he ran away from home and they've not heard from him since.'

'Did you know the family well?'

He smiles. 'Owen works for me. He's worked as my gamekeeper for thirty years. Of course I know him.'

Callum waits for Strabane to fill in the gaps. He's learnt that waiting can be useful sometimes.

Strabane regards him sceptically. 'D'you have any authority or licence for asking all these questions?'

'I'm just trying to get a bigger picture, that's all. For Joan. She's looking for some kind of closure.'

Strabane sighs, and steps out into the courtyard. 'Join me for a stroll in the gardens,' he suggests, and as he closes the great double doors behind him, he glances upwards at the windows above, conscious of Lottie and Sophie up there.

They walk together along the path that leads down to the terraced lawns and sweeping grass slopes that have been given over to flowering meadow.

'We like to experiment,' Strabane says, indicating the drift of wildflowers. 'Lottie's idea. Leave the lawnmower in the barn, let the grass grow to seed. Beautiful, don't you think?'

'It's stunning.'

Strabane glances at him sideways. 'You used to be in the police, I hear?'

Callum nods.

'I can't think why else a local joiner and…' he hesitates, 'forester – if that's what you are – would be stirring up the past. Joan's doing, I take it?'

'It's funny,' Callum says. 'But everyone seems to want to leave the past alone.'

'Except Joan,' Strabane notes.

'Except Joan.'

'Don't you?' Strabane asks, raising his eyebrows.

'Not if I'd lost my grandson, I wouldn't.'

'Fair point.'

'Were you here then?'

'When?'

'The night Robbie went missing.'

Strabane laughs. 'Me? I've been here forever, me and my family in one shape or another. Of course I was here. And my father, and my grandfather before him. Generations down the line.'

'D'you remember anything about that time, the night he went missing? Any small details? Anything might be useful.'

Strabane shrugs. 'It was a long time ago. I remember Owen and his wife were devastated. Of course, who wouldn't be? If one of my daughters took off like that, without saying goodbye…'

'Joan thinks her grandson never left Kilbroch that night.'

'But I thought… I thought he'd taken his rucksack, a few belongings, his passport, that kind of thing?'

It's Callum's turn to raise his eyebrows. 'So you remember something about it then?'

'Well, it was a big event round here. It would be odd if I didn't.'

'Did you know Robbie?'

Strabane shrugs. 'He was my employee's son. Of course

I knew him. Quiet lad. But then, so is his sister. You've seen her about, I take it?'

'She blends into the woods around here, doesn't she?'

'That's about right. Never goes anywhere. Owen did try to get her to normalise once or twice, as far as I remember. She had a stint working in the local charity shop, a spell on the counter at the pharmacy. But she's not one for crowds, as you may have noticed.'

'The neighbourhood must have been very affected by Robbie's disappearance.'

'How d'you mean?'

'Well, a neighbour's child goes missing… you begin to worry.'

'He was sixteen. Almost an adult. We all assumed he just took off.'

Strabane leads the way to another part of the garden, where there are trees and the trickle of water over rocks. It seems to work well, walking and talking like this. Callum always noticed that, during his career as a police detective, people talk more freely and openly when they are outside in the fresh air, walking. One foot in front of the other encourages confession, instead of sitting in a stuffy room, feeling uptight and on edge.

'Besides, there'd always been tensions in the household, as I understood it.'

Callum gives a quick glance sideways at Strabane. 'How d'you mean?'

'Well, Lydia wasn't always happy.'

'She told you that?'

'Of course not, but… you can gauge these things. She used to work for me.'

'Really?' Callum is surprised no one had thought to mention this before.

'We had an agreement. She came up to the castle to clean three or four mornings a week. Part of the deal with

90

the cottage. Owen was my gamekeeper, and his wife put in a few hours too. Takes a lot to run a place this size, you know.'

'I can imagine,' Callum adds, although he can't. 'Did you ever have reason to think she was frightened or distressed in any way?'

Strabane looks a little guarded now, worried in case he has said too much. 'Not in so many words. I came across her crying once or twice.'

'Was that before Robbie went missing, or after?'

'Before, I think. Yes, it was definitely before. She'd come to work upset, try to pretend there was nothing wrong, but you could see there were problems.'

Callum thinks of Joan's photograph album, the smiling snapshots, the two siblings – brother and sister – laughing and smiling, always close. Had their parents argued? Is that why the siblings were so close? He remembers Joan's comment that she'd felt her daughter was struggling in some way.

'You know Lydia committed suicide, right?' Strabane adds now.

Callum stares at him. 'No, I didn't know that.'

Why hadn't Joan told him? Surely that was crucial to any attempt at a belated investigation into what happened to Robbie?

Strabane carries on. For all his initial reluctance, he almost seems to be enjoying himself, dishing the dirt on a neighbour's bad times, a tenant's domestic difficulties. Maybe it made him feel better about himself. That's often the case, Callum has observed. It's the way human nature works. You pass on glad tidings about someone, and you can see it in the eyes – the envy, the niggling anxiety that someone might be having a better time than you. Pass on some calamitous news however, and people love it, longing to know more, with a prurient sense of pleasure. All the likes

91

on Facebook if someone dies or suffers a setback, whereas the tight formulaic 'congratulations' is routinely offered if someone celebrates a success – not that he engages with social media, but he knows the way it works. Human nature is endlessly fascinating and ultimately predictable, if you listen and watch closely enough.

'Couple of years after her son went missing,' Strabane says. 'Guess she couldn't take any more of the grief. Seems a shame though, to leave your only remaining child behind to cope with the mess.'

'Joan never told me.'

'I suppose she finds it difficult to talk about. Tragedy like that. You could barely bring yourself to speak of it.'

'Did your daughters know Robbie at all? Perhaps I could speak to them?'

'Doubt it. They'd have been six and eight at the time. Bit young to be remembering anything, don't you think?'

Callum says nothing.

'It was a long time ago,' Strabane goes on.

'So everyone keeps telling me.'

'Don't let Joan get to you. She has painful memories to bear. When I lost my wife to cancer fifteen years ago, and ended up raising my girls on my own, I said to myself, it's important to bury the past, to move forward all the time. For my daughters' sake.'

Callum looks at him oddly. Don't people normally cherish the past, rather than bury it, if they lose a loved-one to cancer? He stops himself from saying it out loud.

'You must miss your wife very much,' he says now, fishing. A statement, not a question.

Strabane paces slowly, his arms behind his back like a member of the royal family, and assumes a pompous air. Callum can't help but notice the comparison.

'It was hard, yes. But we got through it in the end.'

'We?'

'My girls and I.'

'Oh, of course. Your daughters…'

'Lottie and Sophie.'

Callum smiles at him guardedly. 'They must feel very lucky to have such a father.'

'Oh well,' Strabane laughs, feigning modesty. 'I don't know about that. You'd have to ask them.'

'Maybe I will,' Callum says, scratching his stubble again. 'Beautiful gardens, aren't they? Just beautiful. Nathan does an excellent job.'

Strabane watches Callum now with a trace of uncertainty. 'Was there anything else you wanted to ask me? I mean, if Joan is concerned or worried at all, then obviously we're all here to help. Neighbours and friends.'

Callum smiles again. 'I'll tell her. She'll appreciate that.'

He can feel Strabane's eyes on him as he walks away towards his van. He glances up briefly at the high walls above him, the crenellated turrets, the tower flat, the tall windows overlooking the gorge which lies hidden by trees. He shakes his head. What must it be like to own all of this? He can't possibly imagine.

But he's surprised by one or two things. He can't believe Joan has never told him how her daughter died. Why has she never mentioned it? Too painful, perhaps? Possibly.

He glances in his rear-view mirror and sees Strabane still standing there, staring after him, his hands in his pockets, a studied air of nonchalance on his face.

He turns the key in the ignition and drives away, but Strabane never moves from the spot.

George Strabane moves into the darkened hallway where the shadows lie heavy across the stone flags.

'Who was it?'

He glances up, surprised.

His youngest daughter, Lottie, is standing half-way up

the spiralling staircase, leaning on the bannister. The light pours down onto her from the cupola window above.

'Oh, just Callum from Glenwhilk. He was just passing.'

'What were you talking to him about?'

Strabane smiles and moves towards his daughter. 'When I want to share all of my private business with my daughters, I'll let you know.'

He's pretending a light air of joviality, just as he was pretending nonchalance earlier, but his daughter isn't fooled. She holds his gaze for a long insolent moment that just succeeds in making the fake warmth freeze from his eyes. He walks past her, through to the study, his footsteps ringing on the flags.

Lottie watches him go, scowling.

Lydia

Callum pulls up outside Joan's house, slams the door and moves towards the plant-filled porch. Recognising his bulky silhouette Joan opens the door to him without a word.

'Why didn't you tell me, Joan?'

'Tell you what?'

'Look, I want to do my level best to help you, but how can I do that if you withhold information, if you don't cooperate?'

'I don't know what you mean.'

'Your daughter.'

'Oh. That.'

Leaving the door open, she disappears down the hallway to the conservatory at the back, where she takes a seat.

'I know this is difficult, Joan. But why didn't you tell me?'

'It's... I never talk about it.'

'But–'

She holds up a hand to stop him. 'I can't.'

He sits down beside her with a sympathetic sigh, and takes her hand. She glances down, uncomfortable for a moment, considers removing it, then abandons the idea. He's one of her dearest friends at the moment. She doesn't know how that came about. It just did. Two rough old square pegs, who never did fit into round holes, they had something in common right away, despite their differences in age and gender.

'If we're going to move forward in this case...'

She looks up, surprised he's actually calling it that – a case. A good sign, as it means he's committed to finding out what happened to her grandson.

'If I'm going to make any headway, then I need to know everything. And I mean – everything.'

Joan swallows, takes a deep breath, and summons up her strength and courage. 'There are dark places in my heart, Callum. Places I don't want to go.'

He listens quietly.

'My daughter took her own life. Two years after Robbie went missing. She didn't leave a note, nothing. I don't think it was considered. Perhaps she felt she couldn't cope anymore, couldn't bear whatever it was…'

'What do you mean?'

'Whatever she thought had happened to Robbie. Something weighed heavy on her conscience, and I never knew what it was. It wasn't just anxiety over Robbie, wondering where he was, if he was okay. There was something else. It was as if she knew he wasn't coming back.'

Callum holds his silence, waiting for what she might say next.

'She regularly walked the dog across the fields towards the chapel. One day, she didn't come back. They found her body at the bottom of the gorge, dashed against the rocks.'

'Jesus–' Callum wipes a hand across his mouth, as if to wipe away the deed. Despite their friendship, there was so little he'd actually known about her. He knew she'd had sadness in her life, but such a double tragedy, so close together, must have broken her. And yet, she carried on. Or appeared to.

'It was thought at first that she'd slipped. An accident. Being careless. But I don't think it was that. And neither does anyone else.' Joan looks at him now. 'I think she meant to die that day. Maybe it wasn't premeditated, but she suddenly felt she'd reached the end of the road. If only I'd been there for her…'

'You were there for her,' Callum comforts.

But Joan shakes her head. 'Obviously not. She didn't feel she could turn to me. Not that time.'

She looks up at him then and gives a weak, watery smile. 'And it only takes one time.'

Moments pass, while her gaze fixes on the hills beyond her garden. 'The dog ran home whimpering. They raised the alarm. Owen feared the worst. They began a search. It didn't take long to find her.'

Callum thinks about the gorge tucked away beneath the castle, sheer slopes of slick rock hidden by dense greenery and foliage. It's a beautiful spot, a lethal spot. It was wise not to go too near the edge, even if you knew the area as well as Lydia obviously had.

'Were they sure?' he asks.

She looks at him, perplexed.

'That it was suicide.'

'The coroner ruled that it was, and a post-mortem revealed she was on a heavy dose of antidepressants at the time. Her GP confirmed she had been struggling.' Joan gives a bitter laugh then. 'We all could have told him that.'

Watching her, Callum appreciates that it must be difficult for Joan, opening up all of this now, when she could so easily let the ghosts lie. He admires her bravery and her courage. It was more than he was capable of.

'I just feel I need to do this,' she adds, on a painful sigh. 'For my daughter, and for Robbie.' She pauses, and nods decisively. 'It's the right time.'

Kells Chapel

Callum parks his van at Kells Chapel. It's a place he rarely visits. It's not in use anymore, but belongs to the Strabane family at the castle. It makes a picturesque addition to the landscape, its stepped gable end peeping between the trees.

He opens the gate and walks along the track towards it. An oak tree stands to one side, shielding the building from the wind, its roots snaking towards the ancient mossy stone wall that borders the graveyard.

He places a palm on a protruding slab in the boundary wall, half-way up. If Laura was here, she would be able to enlighten him as to its probable use, for riders attending church on horseback in centuries past, allowing them a handy elevation? For Laura can read the past in the landscape. It's like an archive, if you know how to look carefully.

He passes through into the graveyard itself and is immediately caught by the atmosphere. The crumbling boundary wall merges seamlessly with the land around it, Wuthering Heights-fashion; ancient untended gravestones lean in the sunlight, velvet with moss, speckled yellow with lichen. The porch is locked, as usual.

He makes his way round to the back and stands, leaning against the far wall, where he can hear the torrent of the river beneath. There's a drop just beyond here, down to the beginnings of the gorge, which snakes all the way towards the cliffs at the foot of the castle.

He peers through the trees and thinks about Lydia, the route she might have taken that day, the day she apparently took her life. Ten years is the blink of an eye when you compare it with the passage of time which has crept over these graves.

Did she walk this way often?

Who with?

Was she alone?

What did she think about?

Did she think about her son, was she tortured by memories and the knowledge of what she might or might not have done to protect him?

Did she think about Ruthie, her only surviving child, as she took a step toward the edge of the drop, as she skidded and scraped against the sides of the cliff-edge? Did she try to arrest her fall, reach out to invisible handholds as she fell, grasping at ivy, slippery vines, finding only air?

He wishes he had lived here then. Would that make any difference now, if he had been part of this community when the deaths took place? He shakes his head. Of course it wouldn't. He was busy dealing with his own troubles at the time, trying to negotiate his way around a corrupt police force.

He sighs as he listens to the water below, clattering over the rocks in the gorge. It's the kind of sound that makes you feel alive. He sometimes needs to be reminded of that. What made him think he could retreat to the countryside like this and avoid feeling any curiosity about life? You let people in, you make friendships, and immediately their problems become yours in a sense. It would be good to go through life without giving a shit. That would be great. He's tried it. He's tried very hard to find the meaning of life at the bottom of a bottle. But life just pulls him back in. He's not dead yet, that's the point. He's still very much alive, and ought to count himself lucky for that. Some people don't have the privilege of growing old.

Turning his back on the gorge, he regains the path and makes his way past the mossy gravestones. Most are neglected, their descendants long since perished and no longer here to lay flowers or scrub the moss off the chiselled inscriptions. But one or two are still tended. One in particular, near the boundary wall, where the field beyond encroaches. He picks his way through the graves to stand before it.

Of course.

Lydia MacBride. Wife, Mother, Daughter. Died 17th October 2012.

A small bunch of mixed wildflowers sits in front of the tiny headstone.

Joan would still be laying flowers here. She would not wish to forget, even though she cannot speak of it.

Or Owen? He can't imagine Owen making such a sentimental gesture to his dead wife. Ruthie, on the other hand, was a different matter. She was certainly capable of gathering the prettiest of wildflowers, maybe even stolen from Strabane's own meadow, and leaving them here on her travels.

He glances over his shoulder, senses someone watching him, but there's no one there. Just the wind moving through the branches, and the distant clatter of the burn. He turns and makes his way out of the graveyard, spooked for a moment.

Kells Chapel is a lonely spot. Maybe it's the fact they never use it these days, but it has an air of secrecy about it, as if no one now ought to be buried here. But there is still a community at Kilbroch, dwindling though it may be, and where else to bury a loved one of the hamlet if not here?

Rooks set up a racket in the oak tree as he passes, and as he turns his back on the chapel, he feels eyes watching him. Images borrowed from horror movies fill his mind, the silent dead massed at his back, faceless and unmoving. He refuses to turn around and look.

He opens the gate at the end of the track, passes through, and climbs back into his van.

He feels the need for another visit to Gallows Hill. Maybe he'll find Laura Pettigrew in situ. Another chat with Laura can only do him good, after all.

He turns the key, once, twice, listens to the engine rumble into life, and drives along this quiet road he knows so well.

The Dig

'How are you getting on?'

Laura looks up to see Callum making his way towards her through the bracken. She drops the trowel at her feet and eases herself to a standing position, stretching her back muscles. 'Fine. Plodding on, as usual.'

'Find anything interesting yet?' he asks, glancing around the site.

'Depends what you mean by interesting,' Laura smiles. 'I find all of it interesting.'

He nods, gazing up at the branches of the great oak. 'It's an atmospheric spot, this.'

Laura agrees. 'It is that.'

'Have you had any more trouble?'

'Apart from the midges, you mean?' She laughs, and tosses her hair back. 'No, nothing.'

He glances into the trees at the side, dense pine in two directions, packed so tightly you can make nothing out but darkness. Anyone could watch you from their cover. He wonders if Laura feels that. He rubs his chin again, wondering how best to proceed, thinking, wondering how much to share, how much to withhold.

Laura gets there first. 'So you're an ex-police officer.'

Callum frowns. 'With emphasis on the ex.'

'Once a copper, always a copper, is that right?' Laura grins. 'So what made you give up?'

He sighs, and gazes off into the far distance. 'It's a long story.'

'I'm all ears.'

'Maybe some other time.'

She nods.

'I don't know how many of the locals you've got to know?' he asks.

'Not many, to be honest. I've only been here five minutes.'

'Remember I was telling you about Joan Metcalfe? She's a retired schoolteacher, friend of mine. She's asked me to look into the disappearance of her grandson, Robbie MacBride.'

'When did he go missing?'

'Twelve years ago.'

'Christ!' Then she recollects herself. 'That's a long time ago.'

Callum nods. 'My thoughts exactly. But I've promised to help her. She's a friend. She's paying me too,' he adds, grinning.

'First case as a private investigator?'

'First and last,' he says. 'I gave all that up a long time ago. This is different, because I'm...'

'...doing it for a friend,' she puts in, before he can say the words himself.

He catches her eye and they both laugh.

'Well, I don't know how I can help you,' Laura adds, gazing about the area of the dig, where she has marked out the ghost of a building with string and wire, metal pegs and wooden markers. Her bag of tools lies neatly to one side, a small camping stool beside it, primus stove and flask. 'I mean, obviously I wasn't around then.'

'Neither was I, as a matter of fact. The police closed the missing person's file on him several years ago. He'd packed a bag you see, took his passport, application for a driver's licence, his National Insurance card. Whenever a body is found – in another part of the country – any part of it – no matter how far away – forensics run a quick check to see if they can make a positive identification and bring closure for the family. That's what's supposed to happen anyway.

103

But I don't know whether they even have Robbie's DNA on file. It would depend on how seriously they took the case. The thing is,' Callum adds, staring down at the soil beneath their feet, 'Joan believes he never left Kilbroch. She thinks he's still here.'

A sudden breeze stirs the topmost branches at the edges of the clearing, setting up a faint susurration. They both look up, as if sensing the atmosphere. Laura feels a shiver run down her spine.

'Where d'you think he could be then?'

Callum shakes his head, kicks the dust with the toe of his boot. 'Who knows? But if you find anything, just let me know first, hey?'

She raises her eyebrows at him.

He laughs. 'Don't worry. As an ex-detective...'

'Private Investigator,' she reminds him.

'I never rule anything out.'

'Great,' she jokes. 'So you think I could be digging up more than my Bronze Age broch?'

Callum holds her gaze for a moment. 'Who knows? But I do know someone wasn't too happy about you choosing this particular spot for your dig the other night.'

Her face becomes serious for a moment, losing its earlier levity.

'Be careful,' he warns her. 'If they tried to frighten you once, they might do so again.'

'I don't let things like that bother me,' Laura says.

'Well, perhaps you should!'

She eyes him cautiously.

'I guess I'll leave you to it,' he murmurs, and begins to walk away.

He is surprised when she calls after him. 'Hey!'

He turns to look at her, and she's standing there with one hand on her hip, as if the clearing has become her own little kingdom. 'D'you fancy going for a drink sometime? I could do with a night off, and some new pals.'

He stares at her, not sure whether to be flattered or shocked. 'I'm old enough to be your...'

'Big brother, maybe?' she cuts in.

He shrugs. 'Something like that.'

'It's not a sexual proposition,' she jokes. 'I just need company. And so do you, by the looks of things. We could fail at making small talk together.'

'Okay then,' he agrees, nodding.

Then off he goes, wondering how any of that just came about.

Callum's a man of few words, and those he does utter are often not the right ones. He habitually puts his foot in it. His wife reckons he's on the spectrum, but then don't all wives say that? Ex-wife, he corrects himself. He just knows he's never been good at relationships, always a loner. Not unlike Owen MacBride himself, to be honest.

That's why Callum likes Joan. She's always accepted him the way he is, flaws included. She doesn't judge, she doesn't ask questions – or not too many. And after a few years of friendship, she'd made the decision that he could be trusted – he alone – with the dilemma which haunts her. And whatever they find out, Joan is certain that she can trust Callum to act on his instincts, and in the best interests of everyone.

As Callum walks back to his van, parked on the road below, he thinks about Laura's invitation. Offers of friendship don't grow on trees, young man: he can hear Joan reprimanding him, as if she is walking beside him, at his shoulder. 'Young man' as a term of endearment is stretching it a bit. He's forty-five next month. But Joan likes to maintain her schoolteacher air as a humorous and affectionate façade with those she cares about and is fond of. It's one of her little idiosyncrasies.

105

The bracken has grown waist-high over the summer months and he has to push his way through, carefully negotiating the barbed wire at the bottom.

At the road, he turns and glances back up the rise towards Gallows Hill, where Laura is still working, completely hidden now by saplings of birch and pine, a copse of trees and undergrowth, giving way to forest and woodland. He can make out the crown of the great oak, beneath which she is digging. You'd never guess there was a clearing up there, unless you knew of it beforehand. And you'd certainly never guess its history or its name.

He keeps his gaze fixed on the sky, uneasily. She is isolated up there, hidden from the road.

He makes up his mind to have another attempt at talking her out of it when they next meet. Perhaps she can be persuaded to hasten the work along somehow. Finish early, although admittedly she's only just started. Was a week long enough to achieve all she needed to at Gallows Hill as a site of archaeological interest? How long did she say she was here for? He tries to recall. Was it another two weeks? Another three?

He sees a red kite circling, drawing half moons in the sky with its wing tips, slow manoeuvres that are restful to watch. It's joined by another, then another. He hears their long drawn-out cry. A mournful, aching, wistful note that he loves.

As a boy he grew up in a rough part of Glasgow, surrounded by concrete tower blocks and tenements. It wasn't a bad life, but that's why he loves it here. You couldn't hear a cry like that in Pollok, unless it was from a victim of knife-crime or some other random act of violence. Red kites didn't circle the sky above Dormanside Road where his family lived.

As he climbs into the van, and starts up his engine he thinks about the red kites, how they live off road-kill, or carrion left by other birds. The only vultures in Pollok when he was a boy were the human ones. They didn't perch on rooftops, waiting to swoop, but he was aware of them all the time. Had to be sharp to survive. Some of that built-in caution and wariness has never left him.

Artefacts

After Callum has left, Laura kneels, picks up her trowel and focuses. She's wearing a pair of thin gloves, and as she wipes her eyes, she realises she's smeared soil across her cheekbone.

She sits back on her heels, stares into the trees. Feels the solitude pressing down on her. She's perfectly hidden here. Perfectly screened from the view of the road. She reminds herself she has a rape alarm stuffed in the pocket of her cagoule, a strange gift from her anxious mother who said, 'We always had them in the nineties, dear. I walked the streets of London with my hand over one in my pocket.' She imagines her mother as a young woman walking through Clapham Common, eyes alert for danger. The sad thing is, her mother probably needs it now more than ever, looking as vulnerable as she does. Laura fishes it out, lays it on the grass beside her. Then she's annoyed with herself for betraying her nerves.

Laura wonders now what her mother would have to say if she knew she was here, on her own, digging, when she'd already encountered a fright a couple of nights before. She'd be apoplectic with worry. Which is precisely why Laura never tells her mother anything. It was best not to. She'd only imagine the worst.

She thinks about Callum, with his clumsiness and his shyness, his stubble and his scruffy clothing. She kind of likes him, and she could do with a friend. Laura collects friendships. She likes people, and there are some people she just knows she'll like more than others.

She scrapes away at the peaty earth, gradually revealing more of what lies beneath. She loves the way that landscape is an archive of the past, documenting the distant dawn of all our beginnings.

When a branch cracks in the trees behind her, she turns her head slowly. No one there. Probably a deer, spooked by her presence.

A glint of dull metal in the dirt catches her eye, and at first she's inordinately excited, thinking of her Bronze Age community lurking here in the woods, waiting to be discovered. Of course, there would have been no woods covering this spot at the time. She brushes it down, rubs the surface with the pad of her thumb until a dull sheen forms, and then – with infinite disappointment – she realises it's a Joy Division badge. Nothing so marvellous as a spindle whorl, or a fragment of Bronze Age jewellery.

She lays it flat in the palm of her hand.

'Someone liked Factory Records,' she muses, making a mental note to show Callum. She hears his van door slam on the road beneath and then his engine rumble into life. She could call down to him, but he wouldn't hear. She'll need to leave it till later. She pockets the little trophy in her jeans.

Behind her, someone is watching. Someone who has reason to be afraid.

Laura works on oblivious, the rape alarm three feet away from her on the ground, discarded and forgotten, while the secrets that only an archaeologist can read inch their way out into the open after thousands of years buried beneath soil.

The Past

Callum sits at his kitchen table, carving a piece of wood with the utmost delicacy and precision, so that blonde shavings curl onto the floor beneath his chair. He feels at peace as he works. You need a steady hand for this, so he works in the daylight hours, when his brain is still clear and unfogged by drink.

When he first took on the tenancy at Glenwhilk he was pretty satisfied with the quiet solitude of his new life. Well, maybe satisfied was stretching it a bit, but it was peaceful and had gone some way to patching up the past, putting an end to the pointless round of recriminations and self-accusations. Being an ex-police officer sounded ominous, gave off a taint of corruption, like decay. Oh, there was corruption alright. But it wasn't Callum who was corrupted. He'd been one of the good guys, standing up to the powers-that-be.

As the narrow blade takes off another millimetre of wood, paring it back to the shape he knows lurks beneath, he thinks back to that afternoon, ten years ago now, when the call came through about a botched burglary. He knew without a shadow of a doubt who was involved. A man who kept guns and ammunition in his house, said it was his hobby – a retired superintendent – although everyone knew he was unhinged. He'd met him, seen him, witnessed his odd behaviour, knew that he was not a man who should own a gun licence. And what did he do with that knowledge? He warned them, sent memos advising his superiors that Douglas Hutton's gun licence should be revoked. Did they listen? Like hell they did.

So one afternoon he took the law into his own hands,

and when someone attempted to 'break into his house', he shot them. Several times. In the head. Except it wasn't a botched burglary. It was a teenage boy delivering leaflets.

So, at the Fatal Accident Inquiry, he testified, in front of a public gallery of hushed witnesses. He told them all how many memos he sent to his superiors, how many were ignored.

And the result of that honesty?

Well, Callum lets out a small mirthless laugh. He's looking at the result of it right now. Hounded out of the force, persecuted, pushed to the margins, his life made so difficult he had no choice but to concede defeat and leave the force.

The truth gets you into trouble, he thinks, as he shaves off another layer and blows the yellow sawdust off.

When the media got hold of the story, the public made much of the idea that Douglas Hutton was the victim and ought not to be punished. And the boy who died? He was Romanian, a recent migrant, and lived on the outskirts of a travelling community on the edge of Stirling, so no one cared about him. It wasn't like he was a white middle-class boy from a 'decent neighbourhood, someone we can all relate to'.

He glances at the shavings landing like bright curls at his feet. He thinks about Owen and his silent daughter, Ruthie. Owen's wife, Lydia, who apparently one day decided to slip down into the mouth of the gorge. Joan's inability to let the ghosts lie, her desire to know, to find out the truth. What secrets were they all hiding? What did they know, but choose to ignore or forget?

He holds the blade steady, as he tries to catch that last thought.

Choose to forget?

There's something knotty and difficult here that needs

unpicking, and he's not sure he has the dexterity to do this alone.

Blowing the last of the dust away, he wipes a finger along the shape that has emerged.

He thinks about giving it to Laura, but then feels stupid for even considering the thought. She might take it the wrong way for a start.

He places it on the table beside him, and wishes his son still lived nearby. He'd give it to him.

Twelve Years Earlier

A thirteen-year-old girl stands in the middle of the road, watching her brother as he walks away. 'Robbie,' she calls after him. 'Wait for me.'

He turns on her, scowling, and shouts, 'Go home Ruthie,' and when she won't do as she's told, he yells, 'Go away.'

Her face falls.

She'd heard the shouting earlier, Robbie arguing with their dad. He always seemed to be in trouble nowadays, and any attempts of their parents to discipline him just made the situation worse.

'But where are you going?' she practically howls.

Looking back at his little sister, he hardens his heart. 'It doesn't matter. I've got people to see.'

'Can I come with you?'

For answer, he turns his back on her and marches away into the distance, a small rucksack strapped to his back.

Ruthie frowns after him. She used to go everywhere with her brother. He never left her behind. They were pals, companions. Now he's sixteen he seems to be drifting away from her, shutting her out in ways she doesn't like. He's keeping secrets from them all; he's angry, and that's not like Robbie because he's usually such a good-natured lad, that's what their mum always says about him.

But now everything's changing, and she doesn't like it.

Robbie keeps walking and doesn't turn back to look for his sister again until he's cleared the bend and she's no longer in sight. Wisps of grey smoke drift across the hillside, catching in the trees where clouds of golden leaves cling on. His parents have lit their stove, as have the rest of the few residents around Kilbroch.

He walks on, his head bent, his heart full of rage.

They don't understand what it's like. He feels suffocated by their presence and he needs to escape, get as far away as he can. If only for a night or two. He wants to make them anxious, give them something to really worry about.

His mum tried to reason with him. 'Listen, Robbie. Your dad doesn't mean to get so angry with you. He feels bad. He just loses it when he thinks you're getting out of control.'

'So you're defending him?'

And that was it. Everyone was always defending his dad's actions.

He marches on, the rucksack banging against his shoulder blades, and listens to the rhythm of his own trainers against the road.

Like he said, he's got people to meet and somewhere to go.

Lilac grey smoke merges with the mist, and the peace of Kells Wood settles over the rise of the hill.

And just like that, the past disappears, with all its sorrow and regret.

Time moves on. Leaves fall in amber drifts, cold creeps across the land, snow falls, and the years turn, leaving behind those who are missing, and those who are left.

The Camper Van

Laura packs up her stuff and hauls it down to the camper van in the lay-by, her khaki waterproof trousers protecting her from ticks and midge attack as she brushes through the waist-high bracken.

It's always a comforting sight to see her old camper van sitting there in the trees at the edge of the road, waiting for her. Her home on wheels, for now.

Simplicity is key: this is what Laura has discovered, living this lifestyle for a few weeks at a time. She has a flat on the outskirts of Edinburgh, but nothing says home to her like her sky-blue camper van. She slides the panel door open, launches her stuff onto the bench, stores it away in one of the under-seat cupboards. She has left it a little late, she knows. She arranged to meet Callum in the beer garden of the Kilbroch Arms at eight, but kept working despite the late hour. Now she barely has enough time to tidy herself up, do a quick wash and brush down.

Leaning over the sink, she washes her hands and face, strips off her t-shirt and stands in her bra. Glances into the trees and yanks the curtains closed, just in case. Splashes her armpits with water, deodorises, brushes her hair, pulls it up into an untidy top-knot. Pulls on a clean t-shirt. Examines her face briefly in her sliver of a mirror. She looks okay in a healthy kind of way, but not exactly glamorous. She doesn't care, because that's not what this is about.

They could just as easily have met in her camper van, or at his cottage for a cuppa, but there's something relaxing and celebratory about a Friday night pint. She makes a mental note that if she does drink more, she'll leave the van and walk back.

She hops over into the driving seat, adjusts her mirrors, puts the key in the ignition. Immediately Bjork starts up, her ethereal Icelandic arias spiralling over the treetops, disturbing the quiet.

As Laura drives on, she thinks about the strangeness of this place, something which she'd never anticipated when she set out on her assignment.

As a researcher on six month contracts, she could grab three weeks of the summer, and had secured the permission of the Royal Archaeological Society, the professor of her department, and finally the landowner – although that last one had been a bit tricky. George Strabane hadn't been too keen on the idea of her digging up Gallows Hill, even if it was an unused, remote part of Kells Wood, rarely seen, except by the pheasants and the gamekeeper who kept them alive. And kept them alive for what? She could hear her brother's voice in her head: she was able to quote him verbatim: 'so that a bunch of toffs can take pot-shots at them for a bit of sport.'

George Strabane had been up front in confiding the difficulties of maintaining his land and property. It wasn't a big estate, didn't carry the weight and grandeur of estates further north, so he did it all on a smaller scale. He had to arrange shooting parties for groups of tourists in order to help 'make ends meet' as he put it. Although, to someone like Laura who was immensely proud to own a camper van and a bedsit on the outskirts of Edinburgh, it looked to her like he was making ends meet pretty well. He lived in a castle, after all.

'I mean, who lives in a castle?' she had said to her brother online, when she told him about this place.

'You mean, like a real castle?'

'A real castle!'

She sent pics and a video to confirm it and her twin Simon agreed that – yes, it was indeed a castle. He asked to

116

come and visit, at which point she quickly pointed out she was working.

He scowled at her, but she promised him he could come at the end of the dig, once she'd worked out what she was dealing with.

However, what she had not expected to be dealing with was a freak bogeyman trying to frighten her off and a historic missing persons case, together with a retired (maybe?) police officer intent on finding out the truth – or so he said.

She drives along now, banging the steering wheel to the wild cries of Bjork, then the tempo of the music just as suddenly drops to melodic and lyrical. Through the open window, she can hear the red kites, their stretched wing-tips wheeling with slow grace.

She gazes at the unfolding green of the land with an archaeologist's eye, noting there will be treasures to find here, for the trained expert, or maybe even for the lucky amateur, stumbling upon a find somewhere in those sweeping mounds of earth. To her right are the green fields, falling away; to her left is the natural woodland climbing the hill, and the road she is driving on cuts a narrow path between.

She acknowledges that she feels happy as she drives along, despite the fact someone has been trying to scare her. She refuses to take the threat seriously. She reasons that if they'd wanted to do her any harm, they'd have done it by now. It just makes her more certain than ever that there is something here to find. Certainly, archaeologically speaking. As for Callum's suppositions about Joan's missing grandson still being around here somewhere, maybe that too. She can't help feeling drawn by the drama of it. She is still young enough to be thrilled by intrigue, unaware that curiosity killed the cat.

Callum is waiting for her in the beer garden when she

arrives, sitting at a table beneath the trees, looking more spruce than usual. It looks as if he's actually shaved for once.

'You beat me to it,' she cries.

He acknowledges this with a stiff laugh and she realises suddenly that he's nervous.

'What would you like?' he asks, getting to his feet and reaching into his pocket for change.

'A pint of Schiehallion, please.'

'I'll be right back.'

She scans the lawn, the sparse tables scattered beneath the trees, the lit windows giving a glimpse of the cosy interior. She doesn't recognise any of the other customers.

When Callum returns, he's balancing two pints and skillfully places them on the table. 'You're not cold out here?' he asks now.

'No, I'll be fine.' She nods towards the camper van. 'I've got my fleece if I need it.'

'So,' she says confidently, leaning forward. She can tell already that Callum is not one for small talk and struggles a little in this kind of situation. 'What I'm wanting to know is…' she pauses for dramatic effect. 'What is all this about?'

'You've lost me.'

'The whole private investigator thing?'

He shrugs and shakes his head. 'I've told you, I'm no private investigator.'

'But you were in the police force. Once.'

'Long time ago.'

'What happened?'

'What do you mean, what happened?'

'Well, why are you not in the force any longer?'

He laughs. 'Christ, you don't mess about, do you? Plunge right in, why don't you?'

'It's my style,' she jokes. 'I'm just curious, that's all.

118

And I can tell you're not much of a man for small talk either, so why not just get to the point.'

'And the point is?'

'The point is… I want to know what's going on with this whole mystery case. I mean, it does impinge on me if you put it that way. Someone doesn't like me digging around up in Kells Wood.'

'Maybe.'

'I want to know who. And why.'

'Join the club.'

'So, what d'you think? What's your theory?'

'I don't have any theories.'

'You don't like giving much away, do you?'

'Does anyone?'

Jeez, he thought to himself. It was as bad as talking to Joan.

'You remind me of Joan,' he adds now. 'The retired school teacher I told you about?'

'Who lost her grandson. I remember.'

'She's very direct and straight-talking too.'

'Is that a problem?'

He hesitates, takes a sip of his lager to buy time. 'Honesty can get you into trouble sometimes. Just remember that.'

'Why d'you say that?'

He thinks about his ruined career in the police force.

'Oh, no reason. Just experience, I suppose.'

She would love to probe further, but instead leans back in her chair and gazes around.

'Have you lived here long?'

'Five years.'

'What brought you here?'

He smiles again. 'Nothing in particular.'

'A need to escape? Sorry,' she says. 'It's just, you strike me as someone who's deliberately chosen to hide away in a backwoods somewhere.'

119

'Well, you're right there. Maybe Joan should be employing you, instead of me. Help her solve the case.'

'Two heads are better than one, as they say. Anything I can do to help...' She raises her own glass and sips. 'Oh, I almost forgot.'

She sits up straighter in her chair and reaches down into her jeans' pocket.

'You asked me to come to you first, if I found anything.'

He watches as she draws out a small dull metal object, holds it out to him.

'I found this. At the site.'

He takes it from her, rubs the logo with the pad of his thumb.

'It's a Joy Division badge,' she adds.

'I can see that.'

He holds it carefully, stares at it.

'I was hoping I'd found a Bronze Age artefact linked to my broch, but no such luck.' She watches him closely, sensing his thoughts. 'Could belong to anyone really.'

'Could do. D'you mind if I hang onto this?'

'Be my guest. I don't think it dates back to my Bronze Age structure, unfortunately. Unless Joy Division was around a lot longer than I thought.'

'D'you want another?' he asks.

'Better not. I'm driving. Anyway, it's my turn.'

On the way home, Laura's headlights probe the darkness, picking out the roots of trees on the high bank above her, crumbling stone walls, buckled wire fence posts. Clouds cover the summer moon and a mist drifts between the pines. Her mood is less light on the return journey. She enjoyed her drink with Callum: the chat – no matter how evasive – was entertaining, and she's still intrigued by the idea of what might have happened here once. Stories old and new overlap each other and give her pause for thought. She always likes a good story, even a gruesome one.

As she rounds the next bend, she's surprised by a deer standing in the centre of the single-track road, caught in the headlights. Startled, she slams on her brakes just in time and the creature bounds away, its rump disappearing between the trees at the side of the road.

The camper van has stalled, so she tries to start the engine up again. It takes a couple of times to fire and she glances into her rear-view mirror as she waits. Nothing but darkness ebbing away into the distance. She's passed all the house lights there will be until she gets to the castle, and that's still a mile or two away.

Humming to herself, she releases the handbrake and drives on, a new breeze stirring the treetops above. A heavy August night hangs over Kilbroch, filled with secrets and summer darkness.

She thinks about what they discussed, she and Callum. And she thinks about the tiny badge she found, up on Gallows Hill, what it might mean for Joan's grandson. The police at the time believed he ran away from home, but was Joan right? Did he never leave at all? Was he lurking here even now, in Kells Wood, and was her own archaeological site the same spot where he met his end? It was possible. Certainly, Callum seemed to be hinting as much. But why, and who would do such a thing? Why were they never caught? And why did the police never pick up on the signs?

When a car's headlights appear behind her from nowhere, she's taken by surprise, her thoughts so clearly elsewhere.

The other vehicle gains on her until it's almost tailgating her.

She glances anxiously into her rear-view mirror, but can make out nothing except a blaze of lights blinding her. She can't make out a driver. All she can see is the glare, edging closer and closer. Too close.

'What..?'

She swears as she grips the wheel, trying to keep her eyes fixed on the road ahead. With no streetlights and no road-markings, she needs to concentrate on keeping the van on the road, away from the steep drop. To the left of her the woodland disappears and she's aware of the ground falling steeply away. Her legs feel like jelly and her stomach flips with dread.

'Fuck off...' she mutters to the invisible driver behind her, cursing.

Reaching forward, she presses the hazard lights, eyes quickly reverting to the road ahead, hoping that will work, alarm them enough to make them drop back, but no such luck.

The headlights creep so close they're practically touching her rear bumper, and then – unbelievably – she feels the impact. One crumping thump, before the vehicle behind lets up, but only for a second.

'Shit,' she wails, realising that whoever is behind her means business.

She thinks of Callum's warning, earlier in the beer garden, that she ought to take the threat to her safety seriously, even while she'd laughed it off.

As the headlights speed up towards her again, she takes her eyes off the narrow road for a fraction of a second, but that's enough to misjudge the bend. The sky-blue camper van, faithful friend and temporary home, plummets into the dip on her left.

Radio Silence

Callum is deep in thought as he drives past Joan's house. He notes the warm glow of a lamp in an upstairs window, knows his old friend will be up there, getting herself ready for another troubled night's sleep. How does she deal with her grief, he wonders?

Same as everyone else, he supposes.

With difficulty. And with painful endurance.

He's feeling a little uncomfortable tonight, replaying in his mind the conversation with Laura, thinking of all the stupid things he might have said. He doesn't like letting his guard down.

He pushes a CD into the machine, presses play, and is instantly comforted by the sound of Pink Floyd's 'Breathe' unwinding in the darkness.

'A blast from the past,' he thinks, smiling to himself. He catches himself out being suddenly in touch with his boyhood self, unfettered and free of cares, no regrets yet, no mistakes made, full of joy yet to come.

The road ahead is quiet as usual, fathomless dark despite the summer moon, no street lights for miles.

When he sees Laura's van lying wounded on the verge, its bottom end sticking up at an odd angle, he slows to a standstill. The music is still blaring in his van, so he hits the stop button and a sudden eerie silence descends.

'Shit.'

He flings open his door, and launches himself out into the darkness. Steps carefully to the edge of the verge.

'Laura?' He calls her name, but receives no answer.

He scrambles down the slope, gripping exposed tree

roots and grappling with a buckled fence post. He can hear himself breathing heavily, above the faint hum of his nerves.

He struggles his way to the side of Laura's van where he can see already that the door is wide open. When he gets level, he leans inside. The driver's seat is empty. He looks about him in a panic, calls her name.

Once, then louder.

No reply.

Scrabbling about in the dark, he looks to the right and left, peers into the back of her van, but there's no sign of her.

He walks a few paces ahead on the empty road, stares into the trees.

'Laura!'

One long shout.

But the trees offer no reply.

For one terrible moment he's deeply aware of the darkness and emptiness of the night surrounding him. The silence of the forest seems sinister now, full of some unseen threat, just as Joan had implied.

'This place has something malign about it,' she'd said. 'Don't you sometimes feel it?'

In all honesty, no, he hadn't felt it. Not then. His mind was too full of other things, practical things.

But now he feels it, pressing in on him either side, as he stares into the emptiness, calling out Laura's name and meeting only silence.

He thinks about returning to his van, but decides to search the thicket beside the road, just in case there's any sign of her. A sudden vision swims into his head, of a body being dragged backwards through trees. Laura's body. And he quickly stifles it. He stands there, and shouts her name into the darkness.

Tripping over tree-roots, leaning against mossy trunks,

he breathes heavily. No sign of Laura anywhere. She's vanished.

He taps his back pocket, but realises he's left his phone in the van. He stumbles back along the road, cursing, switches the overhead light on, grabs his phone.

'Police. There's been an accident.'

Around him the trees listen, ash and alder, birch and pine, moving faintly in the summer breeze.

He waits until he hears a voice at the other end.

'There's no sign of the driver. I don't know what's happened to her.'

He pauses, then turns quickly, aware of movement behind him. 'Yes, I'll wait.'

His breath hangs on a thread as he waits to give more information.

In the trees to his right, he notices a flicker of movement and his heart leaps to his throat, hoping it's Laura. Instead, he's almost sure he sees a white figure moving between the birches, ghost-like.

'Laura? Is that you?'

But the figure vanishes.

Laura

He promised the police he'd wait beside the vehicle, but he can't help himself. He has to keep searching. He starts the engine, watches his headlights pick out the road ahead. The moon appears fleetingly, picking out the soft silver birches, then fades once more behind a bank of cloud. While he was standing outside, scanning the dark, his eyes became adjusted to the gloom, but now inside his van, at the wheel, it becomes difficult to see again.

He drives slowly, heading towards the bend that will take him up to the castle. And then he sees her up ahead, a small lone figure, walking by the side of the road.

She turns at the sight of his vehicle and he catches a brief glimpse of her face, her terrified expression as if she is anticipating something much worse. It seems to take her a while to register it's him, and then he sees the relief grow in her eyes.

He stops alongside, leans over. 'Get in,' although he scarcely needs to ask. She's desperate to clamber up into the passenger seat beside him.

'Thank God you're alright.'

She glances at him, surprised at the strength of his concern.

'What happened?'

She shakes her head. 'My poor van.'

'Never mind that. At least you're okay.'

'Only just. Someone…' She takes a deep breath, still trying to absorb the shock. 'They appeared from nowhere. I was driving home, quite the thing. Next thing I knew, there were headlights behind me, and they shunted me.'

'What?'

'They shunted me into the verge, then drove on.'

'Did you get a good look at them?'

She shakes her head.

'Large black BMW-type vehicle. That's all.'

'I've called the police. I'll wait at the van with you.'

Then the obvious occurs to them both.

With the sky-blue camper van crashed into the trees at the edge of the road, where will Laura sleep for the night? It is her home on wheels. She's been parking it outside the castle and waking to the morning birdsong, drinking her tea on the step, gazing at the gardens and estate grounds. Now, where will she go?

'I could... I'll ask Joan if she can put you up for the night,' Callum offers. 'She'd be more than happy...'

'No, it's fine. I'll ask Strabane if he has a room in the castle I could use.'

'If?' Callum says, and smiles.

'I imagine he has a few.'

She appears to hesitate for a moment, and then adds, 'Actually, would you mind asking Joan?'

'Not at all. I'll take you there now.'

They drive on in silence, Laura still in shock and distressed about the damage to her camper van, Callum glancing at her once or twice, checking to make sure she is okay.

At last she says, 'It seems as if my project here at Kells Wood is ill-fated. Gallows Hill is obviously reluctant to give up its secrets.'

Callum doesn't reply.

She shakes her head and watches the tall silver birches loom towards her beside the road as they leave Kells Wood behind and head for the more open countryside, the rolling fields where Joan lives and where Callum rents his cottage. All the effort she has put into securing the funding for this project – the bridges she has had to cross, the red tape she has had to negotiate, the excitement and anticipation she felt – only to find there is a whole lot more to this dig than she bargained for. She has found herself in the midst of some strange set of mysterious circumstances which she barely understands.

She gives a short laugh. 'All I want to do is find my Bronze Age people.'

'If you were of a fanciful frame of mind you could imagine their spirits are trying to tell you something.'

'What's that?'

'Maybe they're saying NO CAN DO.'

'NO CAN DO?'

'Well, words to that effect. What's Bronze Age for *Do Not Embark Any Further on Thy Archaeological Dig*?'

She laughs. 'I didn't have you down as a superstitious type.'

'I'm not. I'm just filling in the gaps.'

'Well don't. Leave that to the archaeologists. I'll put two and two together...'

'... and see if it makes five?'

'Something like that.'

'You'll be alright at Joan's house,' he adds, judging they are drawing near.

There are no lights on, and it occurs to him he should have phoned ahead, to give Joan some warning, but it's too late now.

Glancing out the window, Laura sees a homely-looking villa hidden behind a tall hedgerow, its walls and windows festooned with plants. She imagines it looks bleaker during the less generous winter months, when all the abundance of greenery dies back, but just now it looks inviting, even in the dark.

'Here we are,' Callum says, yanking on the handbrake so that it gives a metallic groan.

Laura stands outside on the gravel, glancing up at the

darkened house. Even here, she feels the past has left its ghosts behind, but she dismisses the thought quickly.

Dan Lennox

'That poor camper van of yours is always in the wars,' Joan says, as she spoons sugar into a hot cup of tea and hands it to Laura.

Laura appears to struggle for a moment. She loves her van, and now she's not even sure it can be fixed. When she and Callum drove past it on the way here, it lay like a wounded beast, its silver back bumper upended to the world in a humiliating posture of defeat. What she really can't get over is that they – whoever they are – did it deliberately. They wanted to cause her harm.

'Who d'you think could have done this?' Joan asks.

Laura shakes her head.

'Well, we'll worry about that one in the morning. In the meantime, there's a spare bedroom upstairs where you'll be pretty comfortable.'

'Lucky for you,' Callum winks.

'But what about the van? I'll need to...'

'We'll sort it out in the morning,' Callum says. 'Well, sorry again for crashing in on you like this, Joan.'

'Don't be silly.'

'I'll leave you to settle in and get back to you in the morning.'

'Where are you going?' Laura asks, with a sudden look of alarm on her face.

'Back to your van, to wait for the police. Someone needs to be there. I'll tell them they can speak to you in the morning.'

'They may want to speak to her tonight,' Joan adds.

'Well,' Callum says. 'I'll let them know where to find you.'

Callum has time to think while he drives back towards the scene of the accident, relieved he has left Laura in a safe place for the night. The woods feel sinister, trees spearing the darkness either side of him as he drives.

When he catches sight of her van, crumpled and upended among the trees on the left, he slows down, pulls over and waits. It feels eerie, especially knowing that someone did this on purpose. But who? A stranger? There are so few people living out here in Kilbroch. The road is a dead-end, leading nowhere except to Broch Farm.

He runs the possibilities through his mind now. The only people who live up here are Owen and Ruth, George Strabane at the castle, himself and Joan. Beyond that, there are a couple of old men, brothers, who live in the Lower Glen Farmhouse, Pat the retired lawyer who occupies a pretty swish renovated cottage at the end of the road, with luxurious lawns, a pond and a fear of being attacked by the victims of former clients of his, and there is the Adebayo family at Broch Farm – Makena and William and their three kids. Apart from that, who else would have any reason to drive up here?

He doesn't want to suspect Owen. Everyone has secrets to hide, but he's pretty certain his friend would not go to such lengths to ensure something is left in the past. He knows Owen. He's spent evenings with him. He can't believe he'd be capable of this.

Laura described a car with bright headlights on full beam, looked like a new vehicle, but beyond that she had no other description. She couldn't see the make or model or registration, or the driver. She'd been blinded by the glare. Just that it was a 'huge black BMW-type thing', although she couldn't swear to it.

Two attacks on her in the course of a single week. It couldn't be a coincidence. Someone wanted to frighten

Laura away, to stop her from digging at Gallows Hill. It all seemed to point in one direction.

A faint wind stirs the pines as he waits for the police to arrive, a reminder of the wildness that descends on this place in the winter months, when the road becomes blocked by snow. The moon appears briefly from behind a bank of cloud and lights up the forest, casting a silvery glow against the trunks of the birch trees.

An owl hoots.

Then, in the distance, he makes out the lights of a police vehicle heading towards him.

'At last,' he mutters under his breath, and wonders who they will have sent.

When he sees his old pal, Dan, climbing out of the vehicle, stiff in his cumbersome uniform, he sighs. Of course. Who else?

There's a young woman accompanying him, and a burst of static erupts from the vehicle for a moment as they gaze about at the scene before them.

Callum steps out of his van and walks towards him, notices Dan's surprised expression and his quick recovery.

'Callum.'

'Dan.'

'Didn't expect to see you here.'

'No. Me neither. How are you?'

'So, what have we got here?' Dan moves towards the side of the road, shines his torch down the bank at the place where Laura's injured camper van lies embedded in the trees.

'This yours?'

Callum shakes his head.

'Where's the owner?'

'I drove her to stay with a friend nearby. She was badly shaken.'

The other officer glances at each of them, wondering how they know each other.

'Callum, you know the protocol. You should have told her to stay with the vehicle.'

'It was deliberate. She was shunted off the road.'

'And the other vehicle?'

'Drove away.'

'Did she get a registration number?'

Callum shakes his head and Dan exchanges looks with his colleague.

'Description?'

Another shake of the head.

'So you don't have any evidence that another vehicle is involved?'

Callum raises his eyebrows and indicates the van itself.

'Mmm, people have done it before for insurance purposes. Looks like a write-off to me.'

Callum suppresses a sigh. And this is the type of officer they keep in the job, while he was forced to leave? 'I doubt she'd get much insurance for it. Or that she'd do it herself. She loves that camper van. It's practically her home on wheels.'

Dan frowns. 'So, a bit of a traveller?'

'She's an archaeologist. Conducting a dig up on Gallows Hill for a few weeks,' Callum explains.

Dan continues to look bemused. Callum knows he doesn't have a clue where Gallows Hill is. Hidden by trees, as it is, very few know of its existence. Once a prominent spot a few hundred years ago when those who fell foul of the law – arbitrary as it was – were executed there, against a backdrop of bare hills, it now lies covered in forest, while the community itself dwindled and migrated slowly northwards. Joan has filled him in on the history of the place, and Callum considers himself a mini expert due to Joan's informative stories over the years.

He knows that his former colleague, Dan, won't have a clue about any of this. He watches him step closer to the vehicle, inspect the back bumper.

'There's evidence of a bump alright. Where's she staying?'

'I took her to Joan Metcalfe's house,' he indicates back the way they have come and Dan nods. Callum also knows he won't have a clue who Joan Metcalfe is. 'You'll have passed her place on your way here.'

'Bit of a remote spot, this, isn't it?' Dan glances around him, and then back at his old acquaintance. 'Can't believe you chose to live out here, Callum.'

'I like it.'

'Seems a waste.'

Callum gives a tight non-committal smile. 'It wasn't exactly my choice to leave the force in the end.'

Dan has no answer to this, but begins to head back to his vehicle. 'I'll go speak with the owner. What did you say her name was?'

'I didn't. Laura. Laura Pettigrew. You couldn't leave it till the morning?'

Dan shrugs. 'We're here now, aren't we?'

Callum gives them directions to Joan's house and watches his former colleague drive away, wondering just how it is that a douchebag like him manages to keep his nose clean all the way to retirement, probably, while men like himself – who feel compelled to tell the truth – are punished for it. Punished and persecuted until their life in the force becomes untenable.

He'd wanted to leave all of that behind, and now here he was, entangled in another case, with questions unanswered and no one apparently interested in answering them, apart from him and Joan. And now, maybe Laura.

The Guest Room

Laura sits on the bed, taking in her new surroundings. A fresh quilt, fluffed-up pillows, comfort cushions scattered near the headboard. A chest of drawers and on it, the photograph of a young woman. All the evidence and trappings of another person's existence.

Laura picks up the plastic frame, examines the young woman's face. She looks happy, smiling but also slightly mysterious, as if she's hiding a secret. Glancing to her left, Laura sees another picture of the same person, this time looking older and supporting a toddler on her hip, standing under an oak tree, her head on one side. She is staring at the person taking the photograph, almost coquettishly, while the child squirms with energy. So much life and joy.

She peers closer, thinks for a moment she recognises that tree, the great oak up on Gallows Hill with its spreading canopy of branches, its dour history. Could it be? Possibly.

She thinks sadly of her camper van, and being unable to spend her nights and days in it. Could it be fixed?

She appreciates Joan's kind offer, but she doesn't feel comfortable with the idea of staying under her roof for the next couple of weeks. Apart from the fact she doesn't want to cause inconvenience, she also can't bear the thought of living in this room for that long. Something about it makes her feel confined and suffocated, smothered by someone else's story. She feels the echoes and memories of another life too powerfully, interfering with the smooth processes of her own thoughts. She needs a blank canvas to work in, not a place cluttered with a stranger's memories.

Joan passes the hallway, catches sight of Laura examining the framed photograph. They glance at each other and a moment of awkwardness and recognition passes between them.

'It was my daughter's room,' Joan says, and Laura nods.

'I'm sorry. I didn't mean to pry.'

Joan ignores the apology, leans in the doorway for a moment. 'I had it made up like this, just in case.'

'In case?' Laura asks, not fully understanding.

'I thought maybe she might need somewhere to stay eventually. After Robbie disappeared... there were problems. We didn't get along so well after that. I felt she and Owen were hiding things from me. I thought she'd turn up at my door one day and I would take her in, let her stay in her old room, just like old times.' Joan's voice doesn't waver. 'But she never got to that point.'

Laura hesitates, afraid to ask, but desperate to know. It's the kind of night, after an incident like this, when confessions and confidences come easily. No holds barred. Laura knows that, ordinarily, this woman would never confide in a stranger, a new acquaintance, but the events of the night have prompted something more.

'Sleep well,' Joan says, and Laura hears her softly closing her own bedroom door.

She knows now that she will do anything but sleep well, despite her exhaustion. All she wants to do is get her vehicle fixed, see if it can be saved. Change has come crashing into her life, spoiling her plans.

She goes to the window, stares out at the fields and farmland beyond Joan's house, the shadowy hills rising under a low moon, silhouetted by a bright white radiance emanating almost from the earth itself. Uneasiness creeps into every atom of her body. As much as she likes Joan, she does not want the clutter of other people's lives, other people's pain. She wants clarity, quietness in order to fulfil the task she has set herself over the next couple of weeks.

She promises herself that she'll make enquiries of

Strabane in the morning, ask him if there's any chance she could use one of his rooms up at the castle. Given that he was pretty reluctant for the dig to go ahead in the first place, she's not too sure of the answer.

Later, as she tries to sleep, she keeps reliving the moment of impact in her head, the glare of the lights in her rear-view mirror, practically blinding her, the narrow road with its perilous bends and steep drop to one side, the disbelief and shock when she realised the lights were almost on top of her, shunting into her back bumper, the sickening dread when she lost control.

And then afterwards, sitting at the wheel, sensing the other vehicle speeding away, leaving behind an enveloping darkness.

The Gamekeeper's Cottage

Early the next morning, Callum pulls up in front of the gamekeeper's cottage, kills the engine, glances around, wondering who is home. Owen will not be pleased to see him, but he has more questions to ask.

He sees Ruthie coming out of a side door. She stops when she sees him, stares.

'Ruthie.' He acknowledges her with a quiet nod, not expecting much in return. It's the best way where Ruthie is concerned. 'Is Owen around?'

Instead of answering, she turns and disappears inside the house. She reappears a few seconds later with her father. Watching her, Callum wonders now if she ever speaks to Owen when they are alone inside the house together, when no one else is around, or if her silence is a permanent fixture. An adult now, it would be impossible for her to live alone without her father's help unless she chose to communicate sometimes. Her reticence and wordlessness is baffling, even while it appears to be accepted by most of those who live in Kilbroch.

Owen breaks into his thoughts. 'What is it now, Callum?'

'Laura found something, up at Gallows Hill.'

'And?'

Callum holds out the Joy Division badge resting in his outstretched palm.

Owen won't look at it, at first. Then, when he draws closer, he grows pale and a look of infinite pain sweeps across his face, followed by one of anger. Without a word, he picks up the badge. Laura has unwittingly excavated a painful memory buried deep in Owen's mind. Taking a moment to recover himself, he says, 'Robbie had one just like it.'

Callum nods, waiting, hoping for more. 'Could it be his?'

'He went camping up there, at Gallows Hill, with a couple of friends, the night before he went missing.'

'Can you remember their names?'

'It's twelve years ago, Callum.'

'I know,' he says, with a look of apology in his eyes, 'But their names could be important. If we can retrace Robbie's exact movements leading up to…'

'I don't want to retrace my son's movements,' Owen says quietly. 'I want to leave him in peace.'

'I understand,' Callum offers, 'I'm just trying to help.'

'Are you?' Owen says, and there's a hard glitter in his eyes which ought to warn Callum off.

But he's never heard mention of these boys before and he's wondering now if they were ever interviewed by police at the time, and if not, why? His entire mind is so focused on that, he once again misses the rage in his friend's gaze.

'Look,' Owen's expression has shut down, his eyes growing hard. 'There's no point. There's no point in you or Joan or I trying to find out what happened, where he is. No point. Tell Joan that.'

'Aren't you at least curious? For peace of mind's sake?'

'Peace of mind?' Owen says, and gives a bitter half-laugh. 'You have no idea.'

'No, I don't, Owen, so tell me.'

'I don't need your help.'

Callum steps back, resigned, and nods. He takes a second, then adds, aiming for a peaceable tone, 'If there is anything I can do to trace Robbie. Anything at all?'

'Yes, there is something you can do,' Owen says, looking Callum firmly in the eye and handing the badge back to him. 'You can stop sniffing about and asking questions that don't lead anywhere. That's what you can do.'

Callum says nothing in reply.

'You're not in the force anymore, Callum. What's the point?'

'The point is, Joan...'

Owen makes a gesture of impatience and fury. 'Oh, Joan!'

'...Robbie's grandmother believes he never left here.'

'And I believe otherwise.'

'She's begged me to help her and she's paying me to do so. So whether you like it or not, Owen, I'll be pursuing this.'

'Some friend you turned out to be,' Owen mutters under his breath at Callum's retreating back.

Opening the driver's door of the van, Callum hesitates, feeling torn. On the one hand he feels guilty about pestering Owen, trying to dig the truth out of him, but on the other, he wants to find some answers and he can't help finding it strange that Owen himself seems to be standing in his way. Surely, if he really believed that the boy had run away, he would do everything in his power to try and find him? Unless, of course, Owen was right and he felt that Robbie did not want to be found?

He sits for a moment, listening to the engine warm up. He is aware that he is being more than a little insistent, intruding on Owen's grief in a way that sits uncomfortably with his sense of loyalty to a friend, but something pushes him on. 'What is it you're hiding, Owen?' he whispers to himself, as he watches the gamekeeper reach his own front door.

Owen turns and glares at him, almost as if he has read his thoughts, before disappearing inside.

As Callum drives away, Owen is very much on his mind.

*

140

Inside the house, Ruthie has been listening. She doesn't speak, but she has spent a lifetime listening to others, and as she watches her father cross to the sink and wash his hands, she waits, wide-eyed, hearing again those words of her father's. 'He went camping up there, at Gallows Hill, with a couple of friends, the night before he went missing.'

A memory tugs at her.

And then her father, saying, 'There's no point.' His guarded hostility towards Callum, as if he perceives a threat to their closed-off private little world. A sudden darkness seems to heave at the edges of her mind, a darkness she does not want to let in.

Her father turns and looks at her. He looks tired and weary.

As she heads back into the hallway, she glances up the staircase and stops in her tracks at the sight that greets her. She has just glimpsed the ghost of a child standing there, on the landing. She is standing very still, hoping to be invisible, listening to her parents shouting at each other in the kitchen below. It is the ghost of her younger self. A time-slip which takes her by surprise. She often has these moments, but they never fail to alarm her, so realistic they seem.

Pained voices shouting themselves raw.

'Our son, Owen! Our son!'

'Don't you think it hurts me too?' Her father, bellowing back.

'The truth,' her mother cries. 'That's all I'm asking for. That we tell the truth.'

'Oh yeah? The truth? And what d'you think that will do to her?'

'This is destroying us!' Her mother, wailing.

'Telling the truth will destroy us.'

A thirteen-year-old Ruthie sits on the middle stair and listens, while the voices echo from downstairs and the rest of the house lies empty.

Words.

Ruthie knows that words hurt. They penetrate like bullets. They are better left unsaid.

Breakfast

When he turns up at Joan's, he finds her and Laura sitting at the table, a pot of tea between them, evidence of toast and jam, already eaten. It looks almost convivial.

'How are things?'

Joan nods without saying anything.

'A police officer came to speak with me late last night,' Laura says. 'Wanted to know the details of what happened. Although, the way he spoke, you'd think I'd wrecked my own van on purpose. Where do they get these police officers?'

'Good question,' Joan chips in.

'I know him, actually,' Callum admits. 'Former colleague.'

'Oops, sorry,' Laura says.

'We weren't that close.'

'Anyway,' Laura rises from the table. 'I'd better make some phone calls. I need to get the van looked at, find out if they can rescue her...' she trails off, not wanting to think about the possibilities. 'I fixed it all up myself, you know,' she says now. 'Inside and out. It was a pet project for two years.'

'Well, let's see what they say,' Joan murmurs reassuringly. 'In the meantime, you're welcome to stay here until you get it fixed.'

Laura hesitates. 'That's very kind of you, but I was thinking of asking Strabane, up at the castle. Two weeks is a long time to put on you while I'm working.'

'Working?' Callum says.

Laura looks at him.

'You're not thinking of carrying on with the dig, surely?'

143

'Why wouldn't I?'

'Because there's someone threatening you, and the only reason for that is they don't like you digging around on Gallows Hill.'

'Maybe.'

'There's no maybe about it.'

'Listen, it's really nice of you to look out for me like that. I appreciate it, but I think I can make my own decisions. I have done so for all of these years.'

Callum looks chastised and there's an awkward silence. Joan avoids looking at the other two, sensing a developing tension and closeness between them that takes her by surprise. She's no fool. She misses nothing.

'Anyway,' Laura holds up her mobile and disappears outside to make a few calls.

Joan and Callum are left alone at the table with the abandoned cups and plates.

'Touchy,' Joan murmurs, smiling.

He nods. 'I can't blame her.'

'I suppose she's had her heart set on this project for a long time, and she's got the site all set up.'

'Doesn't seem like a good idea to continue though, don't you think?'

Joan sighs and looks desperately sad for a moment. 'What do you think she'll find there?' she asks now.

'Apart from a Bronze Age broch you mean?'

Joan nods.

'I don't know, my friend,' he says quietly. 'I don't know.' He lets a moment or two pass before adding, 'D'you think we should call the police, get them to reopen the investigation? Tell them what you suspect?'

Joan shakes her head. 'Not yet.' She wonders for a moment if it's because she's afraid of what she might find out.

'You run a fine bed and breakfast, anyway,' he jokes, rapidly changing the subject.

'Why, thank you for saying so.' She straightens herself and moves to the sink, clattering the plates together.

'No, Joan, leave that. I'll do it,' Laura cries, popping her head back through the doorway, before disappearing again.

Joan sits opposite her old friend and leans on her stick.

'I went to see your son-in-law this morning,' Callum confesses.

'Oh yes?'

'I forgot to show you this.' He holds out the tarnished and dulled piece of metal which Laura found. Joan looks at it, bemused. 'I showed it to Owen.'

'What did he say?'

'He said it belonged to Robbie, that he'd been camping up there, on Gallows Hill, with a couple of mates, the night before he disappeared.'

Joan is silent, frowning, trawling back through her memories. 'That's probably true.'

'He couldn't remember their names.'

Joan sighs. 'I know they were worried about him.'

'In what way?'

'Lydia had mentioned something about him hanging out with the wrong types, getting involved in things she didn't like.'

'Like what?'

Joan sighs. 'I don't know.'

Callum runs through the possibilities in his mind. Smoking cannabis, drinking, something worse? It was an old, old story. Parents always worried about their teenage children and their unknowable dark secrets. Some kept their noses clean, and could be trusted. Others ventured into risk-taking. Which was Robbie?

As if in reply to his unasked question, Joan adds, 'He

was a good boy, Robbie. Kind. Always quick to think of others.' She sighs before adding, 'His sister adored him.'

'Ruthie,' Callum says the name, as if testing it out on the air, that strange creature who never spoke. 'I saw her there. She went and fetched her dad for me. But didn't speak, as usual.'

'She never does.'

'Have you ever known her to speak since her brother vanished?'

Joan shakes her head sadly. 'I'm the last person she would speak to. Owen warns her off, probably.'

'What was she like when she was little?'

'Ruthie?' Joan's eyes glaze over momentarily as her thoughts drift back years. 'I suppose she was always a sensitive child, quiet, but certainly not silent. Robbie's disappearance changed her.'

'They were close as children?'

'Very.'

'She must have missed him deeply.'

Joan stares at the table for a moment.

'Why did you and Owen fall out so badly?'

'I was angry with him, I guess. And I suspected he was hiding something.'

'Before Lydia died?'

'Before and after.'

'It seems odd,' Callum sighs.

'What does?'

'Surely Owen would have his child's best interests at heart and want her to maintain links with her grandmother, the only other living relative nearby?'

Joan is silent for a moment or two.

Callum casts his mind back to his own difficult childhood in Pollok. A brief flash of memory, his mother snatching an ice cream cone from his hand because his paternal grandmother had bought it for him. Shouting on the street, two women yelling at each other, and himself and his brother crying as vanilla mush dribbled on the pavement.

'Your father was a bastard, just you remember that,' his mother finished, dragging them both away by the hand, leaving the 'vindictive old woman' staring after them.

Experience taught him that that's exactly what parents did all the time, causing rifts which affect the next generation, inflicting their grudge-holding on those who follow, although in his own mother's case he knew she had ample justification.

'It happens,' Joan says.

'But you're her grandmother.'

'Makes no difference. Things are as they are. Nothing can change that.'

'There. That's that sorted,' Laura says, coming back into the room. 'They'll be coming for the van in the next couple of hours. I'll need to wait beside it.'

She glances from one to the other, sensing she has intruded on a sensitive bit of conversation, but no one bothers to enlighten her, so she makes a move to finish the washing-up.

'I'm heading that way. I'll give you a lift,' Callum says.

Owen

After they have left, Joan pulls herself up the staircase, glances into Laura's room, the room she always kept waiting for her daughter, and now continues to do so, even though she knows she will never see her daughter again. She pauses on the threshold, looking in. It is strange to see it lived in, evidence of another presence scattered about the room, the pillow dented, the duvet crumpled despite the bed having been made. There is a hollow where Laura sat earlier, perhaps to pull on her shoes. The rug is slightly rucked.

Joan bends and straightens it and when she stands, she comes face to face with the picture of her daughter on the dresser. A younger, happier version of Lydia, before the darkness and the shadows began to crowd in on her life. Laughing, carefree, spinning her toddler son around on her hip. She has others, snapshots of the same afternoon, raising him in the air to the tune of the Lion King. *The Circle of Life*. Joan remembers that Lydia loved to play it to Robbie as a baby, and hold him up in playful imitation of the lion cub in the film, spinning him round.

She reaches out one finger and gently strokes the photo, the two faces smiling back at her, lost in the mists of time. Robbie and Lydia. She can't let them both go. She can't let them rest in peace until she knows what happened to them. And she trusts no one else but Callum to do that for her.

She feels caught out in an act of voyeurism in her own life, snooping about a room that is now the temporary abode of a house guest.

She thinks about how she was never able to remove Lydia's things. She'd kept it neat and tidy, ready for a

148

surprise visit when the darkness seemed to descend on her daughter's life after Robbie disappeared, in case Lydia ever needed a place to rest. And then, when she lost Lydia too, she couldn't touch anything for fear of expunging the fragments of her childhood that still resided there. She didn't even want to disturb the air. She kept it like a shrine, only venturing inside to dust the photo frames, the surfaces, to smooth the pillow where her daughter's head would never now lie. She sometimes wonders why she inflicts such pain on herself, but why not? The living have nothing to lose any more. All they have are the memories, and the fear of losing them.

She's still in her daughter's room when she hears a car pull up outside. She hobbles to the window, thinking it will be Callum back again. She leans on the window sill and looks out. She can't see whose vehicle it is, as it's parked beyond the tall hedgerow that separates Joan's land from the road to Kilbroch.

When someone bangs on the front door she moves across the landing to the stairs.

'Alright, alright,' she mutters to herself when the thunderous knocking is repeated. She can see a dark hulking figure behind the glass and her heart sinks.

She opens the door and stares at her son-in-law, who has never set foot near her house for more than ten years. 'Owen?'

But before she can say anything more, he launches into a tirade. 'What are you thinking of, stirring things up for me and Ruthie?' he says, glaring at her with such desperation on his face she almost feels pity for him. 'What's the point? Getting Callum to ask questions, prying into other people's grief? You might like the attention, but I don't. Think of Ruthie.'

'I am thinking of Ruth.'

'Think of what this will do to her.'

149

'I have…'

He cuts her off again. 'You might not be able to accept it, Joan, but neither of them are coming back. They're gone. And all we can do is live with it.'

'With the guilt, you mean?'

'What are you talking about?' he snaps.

She feels frightened now, but her fingers grip the side table. She's left the door wide open. Her angry son-in-law has a clear view through the hall and down to the kitchen, and could step inside and slam the door behind them both if he so chose. But she doesn't care anymore. She doesn't care what risks she takes. 'I want to know what happened to my daughter, and why.'

'You know what happened to her,' he cries. 'She killed herself.'

'But why?'

'You'd have to ask her that. And she's not here, so no one's going to tell us. So,' he stops suddenly, unable to continue.

She knows he must have carried so much grief of his own over the years, so heavy a burden, but still she cannot dismiss the notion that some of that grief is caused by guilt. How much does he know, and how much is he withholding? She waits for him to say more, waits for him to leave.

Behind the high hedge is his Land Rover, and there's no one about for miles around. There never is.

Joan is used to a life of seclusion. They all are. Miles of farmland between each house, a scattered community who know one another's business despite the distances between their houses. He wouldn't dare do anything now, would he? She looks at him, almost wanting to provoke him into anger to see what he is capable of, to see if any of her suspicions about him have, in fact, any basis in reality.

'I will find out what happened to Robbie,' she says now, in a low voice.

Owen stares at her as if she's gone mad, and shakes his head. 'You don't know what you're doing.'

'Don't I?'

'Playing private detective with your ex-cop friend.'

She almost laughs then when he adds, 'This isn't an episode of *Happy Valley*. This is my life you're interfering in.'

'And mine.'

'No, not yours. She left home, remember. She was my wife. And she was the mother of my children.'

'She was my daughter,' Joan chokes back the words.

'Well, maybe you didn't know her as well as you think you did,' he ends on a bitter note.

She stares after him in shock as he turns his back and walks away. She waits while he starts up the engine on the other side of the hedgerow and listens as his vehicle speeds off down the lane. Then she listens to the silence afterwards.

Pat

Callum had waited with Laura for a short while before the pick-up truck arrived to haul the injured van away. She'd reassured him that she didn't need company, she could manage just fine, so he left her to it and drove on to the end of the single-track road, around the bend, over the summit of the next hill and out onto open farmland, where only a renovated cottage stood to one side, commanding a view of the surrounding hills.

He knew Pat lived here, the retired solicitor. Lawns swept down to a pond where reeds stood tall in the sunshine and a glimmer of glass could be seen through the trees, evidence of a sunroom extending off the main building. It was a luxurious conversion and a perfect retreat for the Glasgow lawyer, a hideaway from a life of seediness in the law courts, defending the criminally suspect. Callum knew that much because, despite his own reticence, he was often good at getting people to talk.

He slows his red van beside the cottage, glancing across at the vehicle parked in the open driveway in front of the cottage. A black BMW. Powerful engine. Powerful headlights, probably. Enough to blind anyone if you put them on full beam while you rammed into the back of someone else's vehicle.

He shakes his head. He knows Pat. Pat is harmless enough, a good sort.

Even so.

He gets out of the van, walks alongside the vehicle, bends down to inspect the front bumper. Shiny, clean, brand-new, well-maintained. With a mark. A tiny mark, and a dent.

'Callum?'

Pat is framed by the open doorway of the cottage, watching him. 'Can I help you?'

There's a moment of awkwardness, and Callum notices Pat's eyes slide to the mark on his front bumper, before looking back at him.

'There was an accident last night. Wondered if you saw anything?'

'You mean the van?' Pat says. 'Yeah, I saw it crashed into the ditch on the side of the road. Quite a bad one.'

'It belongs to the archaeologist. Laura.'

'Is she okay?'

'She's fine, but it could have been much worse.'

Pat nods. 'Yeah, I saw the damage, but,' he hesitates for a moment and meets Callum's eye. 'I thought the police would be dealing with it.'

'They are.'

'You getting drawn back into undercover operations, is that it?'

'Not likely.'

'Then why?'

'I'm just looking out for a friend.'

'I see. Is that what they call it?'

Callum glances at the hangar on the far side of the lawn. He wants to ask the retired lawyer, 'Is it true you keep a light aircraft in there, as a quick getaway in the event of a revenge attack from one of the victims of your former clients?'

Rumours move about the isolated hamlet of Kilbroch without anyone trying. Nothing gets past the scattered residents hereabouts. Except, of course, it had. The disappearance of Robbie twelve years ago. No one, apparently, knew anything about that.

Pat steps out into the driveway now, hands in the pockets of his jeans, and leans down to the mark on his bumper.

153

'Must get that fixed,' he says now. 'A trolley in Tesco's car park, would you believe?'

'There's not a mark on it, apart from that,' Callum observes.

'Well, let me know how you get on. Helping out your friend,' he adds. 'Although I'd be careful. It's not always a good idea to interfere in police business. I thought you of all people would know that.'

As Callum turns away he revises his opinion of Pat. Not such a good sort, after all.

The Camper Van

While Laura waits beside her vehicle, she can't escape the notion that she is standing beside a wounded beast, one whose injuries she can't bear to look at. She'd worked tirelessly on that van for months, looking forward to the time when she could drive away into the hills and camp out in the wilds. She loves this about Scotland, the accessibility of some of the wildest spots in Britain. It was a dream come true to own a van like this. She would pack a bag and head off spontaneously for weekends beside lochs, at the foot of mountains, on islands, parked up beside beaches. She'd stay for a night then move on.

She'd had it kitted out with tasteful furnishings and kept a shelf of books over the bench seat that magically transformed itself into a bed, her favourite paperbacks, and some precious hardbacks about archaeology and nature writing. It occurs to her now that she'll need to empty all of these things, shift them and store them elsewhere while the van is being fixed. If it can be fixed.

She gazes along the winding road, lined by yellow whin bushes and natural woodland, birch and alder dripping with moss and greenery. But rather than admiring the view, she feels a knot of anxiety in the pit of her stomach, like waiting for an ambulance to arrive and for the paramedics to tell her what the damage is.

It's an unpleasant job, but she begins to empty the van of some of her belongings and dump them on the side of the road. She'll need Callum's help to keep them somewhere for now. So when he pulls up a few moments later, and asks, 'Still no sign?' she's insanely grateful.

Glancing at the heap of stuff at the side of the road, she says, 'I don't suppose…?'

'Yeah, of course.' He climbs out and together they begin to load the books, cushions, blankets, cups and pots into the back of his vehicle.

Laura realises she feels kind of homeless without her camper van. She sighs, a hand to her forehead. 'I can't dump all of this on Joan. She's got enough to be dealing with.'

She also hasn't asked George Strabane yet if she can use a room up at the castle for the duration of the dig.

Before she can say anything further, Callum comes forward with an obvious offer. 'Look, why don't you store it at mine for the time being? There's not much and I've got plenty of room. It's just me.'

Before she can respond, he adds, 'Looks like the cavalry have arrived,' as they glimpse a huge lumbering recovery lorry struggling to negotiate the narrow width of the road in the distance. It advances slowly towards them.

'I'd be grateful,' Laura says.

'No problem.'

He climbs into the van and backs it up to the next turning-space to allow the truck the road, and waits while one of the mechanics jumps down to speak with Laura.

'I know it's hard to say,' Laura begins hopefully, 'but d'you think you can save her?'

The mechanic takes a look at the van, and winces. 'Not sure about that. You'd have to check with your insurance people.'

It's not the verdict she wants to hear, and her heart plummets.

'Things are definitely not going according to plan,' she comments to Callum afterwards, as they watch her home on wheels be loaded onto the back of the truck and disappear into the distance, its sky-blue bodywork raised high above the hedgerows.

It breaks her heart to see it being hauled away like that. She knows it's only a lump of metal and she ought to be grateful for that – but still, it hurts.

Kilbroch Castle

As Laura stands in the centre of the hallway, she is aware of wood panelling, dark portraits in heavy frames and a weight of history in the air. A stained glass window halfway up the spiralling staircase lets in beams of sunlight which land on the flagstones in quivering lozenges the same colour as boiled sweets.

She is enchanted, yet unsettled. It's like entering Bluebeard's castle, a fairytale kingdom in which anything could happen and where things might possibly go even further awry.

Contrary to what she'd thought, George Strabane seems only too delighted to lend her a room in the castle. His manner is polite, urbane, charming even, while his daughters watch from the sidelines.

The idea of staying in a castle goes some way towards compensating her for the loss of the camper van. In all honesty, she prefers waking up to the birds and drinking her morning tea on the steps, but failing that, a room in a castle is no mean accomplishment. So why can she not shake off the feeling that something is not quite right with the Strabanes? She can't quite put her finger on it, but one of the daughters, the youngest, seems to carry an air of resentment about her like an extra suitcase nobody wants, as if she is angry with her father. Laura suspects the girl sees her father's urbanity as an act of some kind and wants to blow a hole in his hypocrisy... something like that. Although she could be wrong. Everyone has their own story to tell, and we don't always pick up an accurate version of someone else's narrative.

'So you'll be carrying on with your dig then?' Strabane is asking.

'I've still got three weeks left. I want to see what I can do in that time.'

'I'm sure Josie will have a spare room made up ready. We usually do,' he says. 'But tell me, you must still be pretty shaken about what happened last night?'

She nods.

'I'm surprised it hasn't put you off.'

'I don't let anyone put me off that easily.'

He looks at her. 'You sound as if you think it was deliberate.'

'Oh, it was deliberate alright. I know for sure, and that's what I told the police.'

'Have you thought they might be trying to threaten your life in some way? If so, it hardly seems a sensible course of action to continue with the dig.'

She meets his eye. 'They'll need to try harder than that.'

She wonders what makes her so bull-headed and awkward. She knows he's right to some extent and that it's probably not a sensible plan to continue, but apart from being bullishly stubborn, it's the only chance she's got. She's dreamed about it for months and she can't swerve from her course now. She has a job to do, a task to finish, and she will finish it. Nothing and no one will stop her, insane as that may seem to others.

All this while Laura is conscious of Lottie, his youngest daughter, watching her father with a look that is... not quite sullen, but almost. As if she carries an unwanted secret that she wants to blurt out to the world. As if she wants to challenge her own father, call his bluff. Laura can't blame her. There is an oily smoothness to him which must rankle. She can't imagine he's an easy man to live with, or to have as a father. There's something about the way in which he refers to his poor dear wife who died of cancer, and how he

159

cared for her himself for two years before she died and then brought up his girls on his own. So quick to sing his own praises in that respect, as if he is painting a certain picture of himself as a noble, fine, selfless family man.

She wonders what Sophie and Lottie would really say if quizzed about this version of their father. She makes a mental note to mention it to Callum later.

'Is Josie your housekeeper?' Laura asks now.

Strabane turns to stare at her. 'She comes up to clean the rooms three mornings a week.'

Laura nods. Glancing at the spiralling mahogany staircase, she can't help feeling that the many rooms of Kilbroch Castle would require more than the efforts of one woman to make it hospitable.

'Owen's wife used to clean for us three mornings a week. Came with the territory. Part of the package, if you like. Gamekeeper's cottage, job on the estate. Yes, we missed her terribly when she died.'

Laura feels the skin on the back of her neck prickle, as she follows Strabane up the staircase. 'I didn't know you knew her.'

'Knew her? Of course I knew her. She was my gamekeeper's wife.'

'It's very sad, what happened to her.'

She senses his back becoming slightly rigid, although she could be mistaken.

'Joan was telling me,' she explains. 'When I stayed last night.'

'Yes, poor Joan,' Strabane says, not turning to look at her as he proceeds up the stairs. 'We've had our tragedies out here, but then, hasn't everyone? Although,' he adds, 'I thought it was the more distant past you were interested in?'

He pauses on the threshold of a room, and she smiles awkwardly as she moves past him.

'I'll leave you to it then.'

160

'Thanks. I'll be going out later, to the site.'

'I assumed you would be,' he adds. 'No need to keep me informed of your movements. Come and go as you please. I'll not disturb you.'

Putting her backpack on the bed, she crosses to the long window. A view onto the gorge below, where the burn is hidden by trees and dense greenery. When she pushes the sash window up, she can hear the sound of water against rocks, together with the murmur of the trees, and birdsong.

She can't help feeling overwhelmed by the castle. Who wouldn't be? Floors which creak and slope beneath their layers of vintage rugs, oak-panelled walls, corridors which beckon and conceal. She wonders if Callum knows that Owen's wife had worked up at the castle three mornings a week? Would Joan have mentioned that fact, and if not, why not?

Up at the dig, it's a relief to concentrate again on the few square inches in front of her nose, gently scraping the soil, brushing it away, revealing more of the distant past. It's good to focus on something other than the present and the messiness of recent events.

The arms of the great oak reach above her, and around her are trees and bracken and whin-bushes scenting the air with their subtle perfume. Kells Wood enfolds her in its silence and mystery. When she hears someone approaching, pushing their way through the narrow path she has been making in the bracken, she already knows who it will be.

'How are you getting on?'

She sits back on her heels. 'Fine. Time for a break, actually.'

She's grateful to see Callum hold up a flask of coffee.

'I miss my tea-making facilities in the van,' she says.

'I bet.'

161

Perched on stones, they sit facing each other, sipping the hot liquid and catching up on the day's events.

'What's it like staying up at the castle?'

'Spooky, actually. The place is like a mausoleum.'

'I can imagine.'

'Actually, I wanted to run a couple of things past you. About Joan's missing grandson.'

He nods. 'Assisting a private detective with his investigations?'

'Something like that. Strabane told me that Lydia worked for him three mornings a week up at the castle.'

He nods. 'Yes, came with the job, apparently. Free accommodation, I imagine, for the gamekeeper and his wife.'

'I wasn't sure if you knew.'

'No, it's good to verify these things. Anything else?'

'Yes, there is actually. I was wondering what you thought about Strabane's daughters.'

'How d'you mean?'

'The youngest, I think it is, Lottie. She strikes me as someone who resents her father for some reason.'

'Don't they all?'

'Yes, but there's something different about this. There's an atmosphere between them. My hunch is that she knows her father puts on an act in the presence of others for some reason, and she doesn't like it. She wants to show it up for the performance that it is. I wondered what you thought about that?'

'You could be right. I get the same feeling.'

'Hey,' she jokes, nudging him. 'I could be an insider source of information for you, if you like. Keep my ear to the ground while I'm staying at the castle. That kind of thing.'

He laughs, and sips his coffee. 'I think we need more than hunches. We need evidence.'

162

'Do you think Robbie did run away, like the police said? Or d'you think Joan is right?'

'What, that he's still here somewhere?'

She nods.

He sighs. 'It's been twelve years. Who knows what really happened? I know what Joan suspects. She doesn't trust her son-in-law and she wants me to probe him, but… I somehow hope she's wrong about that. If the boy didn't run away and someone else is responsible for his disappearance, chances are it was someone in the area.'

'Someone he knew?'

'Whether they are still here, though, is another matter.'

Laura blows on her coffee to cool it. 'It would be strange if Robbie was still alive and well, and only a few miles from where we are now.'

Callum glances at her sideways.

'Imagine,' she adds, 'if he just walked right back into their lives? How would Joan feel then?'

'Elated, I imagine.'

'And Owen?'

There's a long silence while they both contemplate the impossible.

'It has happened before,' Callum says quietly.

'What has?'

'A missing person walking back into everyone's life.'

Callum casts his gaze around the clearing, wishing he could roll back time. Laura wants to roll back the centuries, but a mere twelve years would do him just fine.

'Penny for them?'

'Owen mentioned two boys that Robbie was friends with at the time. They camped up here, the night before he disappeared. He doesn't remember their names though. Which seems odd.'

He imagines the scene back then, Robbie and his two mates, building a fire, probably drinking, smoking maybe,

163

sleeping under the stars, trying to freak each other out with ghost stories about Gallows Hill that they'd picked up over the years.

'There's no record of two teenage boys living in Kilbroch at the time, I've checked. It's a small population, obviously – so I imagine they came from Dunbrochan. Maybe they knew Robbie from high school?'

'Will you try and trace them?' she asks him.

'Difficult without names, but I'll try.'

'If only Ruthie would speak,' Laura says now, and Callum looks up at this.

'If only.'

They are both entertaining the same thought.

What might Ruthie be able to tell them if she would only break her self-imposed vow of silence? She is a source of unplumbed secrets which they would love to tap.

Joan's Grief

'I don't know,' Joan says, shaking her head as Callum quizzes her. 'I can't think.'

'Listen, Joan, if you want me to help, you have to tell me everything.'

Callum watches his old friend. He knows that she is stubbornly convinced that Owen is their lead, that all routes lead back to him, but Callum is not so sure she is right. 'You can't think of any names then?'

'The two boys he went camping with?' She shakes her head, frowning, searching the files of her memory, made faulty through trauma. 'He had so many friends. Although...'

Callum waits.

'Lydia thought he was having a hard time at school.'

'In what way?'

'She felt he was being bullied by some of the other kids.'

'Okay.'

'But I don't know much more than that.'

'Is there anyone else Lydia might have spoken to about this? Close friends?'

Joan looks deeply sad. 'I don't know that she spoke to anyone. If she did, she never told me. Like I said, I always had the feeling she kept things locked up. Even from me.'

She turns away from him to find a chair. 'I'm sorry,' she adds. 'This is all so hard.'

'I know,' Callum says softly, and touches her shoulder.

'Why did she do it, Callum?'

He doesn't answer that.

'Why didn't she just come to me instead? I could have helped her. Or tried to, at least.'

Callum doesn't like to see his old friend suffer like this. He prefers it when she soldiers on, hiding her feelings behind a façade of stoical resolve. To see her vulnerability alarms him in some way, making him realise how much he has come to depend on her over recent years while living here in what he has always thought of as glorious isolation. He has probably become more enfolded in this community than he had suspected.

Words

The whin bushes along the edge of the road scent the fields with coconut, and in the woods the bracken grows so tall that the pathways where Ruthie used to walk become almost impassable. The feed bins are full and the pheasants and grouse bob their heads in the pen. They can be released soon, to wander the fields and woodland.

The water in the burn, usually in spate, becomes quieter, narrower, a mere trickle over the stones – even the falls are reduced to a thread – and the vines hang heavy down the sides of the gorge. The rock-face on one side is slick with moss; on the other, the turrets of the castle loom above the dense dark greenery.

Ruthie walks here, alone as always, invisible. She's not supposed to. This is Strabane's land – the gorge – part of his garden estates, technically private property. His daughters come here to bathe and swim. Witches were drowned here once, local legend has it. They call it the Drowning Pool or the Witches' Pond. Bit of a giveaway as to its former use in days gone by.

Only one or two windows of the castle overlook the gorge. Ruthie knows that you'd have to be pressed up hard against the glass to see down into it and even then you probably wouldn't see much. She's not sure which two rooms the Strabane girls occupy. She knows that lots of the rooms are empty, full of furniture that is, but rarely visited.

Her mother, Lydia, always maintained the castle was haunted, she remembers that. She thinks of her mother now, how she went there to clean several mornings a week and knew the place so well – well enough to absorb its eerie atmosphere and experience one or two anomalies. She took Ruthie with her when she was little, hefting her in the car-seat, plonking her on the long dining table while she worked. As Ruthie grew older, she left her behind with her grandmother.

Lydia claimed the old place had its resident ghost. One story was very familiar as her mother repeated it so often, how she once placed Ruthie in her car-seat on the long dining room table, bent to plug in the hoover, and when she stood up the car-seat simply wasn't there anymore. It was twenty feet away, at the far end of the table, with the baby – herself – still sleeping inside.

'There was no one else in the castle at the time,' Lydia maintained. 'Not a soul. The family were away. In the Cotswolds.'

'Maybe it was Nathan, playing a trick on you?' Robbie had cried.

But their mother shook her head. She was adamant she always locked herself in the castle when she was cleaning there on her own, in case of burglars or prowlers. She'd watched too many dark dramas and thrillers to do otherwise.

When they were growing up, Robbie and she had laughed at her stories, and Owen told her not to freak the kids out.

Who knows what the truth of it was?

Ruthie thinks of her baby self now, strapped into that car-seat, and finding herself mysteriously whisked down the other end of a twenty foot long dining table. Was she asleep at the time? She remembers nothing of it.

She doesn't often think of Robbie, or her mum.

So long ago. A different life.

There were words before.

Now all the words have fled, except the ones inside her head.

A Hopeless Case

Callum rounds the bend and sees his own ramshackle cottage come into view. He frowns as he notices a police vehicle parked outside. His old colleague, Dan, is standing beside it, his hand on the roof, waiting for Callum to pull up.

Tyres crunch over the gravel and dust plumes around them.

'You took your time,' he says immediately, as soon as Callum comes level, winding his window down.

It's a hot summer, unusual for this part of the country, and Dan looks hot in his uniform.

Callum looks at him curiously.

'We've had a complaint, Callum,' he begins.

'A complaint?' He raises his eyebrows, wondering what will follow.

'That's right.'

'D'you want to come inside and tell me about it?'

'Outside will do.'

Dan shifts slightly, redistributes his weight, of which he carries too much. Callum notices the lazy movement, recognizes how his old colleague, always slightly heavy, swapped legs as he spoke, resting one hip as if it was too much bother to stand upright.

'One of your neighbours has raised concerns about you meddling in police business, Callum. Stirring things up, asking questions…'

Callum nods along as if he half-expected it, although in reality he's shocked.

'So, who…?'

'I'm not at liberty to tell you that. Complainant's identity remains confidential…'

'Of course. But if it's one of my neighbours… I could make an educated guess.'

Dan nods. 'We've had more than one complaint.' Dan takes a step closer to him. 'People are concerned about you stirring up a hornet's nest.'

'A hornet's nest?'

'Well, maybe the wrong metaphor, but you know what I'm saying. People don't like it. You weren't living here back then, but a lot of people were deeply disturbed and troubled by what happened.'

'Robbie's disappearance, you mean?'

'No one wants that to be revisited. It's not your place to be picking over old wounds.' Dan shakes his head. 'Don't go there, Callum.'

'The police are satisfied they did everything they could at the time, then, to find the boy?'

Dan stares at him without answering, a look of weary patience on his face. 'You were a good detective once, Callum. But those days are over.'

'Well, there's a turn up for the books. It was me who used to tell you that.'

'So listen to your own advice, then, and leave it.'

'Is this an official warning?'

'Not yet.' Dan holds his gaze, and there's something glinting there which Callum doesn't like. 'But next time, it will be.'

He smiles and nods. He can't resist adding 'Gee, thanks for the courtesy visit.'

Dan turns back, shoots a look of injured pride at Callum's tone. 'It's not a courtesy visit. You always were too mouthy.'

Callum says nothing as his former colleague opens the door of his vehicle, hefts his bulk into the driver's seat, and slams it shut. He watches the dust clouds rise as Dan drives away. Stands still in his yard, conscious of the hills to either side of him, the solemn silence, the sheep on the distant rise, the bees and insects in the tall grass, the smell of the logs piled high under the corrugated tin roof of the shelter.

He takes a moment.

Someone made a complaint against you, one of your neighbours. It has to be Owen. More than one complainant? Who else would be bothered, or notice that he has been asking questions, 'stirring things up', as Dan puts it? He thinks of Strabane up at the castle, Pat in his luxury conversion.

More importantly, why should it bother them? Surely, if they had nothing to hide, they'd be delighted to know that someone was trying to trace the boy, answer some of the questions left hanging? For Owen, maybe, he can understand the reluctance, the pain of revisiting such a traumatic event.

The last thing he wants to do is cause offence. Although, is it? Really?

His detective's brain has always been set on auto-pilot, determined to find the answers, to dig away, following lines of both logic and illogic, things which make sense, and others which don't make any sense at all. He hasn't always been successful. Investigations like this one, for example, seldom are. People go missing all the time, and are never found.

Theories had circulated at the time as to what might have happened to Robbie.

He ran away from home, hitched a lift, and ended up down in Dover, disappeared to the continent. Or vanished in London. Or was murdered en route by an anonymous itinerant lorry driver, his body abandoned in a ditch somewhere but never found. He committed suicide, but didn't leave a note, took himself off somewhere to die

171

where no one would ever find him, fell off a cliff, joined a group of travellers, changed his identity.

Or – Joan's theory – he never left Kilbroch at all.

They'd searched the area at the time, painstakingly. They searched sheds and barns, ditches and culverts, fields and ravines. They searched the gorge, they searched the castle and its surroundings. Although Callum thinks now of all those innumerable attic rooms and basements and wonders how thorough that search might have been. After all, George Strabane was an influential man. No one would want to offend him. Teams of divers swept the river, sniffer dogs searched the woods, with all the available technology at their command, infra-red, heat-sensors, although if a dead body had lain for days there would be no warmth evident. Search parties of local residents had gathered, Owen nervously leading the way, dividing the land between them – the fields, the lanes, the woods, the gardens.

So, how come Joan was so convinced that her grandson Robbie was still here? After all that? She didn't know, was the truth. She was just guessing. Following a deeply-embedded hunch which told her that her grandson had not gone far.

'But what if he'd been taken?' people had suggested. 'He could be anywhere by now.'

When Callum put this to her, she had lifted her head and gazed straight into his eyes with cold certainty. 'He was not taken. He's here.'

And that was all she would say.

White witch, female intuition, whatever it was, she felt it.

And although Callum is not inclined to work on such tenuous leads, he can't let his old friend down. He couldn't refuse her. He's just not so sure he'll be able to provide her with any answers in the end. And now, he has been politely warned off the case, threatened with an official warning.

He takes a deep breath, wondering what his next move will be.

Back inside his own kitchen, he takes down the snapshot of Robbie and his sister that he had pinned to the fridge. Robbie is so fresh-faced and young that it seems impossible he would ever grow up. Then there is the one of his mother, Lydia, her profile half-turned from the camera, happy, yes, but slightly mysterious, as if there were things on her mind, things she knew but was not at liberty to divulge.

'Hopeless case,' Callum murmurs to himself, studying her profile. 'Hopeless.'

Joan's Ire

'He did what?' Joan says, her voice rising.

'Warned me off.'

Joan is furious. She can't believe it. 'What business do any of them have...?' she splutters, at a loss for words. 'It's up to me if I want to find my grandson. No one has the right...'

'Calm down, Joan. I know. No one has the right to prevent you from...'

'Or you...'

'Well, actually, they do have the right to stop me,' he points out.

'But you're not going to, surely? You're not going to let them stop you, are you?'

He shakes his head. 'But it's going to be difficult.'

'Anyone tries to give you a police warning – including that old colleague of yours, fat Dan – they'll have me to deal with.'

'That's reassuring, Joan,' Callum says, dead-pan, and she gives him a quick glance.

'You're joking.'

He nods. 'When did you start calling him fat Dan?' he adds, laughing.

'Just now.'

'He's actually not that f...'

'Pound or two of extra blubber on him,' Joan states sharply, enjoying the sound of her own voice, knowing she is being outrageous. 'Old women like me are allowed to speak their mind, Callum,' she tells him.

'I know that, Joan. But if you don't mind, I'll not refer to him as fat Dan. I'm in enough trouble already.'

Her eyes glitter with humour, before the anger returns, a dark veil across her face. He suspects she has always spoken her mind, even when she was a very young woman.

'I trust you, Callum.'

He thinks about this for a moment. It seems a big responsibility, for someone to put so much trust in his efforts. And he wonders why. 'What if I fail?'

'To find anything?'

He nods.

'What's important is that we try. When are you seeing that son of yours?' she adds.

'She wants a divorce.'

'That's not what I asked. I said – when are you seeing that son of yours?'

He lowers his gaze to the floor and shame floods him.

'You should try harder to see him, Callum.'

He knows she's right, but it hurts to think of all that, makes him uncomfortable, the mess of his personal life, the things he should do, ought to do, but somehow never manages to do.

'You're a hard woman, Joan. And you keep me on my toes.'

'Someone's got to. So Laura won't be coming back here to stay then?' she asks.

He shakes his head. 'She's opted for the castle.'

'Can't say I blame her. Bit of an upgrade. Hopefully she'll get that van of hers fixed and back on the road. Nice girl.'

'Mmm,' Callum makes a non-committal noise.

The Shoot

Owen's quad bike veers across the field then comes to a standstill on the brink of the hill. Open sky all around him. He and Ruthie live so much amongst the woodland, it's good to get clear of the trees sometimes. He remembers when he used to come up here and admire the grand vista, layered mountains piling up in the distance, their summits dusted with snow. He's been living his life under a cloud of grief for so long now, he can't remember what it feels like to be free of it. If he could put the clock back... revert to an earlier version of himself...

But you can't change the past.

You can't alter the decisions you make. You have to live with them, the mistakes.

The breeze touches his face. That horizon. He has always loved it, the way you can see into the melting distance, with its promises that beckon but never quite materialise or satisfy.

Lydia had wanted to leave. She wasn't always that settled in Kilbroch. She'd been troubled by morbid imaginings, following a bout of postnatal depression after Ruthie was born which never quite went away; things he didn't understand, although he tried.

He was too taciturn, not the greatest conversationalist in the world, and he'd sometimes thought Lydia needed someone more sophisticated than himself, someone more cultured, who could talk about art and books and poetry and stuff.

'I'm just sick of living here sometimes, Owen. All people talk about is sheep.'

'Not just...'

'And pheasants.'

'Well, the shooting season is what keeps a roof over our heads.'

She'd given him a look then.

He thought it would change when her mother, the biology teacher, moved nearby. A handy babysitter, offering support and stability. So it surprised him when she didn't seem all that pleased. There was tension there, although he didn't know what that was all about. Probably never would, now.

Would things have been different if he'd agreed to her demands and left the area? But what would he have done to earn a living? Where would they have gone? All he knew was this place, and places like it. All he knew was a life outdoors, serving an estate like Kilbroch Castle. He refused to think of himself as serving George Strabane. The man was immaterial, incidental to the job itself. All he wanted was to be outside, to live far away from other people. What other kind of employment offered this privilege?

He tries to imagine life on a housing estate, like the boxy sprawls he can see on the hillside in the distance if he drives to the highest field and stands up on the footrests of the quad bike. Lydia pretended she'd love to live in one of those houses, like her friends, the ones she'd met through the kids' schools, but she'd have hated it just as much as him. Surrounded by nosy neighbours, every window overlooked by a hundred other windows, people staring into their rooms, looking into their lives, sending a searchlight there, living all the time under that public glare.

Lydia's depression would have worsened in a place like that, he's certain of it.

Although…

He hears a sound in the distance, the crack of a rifle shot, followed by others.

He remembers the early shoot planned by Strabane and smothers his alarm. He hadn't realised they'd started already; Strabane offering his paying guests an afternoon of sport.

The beaters are moving through the woods, flushing the young birds out from their haunts. Ruthie is in the kitchen when one of the shooters leaps their dry stone wall with a hunting rifle. A dark figure outlined by the light behind him, he looks like a ghost from the first world war.

Ruthie freezes when she sees him, drops the bowl she's holding so that it smashes on the flags at her feet. She hardly notices the sound. Time seems to elongate, a frozen moment which holds her in its grasp, like a fly in amber, trapped, forever struggling.

Something is struggling to get out. A memory, a scream, a hideous something from a time before. She opens her mouth to cry out, but no sound emerges at first. Then a wail, a long thin wail of pain, as she crouches on the floor, her hands covering her ears, trying to block the world out.

And this is how Owen finds his daughter when he steps through the door. Owen looks up through the kitchen window into the eyes of the man with the rifle. Who shrugs, as if it's of no consequence.

Immediately, Owen is out the door, into the garden. 'What the hell are you doing?' he shouts.

The man with the rifle looks at him as if he's gone mad and gives a nonchalant shrug. 'What does it look like?'

'What the hell do you think you're doing?' Owen repeats. 'This is private property.'

The man puts up a hand in self-defence.

'You can't just charge in here and think you own the place.'

'Steady on, man,' he mumbles, looking shocked and blundering back the way he came.

The pheasant he was in pursuit of scuttles off into the undergrowth, to live another day. But Owen doesn't hear the clack of its wings. All he can hear is the roar of his own blood: the anger, the rage, the indignation.

Men with rifles clambering all over the place, into private gardens, thinking they own the land just because they're Strabane's paying guests.

He's furious.

When he returns to the kitchen he finds Ruthie kneeling on the flags with the broken bits of pottery around her, her face white.

'It's okay, love,' he coaxes, placing an arm around her shoulder, but she shrugs him off and dashes away up the staircase.

A door slams above and he knows she will stay there for hours, until she feels ready to face the world again.

Callum is on his way to visit Laura at the dig when he hears raised voices ricocheting across the glen. Shouting, their voices spilling out into the courtyard in front of the castle, with no regard to who might be listening.

Owen is incensed, enraged, you can tell that at a glance.

'… think you own the place.'

'… news for you, Owen, I do own the place…'

'Barging in… private property… terrifying the life out of her.'

The shouts float over the heads of those listening, those scattered about the glen: Nathan the gardener, pausing at his work near the greenhouses, Sophie back from her jog, Lottie in an upstairs room of the castle, leaning close to the glass, peering down.

Callum stops the van, his elbow resting on the open window, and listens to the dispute. The fact that Strabane is Owen's employer seems to matter not one jot.

'… should be used to rifles by now, man. It's your job…'

'You know I don't own a rifle anymore.'

Callum misses the next exchange which takes place at

a lower decibel, as Strabane mutters close to Owen's ear. Then, incredibly, Owen leans back and takes a swing at the other man, lands a punch on his jaw.

Callum is out of the vehicle in a flash. 'Hey, steady on,' he says, separating the two men, calmly peeling Owen away from further conflict with his employer.

Strabane wipes his jaw where the impact hit, then glares at his gamekeeper. 'Consider yourself an ex-gamekeeper,' he mutters.

The mood instantly deflates.

Owen, still seething, shrugs off Callum's arm and stalks away, his footsteps crunching on the gravel.

As he watches him go, Callum can't help feeling empathy for the man. Would he lose his job and his home now, his gamekeeper's cottage where he'd lived for years, and the woods where he'd worked every day of his adult life?

Whatever anyone else thinks of the man, the suspicions they all harbour against him, Callum can't help feeling pity for him.

He turns to Strabane, wondering if he will follow through with his threat.

Another figure appears, a lanky man in tweeds, rifle in his arms, and looks from one to the other. 'Didn't mean to cause any upheaval, old chap.'

Strabane shakes his head, but says nothing, still too shocked by the punch landed on his jaw.

'I don't know what his problem is. A bit OTT, that's for sure,' the man with the rifle adds.

Callum looks at him. 'Perhaps if you'd given him and his daughter some warning, rather than leaping their garden wall?'

'It's just a damn sport, man. He should be used to it by now. Isn't he your gamekeeper?'

'Ex-gamekeeper,' Strabane sighs.

Lifting his gaze, Callum notices Nathan the gardener looking across at them with a knowing look in his eye.

The castle looms above them all, its high walls dominating the glen it sits in, while the many windows glint in the sunlight. In a first-floor bay window above, Lottie steps back into the shadows, her eyes clouded with resentment.

Sophie stands in the open doorway of the castle. 'What was all that about, Pa?' she asks.

Strabane shakes his head, his lips twisted in a bitter smile. 'Nothing for you to worry about, darling.'

She eyes him doubtfully.

Strabane then locks eyes with Callum and says, 'You see what I mean? A man like that,' he shakes his head. 'Such a foul temper on him. We've tolerated him for years because we know what he went through, but...'

Callum says nothing in reply.

'But I think,' Strabane adds, 'he has just reached the end of the road.'

Excavation

The trees around Laura seem to breathe with quiet intent as she kneels in the dirt, brushing away the ancient layers of soil. It's strange how you don't have to go that far down before you hit a different time period, Laura thinks, as she moves her head from side to side to ease the tension in her neck muscles. She stretches, sighs, glances briefly around the clearing, then carries on with her work.

All of her concentration is focused on the two foot area in front of her nose, as she fixes her gaze on the earth and the small details imprinted there which only she can read. Slowly, carefully, painstakingly, her Bronze Age broch is beginning to take shape. She's found the boundary wall, and she imagines the people who lived here on this spot, three thousand years ago, before there were any trees planted on this hill. This would have been a prominent spot, and their view across the landscape unimpeded. In other parts, where cities like Glasgow now stand, a dense Caledonian forest would have been thriving, filled with bears and wolves.

What were they like? What did they eat? What did they talk about? What did they wear? How like us, and yet unlike us, were they?

These are always questions which preoccupy Laura, and frustrate her because she cannot always find the answers. But the quest itself is sometimes enough, a passion which absorbs all of her attention. It makes life exciting for her, the knowing and the not-knowing, the mystery, the way the past can tease you into submission. It sets fire to her imagination, inflames her curiosity and her desire to know.

As a child, she'd always loved museums. The first time she visited one on a school trip when she was eight years old she was fascinated. She couldn't believe these places existed, whole rooms and buildings and galleries and airy light-filled spaces given over entirely to the discovery of knowledge. And her eight-year-old self made a promise to revisit this experience, to do something in life that would always ensure she could retain that sense of wonder.

She's trying not to think about Callum, and Joan, and Joan's missing grandson, and the badge she found here, at the top of Gallows Hill, lying in the soil where it had lain for twelve years. And she's trying desperately hard not to think about her damaged camper van, and how someone – she doesn't know who – possibly does not like the idea of her continuing with her exploration here.

She bends her head, scrapes another careful teaspoon of dry dust and sand from the layer beneath. The close observational skills and the obsessive attention to detail required often reminds her of doing a jigsaw puzzle, or an embroidery cross-stitch where the stitches are so small you can barely tell them apart. All you can see after a while are the tiny infinitesimal details in front of your eyes, as the rest of the world recedes.

Only it doesn't disappear. Not entirely.

It's still there waiting for you, the minute you lift your head.

When she finds her first bone, she pauses, and the world seems to fall still around her. Nothing moves on the pine-scented air. She's not sure at first what she's seeing.

A piece of fabric, badly deteriorated, the threads of which look suspiciously like nylon.

She sits back on her heels in slow realisation.

It doesn't look as if Robbie is ever coming home now.

Findings

Joan is standing on the lawn, unpinning her washing from the line, when she recognises Callum's dusty red van bounce along her drive. She continues to unpeg the sheets, dropping them into the basket at her feet.

Callum walks around the side of the house to join her.

'Not bothering to fold?' he jokes.

'You know me. Haven't got time for that.'

'I've just been up at the castle.'

She turns to him. 'What's new?'

'...in time to see a huge fight between Owen and Strabane.'

She drops the last sheet in a bundle and stares at him.

'A fight? What about?'

He shrugs. 'I was hoping you might be able to enlighten me. Can you think of any reason why Owen and Strabane would bear a grudge, or have an issue with each other, apart from their relationship as employer and gamekeeper?' He is thinking now of the passion and rage that fuelled their confrontation.

Joan shakes her head. 'That bad, was it?'

Callum arches his eyebrows. 'Owen landed a punch at Strabane, who claims he is now an ex-gamekeeper.'

Despite Joan's distrust of her son-in-law, she flinches at this information. He can see all the thoughts running through her head, anxiety about whether Strabane will carry through with his threat, whether her granddaughter and Owen will be made homeless and forced to leave the cottage that has been their home for thirty years. Where would they go? What would they do?

'One of the paying guests up at the castle decided to

184

leap over Owen's wall into their garden while he wasn't at home. But Ruthie was, apparently. He claimed she was terrified, seeing a stranger with a rifle in their back garden. Understandable.... So, Owen took matters into his own hands.'

Joan is silent, taking all of this in. 'There's more to this,' she murmurs.

'What d'you mean?'

She sits down on her garden bench, and invites Callum to do the same. 'There's always been something between those two. Some sort of animosity.'

'Strabane is his employer. I suppose there might be tension at times.'

'I know that, but there's something else. Something personal and I don't know what it is.'

Callum stares at her profile, hoping for some answers, but again the facts, the real truth behind Robbie's disappearance, slides out of reach. It seems there are mysteries here, complications which not even those closest to the family are able to disentangle.

He waits patiently for a moment or two, then adds, 'There's something else that's bothering me.'

She listens, still gazing at the gently sloping hills beyond her garden, fading away into shades of mild green and violet.

'Why would Owen not own a rifle?'

'What?'

'I heard him. I heard him shouting back at Strabane before I separated them. He said something about not keeping rifles.'

There is a pregnant pause, before Callum adds, 'Why would a gamekeeper not keep guns in his house?'

'He used to,' Joan adds. 'He used to drink too. And now he's teetotal. Almost.'

Callum frowns. 'He's a gamekeeper. Doesn't that strike you as strange?'

'The not drinking? Or the not keeping guns?'

There is a long silence between them and he notices that Joan has grown deathly pale. 'I'm telling you, Callum. My son-in-law is guilty.'

'Guilty of what, Joan?'

He wants her to spell it out. He knows he's being cruel, pressing down on a wound that is still raw, but he's floundering in the dark here, and he can't see a way forward, and he doesn't entirely believe that Joan's instincts are right.

But she just looks at him with a long knowing look, then turns her face toward the hills.

'I don't believe Owen would do that to his own son, Joan. He's not that kind of man.'

'And you think you know him? After living here, what, five minutes?'

He doesn't reply, stung by her retort.

Any bird of prey gliding over Kells Wood at this moment would see Laura alone in the centre of a clearing, thick woodland at her back, a small area marked out by tape and string in front of her. It's not a crime scene.

Yet.

Above her the trees breathe.

She leans forward, eyes focused on what lies before her. She brushes it down, a fibula maybe. It looks too new to belong to her Bronze Age community, too complete, although you never know. And then of course there are the threads of nylon, too closely mixed in with the bone fibres to be unconnected.

She sits back on her heels, hardly noticing the discomfort of her cramping muscles. She expected to find

186

tiny discolourations of soil, the remains of boundary walls, not this.

There is a tangible presence moving like breath through the trees, a sense of menace on the air, which Laura tries hard not to log into. She keeps her mind steadily fixed on the facts. When more of the bones emerge, she stands quickly, grows pale, fumbles in her pocket for her mobile. After taking a couple of pictures, she looks for the last caller on her phone and presses the number. Her fingers are so nervous she drops the device in the long grass at her feet, even as she hears the disembodied voice of Callum on the other end.

When she retrieves it, he's not there anymore, so she tries again.

He picks up instantly.

'It's me, Laura. I've found something I think you should see.'

Exhumation

The atmosphere at Kilbroch has changed. A white police van is parked in the lay-by beneath Gallows Hill and a forensics team from Edinburgh are pushing their way up through the waist-high bracken. Laura's quiet little spot in the clearing, where she was slowly and painstakingly uncovering the three-thousand-year-old remains of a Bronze Age broch, is now crawling with men and women in white suits. Her quietly sectioned-off archaeological site has been invaded and is now cordoned off for other reasons.

Laura stands beside Callum, at a distance.

The chief crime scene investigator lifts her head and gives them both a cursory glance. 'We need the area cleared,' she says.

And in those words Callum feels himself ostracised, on the outside looking in. He has to remind himself he's not a police officer any more. He's a drop-out living in a run-down cottage, doing odd jobs for people and selling firewood. It's what he chose, until Joan forced him into a state of curiosity again.

The peace of the clearing has been replaced by the static of walkie-talkies and police radios. Both Laura and Callum have suddenly become ousted.

As they walk away Laura asks, 'D'you think they're looking at a crime scene?'

'Your guess is as good as mine. They'll have to wait and see what the pathology report comes up with.'

Down on the road, Joan's red car has pulled up and she's standing beside it, distraught. When she sees the other two she takes a step towards them. 'Is it Robbie?'

'They don't know, Joan,' Callum comforts her. 'We'll

have to wait and see,' but he knows that the waiting will be agony for his friend.

He can only wonder what Owen and Ruthie must be feeling, alone in the gamekeeper's cottage, hearing the police activity building in the glen.

Not many people live along the road up to Kells Wood, but rumour seems to move as if by osmosis, from house to house, and the crows above Gallows Hill lift up from the branches with a nervous cawing, telegraphing their unease to the world.

Watching his friend, Callum feels her pain.

When she appeals to him for help, to find out what's going on, he can only reiterate what she already knows. 'My hands are tied, Joan.'

'But surely, you can pull a few strings?'

'The law doesn't work like that. And besides, I'm not Police Scotland's favourite ex-copper. I'm an outsider as much as you.'

Even as he speaks, a police vehicle rounds the bend beyond the trees, filling the narrow road, and his old colleague Dan rolls down the window. 'Was it you, found the bones?' he asks pointedly, directing his comment at Laura, and there is an arrogance and swagger about the way he doesn't bother with preliminaries.

She nods.

Then he turns his attention to Callum. 'Always on the scene, aren't you, mate?'

'Why wouldn't I be? I live here.'

'When will they be able to confirm the identity of the victim?' Laura asks, stepping forward and making a huge effort to be polite in order to glean as much information as she can, for Joan's sake.

Dan's expression closes down, and he looks at her coldly. 'I would query your use of the word "victim",' he says. 'It's an ongoing police investigation.'

Joan bristles at this. In her view, the so-called police investigation has done nothing, over the past twelve years, to inspire her confidence, being largely non-existent. Callum tenses, realising what's to come.

Joan pulls herself up a good two inches taller and directs her own hard gaze back at the police officer. 'The ongoing investigation refers to my grandson, who has been missing for twelve years, and I have a right to know what is happening up there.'

'With respect, Mrs Metcalfe, no one has a clue yet what is happening up there, and nor do we know who those bones belong to. When we have a positive ID, I'm sure you will be the first to know.'

Joan breathes deeply, holding in her anger. While she knows he is right, it hurts to be spoken to in that tone, particularly over a loss which has impacted her life for so many years. A loss more terrible than any Dan Lennox could possibly imagine.

As they watch the police vehicle drive away, Callum rests a comforting hand on Joan's arm. 'Man has the sensitivity of a bulldozer.'

Laura turns to Joan. 'Come on, let me take you home. As I've been booted out of my own dig site, I'm officially taking an enforced break and I could do with a cup of tea.'

She winks at Callum over Joan's head and he watches while the two women head for Joan's car. Joan is a forthright, confident woman, but she looks smaller, somehow, as if the shock has doused the fire in her. She is glad to be led, glad of the company.

Her thoughts over the coming hours, while they wait for further developments, will be dark and painful.

Callum glances back at the police tape flashing blue and white through the bracken in an incongruous manner, and sighs. He wishes he had more power. He wishes he wasn't on the outside, looking in. And he also wishes he could switch it all off and slip back into the tranquillity of his quiet life before Joan turned to him for help.

While the forensics people work at Gallows Hill, exposing the dark earth and revealing the bones of whoever lies beneath, one lone figure stands apart in the trees. No one can see her. No one ever sees her. She walks the woods, invisible, finding secret pathways through the dense thickets, parting the tall grasses, bending beneath the overhang of dark twisting branches. She seeks out the same pathways normally haunted only by deer. And she watches events unfold.

It is impossible to know what she is thinking as they dig up the bones that lie buried there. Does she know what they will find? Her eyes are wide with untold pain which she has carried now for so long it has become part of her. It is all of her. She knows nothing else, other than these woods.

She creeps as close as she dares, crouches down, and watches from a distance, listening to her own heartbeat. She knows that people in Kilbroch think of her as weird, but she doesn't care. All she ever wants is to hide from other people. She wants to be alone, because there isn't any other way of being, as far as Ruthie is concerned.

As the men and women in white suits pull back from their find, she sees one in particular step forward, camera in hand. She winces as they lean in close and take photographic evidence. Each click is like a camera shutter in her soul.

She turns away and wanders back through the trees, brushing aside branches, retracing her steps. No one notices her, which isn't anything unusual. She has walked these woods for years as a barely visible presence and this is just one more day in her life, except that it is different.

As she glances sideways, she stops still and stares. Up ahead are two children, one taller than the other, a boy and a girl. They are staring at her. They look as if they belong to these woods, as if they have been here forever and will continue to dwell here in the darkness even when the rest of the world rolls forward into the future. Then they turn, and she hears their laughing voices before they vanish into the mists of time.

Memory, pulling at her, tugging at her sanity. Memories and forgetting are all she has, and she does not know which offers the most comfort, which has the most power over her life.

The gable end of the gamekeeper's cottage where she has lived all her life comes into view through the tangle of trees, beyond the green slope leading down towards the ramshackle back garden with its four foot stone wall, which the shooter had leapt over earlier, startling her so badly. Her father's homemade conservatory glints in a brief flash of sunlight.

Should she tell him?

How will she find the words?

And what is that darkness that lurks inside herself, the knowledge she bears? She hardly knows herself. Amnesia, forgetting, has been the answer for all these years, a place where no one can touch her, a silence so complete it bears her along like a river, like the burn at the bottom of the gully where her mother fell to her death.

So many memories to forget, so many secrets to hide, but for now they lie locked within her.

No one has the key to release them, least of all Ruthie herself.

They can dig and they can dig, the men and women in white suits, they will never make her retrieve the past or unlock those bittersweet memories.

Some memories need to be buried in a place so deep and dark and secure that no one will ever find them, and that's exactly where they should stay.

Compensation

Laura fills the kettle at the sink in Joan's kitchen, sets it to boil, leans against the counter, watching the older woman with concern.

'You okay?' she asks.

Joan nods. 'I'm fine.'

Laura waits patiently for the kettle to boil, opens cupboards, drops a tea bag into each mug. When the door opens, startling them both from their thoughts, Laura is relieved to see Callum standing before them, his gaze lowered.

'Is it him?' Joan asks quietly, whispering his name softly. 'Is it Robbie?'

'They don't know yet. They'll need to do a post-mortem. Once they have the coroner's report they'll be able to release more information.'

'What kind of information?' Laura asks.

'Establishing the cause of death, for one thing.' He shifts his gaze to his feet and adds, 'Only then will they be able to identify the body. They need to take a DNA sample and see if they can find a match.'

'A match?'

'With Robbie. The difficulty is they no longer have Robbie's DNA, so...'

'So what can they do?' Laura asks.

'Well, there are some options,' Callum says.

'Such as?'

'They could take a sample from a sibling.'

Joan, listening to all of this, shakes her head. 'Ruthie will never subject herself to that.'

Callum agrees. He knows enough about Ruthie to

realise she will never submit herself to any kind of process or meddling from authority. But he knows how these things work, what needs to be done, what will be expected of her.

'With missing persons' cases in the past, they've been known to do just this. It's not distressing. All they need is a hair, or a sample of saliva, from someone who shares the same DNA as Robbie, and then, if it's a match, they'll know.'

'What about me? Couldn't they take a sample from me?'

Callum shrugs. 'Maybe. We'll see what they say. But whatever happens, Joan, we've just got to be patient now, and wait.'

She lifts a hand to her forehead. 'Easier said than done.' Then she adds, 'I know it's him. I know it's Robbie.'

For a moment, a thought occurs to Callum. What if it isn't Robbie after all? What then? Where will Joan go from there?

He rests a heavy hand on her shoulder and presses down. She lifts her own and pats his knuckles, a gesture of affection which is rare with Joan.

Laura, watching them both, feels deeply sorry. When she first came to Kells Wood to scope out the site, she'd had no idea that she would become so involved with these people and she can't help feeling attached to them both, as if they share a common purpose. Although she hasn't known them long, they have both been so kind, and she feels less and less inclined to give up on her dig and simply go back home to Edinburgh. She can't walk away from all of this without first finding out the truth and being there for these two people in some capacity.

'It seems so strange that a strand of hair from Ruthie's head could give them everything they need to know,' Laura murmurs.

'Well, not quite everything,' Joan says.

Callum catches her eye.

'It still won't reveal what happened to Robbie.'

'No, but it means they'll be a step closer.'

Joan snorts her disapproval. 'As if they care about that. Once they've established who the bones belong to, if – as you say – it's a match – they'll see the case as closed. Missing person found.'

'Not necessarily,' Callum says. 'If it is Robbie, they could be looking to open up a new murder enquiry.'

The atmosphere in the kitchen is tense, as each three hold their own thoughts.

'It's only speculation at this stage,' Callum adds. 'We don't yet know what the results will be, but as Dan said, if it is Robbie in that grave, you'll be one of the first to know.'

One of the first? In that statement they can both hear the indirect reference to her estranged son-in-law, Owen, who lives not two miles from her own house, but whom she never visits, and vice versa.

Joan releases a small bitter laugh. 'Am I supposed to take comfort in that?'

Callum sighs. 'I know it's difficult, Joan. But once you've opened Pandora's box, you can't close it again. You knew that.'

'And you think not-knowing was ever an option?'

Callum's eyes cloud over for a moment, lost in his own memories. He can remember telling the truth on a witness stand, at a public enquiry, in front of a sea of curiously blank faces, a gallery of hushed witnesses, and it did him no good at all. It may have served some service in establishing the facts behind a hugely traumatic shooting which rocked the country and devastated an entire community, but it did nothing to ensure that justice was done. And the end result? He became the scapegoat for the police force, the one shunned by his colleagues, hounded out of his job by his superiors by pointing out the weaknesses inherent in the force.

That's what telling the truth results in, as far as Callum can work out.

But he doesn't divulge any of this to Laura or Joan. He keeps his own bitter thoughts to himself, to mull on another evening, as he nurses a lonely bottle of whisky in the solitude of his sitting-room, in search of his own form of amnesia.

Joan is so convinced that the truth matters, but Callum is not so sure of this.

Sometimes, once the truth is out, people choose to ignore it and everything slips back to normal, injustices still in place, with nothing to compensate the victims.

Ghosts Never Haunt the Innocent

Time moves slowly over Kilbroch and Kells Wood. Evening creeps forward through the trees, and the search goes on at Gallows Hill even as darkness descends. Then the hum of the generator takes over and the harsh glaring light in the clearing disturbs the wild creatures who normally inhabit this lonely space.

Ghost-like presences in luminescent white comb the area, using their expertise, while a cold crescent moon shines down from an indifferent sky.

Laura remains at the castle, reluctant to leave.

Her job here is not done, and it may yet be that she can resume her own investigation at some stage. Those distant Bronze Age people whom she is seeking have left nothing of their spirit behind. Laura does not believe in ghosts. She knows that the only evidence humans leave behind are the physical remains: fragments of bone, fragments of pottery or clay, fibres, threads, beads, a Joy Division badge encased in dirt, the shadowy echo of stone ramparts in the earth, and eventually, as the centuries roll on, a tide of plastic we can never be rid of. Landfill, toxic waste. Laura has investigated the remains of crannogs before now, on the edges of Loch Tay. It involved diving beneath the water and identifying the fallen waste that would gather beneath the site of a crannog, a watery midden entombed in the clay. If only middens were all that we are dealing with nowadays, she often thinks.

Nowadays the waste we leave behind does not deteriorate. It remains.

So what now remains of Robbie?

A teenage boy disappears twelve years ago, and was

known to camp up here in the woods, on this very spot? In fact, according to some, he was camping here with friends the night he vanished. Then no one ever sees or hears from him again, and the friends he was camping with? No one even remembers their names.

Up at the castle Laura spends a lot of time lying awake in the vast bed, aware of the darkening night outside. The rooms and the corridors creak. Ivy clambers up the central tower, speckled with night roses that give off no scent. She lies still, listening.

She is not used to lying in a room as vast as this, tall windows lined with heavy drapes designed to keep out the draughts. It smells of mothballs and ancient memories. Beyond her room are dim stone passageways, lofty chambers with dusty chandeliers hanging from a central ceiling rose. The light switches are ancient and hum in a disconcerting manner at times. She's almost sure she received a shock from her bedroom light switch when she clicked it off tonight, accompanied by a momentary buzzing.

Laura sleeps, eventually, and above her jackdaws roost in the crumbling battlements. Below the castle lies the dark glen, hidden by trees.

In the sunken garden a set of stone steps is set in the rock-face, behind an iron gate too stiff to move. Rust-coloured pines, silvery birches and soft green larches guard the way. But you can budge the gate, if you try hard enough, and then you have to step your way carefully down the slippery steps, slick with emerald green moss, treacherous underfoot.

Then down into the dreamy glen, with its mysterious path which winds next to the burn. On the opposite bank is the high rock-face, hung with ropes of vine, slippery with moss, down which Robbie's mother fell. A fallen tree lies halfway across the burn at its widest point, and further on is a bridge that leads nowhere and is no longer in use. Further still, and you hear the falls, a lovely mellow sound, falling perpetually into the hollow they call the Witches' Pond, or the Drowning Pool. Its surface flickers with silvery shards of moonlight.

Few people come this way, especially since Lydia died here ten years ago. Sophie sometimes jogs on the ridge high above, but her father warns her to be careful.

Laura has investigated it before now, in her moments of boredom while the dig is suspended, and has found it a strange, atmospheric spot. She dreams of it now as she lies in her bed in the castle. She feels the brush of the night air against her bare arms, softly stirring the silver birches. Everything is bathed in an eerie glow. Glancing down at her feet, she sees they are bare, and has a moment of lucid thought when she wonders if she is sleepwalking.

The murmur of the burn and the purr of the waterfall are like music in the background, lulling her into a false sense of security, so that it takes her by surprise when she sees the body lying there on the rocks, arms splayed and twisted, neck broken, blood pooling on the rock beside her head.

She feels herself falling, slipping, the stones crumbling away from under her feet as she struggles to gain purchase. She jerks herself awake so violently that the bed jumps – or feels as if it does – then she lies there, perfectly still, staring up at the empty space above her head, blinking.

The ceilings are so high, and for a moment she longs for the cramped safety of her camper van.

She leans over, finds her phone on the bedside table and checks the time.

Four a.m.

Too early to get up. Too late to slip back into a cosy dream world.

She hears a harsh cry, and sits up.

She pushes the quilt aside, steps across to the window. Although it's summer, it seems to be forever winter inside the castle, and as she holds the drape aside, a draught wraps itself around her shoulders.

A fox crosses the lawn below, stands still for a moment on its moonlit path, one paw raised, staring at the bulk of the castle. Laura wonders for a moment what it sees. Does it see her lonely figure standing at the window, high above, holding the drape aside? She must look ethereal from this distance. Like a captive princess locked in a tower.

To Laura, this is what the work of an archaeologist is like. It is like stepping outside yourself and looking back, to see what others might see. It's taking the long view. But more and more lately, she finds that looking back at the past gives one a different perspective on the future. She begins to see herself as an ancestor, a predecessor of those who will come after. She sees modern society on the timeline and realises, with shocking clarity, that we as humans are not at the beginning of our journey, but that the journey has perhaps already been, and we are somewhere near its end. It's just that we never knew it until now.

Gloomy thoughts, perhaps brought on by the atmosphere of the glen and the recent discovery up at Gallows Hill, but she cannot help herself.

'You've always been a deep one,' her twin Simon tells her.

And she has.

In another part of the castle, one of the windows downstairs is lit by a small lamp. George Strabane sits at his desk, his chin in his hand, brooding. He knows that on his land right now, a team of forensics are scouring the clearing on Gallows Hill, before exhuming and removing the remains of whoever they have found there. He stares hard at the wall, frowning, then slams his hand on the desk.

That's the last thing he'd wanted, people sniffing around the estate. He should have known not to encourage Laura. It

200

was one thing to suffer an archaeologist inspecting Gallows Hill in search of an ancient broch, quite another to have a crime scene investigator picking over the site with her team of white-clad minions.

A dead body. On his land. On his watch.

He mulls on the fact that Laura knew he was reluctant to allow the dig to go ahead in the first place. What will she take from that, now they've made this gruesome discovery? Will she think to herself, why the reluctance? Will she report his reluctance back to anyone else, like Joan for example, or that jumped-up busy-body of an ex-detective who rents a cottage from him? And what will they make of it, now a body has been found?

Ironically enough, she is sleeping under his roof this very minute. He can't help thinking that she will be well-advised to leave this place and never come back. Should he communicate that thought to her in some way?

Outside, the fox disappears into the undergrowth, its coppery coat streaked with silver.

Strabane is still awake when a pale dawn floods the perimeters of the estate and the early morning mist picks out cobwebs between every spike of grass.

Something keeps him awake. His conscience?

It is a fact that ghosts never haunt the innocent.

Glass Houses

Owen is in his back garden when they arrive, one male, one female.

He hears the car doors slamming, and as he does so, it feels as if all his nightmares of the past twelve years have come to haunt him. The sun slides behind a cloud and he feels the shadow of it pass across his soul, darkening what small glimmer of light he has tried to live his life by.

Ruthie is sitting at a table in the conservatory, surrounded by hanging plants, her chair pulled up to a folding table on which is arranged a half-completed jigsaw. She spends hours on these, carefully slotting the tiny pieces together, gradually forming a picture. This one is of an improbable scene in Japan, a place she is never likely to visit, with spartan trees and ethereal-looking mountains, more sheer than any in Scotland. It's a copy of a painting, executed three centuries earlier by a famous artist using ink and calligraphy brushes.

He has always encouraged her because he knows it occupies her thoughts, serves some process in her mind that is important to her, somehow. Slotting the pieces together to create a whole, returning a fragmented vision back to what it once was. He's noticed that she sometimes looks at peace when she's working on it.

He can see beyond Ruthie to the two suits approaching along the side of the house and he knows that her world is about to be shattered. She cannot see them yet, doesn't even hear them from inside the glass lean-to, so engrossed is she in her puzzle. He built the glass-house, as they called it, especially for her, filled it with plants, dragged some furniture into place, so that she could sit here in the

202

sun, awash with aqueous green light, surrounded by leafy tomato plants, and work on her puzzles.

As they walk down the side path an odd phrase arrives in his head from nowhere, prompted by the thought of the lean-to he constructed.

People in glass houses...

Has he thrown any stones? Not that he knows of. Is his life fragile? You bet it is. These people are about to shatter it, and with this knowledge he feels all the ghosts he has tried to bury come tearing and screaming out of the darkness.

But Ruthie, thank God, sees nothing.

Knows nothing yet.

Remains blissfully ignorant, still absorbed by the pieces of a puzzle describing inky mountain ridges, topped by regal pines; protected by her silence, a silence that perhaps – he admits to himself – he has gone some way to preserving.

He is sometimes brave enough to ask himself: who am I trying to protect?

'Mr MacBride?' a voice says.

Owen looks up.

'We'd like to have a few words with you, if that's okay?'

He cannot help himself. He feels intimidated by their power, their authority. Their presence has no place in these woods, which only things of nature inhabit. It's his kingdom, a world set apart from others, even though none of this belongs to him: he is only the caretaker, a custodian with little or no true power, who spends all of his days nurturing the woodland and the pheasants who breed there. He has protected it all for so long, and now here they come, tramping through it with their need for truth, desperate to dig up what is best left hidden.

He stares at them, and then at Ruthie through the glass.

'You don't know what you're doing,' he tells them.

The officers exchange a quick glance, and step forward. 'Perhaps it's best if we explain right away, Mr MacBride,' the woman begins. 'You're aware that an archaeologist has been working in the area? We've found bones lying in a shallow grave which could belong to your son.'

They wait for a moment, expecting a cataclysmic reaction, but Owen remains calm, although beneath this calm is a terrible fear.

'We can't be certain at the moment, but one way to get a positive ID and confirm this, is…' the officer glances towards the glass lean-to, 'if we take a DNA sample from your daughter.'

Ruthie stands up suddenly, noticing the intruders for the first time. She stands frozen for a long moment and as they step closer, she knocks over the table without a care for her work completed so far, scattering the tiny pieces, breaking up the puzzle she has almost finished. Although she can't hear their words through the glass, communication is nine tenths non-verbal and she has gathered a pretty clear gist of what they are here for.

'Is that necessary?'

'I'm afraid it is, Mr MacBride.'

Both glance sideways at Owen's daughter.

'I'm not sure that's a good idea.'

The officers meet his gaze.

'It's not a request, Mr MacBride.'

At this, Ruthie backs away, through the open door behind her, into the house. Owen makes a move towards her, but she disappears inside. She stands for just a moment in the hallway, that long hallway in which she once stood and overheard conversations between her parents so many years ago now, where memories flicker in the shadows.

She hesitates for only a second, then heads for the door to the front porch, the door they never use, grabs the keys and yanks it open. She is out onto the drive in seconds, the sweeping driveway that runs up to the castle, but instead of heading up that way, she turns right. She can hear footsteps behind her, figures appearing from the side of the house. She pushes her way into the thicket of rhododendrons that line the road, and is instantly swallowed into the undergrowth.

She runs along secret tracks, pushing aside branches, trying to lose herself.

She hears a shout behind her, but nothing will make her pause or turn back.

She crashes on through the trees, following a path only she knows, on through the labyrinth of Kells Wood.

Kells Wood

A huge upended oak lies on its side, brought down by last autumn's storms, its crown softly decaying into the moss and stones, its bare earthy roots exposed. Ruthie makes her way into the crawl space on her hands and knees, and sits there, among the spiders and the insects, listening to the noises of Kells Wood all around her.

She's too old for this kind of caper, she knows. But she's never really grown up. She has been kept in a kind of stasis, frozen in time, unchanging. A state of denial from which she has absolutely no intention of waking up. There are memories buried deep, so dark that it would spell death if she unearthed them.

She can hear her own panicked breathing begin to slow as she focuses on the movements of the birds in the undergrowth, the cry of a red kite carving the silence up above. She doesn't want these intruders marching through their cottage, through their lives. Even if her father thinks it's for the best.

He has never known what is best. Parents never do, do they?

A line was drawn in her life, twelve years ago.

Before and After.

She and Robbie playing in the woods, she and Robbie walking home from the school bus together, she and Robbie in league against the rest of the world. Robbie protecting her at school when she was bullied, standing up to the class of 1C when they turned on her because they had nothing better to do and they were an odd mix that should never have been put in the same class together in the first place.

(They changed the register the following year, after it was identified as the class from hell).

It was always her and Robbie against the rest of the world.

And then... he vanished.

One day he was simply not there anymore, and she can't even remember how it happened, or the last time she saw him.

When the police questioned her at the time, she had no answers. Her parents had watched anxiously from the sofa as she was interviewed, until her mum stepped forward and demanded, 'That's enough. Can't you see she doesn't know anything? She's upset.'

And then the muddy, murky years that followed until her mother stepped out into the gorge one afternoon and never came home, leaving Ruthie and her father on their own.

She chose oblivion over us, Ruthie thinks. She let the air catch her, except it didn't, did it? It slammed her hard against the watery rocks beneath, and her blood mixed briefly with the green of the mosses, and they found her there, her hair rippling sideways in the current. Her body opened up in abandonment like a flower, lotus pose, cactus arms branching sideways in a gesture of complete relaxation. Like Ophelia.

A pre-Raphaelite image which – although Ruthie never saw her mother's body – has remained with her ever since, like the plate illustration in one of her grandmother's old copies of a play called *Hamlet*. Ruthie had stared at this illustration for long hours at a time as a child, the woman floating in the shallow water, long hair threaded and looped with delicate flowers, the stream supporting and flowing over the ripples of her hair and gown. And when her mother died, this was always the image Ruthie thought of.

Ruthie was fifteen when she lost her mother, thirteen when her brother disappeared.

She remembers she used to listen at doors a lot, trying to find out the truth, but she also remembers that she didn't try very hard. She didn't want to know, because the truth was something horrific, a yawning, gaping hole in the rock-face that would take her down into Hell, just like the stories she used to read about Orpheus and Euridyce. He shouldn't have looked back but he did. And she stayed forever underground.

Robbie.

She whispers his name now.

It is always on her lips, but she doesn't want to remember. She loved Robbie, and Robbie loved her.

'Ruthie!'

She hears her name being called in the distance, and the crash of footsteps through the bracken.

She keeps still, and only the spiders and insects make any movement where she crouches.

The Gamekeeper's Cottage

Back at the cottage Owen regards the two officers and shrugs his shoulders, opening his palms wide.

'She's her own person,' he says. 'I can't make her do anything. And neither, I suspect, can you.'

'Mr MacBride,' the woman says, stepping forward. 'Could we step inside for a moment?'

Owen glances around the garden and then back at the house. 'Why?'

'Well, it might be more comfortable, for a start.'

'You can say what you've got to say out here.'

'Okay.' She takes a deep breath and nods. 'We haven't yet received the post mortem report on the body they found at Gallows Hill, but we are beginning to piece things together.'

'I thought you said you needed a DNA sample.'

She nods. 'We do. A DNA sample would make all the difference and we will need to pursue that.'

Owen swallows, and waits.

'You haven't asked what picture we are putting together, Mr MacBride.'

He refuses to reply.

Then she changes tack, glancing around at the few outbuildings behind the house. 'Do you keep guns, Mr MacBride?'

'Not in the house, no.'

She glances again at the sheds. 'And outside the house?'

He shakes his head.

'D'you mind if we take a look?' she asks, stepping forward to investigate.

Her colleague moves towards the door of the first outbuilding and notices the padlock.

'Do you have a key, Mr MacBride?'

'Don't you need a search warrant for that?'

She smiles and nods, maintaining her firm but conciliatory manner. 'It would be odd, don't you think,' she adds, 'for a gamekeeper not to keep guns on his property?'

Owen shrugs. 'I breed pheasants for others to shoot. I don't shoot them myself. It's not rocket science.'

'We'll come back, Mr MacBride, with a warrant.'

Then she turns and makes her way back down the side of the house, followed by her colleague.

He listens to their vehicle drive away until the sound of it fades in the distance, then collapses on the garden bench, his head in his hands.

All of it, he feels, is too much for any one man to bear.

DNA

Callum is tinkering with the engine of his van, the bonnet up, his head down, unaware of Dan's police vehicle slowly inching its way over the dirt road to his cottage.

He looks up and turns to face his somewhat unwelcome visitor. 'How's things?' the usual terse greeting.

'I promised I'd let Joan know when we had any news,' Dan begins, climbing out of his car and standing with the door wide open.

Callum squints at him, raising one shoulder. 'So, why are you here and not at her house?'

Dan concedes this with a small nod. 'I promised I'd keep you in the loop.'

'No, you didn't. You warned me off the case, said I had no right meddling and there'd been complaints.'

Dan takes a step forward and releases a heavy sigh. 'Why so defensive, Callum?'

'Can't think.'

'I'm trying to help you here.'

Callum doesn't respond to that.

'They managed to take a DNA sample from Ruthie, in the end.'

Callum tenses, waiting for what comes next.

'They got a positive ID.'

Callum feels an audible intake of air, an involuntary shudder. How will Joan receive the news, how will she bear it? With relief, maybe, confirmation of what she knew, that her grandson never left Kilbroch twelve years ago at all.

But Dan's next words come as a hammer blow. 'They've taken Owen in for questioning.'

'Is he under arrest?'

'Not yet.'

Callum thinks of Owen and the last time he saw him, the pain in his eyes, the anguish.

'When will you tell Joan?'

'Soon. Now, in fact. I thought that you might like to be on hand. I take it you're pals. She might need a listening ear. There'll be a funeral to arrange.'

Callum is surprised at Dan's forethought and concern, almost touched by it. 'Will Owen be allowed to attend?'

'I imagine so. They're holding him for 72 hours, until we can get enough evidence. But he'll be allowed to attend his own son's funeral. Compassionate grounds.'

'And Ruthie?'

'We're going to interview her.'

'With difficulty.'

'Aye. It won't be easy to pin her down. I wondered if you'd be prepared to help?'

'Me? What can I do?'

Dan shrugs. 'You seem to be familiar with everyone around here.'

'That's maybe because I live here.'

'Aye, but Joan trusts you so I thought maybe her granddaughter...'

'They're estranged from one another. Haven't spoken in years. Not since Ruthie's mother died.'

Dan considers this.

'Aren't you forgetting a little something as well?' Callum adds.

'What's that?'

'I left the force several years ago.'

Dan pulls himself up. 'Oh aye, I know that. But, you're a self-styled private investigator it seems.'

'Not really.'

'Joan's taken to calling you that.'

'I've been helping her, yes, as much as I'm able. But it became a little tricky once I was warned off.'

Dan lowers his gaze ruefully, unwilling to admit his error. 'I just thought you might be able to get Ruthie to talk, that's all. If you do, and if you manage to find anything out, we'd be grateful.'

Callum stares at his old colleague, dumbstruck, and watches in silence while he climbs back into his vehicle and drives away along the sandy track to the road. He stands staring after him for several long minutes before returning to the problem of his tricksy engine.

Rain clouds are rolling in from the far hills, blotting the horizon. He can't help dwelling on how Joan will take the news. And what of Owen, sitting alone in a police cell up at the station in Stirling, knowing his son's body has been found and that he is suspected of having something to do with his death. He must surely be worried about Ruthie, alone now in the gamekeeper's cottage which she has lived in since birth. And if his last encounter with Strabane was anything to go by, it might not be her home for much longer.

All these thoughts and more come pouring through Callum's mind, and again, despite the facts, he can't help feeling pity for Owen.

Joan is standing at the kitchen window, gazing at the far hills where the grey clouds scrape their bellies across the distant peaks. She can't tear herself away from the view. It eases her thoughts, stops them spinning, to focus on that far horizon. Somehow it relaxes the tension in her shoulders, soothes the ache in her head.

When she hears a light tap on the door, she barely moves. She recognises Callum's knock.

When she lets him in, she can tell by his face that he already knows.

'You had a visit then?' he asks.

'From that friend of yours? Yes.'

'He's not my... he's my ex-colleague.'

'Well, whatever he is, I don't like him,' she snaps. He's glad to see she hasn't lost any of her old sharpness.

'You pleased now?' she asks.

'Me? Why would I be pleased?'

'Oh, I don't know. Because they're finally questioning my son-in-law?'

'Are you?'

She takes a moment to gather her breath. 'How can I be pleased? My daughter and my grandson are both dead. They found him, though. Here in the woods, where I knew he'd be.'

'Yes, they found him.'

She sighs again. 'So, should I accept it as some form of closure?'

He doesn't reply to this.

'I can't help thinking of Ruthie, all alone up in that house. What must she be thinking?'

'I could try and talk to her.'

'I'm her grandmother. That's my job.'

Callum acknowledges this with a silent nod.

'So,' Joan says, turning to him with a smile which somehow carries an ominous question mark somewhere within it. 'Case closed?'

He stares back in silence, wondering if she is demanding an answer, if she wants him to come down off the fence and express what he really thinks. 'You think so?' he asks.

'You're the private investigator. You tell me.'

'That's what you're paying me for, I suppose.'

'I haven't paid you yet.'

'I had noticed.'

'Well, you haven't solved anything, have you?'

He gives a dry laugh.

'You don't change, Joan. No matter what you're going through. You're a breath of fresh air.'

'That's not what most people say. They usually use a few choice words, but not those.'

She looks thoughtful for a moment and he senses the inner pain she's struggling with, that she won't admit to. He thinks of his own son, how he rarely sees him.

'Those clouds don't look good,' Joan comments, changing the subject abruptly, and as if on cue, they hear a growl of distant thunder.

'Will you be okay?' he asks.

She smiles sadly. 'I have been all these years, Callum. I'm sure I'll cope.'

As she sees him to the door, she keeps it in, all the pain and the heartache and the sorrow, the knowledge she has carried that her young grandson never left this place twelve years ago when others thought he had run away. All those sightings – people who'd seen him catching a bus to Perth, at Stirling Railway Station buying a ticket to Edinburgh, to Glasgow, hitching a lift on the A9 and climbing into the cab of a dodgy-looking lorry driver. All those false reports, false alarms, glimpses of him in the port at Dover, making his way abroad, making them believe that Robbie had run away when she had known he would never do that. He was here all along, in the woods nearby, not far from all of their houses, still in their thoughts but silenced by the earth that stoppered his mouth, turning his young body to bones.

She remembers the day he was born. Her first ever grandchild. Lydia sitting up in the bed, exhausted but beaming, the small bundle that was Robbie in her arms, and Owen hovering nearby, an unwelcome presence with his silence and his austere expression. She'd never really thought about it then, but there was something... Lydia was never quite at ease when he was around. That's the way Joan interprets it.

215

Jealous old woman, not wanting to share her daughter? Or perceptive and insightful?

Was the seed already planted then, his capacity for violence? For she knew he'd always struggled with Robbie, had been overly strict at times, heavy with the discipline.

Is that how it happened, she wonders? His rage going too far?

She thinks of her son-in-law, alone in that cell, having no one to confide in. What will he tell them? What will they find out?

She can't forgive him. She can never forgive him.

She believes he drove her own daughter to suicide. And how did that come about? Did Lydia find out eventually what had happened to Robbie?

They might be holding her son-in-law in a cell for now, but there are still so many unanswered questions as far as Joan is concerned, and she hopes Callum will be the one to help her find the answers.

For it's not enough. Finding where Robbie lay all this time will never be enough. She has to know why and how. Callum understands this.

He won't give up. She knows it.

Excavating the Past

He comes across Laura, walking along the lane, a small rucksack on her back. She has been forbidden to approach anywhere near the scene of the dig, but is irresistibly drawn back to Gallows Hill, to the natural woodland that covers that part of the land.

He pulls up beside her and winds the window down. 'I was hoping I'd see you.'

'Oh yes?'

'What are you up to?'

'I was just going to dive into the woods there, for a wander.'

He smirks. 'Trying to get close to the dig again?'

'Well, I know I'm not technically supposed to, but no one said anything against a stroll in the woods.'

'D'you mind if I join you?'

'Be my guest.'

'Hang on.'

He reverses the van and parks it in the only lay-by, then jogs back up the road to join her.

They take a left through a gap in the ruined remains of a wall and into the limpid green light cast by the trees. Immediately they have to watch their footing, wading through ankle-deep grass with leaf-rot, moss and fallen branches underfoot. Splashes of green moss climb the trees, giving the illusion of damp pillars in a ruined cathedral.

'I've been thinking,' Callum begins.

'About?'

'Owen.'

'What about him?'

He hesitates for a fraction of a second. 'I think the police might be barking up the wrong tree.'

'I'm listening.'

'I saw Dan earlier. My old colleague? Although they've yet to prove it, they're convinced they're onto something with Owen.'

'Have they arrested him?'

'Not yet, but they're questioning him. They think he's their chief suspect.'

She looks at him quickly. 'But you're not so sure?'

'Maybe you'll say I'm biased…'

'Well,' she considers, 'No one likes to think the worst of a friend, someone they've known for years.'

After a moment's reflection Laura suggests, 'It could have been an accident?'

'I've thought of that, but if it was, I can't help thinking Owen would have confessed by now.'

'Unless he's not the man you think he is.'

Callum takes this in.

'So,' she adds, 'if you don't believe he is responsible for Robbie's death, who is?'

Callum doesn't answer at first.

The leafy gloom creates a perfect backdrop of privacy.

'I can't share any of these doubts with Joan, of course.'

'Why not?'

'Because she wants an answer. She wants to believe it was Owen, to see her son-in-law convicted. After all, she's harboured a grudge against him all these years.'

'I'm not so sure about that,' Laura says.

'What do you mean?'

She examines the ground as she walks, broken up by mossy runnels and ankle-snapping dips. 'I don't really know, other than… I sense Joan has her doubts too. I'm not so sure she thinks Owen is responsible, after all.'

'You sense it? How? Has she said anything?'

'No… not in so many words.'

'As far as the police are concerned, they think they've got their man, they just need to find some evidence,' Callum continues.

'What is Owen saying?'

'Nothing. As far as I can gather from Dan, all he will say is "No comment". He neither defends nor condemns himself. But his silence is in itself damning. It's certainly not helping his case any.'

'If he was innocent, d'you think he'd still say "No comment"?'

Callum shakes his head. 'I just don't know.'

They've disturbed a deer quietly grazing, and as the creature stares at them, they stare back, until it crashes away through the trees, its white rump flashing. They are nearing the site of Gallows Hill and through the leafy gloom they can see the flicker of police tape and the movements of the forensic team.

They instinctively stop, and watch from a distance.

The woman in charge of the operation senses their presence and glances up at them. They don't approach her and she doesn't encourage them, merely gives them an off-putting stare before continuing with her work.

'Makes you feel very much on the outside, doesn't it?' Callum says.

'It should be me digging that soil,' Laura adds wistfully. 'There's still a Bronze Age fort lying under there.'

She thinks of its latent history, the ground now scored by the trenches of recent events. Recent murders seem so very sordid compared with the mystery and appeal of historic ones. She looks up at the wide old oak and imagines lifeless corpses swinging from its spreading boughs. There is no dignity or grandeur in any of it. In fact, she realises, it is all full of cruelty and indignity, no matter how far back in time you go.

'Are you sure Owen is innocent?' she asks him, watching the scene before them.

'Of course I'm not. I'm not sure of anything. But I'd like to believe he is.'

They look at each other in silence.

Laura thinks briefly of Strabane and the sense she has that he likes to portray a certain image of himself that doesn't always ring true, the sense she has that he is a controlling man around his daughters.

She thinks of mentioning this to Callum again but before she can, the head of the forensics team has broken off from the cluster of her colleagues and is making a bee-line for them.

'Uh-oh,' Laura murmurs and nudges him. Callum politely stands his ground, smiling.

'I thought you understood this area is now a crime scene?' she barks.

'Oh yes, of course,' Laura says. 'We were just going for a stroll.'

'A stroll?' the woman repeats ironically and makes it utterly clear by her expression that she is not giving them the benefit of the doubt.

Laura nods and Callum glances off to the side, as if the sight of the distant hills above the treeline holds some object of deep fascination for him.

The Chief Forensics Officer eyes them up and down, then rustles back to join her colleagues, calling over her shoulder, 'Make sure you don't venture any closer.'

Laura and Callum exchange glances.

'D'you think they'll still be working away here at night, after dark?' Laura asks him.

He shrugs. 'They're still looking for clues.'

He gazes about him uncomfortably. 'She's right, though,' he adds. 'We should let them get on with their job. Guess we should head back down.'

220

Burial

They gather on the edge of the graveyard next to the crumbling wall which separates this ancient burial ground from the hills beyond. They are sheltered by a kingly-looking oak.

Callum looks up at the sky, dirty with rain clouds. It's been strange weather. Weeks of intense heat and unbroken sunshine not common to Scotland, followed by the threat of thunderstorms. There is a faint growl in the distance, as if someone up there is shaking a piece of aluminium, but the storm moves elsewhere for now.

He stands beside Joan, feeling her icy resolve. Her nerves are like steel. Her eyes are dry.

'I shed all my tears long ago,' she'd told him before the service.

Kells Chapel was opened up especially to receive Robbie into its aisle for the last time. He was baptised in its stone font, and now he will be laid to rest in its grounds, alongside his mother.

Few words were said. No one felt inclined to offer any kind of address. It was kept simple and informal, quiet and quick.

For one thing, the family didn't wish to attract media attention.

The ground lies open before them and this time Robbie will be laid to rest with more dignity, surrounded by people who loved him, although Callum can't help wondering if he was better off lying undisturbed on Gallows Hill. Ruthie stares quietly at the coffin and blinks back tears. Her father, Owen, stands apart, gazing up at the sky as if he cannot bear to look down at the ground where his wife and son now lie, for Robbie will join his mother, in the same quiet tranquil spot.

And yet the tragedy that has swept this family is anything but tranquil. It has stormed through their lives, causing destruction and unimaginable pain.

Owen and Joan do not look at each other once, but neither do they show anger. Both seem uncannily and silently united in their grief.

Callum, watching, wonders about that, what it says about Owen's apparent guilt or otherwise.

No one questions Callum attending the funeral. Joan requested his presence and wouldn't hear of him not being there, among the few mourners. And of course police officers were in attendance too. They stood, some metres away, in full uniform with their arms folded behind their backs, proof positive if anyone needed it that Owen is still their chief suspect and would be taken back in for questioning again as soon as this afternoon's formalities were over.

At least they have reopened the case, Callum had said to Joan earlier, although it was small comfort.

George Strabane is at the graveside, standing a respectful distance apart with his daughters, one of whom looks particularly surly. Callum can never tell which is which. One of them jogs a lot, he knows that.

Strabane, Callum notes, glances at Owen from time to time, and he wonders what thoughts must be going through the minds of these two men, employer and employee, since their recent violent confrontation. Now they stand at a graveside, with the question of what happens next unresolved.

Afterwards, the mourners separate, drifting awkwardly between the gravestones, politely trying to avoid stepping on the dead, or disturbing their centuries of sleep in the earth.

A quiet burial is what the family wanted and this is what

they have been given. Robbie has been laid to rest, at last. But it seems an inadequate end to all that searching and hoping, all that waiting and longing.

Joan, Ruthie, Owen, none of them are at peace.

Night

There's a sombre mood lying low over the narrow glen of Kilbroch. Most know that the missing teenager's body was found and buried, twelve years too late, and that his father has been taken in for questioning.

A terrible tragedy, some say, fulfilling the old stories they used to tell about the Kilbroch fairies, how the first-born of every family in the glen will be cursed. It seems that one family in particular has been singled out for that curse, and are paying the price. What could be more tragic than a father being questioned about the unexplained death of his own teenage son?

It hasn't been proven yet, mutter some. He's only being questioned. They've yet to issue a formal arrest. Ah, but it's bound to be him. He was always a surly bugger. Where there's smoke, there's fire.

They mutter these, and other vague comments which bear little or no relation to reality. For no one knows the truth. The locals are only guessing. And what none of them are aware of is that the police already know the cause of death. They're simply not sharing their information with anyone else yet, not until the funeral is well and truly over.

That night, Laura lies in her room up at the castle and mulls over recent events. She did not attend the burial since it was a quiet family affair and she had no wish to intrude. It was not as if she knew Robbie, but she had seen their figures in the distance, their cars parked at the gate, heads bowed as they gathered at the graveside, the scar in the earth reopened before them.

Twelve years had slipped by without a stone to mark where he lay and it seems strange that he now lies beside his own mother, that one so young should have so few at his burial to mourn his passing. The world had moved on without him.

Laura knows from her work that this is the natural way of things. Our own feeble bodies will decay faster than the cheap supermarket cups we drink from.

Rumour has it that the forensics team have packed up and abandoned their work in the woods. Now that Gallows Hill is no longer a crime scene she is hoping she can resume her work, and has no intention of leaving yet. She feels too invested in the whole thing and she's made some surprising connections here.

She doesn't want to leave Callum and Joan for a start.

– OMG Laura, her twin Simon messages her on their private chat, which they call Terrible Twins. It's a lifeline to their childhood, a solid comfort when they are miles apart.

– Don't be stubborn. Get the hell out of there.

– Why?

– That creepy guy at the castle for a start!

– I'll be fine, she tells him. – They're questioning his father. I can't help feeling sorry for him.

– Sorry for him? What if he's guilty?

– I'm not sure they've got their facts right.

– And you'd know, would you? What does your policeman friend think?

– He's not in the police. He used to be. But I think he's not sure either. It's complicated.

– Show me the castle again, Simon begs suddenly. – Take a video of the landing.

– No way. It's someone's home. How would you like someone snooping around your flat, videoing it to share with strangers?

– I'm not a stranger. It's me. Your twin brother. AND, I don't live in a castle.

– The answer's still no.

– Spoilsport!

– Maybe later.

Then their little conversation goes silent, as it so often does. No warning. Just a few fond comments then onto something else. It's good to know he's always there. Maybe that's why she keeps her phone close, knowing he is only a ping away, the brother who shared the same placenta as herself.

'Yuck,' he says, when she reminds him of that fact. 'Too specific!'

She is often asked if it's strange, being a twin, but Laura doesn't know anything else. She can't imagine not being a twin. And what she does know is that if anything ever happened to Simon, a part of herself would always be missing.

'Like an amputation?' someone once asked.

'Worse than that. You can still live without a limb. But you can't live without your heart.'

She thinks of Ruthie whom she met in the woods some days ago, when the dig was just underway, before she found the bones. What must it have been like for Ruth, to lose a brother and to live without him all these years?

She hears a noise, a creak on the floorboards of the landing just outside her door. She pulls herself upright against the headboard. There are no lights on in her room, just the glow from the screen of her iPhone.

She knows that most of the rooms in this part of the castle are empty. Strabane's daughters, Sophie and Lottie, occupy another wing. She concentrates her attention on the space beneath the door. She wants to tell herself it's her own imagination, but she can see movement there, the strip of light shifting, as if a pair of feet are standing just the other side. Waiting.

She doesn't move, tenses every muscle, listens with every fibre of her body.

226

Another creak, and then she has the sense that someone has moved away, down the corridor.

Throwing off her duvet, she's across the room in six steps, gently drawing the door open. It occurs to her now that there is no lock. She's not in a hotel, so why would there be? She is sharing someone's home, after all, even if it does happen to be a castle.

She looks both ways, but the corridor outside is empty, faded antique rugs stretching away left and right, bookcases dark with books, a slant of moonlight falling through the one arched window high in the wall.

She has the unmistakable sensation that someone has been here only recently. The air is disturbed, that faint essence of another presence. Sophie or Lottie, she wonders? More alarmingly still, Strabane?

Back in her room, she taps her screen awake for comfort.

– Hi bro, someone creeping about outside my room. Think I've got the heebie jeebies.

She waits for his profile pic to drop down, to show he got the message. But he's offline.

She tiptoes across the room – although she doesn't really know why she's tiptoeing, she might just as well walk normally – and slides a chair under the door handle.

Just in case.

She thinks she'll sleep better that way.

A couple of miles away, Joan too is restless, staring up at the ceiling. She buried her grandson today and laid him to rest beside his mother. Ten years ago she stood at that same spot and watched them bury her only child, her beloved daughter, who'd been in trouble of some kind but had never felt quite able to share whatever it was that she was suffering. At his hands? That man?

She had stood under grey skies that time, with a bitter wind whipping the fields. Now history has come full circle, but sleep will be a stranger still. Why is it that she feels absolutely no sense of closure? She still does not understand what happened, or why.

She drags herself out of bed, moves across the landing, lit by a pale glow from the window, and steadily descends the stairs, gripping the hand rail. If she cannot sleep, she wants to be in her sunroom, surrounded by her plants. It still looks beautiful in the darkness, her wooden desk scattered with pens and paintbrushes, bursts of bright colour on a china plate she was using as a palette board. It smells of life, something green and growing; she only wishes that it could inspire hope the way it did when she was young.

A positive force still pushes her on. She continues to put one foot in front of the other on this journey we call life, despite the darkness, despite the loss. To give up now would be a betrayal of everything. It would be as if Robbie and Lydia never existed.

So she reads books, she learns, she continues to grow and teach those she comes across. Every day is a school day, and she's humble and wise enough to realise that this planet and its destiny are far bigger than the messiness and pain of their own twisted lives. She still retains her sense of wonder and awe, in spite of everything. Even though it hurts, and her body is tired, she still feels that immense force of life urging her forward.

She sits at the chair before her desk, rests her chin in her palm, and gazes out at the dark green immensity in front of her, filled with inky night. It's been a strange summer, with that girl Laura descending on them all, and unearthing what they had all failed to find. She supposes, when she thinks of it like that, that Laura has been a catalyst. Without her, they would never have found Robbie's body and they would have continued to pretend that he had run away, whereas Joan knew differently. She had known he was here all along. It just needed someone to believe her.

And does knowing that he died here twelve years ago make it any easier to bear?

Of course it doesn't. Not really.

Bricks and Mortar

Early the next morning, Laura stands on the terrace below the castle and regards the glen beneath. The thick trees are stirring, dancing faintly in the soft breeze as it picks up. She can see Sophie jogging below, a small figure appearing now and again between the dense green foliage, her trainers hitting the rocks along the path, picking her way expertly. She runs all the time. It makes Laura exhausted just watching her. It's as if she is in training for life, trying to run away, but from what?

They live in a castle in the middle of idyllic countryside with their father, which one would assume must be an enviable position to be in, but she always has the feeling that both daughters are trapped. She doesn't know why, it's just a vague hunch she has.

– One of your hunches, Simon tells her, when they chat online.

– Well, you've got to admit I'm pretty good at that sort of thing.

– That's true. What makes you think they're trapped?

But at that point she had to concede she didn't know. She had no evidence to go on.

Below her, the little lone figure of Sophie runs along, marking out her boundary, running as fast and as far as she dares.

'Penny for them?'

Laura spins round suddenly to find George Strabane standing in her shadow. She glances behind him.

'I didn't hear you coming,' she says.

He gives that urbane smile of his.

She's holding her coffee cup in one hand and has the other

in her jeans pocket. Relaxed as usual, always comfortable in her own body. She looks away from him at the treeline. 'I was just watching your daughter jogging. She never stops.'

'It seems to be her passion. Everyone needs a passion.'

She glances at him, suddenly remembering the creaking floorboard outside her bedroom door last night. 'And what's yours?' she asks him.

'Mine?' He laughs awkwardly. 'Pretty obvious, I'd say. This.' He gestures around him. 'All of this.'

'Your property?' she says, conscious that she is reducing what he means to the level of bricks and mortar, acreage, the idea of possession, even though she knows it's probably more than that.

He frowns and corrects her. 'Studying the bird life, maintaining the garden and restoring it to what it once was. Yes,' he nods with that veneer of calm. 'All of this is my passion.'

'I'm not surprised. If I lived here, it would be mine too.'

His eyes narrow slightly in a way that can hardly be noticed, and she wonders about him again. His heroic story about how he selflessly cared for his wife during her illness. He doesn't seem the sort, somehow, to happily attend to the physical needs of another with quiet and uncomplaining patience. It's as if he has carefully crafted an idea of himself which he encourages others to believe in.

'You're too suspicious, sis,' Simon tells her.

But she disagrees. She's not suspicious enough. Callum is teaching her to look at things differently, especially after the events up at Gallows Hill.

Strabane takes a deep breath then and looks at her with studied sincerity.

'I guess you'll be leaving soon?'

'What gave you that idea?' she asks.

'Well…' his brow darkens.

'As far as I'm aware, the forensics team have left the hill

231

and they may let me carry on with the dig. I'm waiting to hear about that. I'll let you know as soon as.'

'No hurry.' He steps backwards, away from her, smiling again. 'Terrible business,' he murmurs, 'Terrible business. Still, the funeral went well. And that's the main thing. For the family, I mean. Time to put the whole sorry business behind us.'

Strange choice of words, she thinks. A general lack of sincerity in his manner rankles, but she hides it well.

'It's very kind of you to allow me to stay here,' she adds.

'Not at all. We have plenty of room.'

She nods politely then watches him retreat to the lower lawn where she can see the gardener waiting. She watches the two of them consult one another, the gardener nodding his head slowly and listening, as if he has spent all of his life listening to one landowner or another telling him what to do, how to keep the garden alive, when he has known all along how to do it himself, without any need of advice. She can see that the gardener – Nathan, she thinks his name is – humours his employer.

She downs the last of her coffee and heads for the main door. She needs to make some phone calls about her vehicle.

Before she heads inside, Sophie appears from an arched doorway in the wall. She has jogged up the steps from the glen below. She comes to a halt, perspiring and resting her hands on her hips, breathing fast.

'That was some run you did there,' Laura says politely, friendly as ever.

'Thanks,' Sophie says, glancing quickly across at her father and Nathan on the lawn.

Laura follows her gaze, noticing the slight frisson of anxiety. 'You in training for something?'

Sophie shakes her head, smiling. 'I like to keep fit. I like the buzz it gives me, the adrenaline rush.'

Laura feels suddenly keen to engage her, to know more. 'D'you go far?'

Sophie frowns, and gestures with one hand. 'Just nearby.'

Laura nods and smiles. 'I suppose you'll be off to university shortly, at the end of the summer?'

'Yeah, I'm not really sure about that. Maybe,' Sophie says vaguely.

'What would you like to do?'

Sophie seems to find this too difficult to answer at first. 'I don't know. Conservation maybe?'

Laura gives her a friendly reassuring smile. 'This is a beautiful place. If I lived here, I wouldn't want to leave it either.'

She catches Sophie's worried frown.

'I need to keep an eye on Lottie. Can't leave her alone.'

'Why not?'

Sophie shrinks into herself and Laura has the sense that she has trespassed on forbidden territory.

'Well,' the girl says, heading for the vestibule. 'Best get a shower.'

Laura nods, watching her go, then turns to observe Strabane still talking to his gardener. The heat feels oppressive. She wonders how long that storm will be kept at bay.

Ruthie

The gamekeeper's cottage looks dark and quiet, but Callum knows she is in there somewhere, on her own, perhaps wondering what will happen next. How lonely she must be, traumatised by her brother's burial and her father's absence.

He glances up at the darkened windows in the eaves, knocks on the front door, the one he knows they never use, stands back and waits. No answer. He knew there wouldn't be. The rooks argue in the trees above, then fall silent; he hears the familiar cry of a red kite coasting on the air. A long lonely call that always slows his pulse rate. Its flight above Kells Wood never fails to lift his mind from humdrum worries, reminding him why he chose to live here in the first place.

He waits a further minute, then moves off down the side of the house to the garden which Owen keeps well-stocked, despite the burden of sorrow he carries. A raised bed of vegetables, some tired sunflowers, tall and gangly with yellow faces, a deliberate scattering of wildflowers. He wonders momentarily if he should take some comfort in gardening himself. Ought to, living out here, in a cottage with land attached. But the soil is poor where he lives. Owen has told him this.

He thinks of their companionable evenings together at the Kilbroch Arms – well, as companionable as Owen ever gets. Terse maybe, but there'd been an element of trust between them once. Has he betrayed that trust, he wonders, helping to point the finger of suspicion in Owen's direction?

He pushes down a moment of guilt, peers in through the glass lean-to. No sign of Ruthie. He notices a tray on the floor, with the pieces of a jigsaw puzzle scooped onto it, but some are left lying on the stone tiles as if there was only a half-hearted attempt to gather up the mess.

A flicker of movement in the glass startles him, a reflection behind him, a tall figure darkening the brightness. He freezes for a moment, then spins quickly on his heel.

Dan.

'No sign of her then?'

'What do you think?' Callum says, then immediately notices what Dan accused him of earlier, a defensive tone which he just cannot seem to shake when addressing his old colleague. Resentment is still buried deep somewhere.

'How is it all going?' Callum asks him now, knowing he might be speaking out of turn.

Dan smirks. 'With the case, you mean?'

Callum says nothing.

'I think the police are doing their best to find out how Robbie was killed.'

'And your best is?'

'We got the right man. We just need to prove it. I was hoping *she* might be able to help us with that,' Dan nods his head towards the back of the house, the gesture making it clear who he is talking about.

'You think she'll clype on her own father?'

'There are other ways of establishing the truth.'

'Is that right? And you care about the truth, do you, Dan?'

Dan doesn't reply, but Callum can't resist a final dig. 'The police always care about the truth, right?'

Dan's expression turns sour, and a surge of cold, dark anger flickers in his eye for a moment. 'I'm not going there, Callum. You know that.'

'Going where?' Callum asks.

'You know.'

'No, I don't know. Tell me.'

When Dan won't reply, he pushes him a bit further. 'Who was it who handed him a licence, Dan? You tell me that? A gun licence to a man like that. And look what he did with it?'

'It was years ago, mate. Let it go. That's all been put to bed.'

'Not by me, it hasn't.'

'There was a public enquiry,' Dan mutters.

'At which I testified, Dan. I told the truth. About the memos sent. I told the truth and then I was hounded out of the force for it. Made them look bad. Made them look like it was their fault.'

'You should let it go. You were a good detective, Callum.'

'Until they ruined my career, you mean?'

Callum feels as if he has waited years to say this, to get it off his chest, but he's not done yet. He'll probably spend the rest of his life wanting to shout it from the rooftops, much good may it do him.

Dan shrugs. 'I was just hoping you might get a chance to talk to the girl, that's all. And if you do…'

While they stand there arguing, the sky above them darkens. Someone is watching from the trees, at a safe distance. She cannot hear the actual words but she can sense trouble; there is a buried, unspent anger between these two men. She can feel it simmering on the damp pine-scented air towards her.

She won't approach. She'll let them knock on the door, search for her, but she'll remain hidden.

There is nothing new under the sun they can tell her.

Gallow Falls

After leaving Dan at the gamekeeper's cottage, Callum heads west over the fields, brushing through knee-high grass. Some instinct draws him this way. And as he walks, he realises this is the route Owen's wife would have taken, the day she died. He is retracing her last footsteps, towards the top of the glen.

He doesn't know why.

Frustration, perhaps, at the course of events, the failure to locate Ruthie at the house, to ask her some questions but also – in his own mind – to check that she is okay.

Although, he has to admit he also feels a latent sense of triumph at speaking his mind to Dan, at last, after all these years, calling a spade a spade.

There were reasons Callum had left the force and none of them were fair. Just over ten years ago a massacre shook the tiny town in which they both lived, not seven miles from Kilbroch. A local man known to police had managed to acquire a gun licence which was renewed every year, without fail, despite his behaviour causing some alarm and being noted by certain individuals, who attempted to bring the matter to the attention of the Chief Constable of Police Scotland at the time. To no avail. Gun lobbyists were all in favour of members of the public obtaining a firearms licence, but many did not know that it was possible for people to own guns in this country, because it wasn't something they thought about on a daily basis.

Until Douglas Hutton walked into a supermarket and murdered sixteen people, five of them children.

Callum can still remember the feeling of shock that floored him in an instant, because he was known to the

237

police; they all knew him. Callum sent a memo every year without fail, urging that Douglas Hutton's licence be revoked.

But it was too late.

The damage was done.

And he had to live with that on his conscience, that maybe he should have done more, tried harder to get them to listen. Although he had, in his own way. At the public inquiry, a year later, he testified and Lord Cullen ruled in his report that 'the shootings at the supermarket would not have happened but for the failings of Central Scotland Police.'

Of course, Callum's bosses in the force were not too happy with his testimony. They made his life pretty difficult, eventually urging him to quit.

So he did.

And now he lives with the injustice of it all, and with the weary knowledge that wrongs are never righted in the end; those in power will always get away with it.

That's why living here in Kilbroch is a tonic for him. He prefers to deal with people like Joan Metcalfe, even Owen MacBride if truth be told. He prefers the company of his trees, his woodpile, the breeze in his face, the freedom of the land opening up around him. However, there's always a fly in the ointment. Joan has got him embroiled in this, and if it brings him into confrontation with George Strabane, who just so happens to be his landlord, he may run the risk of losing all he has now. He doesn't know what he would do if he lost this freedom, this space, this life.

So, it begs the question, why is he damn well risking it again? He already knows that telling the truth doesn't pay. It just costs.

A narrow pathway skirts the top of the gorge and Callum picks his way through the bracken. He peers down through the trees; layered greenery falls away beneath him. One false step and it would be easy to slip and plummet into thin air, nothing to break your fall until you slammed against the watery rocks of the burn, far beneath.

He stands still, peers over the edge. So easy to misjudge your step, to slip.

He imagines Lydia walking this way, the day she died, two years after her own son had gone missing. Deliberate, as some suggested? Or error of judgement? He never met Lydia, but he thinks of her now. So many different things to different people. A daughter to Joan, a wife to Owen, a mother to Ruthie and Robbie. And what of friends? Did she have many? Any? Everyone has someone they talk to, who knows them. Right? It occurs to him now, that in order to get to the bottom of Robbie's disappearance, he maybe needs to learn a little more about his mother, Lydia.

He imagines her feet sliding from under her, the relentless slippage of gravity, the hard crash through the undergrowth, knowing it was too late to stop herself. They said it was suicide, but was it?

She could just as easily have slipped.

Or been pushed.

He chases these thoughts as he leans close to the gorge, gazes down into the green depths below. It has an almost hypnotic draw. The greenery is shelved and bottomless, like an ocean, screening a dreadful drop beneath, one that can kill. And has killed.

He glimpses sparkling water from the surface of the ducking pond far below, where they used to drown witches, centuries earlier, according to the records and to popular rumour, those poor unfortunate women suspected of being different. Victims, scapegoats, someone to blame.

And what of Lydia?

Is she a victim of some kind?

He knows he needs to learn more about her life, how she spent her days. And her nights. He thinks of her as a misty incomplete presence, a vague outline which no one has quite had the temerity to fill in for him properly yet.

Even Joan does not speak easily of her.

Was she as odd and mysterious as her daughter, Ruth? Is that why?

Ahead of him he can see the old Wash House, a half-derelict crumbling structure perched high above the waters of the burn, where the women of the castle used to come to do the laundry, pulling up buckets of water from below, and hauling it hand over hand to their precarious platform perched over the edge of the gorge.

Some of the old boards are rotten and hanging vines and ropes of ivy partially screen it from view. He treads carefully, enters the half-ruin, leans over the edge. He seems to be courting disaster today, daring the heights to claim him for their own.

There is something intensely hypnotic about peering over the edge into a plummeting depth as if it is pulling you in, luring you to your death. Like the sensation of watching a speeding train hurtling through a station and feeling yourself dragged towards its slipstream. There is an irresistible pull involved, reinforcing both the precariousness and indeed the preciousness of life, how much we cling to it, how easily we could let it go. A sense of power and destruction throbs through Callum's veins for a moment, giddy at the view, as if he himself is somehow responsible for whatever befell Lydia, whether it was suicide or accident... or something else.

Did she come this far?

Did she often stand here and gaze below, and think about the history of this place, the glen and its unfortunate victims, the terrible tales they used to tell? Did it make her wonder where, in all of this, her son lay? Her young son she once held in her arms as a baby, reared towards his turbulent teenage years, and then was left at the end of it all without even a body to bury, and no idea of his whereabouts.

How painful was that? Could that kind of pain make you finish it all, even if you had another child to care for?

Something makes him glance across the gorge to the tall bank opposite. A tiny movement. A figure walking slowly through the trees. He recognises Strabane, lord of all he surveys, skirting the edge of the high ridge opposite. A moment later, Strabane's figure vanishes, swallowed by trees and foliage. There is only so much of the land opposite that you can see across this gulf, with the shady mysterious gorge lying between, the silver of the burn threading its way over the rocks at the bottom.

Callum knows that behind that screen of trees and the high castle walls are the gardens, formal in places, but mostly rambling, with stone archways and ruins hiding and nestling among the tall hedges. Sheltering walls that are nearly as old as the castle itself bake in the heat.

A paradise of a garden, with its own woodland, and sloping banks, an avenue of trees and a natural waterfall which successive gardeners have encouraged to flow over the rocks.

Strabane is a lucky man, indeed. And yet, Callum has always sensed an uneasiness in the man, an anxiety to hold on to what he's got, as if he cannot quite take any of it for granted – although he does.

Callum feels he needs someone else to bounce ideas off about the case, the mystery of how Robbie died, and the strange coincidence of his mother's accident or suicide two years later. He knows Dan is not the man for that and he's a little uneasy about raising any of this with Joan at the moment, worried it will be too raw, too painful for her. She insists that she is able to talk about the case, to examine every aspect of it. She is ruthless in her own regard for the

241

truth and will not allow her own pain to get in the way of that. But…

He thinks of Laura, of how pleasant her company is, for a start, and how easy it is to talk to her. He knows she is as keen to get to the bottom of the mysteries surrounding the case as he is, and she is keen to help Joan.

He wonders for a moment how long she has left in Kilbroch, staying at the castle. It doesn't seem likely she'll be able to resume the dig any time soon. Perhaps it would be best to strike while the iron is hot. He resolves to catch up with her before the day is through.

In the distance, across the gorge, Strabane's figure briefly reappears, as he emerges from a gap in the wall. There one moment; gone the next.

Twin

Back in her room that night, Laura flops on the bed. The castle creaks all about her, with its silences and its secrets, its sense of empty rooms and passageways reaching beyond the place where she lies. She wonders if she has outstayed her welcome. Maybe she ought to cut her losses, catch a train and zoom her way back to Edinburgh, away from this place and its darkest discoveries. But something holds her here. She wants to know, she wants to help Joan, and she wants to see Callum again, although she won't admit that much to herself.

She rolls onto her back and FaceTimes her twin for some sense of confirmation. When his blurry face appears on the screen, her eyes immediately light up. Her other half, without whom she is never quite complete.

He blinks at her without having to say anything, so she immediately launches in, as she does. 'Am I just imagining it all?'

'All what?'

She sighs and rolls her eyes. 'You know what I mean.'

He thinks for a moment, then, 'You? Letting your imagination run away with you? Now *there* would be a first!'

'Stop it, you know what I mean.'

'Why don't you get the hell out of there, if you're suspicious of them?'

'Because I want to know…'

'Know what?'

'What they're hiding and what happened to Joan's grandson.'

'Tell me a bit more about them,' Simon urges.

So she does. She tells him about the quietness of the castle, the delicate birds which Strabane feeds and is able to identify, the veneer of good manners and calm he wears, that she is almost convinced is a front for something else, the two daughters who seem unable to leave home, who nervously guard their territory from strangers, and who – she is certain – harbour some level of resentment and distrust.

Simon hears her out then takes stock, reflecting her own story back at her. 'And so, you have two healthy, happy young women–'

'–Your words, not mine. I didn't say "happy".'

'–who live with their father in a castle, in the middle of gorgeous countryside. One of them goes jogging in the glen while the other lurks in her room and you conclude from this that they are secretly terrified. Mmm, it's just not adding up, sis.'

'Well, obviously, if you describe it like that.'

'And how else should I describe it? I'm just taking my lead from you.'

'Yeah, I can see how it sounds.'

'Seriously, though, he does sound like a creep.'

She stares at him. 'I thought you just said…'

'So I changed my mind.' He takes a breath. 'I still think you're jumping to conclusions though.'

'I know that.'

'It's dangerous to make assumptions, not to mention slanderous.'

'Well, I realise that. It's only you I'm talking to. I'm not shouting it from the rooftops.'

'So you've not told your cop friend any of this?'

'He's not a cop.'

'You've not mentioned any of these hunches to him?'

Her reply is a deafening silence.

'Well, maybe you should, sis.'

'I thought you said it wasn't right to incriminate him with a mere hunch?'

'Don't listen to me. I don't know what I'm talking about.'

'I never listen to you, bro. You're incorrigible.'

'Good night!' he declares. She waves at him, just as he hangs up, and their two faces are frozen for a second, looking oddly similar.

The Key

Joan feels as old as the hills that night as she lies on her bed, strapped down by her thoughts.

She has always marched on inexorably, defying the world to pull her down, and when her pain gets too much, she buries it deep. A memory of Lydia as a little girl floats to the surface and suddenly the child is there with her in the room, as if all those years between have never happened and the future is yet to be. If only we could keep the future at bay, if wishes were gold, if dreams came true.

In the corner of her mind the little girl plays with tea cups and saucers, her favourite pastime, pouring muddy water from one receptacle into another, and offering her parents various beverages, which they would pretend to drink. So long ago, yet it seems like only yesterday. A child with a future ahead of her. They'd lived in the city then, in tall tenements with long back gardens and friendly neighbours with shared sandpits and washing flapping on a communal washing line. Joan had loved the camaraderie of it all. She'd kept a sketch book and drew the people she saw, toddlers and mothers, men and women on bikes, in cafes, watering plants on windowsills, browsing in bookshops, drinking coffees. All those sights and sounds, so much to look at and occupy the mind.

She'd had ambitions to become a proper artist back then, with a studio and a following. And she encouraged Lydia to draw, always leaving felt tip pens and crayons to hand. Her teaching skills were ever present, both in the classroom and in the home.

Joan remembers how she took pride in her work, and her

life, and her mothering skills. She'd thought she was doing a good job.

Until Brian left her and she had to cope alone, back when Lydia was still a little girl. Then the teaching became a necessity and she worked full time to pay the rent. But that's all history now. In the corner of her mind the small child still plays, endlessly pouring muddy tea from one cup to another, an eternal waitress in training.

When she hears a noise downstairs, she's not sure if she's hearing things at first. The click of the front door, a creaking in the hallway. Then a crash, followed by silence.

She sits up, pulse racing, listening to the sudden silence. She knows there's someone down there. Searching for her stick, she crosses the room as silently as she can, grateful for the thick carpets. At the top of the stairs, she hesitates, listening. Is it wise to confront whoever is down there? Maybe she ought to call the police? Of course she ought to call the police.

Having her phone by her side right now would be nice and handy. Only it isn't. She left it downstairs, charging.

There's not a sound coming from below now, but she knows they're still there. She can feel them breathing, the air thick with their presence.

Step by step she descends, peering over the bannister. The shadows in the hallway cloak her. In the kitchen she hears another faint movement. So she reaches her hand inside the door and snaps on the light switch, at the same time holding her stick aloft, ready to strike, like the old fool she is, knowing full well she'd come off worse in any fight.

A blinding glare fills the small room, sudden and stark after the soft darkness. She blinks for several moments before taking in the sight before her eyes. Her granddaughter is standing by the kettle, her dark eyes round with fear, gazing back at her.

'What the—?'

Ruthie glares at her grandmother.

'You could have knocked!' Joan mutters.

'I still have a key. Mum's key.'

'Well, how about that?' Joan says, suppressing her rage.

All these years and Ruthie has never once crossed the threshold here, as far as Joan knows.

'I've remembered something,' Ruthie whispers. The girl who never speaks appears to have found her voice.

Finding Her Voice

They're all sitting in Joan's living room, a tray of tea on the low table in front of them. It's morning now, a faint light fills the room, bathing them in warmth. Ruthie sits tensely on one of the armchairs, uncomfortable with the attention surrounding her.

Her grandmother sits on the chair to her left, and opposite sits Callum, leaning forward, with his elbows resting on his knees, the full beam of his attention fixed on Ruthie.

'Gave me a fright, so she did,' Joan mutters into her cup, 'creeping about like that. Creeping Jesus! Didn't even know she still had a key.'

'It was Mum's.'

'So I gather.'

Callum stares. He's never heard Ruthie speak before and the idea that she can break her self-imposed silence so easily is mind-bending in itself.

'So you say you've remembered something?' he prompts.

Ruthie nods.

'Have you told the police?'

'We trust you,' Joan cuts in. 'Not the police.'

Callum gives his friend a sharp stare. 'I was asking Ruthie!'

'Fair enough.'

He waits for Ruthie to find her voice again. 'I've remembered what Robbie was doing in the woods, at Gallows Hill.'

Callum frowns, waiting for the revelation, hoping it will lead them all to the crock of gold.

'He was camping with two of his pals.'

249

He drops his head and sighs, trying to cover his disappointment. 'We know that, Ruthie. Your dad said as much, that he was camping there the night before he went missing.'

Her eyes flash towards him like a quick bird on a branch. 'He said he'd seen things.'

Callum leans forward, waiting for her to say more.

'Up at the castle. He told me to stay away from that place. And he was angry…'

'Angry?' he tries to coax her to say more. 'With?'

'All of them,' Ruthie says now.

Callum looks confused.

'The adults,' she says eventually.

'The adults?'

She nods. 'He didn't like George Strabane,' she adds. 'He had a fight with him.'

Callum and Joan exchange glances.

'About?'

Silence.

'What was the fight about, Ruthie, can you remember?' He doesn't want to push her, or frighten her back into silence, but if there was tension or conflict between Robbie and Strabane, it's essential they get to the root of it.

But Ruthie begins to close up, unable or unwilling to go any further. She shakes her head slightly from side to side.

Callum struggles to hide his impatience.

'The night he went missing, Ruthie. The night he'd been camping up at Gallows Hill with his pals. Do you remember their names? Your father didn't seem able to recall them.' He doesn't mean to sound cynical and Joan shoots him a look.

Ruthie nods quietly. 'They were in high school with Robbie. Pete Brodie, one of them was called.'

'Pete Brodie?' Callum repeats the name, just to be sure.

He wonders what all this will lead to, if anything. And

250

he also wonders why Ruthie suddenly remembers all of this now, after all this time? Is it to spare her father, an attempt to lay the blame at someone else's door?

He hates himself for thinking this way but it's in his DNA. Once a police officer, always a… that kind of thing. His mother used to say he was born suspicious. Not a very flattering description, granted, but pretty accurate.

'You don't remember the name of anyone else he was with?'

Ruthie frowns, as if trying to recall. 'There was one other, but I can't remember his name. Robbie didn't like him very much and they didn't always get along.'

'And yet they camped out together?'

She looks awkward and averts her gaze.

Callum leans back in his chair slightly, and wonders, what next?

'Thank you, Ruthie.'

Joan sighs heavily and adds, 'Well done.'

'I wonder if he still lives in the area, your Pete Brodie, and what he might have to say about that night in the woods?' he says carefully.

He watches Ruthie's gaze flicker up to his face for a second, anxiously, then flicker away again like a bird with nowhere to land.

Then he observes his old friend, Joan. Despite all she's been through, there's a warm glow about her this morning, a buried delight at having her estranged granddaughter in her house for the first time in years, and it really is odd how there are no preliminaries. They relate to one another as if that deep bond still exists, was never broken, with a wariness, a guardedness, but a worn familiarity like an old coat retrieved from a dusty cupboard where it has been left too long.

'So, I guess this gives us something else to work on,' Callum says.

Joan nods.

'Ruthie, can I ask you something?' Callum adds suddenly, leaning forward again.

She raises her eyes.

'Do you think your dad had anything to do with Robbie's disappearance?'

She struggles for a moment with an inability to find words for what is going on inside her head, then slowly shakes her head from side to side.

Callum glances sideways at Joan, trying to read her mind. She's resented her son-in-law for years now, since her own daughter died, but maybe Laura is right and she too has her doubts about Owen's culpability. He's languishing in a police cell, as chief suspect, and C.I.D. are no doubt satisfied they are targeting the right man with their enquiries.

And yet here is Callum, opening up a can of worms. He knows that's the way Dan and his colleagues will see it. They'll think he's motivated by revenge or bitterness, stirring up trouble where it's not wanted, just like he did in the past, true to character.

He wouldn't pursue any of this, he really wouldn't. He'd continue his quiet life chopping wood if he could, delivering logs, taking on joinery jobs, but he feels compelled by his friendship with Joan. At least, that's what he tells himself.

As he stands to leave, he peers through the glass door to the conservatory beyond, filled with greenery and plants that reach up to the ceiling; one table is messy with painting materials, a box of watercolours with smears of bright colour across it, well-used, a jar of mixed brushes, their feathery points angled in all directions.

Joan watches him.

'Still painting?' he asks.

'Of course,' she says. 'One never retires.'

He looks at her and gives a small half-laugh. He knows what she's implying, about himself and his own work. She's dragged him back into being a detective, a private one this time, and she takes a sort of pride in that fact.

'Well, Ruthie,' Callum says. 'I might ask for your help again at some point. Would you be okay with that?'

A look of alarm flits across her face and this time Joan decides to speak for her. Resting a hand on her granddaughter's arm, she murmurs, 'We'll do everything we can. We owe it to Robbie.'

Again, the look of pain and fear lurks behind Ruthie's eyes and he wonders just how deep was the trauma that made her opt for silence that day, twelve years earlier. He can understand. Silence seems like a blessed release sometimes, a simple refusal to engage any more, with anyone, anything. But it's also a kind of death sentence, a refusal to live.

He leaves Joan's house and the two women behind, his mind boiling with unanswered questions which he hasn't even begun to unpick yet. The layers seem to thicken, tripping him up, unawares. Was it true, what Ruthie was implying, that Robbie was angry about things taking place up at the castle? What, exactly? And why did he warn his sister off?

Although the sun shines brightly on the fields and lanes of Kilbroch, he feels like he's negotiating his way through thick fog. Blurred shapes are lurking there, just a few metres away, but he can't make them out yet.

He'll get there.

He wonders what forensics turned up through investigating the burial site, not that they are likely to share their findings with him. It's been twelve long years and it's unlikely that any evidence will remain, he knows that. All they know is the identity of the body. How it happened, or where, or why, they do not yet know. And since then, over the course of those years, rain has fallen, leaves have built up in drifts, then snow; mist has gathered in the branches above, and deer, pheasants and other creatures have tracked the invisible pathways around the clearing before Laura began to disturb the earth in her quest for the more distant past.

He thinks of time, deep time and shallow time, and how it all merges into one in the end, and it's impossible to fathom. He wishes he could articulate thoughts like these, but he's barely aware of having them. The thoughts have no words to match them.

That's what he admires most about Laura. She seems able to articulate it, in language, and offer it up. Whatever it is.

He shakes his head, drives home through the early morning, tries to banish the first wave of depression that always afflicts him this early. He wishes he could start the days positively, but it's true this 'case' – his first as a private detective – has given him something to focus on. It's become an all-consuming obsession. From being reluctant to engage at all, he now finds himself unable to switch off from it. All because of his friend, Joan. A born teacher.

Leavings

Laura sits on a stool on the edge of the thick woods, clutching a tin mug of coffee. She's back at Gallows Hill. Forensics have left the site for now and she can hear the flicker of police tape being teased by the morning breeze. It flashes blue and white, what remains of it, like a flag.

It irritates her, the way the police and the authorities failed to clear up behind them. A good camper will try to leave no trace of their presence. But this team of forensics was not camping. They were digging deep, like she herself does, to unlock time, to find the past.

Time locks us into the present moment. To reimagine distant time is difficult. We can go back centuries or we can go back minutes, but both are shrouded in mystery and potential misinterpretation, because unless you were actually there... who knows what the truth is? Who can be certain?

She doesn't know that Callum has just visited Joan and Ruthie, but she thinks about the girl and how she has haunted this place more than anyone. Always she returns, stands in the woods and stares, hiding among the trees. Like she did that time when Laura was first here, pegging out her site for investigation. She remembers how the presence of the girl gave her a fright.

Always it comes back to Ruthie.

Laura doesn't finish that thought, because the trill of her mobile disturbs the silence.

When she answers it, her face lights up in pleasure and relief. 'That's fantastic news. Thank you. Yes. That's great.'

When she hangs up, she taps the phone against her knee

like a schoolkid and exclaims to the trees, 'I can't believe it!'

The impossible has happened. They've rescued her camper van. The wounded beast is wounded no more. She is aware that her concerns in life are trivial and light compared with some of those around her. She travels lightly through life, carefree and airborne. She is often intrigued by the baggage that others carry, her new friend Callum in particular. At a pinch, she supposes it makes him interesting. She is still too young to know that people without baggage make easier companions.

Around her the forest breathes, listening, as it was listening that night twelve years ago, the night Robbie failed to return home.

If only the trees could speak, could give up their secrets and tell us what they saw.

But as Laura understands, they do give up their secrets eventually, if only we have the skill to interpret them.

A Tragic Way to End a Life

Callum is standing outside his cottage, smoking a cigarette, when he hears a vehicle approaching slowly along the rutted track that leads to his own yard. He squints his eyes through the smoke, recognises his old colleague at the wheel and lets out a deep sigh.

'Not him again,' he mutters out loud, stubs out his roll-up and grinds it underfoot. As he watches Dan open the car door and walk towards him, he steels himself for another warning.

'Bad for you!' Dan comments, gesturing at the roll-up.

'Noted! Have you come here for my health or can I help you with something else?'

'You can, actually.'

'Another complaint against me?'

Dan pauses and gives a small tight laugh. 'No, actually. I came to fill you in.'

Callum takes a step back, and stares at him. 'Fill me in? Why would you do that?'

Dan shrugs. 'Why not?' Then he releases a breath and his chest puffs out in that way Callum despises. 'We're still holding Owen, for now. But some new information has come to light.'

Callum holds his gaze. 'Oh yes?'

'Forensics have discovered the cause of death.'

Callum waits.

'He was shot at point-blank range. In the chest.'

There is a terrible chill silence.

'It took them a while to establish the cause, because of the state of the... the length of time, you know. There

257

was damage to the thorax and… foxes had… before they covered him over again.'

Callum stares at him. 'How long have they known this?'

'Quite some time, obviously since before the funeral, but they didn't want to say too much at first. Wanted to keep it out of the public domain.'

'So why are you telling me this now?'

'Obviously, they're trying to link the evidence to Owen. But…'

'But?'

Dan shakes his head. 'I was at school with him, long time ago now. I just can't believe he'd do that to his own son.'

Callum is completely taken by surprise. 'So what do you think happened?'

Dan doesn't reply. Instead he murmurs, 'If you find anything out, let me know.'

Callum can't believe his ears. He'd always thought of himself as the pariah, the one out on a limb, an outsider, but here he is again being sought out by his old colleague to share what he knows.

'What makes you think I'd learn anything before you?'

Dan smiles. 'You live here. People trust you.'

He knows Dan means Joan Metcalfe and her granddaughter Ruthie, and the other locals who live on the road to Kilbroch in various cottages and farmsteads. Callum thinks he's mistaken though. The locals here will not divulge their secrets so easily. To them, he's a newcomer. For crying out loud, Strabane's family has lived on this land, *owned* the land in fact, for centuries. George Strabane, or his neighbours, are hardly going to open up to Callum. But Dan is right about Ruthie and Joan. He *is* close to the family and they do trust him. What can they tell him, though? They seem as lost in the dark as everyone else, looking for answers which never seem to show.

'Anyway,' Dan adds, turning aside and nodding. 'Let me know, will you?'

Callum laughs. 'I thought you didn't want me meddling? Remember?'

Dan smirks, but doesn't reply, so Callum pushes him. 'And the complaint from one of my neighbours? Does that still stand?'

Dan opens his car door and pauses. 'I, for one, don't always take that kind of complaint too seriously.'

'That always was the problem with the force,' Callum can't resist adding, a stab in the right direction.

Dan hesitates, pretends not to have heard, but Callum knows he heard alright.

'Well, as I say, people ask questions. I can't stop you.' Then he slams his car door and drives away without a backward glance.

Callum watches him go. The car turns left out onto the lane and is immediately hidden by the distant hedgerows that line the road to Kilbroch.

Callum stands looking at the far hills for a while, marking a line on the horizon. He doesn't really know what to make of the encounter. Is it possible that Dan, his old nemesis, is becoming a touch conciliatory, accepting Callum's skill as a private investigator and acknowledging that he might be able to get to the bottom of this case faster than C.I.D.? Dan will surely not confide any of this to his superiors though. They'll not want to concede that Callum might be able to find the answers that elude them.

As he turns back into his own yard, he thinks about the new information that has come to light. Shot at point-blank range.

A crime of passion? Domestic abuse? An argument that got out of hand? He entertains the thought, painful as it might seem. God knows, Callum is familiar with the pain of family life, the traumas it throws up, the challenges.

259

Teenagers can be tricky to handle at times. If discipline was an issue, as Joan implied, then perhaps there is something in that. Maybe Owen had discovered something about his son he didn't like. Maybe he was afraid for him, afraid of what he was getting involved in? Drugs? Getting into bad company? Perhaps he flew off the handle, a firearms incident, an accident, even? But no, that didn't tally with the Owen he knew. Owen was not a man to get enraged like that, was he?

But Callum saw enough as a policeman to know that anything is possible. You'd be surprised what goes on behind closed doors. He'd always said this to his wife after a long shift, back in the days when he still had a wife.

He wonders then if C.I.D will share what they have found with Joan and Ruthie as next of kin, or if they'll want to keep it quiet for now in case it prejudices or influences the case against their chief suspect in any way.

Time will tell. And he himself is not sure what to share with them. He doesn't want to cause unnecessary distress.

He walks back into his house, closes the door.

He has work to do, two men in their late twenties to track down for a start. And it looks as if his friend Owen's whole future depends on him right now.

Digging

It's later that same day that Callum drives past the gamekeeper's cottage and sees them tearing it apart in their search for evidence.

He stops the van and winds his window down, but no one bothers to enlighten him. They ignore him as if he isn't even there, carrying on with their task, so he drives on again.

Ruthie must be staying at her grandmother's house for now. Probably best, under the circumstances.

He watches them in his rear view mirror, tramping back and forth along the garden path, turning up boxes of belongings, searching through them, and he feels sorry for Owen. Losing his son and his wife, and now this. A team of forensics picking over his home, trying to find conclusive proof that he pulled the trigger which ended his son's life.

And a part of him, a large part of him, hopes they'll find nothing.

He reminds himself of how Owen reacted to the intruder in their garden, the one from the shooting party, with a rifle in his hand; how he yelled at Strabane, was prepared to risk his work and home in a heated encounter about it. How he lashed out.

Owen, a gamekeeper, no longer keeps rifles at his house. Why?

What happened, Owen?

Callum is no longer sure that he wants to find out.

He drives on up the road to the castle and the trees form a lovely aqueous green archway overhead. Joan has confided in him before that she believes this place to be cursed, but if it is, it wears a beautiful disguise most days. Grand beeches stretch away over the landscape to his right, topping the glen, the gorge where Lydia lost her life, and which teems with history – the execution of witches, among other things. They form stately pillars in the sunshine, a natural cathedral lit up from above, splitting the light.

He drives over the cattle grid and into Strabane's territory. The driveway winds up past outbuildings and cottages and barns, bordered by an ancient wall, and then the castle itself quickly looms into view, turrets and tower standing tall against the blue sky.

Every man should own a castle, he decides.

Strabane is continually complaining about the burden it leaves him with, the worries, *like trying to rescue a leaky boat* is one way Callum has heard him describe it. He glances up at the turrets and roofline. He is sure there must be places where the odd damp patch stains the walls, but it doesn't look much like a leaky boat to him.

He's relieved to see Laura standing outside the castle, mobile clamped to her ear, looking much happier than the last time he saw her.

He pulls up beside her, and she waves, finishes speaking on the phone, then hangs up.

'Hi,' she calls to him as he climbs out of the van, slamming the door behind him.

'You look cheerful,' he comments.

'I am!' and she pushes her mobile down into the pocket of her jeans and beams at him. 'My van is fixed!'

'Good news. They rescued it?'

'They did indeed. We'll be reunited later today.'

'And you'll be able to start camping out in her again?'

'Pretty much.'

He glances up at the castle walls. 'You wouldn't rather stay in a castle?'

'Not this one! Anyway,' she adds. 'My van is my castle.'

'Well, I'm pleased for you.'

She studies his face. 'Is there something else? Bothering you, I mean?'

He considers how much to share with her, but he needs to chew it over with someone. He can't share it with Joan and Ruthie. Not yet. And he's pretty sure he can trust Laura.

He glances back at the row upon row of tall windows glinting high above them, with their view of all that transpires beneath. He's aware of being watched, wonders briefly where Strabane is.

Laura follows his gaze, then begins to walk away down the drive, her back to the castle, and Callum falls into step beside her.

'You know they're searching Owen's house,' he tells her.

'Go on.'

'I just don't know what to think anymore.'

Beside them, glossy rhododendrons hug the edge of the driveway in places.

'Ruthie turned up at Joan's house in the middle of the night. Out of the blue. Said she had a key to the house all along. Her mum's. She's been letting herself in.'

'Hence the weird stuff Joan noticed.'

'Not ghosts, after all,' he laughs. He never believed it was ghosts in the first place, but he knew Laura had had a strange feeling when she stayed in Lydia's old room for a night or two. She'd been pretty glad to vacate it, in fact; had even preferred to brave the ghosts that reputedly haunt the castle instead.

'Ruthie said she'd remembered something about the night her brother disappeared, said he'd been camping at Gallows Hill on the night itself. With two lads from school.'

Laura frowned. 'What's strange about that? Owen said as much.'

'But she remembered other things too. Robbie was apparently angry with Strabane, maybe even his parents.'

'Who isn't?'

'But he warned Ruthie off from going near the castle, as if he was frightened for her.'

'Frightened for her?'

'He said he'd seen things at the castle.'

A pause elapses. 'And Ruthie has suddenly remembered the name of one of Robbie's camping pals.'

'That's good, isn't it?'

'Don't you think it's odd that she should suddenly remember now?'

'It was a long time ago. Maybe she racked her brains to find out.'

'Yes, but... there's something so vague about it all.'

'What are you saying?' Laura asks him.

He sighs heavily. 'I don't know.'

'Are you saying Ruthie might be lying?'

'Lying is a bit strong.'

From between the rhododendrons the gardener, Nathan, suddenly appears, pushing a wheelbarrow of compost, close enough to have overheard what they've been saying.

He stares at them and then walks on in silence.

'Dan paid me a visit this morning too.'

'Oh dear!'

'Strange thing was, he was filling me in, wanting to keep me in the loop in case I learnt anything new.'

'There's a turn up for the books.'

'He told me they had already found out how Robbie was killed, but didn't want to say anything until after the funeral.'

Laura holds her breath, dreading some lurid detail.

'So, how did he die?'

'He was shot in the chest. At point-blank range.'

Laura has a sudden vision of Gallows Hill in fading afternoon light, the peace and tranquillity stolen by a single ear-splitting blast, rooks and crows lifting from the branches in a black wave. Then the silence that follows. What happened in that silence?

Who was there? Who heard it and covered it up?

'Well, I suppose that makes it look increasingly likely that Owen is their man,' Laura says.

'But what if he isn't?'

'Then, who?'

Callum looks agonised for a moment, wrestling with his conscience. 'Of course, I could just leave all of this to the experts,' he says.

'You could.'

'It's not my problem, really. I could just stop worrying about it.'

She nods slowly.

'After all, I'm done with all that stuff. I walked away from it years ago.'

She stops walking and faces him. 'And yet?'

'I promised Joan.'

'There's your answer then. You have to keep looking. You have to keep asking questions.'

'I'm just not sure that Owen is the right man.'

Darker things have occurred. He knows that. Domestic abuse is deep and dark and dirty, and the inexplicable does sometimes happen.

'And what about you?' he asks her.

'What about me?'

'How's your dig?'

'I think I might get back to it. I've still got a couple of weeks left. I've got the funding. Might as well use it.'

'They're letting you go back there?'

'Well, the forensics team have left. And no one's stopping me. So…'

'So we both need to keep digging.'

'A lot of it is speculation, of course. In my case,' she muses.

He regards her quizzically.

'Mine too.'

'What about evidence?'

'Evidence can be misconstrued. I suppose, in the end, unless you were actually there and witness something with your own eyes, you can never be really sure of anything.'

Laura reflects on her own work as an archaeologist, trying to plumb the depths of remote time, while knowing that there is, beyond the era of her Bronze Age fort, even deeper time. And her new friend Callum is right. You can arrive at a place and not have a clue what took place there only moments before, as the otter slips into the water, or the wild cat vanishes in the mist. Even in your local supermarket, someone can collapse, medics can be called, and half an hour later you would never know. The tide closes over and the water remains calm. We barely leave a ripple.

But in fact, Laura knows that we do leave something behind. Something worth digging for, as she carefully excavates the soil, millimetre by millimetre, in the hope of finding the truth. Or a kind of truth, anyway. The past, with all its nefarious mysteries.

'Do you ever think about your people?' Callum asks out of the blue.

'My people?'

'In that broch of yours?'

'Of course. All the time. But do you know what's really weird?' she says. 'They never once thought about me.'

'Obviously.'

'They thought themselves very modern, full of bright possibilities.'

Nathan walks past again, clattering his empty wheelbarrow on the cobbles, and they hear him mutter, 'I'm glad some people have the time to stand and chat.'

Callum exchanges a complicitous glance with Laura.

'I thought you had all the time in the world, Nathan.

I thought that was the beauty of gardening?' he says, but Nathan keeps walking and doesn't respond.

Pete Brodie

Callum pulls up in a quiet residential street in the nearby town of Dunbrochan. Even this little suburb feels like an assault on the senses after the endless quiet of the lanes and fields of Kilbroch day after day.

Dunbrochan is a short drive away. You could walk it in half an hour. Kilbroch, now a mere hamlet, used to be the place where people lived, a few hundred years ago, clustered around the castle. But over the years, the population dwindled and in the late 1960s the neighbouring village of Dunbrochan became the focus instead, as new housing developments spread across the hills in an unsightly rash.

Dunbrochan is a desirable residence, its properties sought after. It has good schools, a bustling High Street, train links to Edinburgh and Glasgow and an attractive river running through the middle of it. But it has always struck Callum as odd that the housing developments of the 1970s onwards occupy the most inhospitable sites, the highest points on the landscape where human populations never wanted to build houses before. And when you hear the wind tearing between the boxy semis, you can understand why.

'There's a reason why people never used to build on those heights,' Joan has told him before now. 'We're lucky here in Kilbroch. Here is where people should be living, but luckily for you and I, hardly anyone does!'

Callum parks his van outside a row of detached bungalows and kills the engine. Sudden silence. It's tea time and he can see families through the half-lit windows settling down to normal routines. A routine he is excluded from, by choice.

He's chosen this time of day on purpose, in the hope

of being more successful in his search. He asked around among his few acquaintances at the Kilbroch Arms, located the address, and now here he is.

Lucky for him, Pete Brodie didn't move away from Dunbrochan. Opportunities didn't beckon. Instead he's still here. Living with his mum, according to Rachel Kennedy who works at the Kilbroch Arms and went to school with him.

'We weren't in the same year at school, but yeah, I ken him,' she'd said. 'Still lives with his maw in Irvine Way.'

His mother is a child minder, and plastic toys spill messily across the front lawn. There's a car-port made of corrugated plastic where the sun can't reach but the draughts can, and a few limp articles hang on a clothes airer there looking damp and dreary, as if they will never get dry.

A wave of depression washes over him. He doesn't know why. There's just something about the hopelessness of family life at its worst, when people struggle and nothing seems to be going right. So much dysfunctional disconnect lies behind closed doors.

This isn't going to be easy. It's not as if he has the badge to help him gain access to people's lives anymore, but then again, maybe that's an advantage. He's a 'friend of the family', he reminds himself. Joan has asked him to do this and Owen was once his friend, if only briefly. That gives him the right.

He walks down the drive and is about to ring the bell when the door is flung open in his face. He's greeted with the words, 'Is that my take-away?' as a young man in his late twenties glances at Callum's empty hands.

'No, sorry.'

'Oh.'

'Are you Pete Brodie, by any chance?'

The young man looks at Callum's face now for the first time.

269

'What about it?'

'I live up at Kilbroch. I'm a friend of Joan Metcalfe.'

'Who?'

'Robbie's grandmother.'

At mention of Robbie's name, Pete Brodie grows pale and repeats the name softly as if he's just seen a ghost.

'Robbie?'

'That's right.'

'You're not the polis?'

Callum shakes his head. 'I'm a friend of the family, of Robbie's family. And his grandmother has asked me to, well, to ask some questions.'

'Who is it, son?' a tired-looking woman appears behind him in the hallway, nods once then leaves them both to it.

Pete turns back to Callum, and looks at him. 'What was it you wanted to know?' he asks quietly.

Callum watches him closely, but not too closely. He's after a level of trust. He needs this young man, who knew Robbie at the time of his death, to open up the floodgates, to spill what he knows. If he knows anything.

'Can we talk inside maybe?'

Pete glances back over his shoulder.

'Out here will do.'

Callum nods. 'Okay. You heard they found a body up at Gallows Hill?'

Pete hangs his head sadly. 'I heard.'

'The family, his grandmother, Joan, and his sister, Ruthie, are hoping to get to the bottom of what happened to Robbie that night.'

At the mention of Ruthie's name Pete looks up quickly, a fleeting look of alarm or something else there, which Callum can't quite fathom.

'Ruthie?' he whispers. 'Haven't seen her in years.'

'She's a recluse. Keeps herself to herself.'

'Nae wonder, hey?' Pete murmurs.

270

'What was Robbie like?' Callum asks now. He wants to build up a picture of the normal Robbie, the life they were all leading when disaster struck.

Pete sighs, and then relents a little. He moves away from the kitchen doorway and takes a seat on a nearby garden bench under the car-port, where the wind blows even on a fine day.

Callum is glad of his jacket. He sits next to the boy, preparing to tease out what information he can.

'We were pals at school. Cut about together all the time, before he... before he... we always thought he ran away, you see. Like he'd always said he would.'

'How d'you mean?'

'He wasn't very happy at home. His parents argued all the time. Big fights. That's why he was so close to his little sister. He said he was going to run away. So when he disappeared, that's what we all thought had happened. Taken it into his head to get away. I wish he had now.' Pete pauses and looks at his feet, as if these memories are a territory he's not visited in a long time.

'I had my doubts though. I wasn't so sure. I mean, he'd never leave his little sister behind, d'you ken what I mean?' he adds.

Callum listens, astonished. It's all becoming very odd, as a picture of brother and sister emerges as babes lost in the wood.

'Why would he want to run away?' Callum asks.

'Lots of reasons. He found out his mum was having an affair.'

'Who with?'

'That dude up at the castle, the rich one they worked for. His dad found out and was furious. Really ragin'.'

A vision suddenly opens up in Callum's head, of the gorge and the day Lydia fell to her death. Suicide? Or was she pushed?

'He's a dodgy bastard, anyway.'

'Who is?'

'That dude up at the castle,' Pete says. 'People said he was up to stuff.'

Callum freezes inside. Why had no one cracked a light about any of this before? Did they even know? 'What sort of stuff?'

And it struck Callum then that teenagers so often know what lurks beneath the surface, the real dirt and squalor that goes on behind closed doors and remains hidden from respectable eyes, people whose gaze is averted elsewhere and who do not want to know the truth. Teenagers can be trusted sometimes to get at the root of the evil.

'He used to get vanloads of young girls to turn up at the castle, and he'd film them.'

'What?'

Callum can't disguise his shock. 'But how do you know any of this?'

'Robbie found out. He'd go with his mum up to the castle sometimes. She did the cleaning up there. And he found out what the old bastard was up to.'

'Did Robbie tell you this?'

Pete nods. 'Yep. We all knew. We used to go camping up there and we used to spy on 'em. Watch people come and go. There were weird parties and that. Posh folk, you know?'

Callum has another vision of Gallows Hill on a dark night, twelve years earlier, when Robbie was still alive and well and tragedy had not yet struck; a couple of teenagers making their way secretly up to the castle, peering through the bushes in the dark. Callum knows that you can quite easily make your way into the gorge without anyone noticing. No one up at the castle on a dark winter's night would notice a couple of peeping-tom teenagers hiding out in the gardens below, slipping between the trees, taking shelter in the greenhouse or the orangerie. Callum thinks of Robbie and Pete lurking in one of the old potting sheds; they'd hear tyres churning up the gravel, car doors opening, discreet laughter, young girls stepping down from high vehicles and being hustled quickly into a side entrance of the castle while Strabane's own children lay sleeping upstairs, oblivious.

'What happened to those girls?' Callum asks.

Pete Brodie shrugs. 'Robbie was terrified for his sister. He tried to tell his mum about it. But she didn't believe him.'

'Why not?

Another shrug. 'I guess it sounded too far-fetched. They'd think we were making it up. I didn't blame her, really. For not believing us, I mean.'

There is a long pause while Callum struggles to take this in. 'And what about the night Robbie went missing? You were there with him? Camping at Gallows Hill like you often did?'

Pete glances at him quickly and frowns. 'No, man. Not that night.'

'Ruthie says that you were.'

'It was all a long time ago. None of us can be expected to remember it exactly.'

'So everyone tells me.'

Pete glances at him sideways. 'I'm not lying, you know. I'm telling you the truth. Why would I lie?'

'Did you tell anyone about it, at the time? The weird stuff you'd seen up at the castle, what you both suspected?'

'Apart from Robbie's mum, you mean?' He shakes his head. 'No, man. Why would anyone believe us? And after Robbie ran away... well, I never went back there. I tried not to think about it.

'Except that he didn't run away.'

Pete hangs his head sadly. 'I know that now.'

The sound of plates being slotted together drifts towards them through the open kitchen door and Callum becomes conscious that time is running out, that he only has so many minutes with this young man, this potential witness, (or potential suspect?) before the barriers will come down.

'Was there anyone else with you when you camped up there sometimes? Ruthie mentioned Robbie had two pals he'd camp out with?'

'Aye!' Pete nods and there's a curl of dislike about his lips, which is not lost on Callum. 'Sean Robertson. I don't see him anymore.'

'You stopped being friends?'

Pete nods.

'Why was that?'

'People drift apart, don't they? It was all a long time ago.'

'D'you know where I could find him?'

'His parents still stay at the Quarry Houses. I don't know where he is, though. He went to uni. Don't know what happened to him after that.'

Callum sits in the driver's seat, checking his phone. The Quarry Houses are on the other side of Dunbrochan, a relatively new estate of prefabricated breeze-blocks covered with white pebble-dash facades, decorated with an assortment of elaborate pillars and balconies. Callum is always mildly amused that these houses, built on a former quarry, are not built with stone. Their solidity is a mere facade. Yet they are very desirable properties, sought after, offering a semblance of the American Dream with their shiny new interiors and velvet-neat lawns.

This is where he is heading now, in search of another of Robbie's former school friends, someone who was possibly with him the night he disappeared, or at least in the days leading up to his disappearance.

He sees movement through the window of the Brodie bungalow, a dark silhouette, watching him leave.

Callum wonders now which one of them is telling the truth? Ruthie or Pete? Has Ruthie misremembered? Or is she deliberately trying to obfuscate the facts? He wonders also, what memories he has dug up with his unwelcome visit. Has he stirred any ghosts in Pete Brodie's life? Twelve years is a long time, but perhaps not long enough to bury a ghost. Ghosts have a way of resurfacing.

Salvage

Ruthie sits in her mother's old room at Glentye. From the bed, she can see out of the window, across the empty fields and to the hills beyond. She reaches out. Folded over one chair is a blanket crocheted in soft colours and squares.

'Your mum made that,' Joan commented earlier when she saw Ruthie gazing at it.

She thinks of her mother as a young girl, crocheting away in the soft dark of the winter nights before Ruthie was even born.

She feels the air is thick with the ghosts of her mother's presence – Lydia at different stages and ages, as a child, a teenager, an expectant mother, a daughter who visited the house once she was married with children of her own – but that's partly because Joan has made it so. A shrine to a daughter she lost and still misses.

Ruthie wants to go home, back to the gamekeeper's cottage with its scruffy interiors, but she knows she can't do that while forensics swarm the place, itemising each object as if they are so certain they've caught their culprit already, as if they have unequivocal proof.

She feels suffocated in her grandmother's warm house with its thick carpets and double glazing where the breezes cannot penetrate. Cosy, it defies the winds that blow, but Ruthie feels trapped. She likes the open air and she's used to breezes finding their way through the gaps in the windows of the old cottage where she's lived all her life.

She's not a child anymore, she thinks, as she gazes out of the window. She can look after herself. She doesn't need anyone else. Just the woods. If only the rest of the world would leave her alone.

But she's worried. She's heard them talking about whether they'll be threatened with eviction. If her father no longer works for Strabane, what then? What becomes of the only home she has ever known?

She recoils from the thought with terror, cannot go there. Cannot put any of it into words. Silence beyond imagining screams inside her head. But she just sits, and stares out of the window as if none of it matters.

She can hear a slight commotion on the driveway below, a car horn, footsteps, crunching of gravel, two women's voices, her grandmother's and another voice she half-recognises. She stands up so she can see the driveway. It's Laura, the archaeologist who arrived here only a short while ago and seems to have become firm friends with her grandmother already. And with Callum.

They seem to be in league together against the rest of the world.

Ruthie likes that feeling, it makes her feel safe, although it worries her too.

She peers out and watches the woman below with envy. She envies her confidence, her freedom.

Laura looks positively ecstatic, beaming with happiness. Her camper van has been repaired and Joan shares her obvious delight and relief at the news. 'So, she's miraculously survived?' Joan cries.

'She has indeed. I thought she was a goner, but she'll live to fight another day.'

'I'm delighted for you, Laura. I really am. So we'll see you about for a while yet?'

'Another two weeks if I can wangle it.'

'Well that's just great news.'

'Have you seen Callum at all?'

'Not since this morning,' Joan responds.

'He very kindly offered to store some of my stuff at his

place. I'm dead excited about moving it back into the van, setting up home again.'

Joan smiles. 'If I see him, I'll let him know.'

Ruthie eavesdrops on the two women. It makes her feel safe, but she also wonders how people manage it, to establish such an easy connection like that.

She catches Laura glancing up at the window and takes a step back into the shadows.

Dunbrochan

Callum sits outside the Co-op in his van after picking up a diet coke to quench his thirst. He takes a long draught from the neck of the bottle. He's overwhelmed by what he has just learned and the implications of what it means.

There's so much to share with Joan and Laura when he sees them. Too much to take in. And where will he start? He needs to share his new information with Dan, too, let the police take matters into their own hands, but first he needs to visit Sean Robertson's family home, ascertain all that he can.

This has been just about the most fruitful part of his investigation so far, a simple interview with one of Robbie's old school pals.

Was Pete telling the truth? But why would he lie about something like that? Parties up at the castle, young girls being secretly trafficked into the place. Who attended those parties? And who knew about it?

He thinks of Strabane and the image he chooses to project, of a caring husband and father, looking after his wife until she died of cancer, raising his two daughters alone. His love of nature, the aviary for local birds, the meadow he asks his gardener to cultivate and sow to protect the wildlife. Then he thinks of Lottie and Sophie; one daughter resentful and afraid, the other devoted, one of them afraid to leave the other alone. This puts a wholly new light on the shape of events.

We all have a story that we choose to tell ourselves, an image we like to project, Callum thinks, a version of events, a narrative that suits our purposes. But it is, in the end, just a story.

He thinks of Joan, sitting in her comfortable little house up at Kilbroch, bearing her pain alone, with her paint brushes and her resilience. He'll need to fill her in, although it will be difficult.

On an impulse, he calls Laura.

'Callum, is that you?'

'Yup. I've found out a few things.'

'Okay. Tell me.'

'Well, for starters, according to Pete Brodie, Lydia was having an affair with Strabane.'

'Really? Are you sure?'

'As sure as I can be.'

'So where does that leave us?'

'I can't help thinking this puts a wholly different light on her suicide.'

'How d'you mean?'

'Well, what if it wasn't suicide after all?'

Even as he speaks, he knows that he cannot be sure of anything, he's simply stumbling in the dark, trusting his instincts. 'There's more,' he adds. 'But I think I need to tell you in person. I'm just going across to see if I can catch up with another of Robbie's old school pals. I'll fill you in later.'

He hangs up, and stares through the windscreen at the quiet Dunbrochan High Street; the Church of Scotland building on the corner, next to the library, and the barber's opposite with its twisting red and white candy pole, his thoughts ticking over.

He's thinking now of Lydia and her apparent suicide, falling from the edge of the gorge at the spot they call Gallow Falls. There are two possibilities. Either Owen found out about the affair and in a jealous fit of rage, pushed her to her death. Or Strabane realised that Robbie had been spying on him and knew about his nefarious dealings up

280

at the castle. A dark thought enters his head: did he silence Robbie first, then Lydia?

A cold horror creeps through his veins, and he wonders for a moment if he should have warned Laura further. But where is the evidence? It's all speculation at the moment.

If he's wrong, and Strabane had nothing to do with Robbie's death, or Lydia's, where does that leave them?

He turns his key in the ignition, pulls out into the quiet High Street where the residents of Dunbrochan go about their business. People walk their dogs, drop their books off at the library, sit outside cafes, rummage through the charity shops, and emerge from the butcher's with packages wrapped in greaseproof paper. Even the Bank of Scotland, at the end of the High Street, is housed in a Victorian building with a white-painted front that gives it the surety and complacency of a domestic dwelling. Everything is safe, presided over by the lofty heights of the Cathedral, a vision of safety and durability caught in stone.

Nothing can threaten this pleasant dream of ordinary suburban bliss.

There are no dark secrets here.

Flashback

Ruthie strides through the woods as the shadows lengthen. She knows these woods like the back of her own hand. She can map the invisible pathways trodden only by deer and foxes. It feels good to be outside again, away from the suffocating warmth of her grandmother's house and the bedroom preserved like a shrine. Joan is not aware of the dreary atmosphere that clings to that guest room. She just hasn't bothered to change or update it, and cannot bring herself to throw away the reminders of her daughter's life. That's all she knows. But to others, the vanished presence of Lydia lingers there uncomfortably.

Ruthie peers through the trees, catches a glimpse of the back of the cottage she's lived in all her life. It appears quieter now. No more people in rustling whites trooping back and forth up the garden path, like it's some kind of garage sale where the occupants have died. So why isn't she being allowed back there yet?

She approaches from the back, so that anyone passing on the road on their way up to the castle will not see her.

She inches her way forward through the trees, stands in the back garden, looking up at the quiet house. The lean-to conservatory her father made for her across the back of the cottage, a glassed-in area filled with plants, her small table where she liked to do her jigsaw puzzles.

A memory crashes through the silence.

Her mother's terrified voice, wailing, 'I can't do this, Owen.'

'We have to, for her sake.'

'Our son!'

A momentary flashback arriving through the murk of the

past. Pots and pans clashing on the draining board. That was often how they argued. A kettle dropped aggressively on the burner, with an angry clatter.

Then she closes her eyes and another flashback emerges. She and Robbie this time, his kindness and laughter.

She whispers his name, the name of her long-dead brother. 'Robbie!'

And she sees herself ambling along beside him up the lane. It's autumn. The leaves above their heads are golden, and they're laughing, throwing their heads back, chattering, walking home from the spot where the school bus drops them every day. Just the two of them.

No one else from high school lived up here at Kilbroch, so they were free to occupy their own world most of the time. Ruthie was free of that burden of tight anxiety that knotted her belly at the thought of the ugly school building in Dunbrochan, with its bright overhead lights and its shrieking bells and its corridors full of frightening faces. The woods and fields and lanes of Kilbroch were the complete opposite of everything the school stood for. There were no alarms sounding here, telling her where to go or what to do. There was just herself and Robbie, walking home from school together, before everything went wrong. Before the darkness came.

She can feel the light on her face, pouring down through the golden tapestry of leaves, just as if it was yesterday, as if she is there again, beside her brother, in that precious carefree moment, captured forever. She wishes she could stop time.

Just her and Robbie.

Walking home in the glow of a late autumn afternoon. A blue sky against flaming incandescent trees, the crunch of leaves underfoot, the lane to the gamekeeper's cottage carpeted in gold. Fallen pine needles in drifts like rust-coloured snow. Piles of leaves gathered near the bright mossy walls that line the road.

The world is blue and gold and Ruthie has her eyes half-shut, squinting up at the sky.

Then a door slams and she crashes back into the present moment.

Through the glassed-in walls of the conservatory she sees a figure, standing there, staring out, and for one terrified moment she thinks it's her father, or Robbie's ghost.

But the man morphs into a police officer.

They haven't left, after all.

They're still here, searching for clues.

She pauses for one moment, before vanishing into the undergrowth, as shy and barely visible as the deer which haunt these woods.

Biology

Joan watches the last of the light falling through the tall windows onto all the beautiful details of her desk. A book on plants sits open at a particularly beautiful centrepiece spread of some fine botanical drawings she admires. An old blue jug bristles with an assortment of paintbrushes, and a box of watercolours sits to one side, open, the bright squares of colour as tempting as boiled sweets.

Ruthie has been showing an interest in the desk. She caught her granddaughter examining the objects on it earlier today, and she'd talked to her a little about plant biology, how the process works. Chloroform, photosynthesis, osmosis, plus the secrets of pollinating, all those words and the language of science which, for Joan, unlocks the mysteries of the universe. She knows that Ruthie too has a love of nature, and hopes that one day she will be able to share more of what she knows with her.

'When I taught Biology in school, plant biology was my favourite topic,' she tells her granddaughter, who listens carefully as always, but says little.

'He keeps a wild meadow,' Ruthie had said.

'Who does?'

'Strabane,' came the answer. 'He keeps bees.'

Joan nodded.

And it was all Ruthie would say.

She didn't mention her father or what had happened, or what she thought about it all. No one ever knew what Ruthie thought. No one ever asked.

Joan wonders now if they all make too much effort to protect her granddaughter from the truth. Perhaps Owen had tried too hard to do that too, over the years.

285

And what of her poor grandson?

They have established the cause of death, a bullet wound to the chest. They've matched the bullet used with those stored in Owen's shed. She knows this much. Although, the shotgun which likely caused the crime is rusted with lack of use. There were cobwebs knitted around its barrel, and the shed he kept it in was padlocked, as if he'd locked the thing away twelve years ago and left it there to rot, never wanting to reopen the door to that nightmarish memory. Was that it? And for the first time, she entertains the thought that Owen might not be to blame. Maybe it was an accident. Had any of them ever considered that?

But if so, why the secrecy and the silence?

Pelmore Avenue

The Quarry Houses lie on the edge of Dunbrochan, just before the main road heads into open countryside. And beyond the estate are the Ochils which beckon northwards, topped by changeable skies. The Quarry Houses seem to defy all that wildness, keeping themselves apart – tight, prim and expensive. It's a relatively new estate, filled with aspirations towards the American Dream, with smooth front lawns, spotless paving and shiny new cars parked out front.

He turns left at a mini roundabout, then right, and immediately finds himself lost, like the Minotaur, in a maze of similar-seeming streets with similar-sounding names, each house like its neighbour, with mock wrought-iron balconies, pillars and porticoes, where families are mortgaged to the hilt and running on credit.

He knows he's being a touch judgemental, but he can't help being aware of a fake facade hiding the truth: the aspirations, the pretend affluence, that won't let them admit to being forced to tighten the purse strings.

Try living like me, he thinks, with a van and a rented cottage, and a bursary of freedom. He's chosen his own way of life. Not for him the upholstered comfort in the bosom of a family home. He's tried it and it just doesn't suit him. He knows that if he lived in an estate like this he'd feel suffocated, smothered, like drowning in cotton wool.

He cruises along until he finds the right address.

Pelmore Avenue, number 33.

There it is. Pristine and precise, a lawn so immaculate there is not a hair out of place. Alarm bells are ringing already. Too perfect.

He parks his van, gazes surreptitiously at the neighbouring houses either side.

Plate glass windows gaze back, blank and unseeing.

There's no sign of activity and he doubts whether he'll find anyone in.

The driveway is a bland monoblock, leading straight to a double glass door with lollipop bay trees in pots either side. He touches one in curiosity. Plastic. These trees will never need lopping or pruning. They will remain plastic for all eternity.

He rings the doorbell, listens to a corresponding chime within, but expects no response.

So when a shadow appears behind the glass and the door sweeps open, he's momentarily taken by surprise.

A woman in her fifties glances first at him, then at the bay tree he was investigating. Finally, she peers over his head towards his van.

'Are you here for the lawn?' she asks crisply. 'You're a bit late.' She has an air of rude condescension about her.

'Er, no, I'm not, actually,' he begins, finding it hard to believe the lawn needs any more attention. 'Mrs Robertson?'

She frowns at him in annoyance. 'Yes…?'

'I was hoping to speak to your son? Sean Robertson?'

'He doesn't live here anymore.'

She looks visibly alarmed, and Callum begins to regret not preparing a more conciliatory opening.

'My name is Callum MacGarvey. I live up at Kilbroch, not far from the castle. A friend of mine, Joan Metcalfe, has asked me to help her find out what happened to her grandson twelve years ago.'

She instantly freezes and the blood drains from her already pale face.

'You may remember the case of Robbie MacBride? Who went missing?'

She glances away briefly, scanning the windows of the other houses.

'Your son was a friend of his, I believe?'

'I wouldn't say they were close friends. They were at school together, in the same year.'

'And they sometimes went camping together, in the woods up near Kilbroch Castle?'

'I don't remember that.' She takes a breath, then says, 'Look, I'm sorry I can't help you. I'm sure it's very noble of you, trying to help the family, but I'm afraid there's nothing I can add to clarify matters.'

He's shocked at her steely tone and the formality of her language, which he knows she is adopting in order to create an unbreachable distance between herself and whatever might be unfolding here.

'That's a shame. I was just speaking to a mutual friend of theirs. Pete Brodie? And he was under the impression they were fairly close at one time.'

A faint sound of disapproval escapes her lips. 'I wasn't happy about my son hanging out with those two. They weren't his sort, you know?'

Callum remains neutral. 'Is it possible I could speak with your son at all?'

She makes a small sound in the back of her throat like a laugh, and says, 'I shouldn't think so. He lives in New Zealand and I doubt he remembers much about it. A great deal has happened since then. He's doing very well for himself, actually. He's a doctor,' she adds proudly. 'I'm sorry, I can't help you at all.'

She begins to close the door in his face.

'I don't suppose you have any memories yourself of that time, anything that might help to enlighten the family…'

The door pauses. But only for a second. 'I'm very busy.'

'Mrs Robertson, what if it was your son who went missing twelve years ago?'

She glares at him. 'But it wasn't my son, was it?'

Then the door closes with an emphatic click.

He stands staring at the glass in disbelief, watches her figure recede down the hallway.

No curiosity about the missing lad and his family, no empathy. In Callum's experience, if someone has nothing to hide, they are open, curious, chatty about the past, pleased to be asked, usually, not defensive. Unless they are ashamed of something, afraid to be found wanting in some respect, or seen as less than perfect? He remembers the curl of dislike on Pete Brodie's lips and he wonders how well the three boys really did get along.

One of them managed to escape to a future of apparent success, a doctor in New Zealand, doing very well for himself, thank you very much; another still lives with his mother in a crowded house in Dunbrochan, trapped by his past; the third lay buried beneath the earth on Gallows Hill for twelve years until his bones were finally exhumed, and are now being examined at close quarters by teams of forensic scientists with a murder to solve.

Surely, a woman like Mrs Robertson ought to be full of horror at what had happened to Robbie and ready to help in any way possible?

Callum turns on the doorstep, observes the circle of white houses before him, a cul de sac leading nowhere, but its occupants proud of having come this far. Always with hopes that their children will go further, and who can blame them?

He would be the same, if he had it in him. If life hadn't lit a bomb underneath him, an explosion that took out most of what was familiar to him.

He walks back to his van, takes another glance at the Robertson house, silent and irreproachable, then starts the engine.

Sean Robertson was clearly given every advantage and

opportunity to succeed, and his road to success began here, at the Quarry Houses, from which he had then managed to escape.

'My son, the doctor,' he can imagine his mother saying proudly at coffee mornings or when bumping into former acquaintances in the local supermarket. Not taking a breath, before launching in to inform others what a success story her son has become, despite the fact that – according to Pete – 'he was a dick in school, a snob and a pain in the arse'.

He wonders now how inseparable the three boys really were, and what transpired during those camping trips. In Sean's case, those nights spent camping in the woods were obviously illicit moments stolen away from the cosseting environment of his family home. Clearly, Mrs Robertson's boasts about her son are so vehemently uttered because she knows how fragile the foundations are. Perhaps Sean's school career had been a little chequered and his road to success not as smooth and inevitable as might first appear. Perhaps there were bumps and troughs along the way, in particular making friends with, as his mother put it, 'the wrong sort'.

People's ideas of success and failure are very mixed and varied; Callum has learnt this over the years.

It is with a sense of relief that he finds his way out of the estate, a maze of identical cul de sacs, full of false leads and dead ends. Families are settling down for the night as darkness gathers on the hills.

As he negotiates the final mini roundabout, he feels his lungs actually expand with pleasure. Dusk is rolling in on those far heights, a sight which in winter is freighted with menace, but right now, he feels nothing but relief to be away from that housing development. Behind those fake facades there is a sense of having arrived, instead of still journeying towards something, and yet so many secrets kept behind closed doors. Callum knows better than anyone how truths can be concealed in places like that.

The hills beckon and he drives towards them.

His route home should take him back through Dunbrochan and out the other side to Kilbroch, but he can't face it. He suddenly feels the need to drive this way instead, and take the long way back, a detour to avoid other houses.

He knows he is a vagrant at heart, never wanting to be tied to a sense of smothering permanence, the way his wife had wanted. She would have loved to occupy a house in an estate like this. She'd have been delighted to be Mrs Robertson's next door neighbour, with an immaculate lawn and plastic bay trees in pots. The very idea fills him with panic.

He watches the horizon stretch out before him, the hills expanding against open sky, and allows himself to breathe.

The Castle

Laura sits behind the wheel, in her repaired and restored van, feeling a lightening of mood as she drives along the narrow lane. She's driving on the edge of a glen, with rolling fields sweeping down to her left and trees climbing the hill to her right, the narrow single-track lane bordered by crumbling stone walls topped by yellow gorse in places.

Sitting in the driver's seat of the van gives her some height and she'd forgotten how good that feels. She loves the view from up here. Her little camper van might be old and rusty but it makes her feel empowered, as if she could take off anywhere. Traveller blood, vagrant blood running in her veins. It gives her an instant escape route out of the city and means that she can lay her head just about anywhere.

She wonders if that's what she and Callum have in common. She finds it easy to talk to him, to relate to his outlook on life, not that she knows him that well, but she feels a connection. In a sense, she feels a connection with all of the people here. It's been a trip worth the making, an expedition that has offered far more than a bit of intensive research. Much as she loves her subject, the search for the Bronze Age broch has paled in comparison to other, more immediate concerns.

So strange that she unwittingly uncovered the bones of Joan's grandson, buried there beneath the quiet earth on Gallows Hill.

As she drives back up to the castle, she thinks of Callum's voice on the phone, telling her that Lydia had been having an affair with her employer, Strabane.

Why on earth, Laura thinks, would she do that? Okay, so the man owned a castle, but...

293

She tries to fill in the gaps. Charmed by him, perhaps? Fooled into thinking he was sophisticated, cultured? Perhaps he seemed to be everything that Owen, with his rustic jackets and his muddy fingernails, was not?

And then Callum had said there was more he needed to tell her. She's curious and wonders what else his visits to Robbie's former friends have unearthed. She's desperate to find out and can understand why Callum might struggle to share this latest information with Joan.

On an impulse, she stops the van in the lay-by below Gallows Hill, parks it and climbs through the bracken, along the line of the old broken fence posts to the top, where the trees grow thick and dense and the world, the modern world, seems far away. Here she is hidden from prying eyes, as was Robbie and whoever buried him.

She stands under the giant oak, stares up at its twisted limbs and wonders what it has seen, what it has witnessed. Is this the same tree they used to hang convicted criminals from, in the days when the laird of the castle stood in judgement over his community and made the decisions of life and death?

Surely it isn't old enough to be the same oak?

The roots of another fallen tree lie twisted and gnarled a few feet away, curled into the earth with such tenacity and ferocity it seems they will never decay.

Perhaps that's the tree.

No one is really sure.

Conjecture and speculation are all we have to go on, she thinks, just like with the twelve year old case of Robbie's death. A single shot to the chest, at point-blank range. Who pulled that trigger? And why?

And who buried him here?

Why did they pick this particular spot, she wonders. Was it significant in some way, so that they could return, so they knew where he lay? But wasn't that rather obvious?

294

Better by far to bury him in the darkest part of the woods where no one walks or visits. Well, whoever is responsible, she's pretty sure they now wish they'd dug in a more remote part of the woods, thick with trees, even fifty yards to the left or right of Gallows Hill, rather than in the clearing itself, beneath that evil-looking oak. If they had done that, the body would never have been found, and Robbie's last resting-place would have remained undisturbed.

Strabane had been so reluctant to give permission for the dig, but in the end, he had given it, grudgingly, reluctantly, but nevertheless he had.

Surely he would never have granted it if he'd known what lay beneath the quiet earth on that spot?

She hears an owl hooting and becomes conscious of the encroaching darkness.

It's so very still and so very peaceful. She thinks of what took place here over the centuries. Public executions when these hills were bare of trees and the view of the gallows tree would be clear for miles around. Centuries of seclusion when the population retreated from this area so that it became largely uninhabited, gamekeepers passing through, shooting parties once or twice a year, then quiet and silence. Lovers discovering the spot, perhaps. Campers, then teenage boys with a tent. And then, latterly, the murder of a sixteen-year-old boy twelve years ago. All these events and happenings are separated by the quiet passage of time and the inevitable changing of the seasons, in an endless cycle of light and dark, heat and cold, snow and rain.

She shudders. As she gazes about at the trees and the patch of luminous sky above, she tries to hear the crack of a single rifle shot splitting the air, as it did that day, twelve years earlier. The birds would have lifted into the sky with a cacophonous clatter of shock. Was there anyone nearby to hear the sound?

This is a rural setting. Distant rifle shots are heard all

the time, depending on the season. Sometimes it's the shooting season and they're after the pheasants cultivated by gamekeepers like Owen. Sometimes it's a farmer scaring crows. And sometimes it's a single bullet bringing tragedy and the end of life.

In this case, far too soon.

Dusk is beginning to soften the edges of the trees and paint the sky with a luminous sunset. The light-fade this far north is so gradual in the summer, it can take you by surprise. It's normally so late that you begin to give up on the idea of night completely, until you realise it has crept up on you after all.

She drives past the gamekeeper's cottage, where the windows are dark and unlit, marked by tragedy. She can almost feel the shadow of evil hanging over it. Or is that sorrow?

She finds it hard to tell.

She drives the camper van under the tall elms up to the castle, and the acres stretch out either side of her. As she rattles over the cattle grid into the castle gardens, she notices a smartly-dressed figure emerging from one of the many outbuildings that line the driveway. Strabane glances in her direction and she catches a momentary look in his eye that unnerves her, which he quickly hides as he then lifts a hand in greeting and keeps walking.

She wonders if she should stay parked in the lay-by beside Gallows Hill tonight? Which would be safer? There, or here?

She's reluctant to go to Joan and park in her driveway. She doesn't want to have to mention what she's just learnt about her daughter, about Lydia's involvement with Strabane. And besides, she doesn't want to intrude on the uneasy peace which is growing between Joan and her granddaughter after so many years of estrangement.

She drives up to the castle in the van, still curious, a little watchful.

She opens her door, hops down from the driver's seat, thinking Strabane has disappeared inside.

But he's still there, standing on the terrace nonchalantly, hands in pockets, lord of all he surveys. Unruffled. Complacent. Secure in the knowledge that his wealth buys him immunity from the worries and cares which trouble others.

He turns at the sound of her feet on the gravel, but keeps his body so still that only his head moves. The effect is unnerving.

He watches her, making no effort to meet her halfway.

She walks towards him, beaming.

There is something lizard-like in his expression.

'She's been fixed!' she announces.

'Who has?'

'My van!'

'Ah. So I see.'

'So, I won't need to impose on your hospitality any further.'

'That's a shame.'

'Forensics appear to have vacated Gallows Hill, for the time being.'

'Now they've got their man, you mean?'

'I thought they were still investigating.'

Strabane shakes his head. 'They know... We all know... sad as it may seem, and a shock to the whole community.'

She hates that he's taking the moral high ground, but then what can you expect? And maybe he is right, after all.

Owen, according to Joan, has always been a surly man. And who knew what had happened to make Ruthie so silent? You never knew what was going on in people's minds, how the dynamics of families played out in private, and perhaps that is true in this case. Maybe Joan was right to have so many reservations and suspicions about her son-in-law.

'So, I'd like to resume the dig, if I may? If you're still okay with that, I mean?'

He holds her gaze for a moment longer than is comfortable. 'Of course. Be my guest.'

It occurs to her that he seems an awful lot more relaxed about the prospect of her digging around on Gallows Hill now that the forensics team have abandoned the area, content they have found their man.

Glancing at Strabane, she realises that a man like him, with property, wealth and power, really does appear to be untouchable. No one had been quick to investigate him, and certainly not thoroughly. In the eyes of the authorities, a man like Owen is far more likely to commit such a crime than a man like Strabane with his manners and his glorious acres, a friend of the present Tories, and a seat in the House of Lords.

He catches her observing him a bit too closely.

'Everything okay?' he asks, and his eyes glint in the evening gloom.

'I saw your daughter jogging earlier,' she points vaguely in the direction of the gorge, to change the subject.

He nods, but doesn't reply.

'She does an awful lot of jogging,' Laura remarks, half-laughing.

'Gives her something to do.'

'She didn't get a place in uni, or anything?'

'Why d'you ask?'

'Well, it just seems strange that she hasn't left home in all these years.'

'And your point is exactly?'

'Oh, I don't have a point.'

He laughs then. Her self-deprecating manner can be infectious and amusing.

'Maybe she likes it here?' he adds.

'Who wouldn't?'

'Will you be staying up here tonight, in your van?' he asks.

'Oh, I wasn't sure.'

'You're welcome to park here, as you did before, if it makes you feel any safer.'

She frowns, thinking of the attack on the van she experienced at Gallows Hill in the early days of the dig, and then the incident on the road, driving back from the Kilbroch Arms.

She nods. 'Mmm… maybe I will.'

He smiles his suave smile.

The Gorge

Dusk veils the bottom of the gorge and a mist creeps with stealth between the birches and the overhanging vines that wet the sides of the rocky cliff walls. No one walks here at this time of night.

Usually.

Ruthie takes her time, stepping carefully. She knows it like the back of her own hand. She likes to come here when no one else does, when there's no threat of encountering Sophie or Lottie, or even Strabane on one of his leisurely ambles about the estate, or Nathan the gardener, repairing fences or steps. Daylight hours are when the others might come here.

Gallow Falls.

This is where her mother fell to her death. She knows this, but it doesn't make the place haunted for her. She also knows that the Drowning Pool is a spot where they used to drown witches, women, girls, anyone unusual or different – like herself. History lies thick on this land, leaving its mark behind in the form of stories and myths that the locals like to keep alive.

It's a beautiful place.

Moonlight touches the sides of the rock walls, where the vines hang, and water drips.

She's not afraid of the approaching dark. She's afraid of other things that lie inside her head. A Pandora's Box she does not want to open. If she opens it, if she ever finds the key, a monster will emerge and she will never again be able to fold all of its monstrous black body back into the box. It will creep through the world, on wicked legs, speedy and disgusting. It will spread its poison.

That is what she must avoid, at all costs.

Memory is the key.

But as everyone knows, memories can be unreliable. We

twist and pervert them to tell our own version of the truth and we don't even know we are doing it.

The true version is so evasive, lurking just out of sight, that even the experts often miss it.

It has been said that the figure of a woman can be seen here in this gorge, late at night, as the mist gathers, or in the early hours, just before dawn. She stands at the top of the ridge, looking down, and no one really knows why she appears.

Is she a presence from a time before?

Or was she a glimpse of the future which eventually came to pass?

When Ruthie glances up, she sees what she thinks is the outline of a figure standing there, until the rustle of a creature in nearby undergrowth causes her to turn her head. Small feet disturbing last year's fallen leaves. Hedgehogs make a surprising amount of noise.

When she looks again the figure is gone.

The ridge above her is still light. The top of the gorge where she saw the outline of a person holds only the shapes of trees now, gathering their skirts of shadow about them. To Ruthie, sensitive as she is, it is as if this entire forested landscape is alive with presences, shapes and phantoms that talk to each other and make music with the slightest of sounds or movements. An orchestra of living souls that light up the night sky.

A tree is a woman, and a line of trees is a parade of women waiting in line for their turn to jump, to leap out into the air where no one will catch them.

Ruthie is a mysterious girl, a mad woman in the attic, a stranger to this world that no one knows what to do with.

The best thing they can do is leave her alone.

Let her be.

But the one man who knows how to do this, Owen, is

currently under lock and key. Perhaps this means she is safer than before? Or perhaps not.

The Outbuildings

Laura draws her little curtains across the windows of the van, against the coming dark.

She switches on a small battery-powered lamp that casts a cosy living-room glow, opens a notebook and bites the end of her pencil, thinking.

She has a glass of red wine at her elbow, feels all the peace and contentment of owning her own four walls again, flimsy as they may seem. She doesn't miss the interior of the castle with its high ceilings and its long passageways disappearing into darkness. She likes the fact she can hear the birds settling down for the night, that they will wake her in the morning, and that one step will take her outside into the fresh air. Inside the castle, she felt separated from nature by thick walls, years of history, centuries of stone, which is odd when you think that she is so driven by the passage of time and her need to uncover hidden layers of the past.

When the lamp suddenly begins to falter and fade out, she rummages about for a replacement with no luck. It needs recharging, so she resorts to the old-fashioned methods. Strikes a match and lights a candle.

After a few minutes she leans forward, pushes the curtain aside and peers out. Blowing out the candle, she lays the notebook flat on the table, face-down, slides the door open and jumps down onto the gravel. The cool evening air is filled with quiet.

A mist is emerging from between the trees at the forested edge of the gardens. She gazes across the acres, feeling the presence and height of those castle walls at her back.

Who owns a castle? Simon had squawked with laughter on one of their recent calls.

Strabane does, she'd replied.

And one day, she supposes, his daughters will. Maybe that was reason enough to stick about rather than go to university, and maybe there is nothing sinister or amiss in their choices to remain close?

Maybe she just fails to understand how the other half live. The wealthier half, the landed gentry.

Tall walls imprison one side of the vast acres, keeping them from spilling over to merge with the endless countryside. These sheltering walls help to create its own little micro-climate during daylight hours, adding to the warmth and the feeling of a secluded paradise.

A pheasant struts and strides on the lawn, on the edge of the meadow, despite the late hour, its plumage bright and regal in what little light is left.

The view is dreamy, mesmeric almost.

Laura feels herself lulled into a false sense of security. If she were Sophie, no doubt she too would want to stay here forever, watching the seasons pass, although boredom might kick in eventually.

Hearing a car door slam, she sees Nathan the gardener in the distance, preparing to leave for his own home at the end of a long day's work.

She waves and he lifts a hand in a vague salute.

His car circles the gravel driveway and pauses alongside her.

'An evening stroll?'

She glances about at the gathering shadows. He has been working very late tonight, but then, she supposes, he loves his job. His hours are more or less his own to dictate.

'I was wondering if I could borrow a torch or a lamp of some kind?'

Nathan nods towards one of the old outhouses.

'You should be able to find a hurricane lamp in there.'

He switches off his engine and makes a move to unclip his seat-belt but she stops him.

'Don't worry. It's okay, I'll manage to find it myself.'

He glances at her.

'On the shelf. To your right.'

'Thank you.'

'You're staying up here tonight?'

She nods.

He releases the hand-brake and mutters, 'I'll see you tomorrow, then.'

She watches the tail-lights of his vehicle retreat along the driveway, accompanied by the crunching of gravel, then the rattle of the cattle grid before the car vanishes behind the trees.

A sudden silence descends. It's peaceful but she feels indescribably lonely. And she doesn't know why.

She glances over her shoulder again. One or two lights have appeared up in the castle, but most of the windows remain dark. She wonders briefly who is watching her, if anyone.

She wanders towards the outhouse Nathan had pointed to. It is fronted by double doors, like a barn, and it takes an effort to yank them open. It's dark inside, too dark to see by, so she takes her phone out and uses the torch on it. A cascade of white light picks out shelves along both walls and a beautiful classic green sports car. Laura doesn't know much about cars, but she knows she likes this one. She's always admired vintage cars since she was a little girl and played with her brother's toys. For some reason, he would always be the one to be presented with a car, she with a doll. The usual gender divide. But it was the vintage make of some of those models that really attracted her, with their shiny trim and polished gleam.

She creeps closer to the MG, smoothes a hand along it.

What a beauty. Just one of Strabane's toys.

Then she turns her attention to the shelves, on which she can see the hurricane lamp. She trips over something and reaches out a hand to steady herself. Takes a look around. She can't help it, curiosity grips her. Behind the vintage car is another vehicle, but this one is sheeted in heavy canvas tarpaulin.

Taking an end of it, and still holding her torch light aloft, she lifts it, throws it back to reveal the vehicle beneath. A hulking black four-by-four.

Why would a car this new be tucked away here instead of in use? It's the rear of the vehicle she can see. Glancing once behind her at the open door, she moves around to the back of the building, lifts the tarpaulin, grazes her torch light over what is revealed.

A damaged front bumper.

Instantly her mind leaps back to that night on the road, the glaring headlights in her rearview mirror, the shock of the impact as the driver behind nudged her van, once, twice, crashing it into the undergrowth before driving on into the night.

The blood drains from her face as she realises what she is looking at and where she is. Isolated, here at the castle, camping alone in the forecourt, Nathan the gardener having left for the night.

Instantly she slides off her torch light, taps the screen.

Callum's number. She needs to look for the last caller, but the door has creaked open behind her. She doesn't dare turn around at first.

'Find what you were looking for?' he asks.

Strabane.

She turns to face him.

She can only see his silhouette in the entrance, framed by what little light still falls outside. His voice doesn't sound too promising.

'Yes,' she says brightly. And she makes a grab for the

hurricane lamp, holds it aloft. 'I needed this. Nathan very kindly…'

She feels the words dry up in her throat. Strabane doesn't move. And he's blocking her exit.

She walks towards the doorway, but he steps sideways in front of her. She still can't see his face, but she can read his body language clearly. He has changed. He's not pretending anymore and he doesn't care who knows it.

The phone is still in her hand, if she just managed to press the last caller and then slide… but it's too late, and she knows it.

She tries for head-on confrontation or diplomacy instead. Confront the issue, see if she can talk her way out of it.

'So it was you? Who tried to drive me off the road that day.'

His silence does not bode well.

Holding the phone in her hand, she touches the screen, hoping she has dialled the last caller, hoping the call will connect with Callum, that he will hear her voice and understand. But she has no way of knowing if it's worked, if she's hit the right number, or any number at all.

'I don't get it,' she says, still trying to talk her way out of it. 'You could have just refused to let the dig go ahead in the first place. It would have been easier, don't you think? Less trouble?'

'You were very insistent.'

She glances to the shelf on her right, looking for a heavy object.

'A simple no would have sufficed.'

'You don't seem the type to take no for an answer, Miss Pettigrew.'

He'd always addressed her as Laura before, but he's aiming for humour.

'It's Ms, not Miss.'

And now Strabane has leant forward and is calmly taking the phone from her hand.

'I didn't kill Robbie, by the way,' he says. 'Despite what you think, and what's about to happen now, I'm not a murderer. I might be many things, but I'm not that.'

She considers fighting, but decides she'd rather wait till they are outside again, for fear of being pushed back and locked inside.

Later, she will wish she fought.

Places bear the marks

Over the lanes and fields of Kilbroch, night descends. But it never gets really dark this far north during the summer months. A grey light edges the world. An owl sits in the branches above the abandoned gamekeeper's cottage and watches. The cottage is silent now. Years ago a family of four lived here, under these quiet eaves. Now two of them are dead. Owen is held behind bars and his daughter has been forced to relocate to her grandmother's. So the windows are dark, the lamps unlit. Memories stir within and without and the silence of Kilbroch bears witness.

Places bear the marks of those who have gone before, Joan always thinks. She tries not to drive past the gamekeeper's cottage if she can help it. It holds too many memories. Sometimes she is forced to pass it on her way to the castle, but she will avoid it if possible. She knows that her daughter believed in ghosts. She spoke about it often. She said she felt someone watching her when she was working up at the castle. Hardly surprising, Joan had responded at the time, with that creep Strabane hanging about. But Lydia had been certain she'd experienced strange things, objects being moved from where she'd left them. And what was that story she told once? She was working up there with Ruthie as a baby. She'd placed the car seat on the long twenty-foot dining table, bent to plug in the hoover and when she straightened up again, the car seat was at the far end of the table.

'Someone moved it,' Joan had said.

'In the time it took me to bend down and plug in the hoover?' Lydia had replied. 'There was no one else there.

The castle was empty. They were all away in Sardinia at the time.'

'Well, maybe Nathan...'

'He wasn't there either. And I'd have seen him.'

Joan had dismissed all of these stories as superstitious nonsense. But she knows now that people do leave a part of themselves behind. They change the ingredients of a place, the cocktail of remembered smells and sounds and memories. They imbue it with their lives.

That is why she chooses to avoid the gamekeeper's cottage.

After Lydia died, she experienced her own string of unexplained events; objects no longer being in the place she left them (although that could be age, granted), the sound of someone moving about the house at night, things going missing. She'd kept Lydia's room unchanged and listened for her footstep on the stair, although she knew it was crazy. Sometimes she had even hoped it was Robbie visiting her in secret, that he was still alive and that one day he would walk back into their lives. Now she knows that Ruthie had had a key all along and could have been the cause of most of these occurrences.

Joan, the rational scientist with a love of art, knows there is usually an explanation, and if we haven't found one yet, that doesn't mean to say that a rational explanation doesn't exist. She is old enough and wise enough to know that there are many things we cannot explain. But she spends a restless night, looking out at the dark.

She knows Ruthie leaves the house at night to go wandering. She heard the stairs creak earlier.

I am not her gaoler, Joan has told Callum. My granddaughter is free to come and go as she pleases. But where does she go at night?

To the woods, no doubt, and back to that cottage with its awful memories. For some reason, her granddaughter loves it there, although Joan can't for the life of her think why. Nasty, cold, draughty place, with its gappy window frames, and its uneven tiled floors.

And its memories.

What goes on in that head of hers? She wishes she could keep her safe, that she had kept her daughter Lydia safe. But Lydia was a grown woman. Ruthie is a grown woman. And you can't keep the people you love prisoner, although it's tempting to try, especially with hindsight, looking back on it all.

She thinks of her friend, Callum, stares out at the point where she knows his cottage lies. He's been a friend to her these last five years and in recent weeks, especially.

She feels old and worn out. But she ought to feel glad. Ruthie is here.

Most of the time anyway.

She is safe inside these walls, under this roof and when she chooses to go elsewhere, Joan will always help her. She won't be able to return to live at the gamekeeper's cottage though, now that Owen is under arrest and has fallen foul of Strabane.

Ruthie will struggle with that, she knows.

Ruthie doesn't know any other life. She doesn't want any other life. To adapt, for Ruthie, is not an option.

It's going to be hard, and at her age, Joan is not sure she has any fight left in her. But then she thinks of Lydia and knows that she must continue to fight for her sake, for her daughter's sake, to keep Ruthie safe. And to find out what happened to Robbie.

Robbie's Room

Ruthie, wide awake despite the late hour, walks along the lane until she sees the chimneys of the gamekeeper's cottage appear from between the trees bathed in the light of the moon – the house where she grew up, with all its attendant memories, good and bad.

This is the same route she used to take every afternoon after she and Robbie were dropped off by the school bus, the two of them walking together under the trees, laughing, their voices sometimes echoing into the woods at either side, having a fine old time. Until Robbie changed and began to grow dark. Maybe he was just growing up, that's what happened. People changed and they grew up, and they didn't want to be hampered by their little sisters anymore. But that wasn't Robbie. She and Robbie were different. They faced the rest of the world together, head on. Robbie always took her side, defended her against the criticism of their mother, for Lydia could be critical – she remembered that. Their mother loved them both, but she complained at Ruthie's quietness, was troubled by her introverted nature, perhaps fearing it would be a disadvantage and lead to no future.

'Why can't you be like the other girls?'

Had she really said that?

'Ruthie's fine just the way she is,' her brother defended her.

And then her father, Owen, muttering 'You're too hard on her, Lydia. Give the girl a break.'

When Ruthie arrives outside the gamekeeper's cottage there's no sign of the forensics people. They've scoured the place, carted away boxes of 'evidence' to sift through – much good may it do them.

The door is locked, but Ruthie makes her way along the side of the house, lifts a stone from the wall and returns to the darkened front porch which is framed by its own pointed rooftop. Idyllic, some would call this house, with its flowering plants and its curtains of ivy and jumbled chimney pots, if they didn't know the history of the place and the identity of the family who lived there.

The MacBrides, *those* MacBrides, who'd been cursed with ill fortune.

Ruthie stands in the hallway, silent now, uninhabited. The clock that never ticks and which they stopped winding after Robbie disappeared casts its own shadow.

Memories, voices, ghosts.

She wishes she could go back in time, stop the clock before the actual events that shaped their lives forever.

Everyone is flawed. Her own parents were badly flawed. She herself is flawed.

No one is perfect.

She walks through to the kitchen and sees the mess the team of forensic officers have left, trooping in and out with their white coveralls on, believing it will make a difference.

None of them know the truth.

Through the kitchen she can see the glint of the moon falling into the lean-to conservatory.

She pales when she notices a movement in the garden and sees a figure at the window, staring in, until she realises it's herself, staring back. An image which she barely recognises, for Ruthie doesn't often look at her reflection. She prefers to avoid the darkness she sees in her own eyes.

With a sigh, she turns and makes her way up through the empty house, her feet creaking on the staircase, until she reaches the eaves.

Then she curls up on what used to be her brother's bed.
Twelve years is nothing.

Twelve years is the blink of an eye.

It is no more than a heartbeat away.

The Moon Hangs Low over Kells Wood

Callum arrives home late, checks his phone. It soothed him to drive over the hills the long way back to his cottage. He feels contaminated by his brush with the housing estates in Dunbrochan. He never did like those places and after visiting the Brodies and the Robertsons, he feels the need to cleanse himself. It clears his mind, purifies him, to get out into the open countryside where he belongs. A fingernail moon hangs caught between the branches of the trees above Kells Wood. He parks the van, stands listening to the peace and silence which surrounds him in this place.

Inside his kitchen he opens the fridge automatically to the jingle of bottles. It's late. He could avoid popping open a beer and chalk up a night free of alcohol for once.

He hesitates while the shelf in the fridge tinkles temptingly.

The urge, the impulse, has become an ingrained habit over the years which is hard to break.

He's tried various things. Drinking fizzy water instead, so that the pop and the fizz still act like a slight celebration. It works sometimes. But his body craves the deep belly hug of the alcohol, that first sip which cracks open the tension in his body and releases him into peace.

A peace which never lasts long and usually just leaves a dry mouth and a residual headache the next morning. He doesn't drink to excess all of the time, but he drinks too much. Every day. Without fail.

Tonight though, he thinks he might forgo.

He slurps orange juice from an open carton instead, disappointed by the sour taste which is a poor second. Clicks off the light switch and heads to bed.

The Curse of Kilbroch

Strabane doesn't sleep. The historic curse of Kilbroch has him in its clutches, tormenting him.

He's not unduly worried. He has got himself into tight fixes before, and he always knows a way out of it. He's untouchable. Or is he?

He thinks he might have committed his first mistake. He didn't need to hurt Laura. It was unnecessary really. All he wanted to do was frighten her off, try to discourage her from digging, not because he was guilty of Robbie's murder, but because he didn't want the attention. It made him nervous, edgy.

He had known what she would find in that soil, if she dug deep enough. Chances were she might not hit the right spot, she might just avoid disturbing Robbie's last resting place, if he was lucky – and it is true that luck has followed him all the days of his life. So he could have let her just get on with it. Which he did, partly.

Until she and Callum started sniffing around again, trying to point the finger of blame. And then of course they found Robbie's body, where he knew it would be all along. Police attention was the last thing he wanted to attract to Kilbroch Castle.

He draws some comfort from the fact that he knows the Chief Constable, can pull a few strings perhaps – if there are any strings there to be pulled. It's always a tricky business. Even when you're untouchable you can never be completely sure if you'll come out of it unscathed.

But this is a bad one, and he has to admit it.

Hosting parties for his cronies in a secret location is one thing, underage girls being quietly shipped into the castle grounds under cover of darkness, the remoteness of the spot affording all the privacy they could desire. People in power have turned a blind eye to that sort of thing for years, he knows that. Members of the royal family, politicians, high-ranking judges, they all know someone whose reputation is a little besmirched, but it's usually a question of Hear No Evil, See No Evil.

However, even Strabane has to admit that this is a little different.

Lydia's death was manslaughter, not deliberate, so it seems to him fair enough that they concluded it was suicide. But this business with the archaeologist woman… well, it's a little different.

How will he explain it away, for a start?

He's angry with himself for acting on impulse. It's strange, what you don't know you're capable of. And he has her phone to dispose of. And the van.

He thinks of Nathan. A good loyal sort, has worked for him for years. He considers this carefully. Mmm, with the help of Lady Luck he could easily pin the blame on Nathan. All he has to do is speak to the right people in the right places. Easily done for a man in his position, with his wealth and power.

Untouchable.

That's what he believes himself to be.

The walls of his family seat loom above him. Bricks and mortar, that's all it is, although the world believes differently. For much of his life he has considered it to be a burden instead of a privilege.

Inside those walls are his daughters. He keeps them there like little songbirds. Women have always been his undoing.

He thinks of Lydia. She was beautiful, in her own way. But she was stupid. Stupid to trust him, of all people.

He remembers the night of her death, how they met in

secret, how they argued, how she struggled with him and fought.

A wind was stirring the trees above the gorge and Lydia was distressed, weeping, still unable to get over the disappearance of her son. Strabane had pretended to sympathise, although he didn't much care either way. If the boy had decided to leave home, what could anyone do about it?

'He'll come back,' he told her.

'No.' He remembers how she shook her head, adamant. 'No, he won't.'

And there was a darkness in her eyes at that moment that made even the psychopath Strabane take note.

'How can you be so sure?' he had asked, and he was suddenly, beautifully aware of the beginnings of a revelation, as if he was tugging on a length of silk that would unravel with slow inevitability to show him something stupendous, something wonderful. It was like stripping a woman of her clothes, undressing her of power with one simple tug.

'Because we buried him,' she sobbed.

'What did you say?' He whispered the words quietly, waiting for the rest of this beautiful confession.

'We buried him. Owen said it was for the best. That we would always know where he lay.'

Strabane struggled to hide his delight. To be able to manipulate her, to use her. He knew from that moment on that he would always have that hold over them, the whole family. Robbie might have been a witness to unsavoury activities at the castle that Strabane would rather keep secret, but he had a hold over the whole damn lot of them now. They would never be able to tell anyone what Robbie had seen. All he had to do was threaten them. He couldn't believe how magically convenient it was.

But he remembers how Lydia had looked into his eyes that night, as the wind moved through the high branches, and realised – too late – that she'd made a mistake in confiding in him.

'Robbie saw what you were like,' she whispered. 'He saw you.'

Strabane laughed and shook his head. 'Well, he won't be telling anyone about it now, will he? You said so yourself.'

'You…' she lashed out at him.

Strabane remembers the moment she fell.

He did love her, but love has its limitations.

We all have a story we tell ourselves. And this is his: Lydia fell to her death that day at Gallow Falls, not because she slipped or because she wanted to end her life, but because they argued. He was with her when she fell, and while he might not have pushed her, he knows that she wouldn't have lost her footing if they hadn't fought.

Events have a way of spiralling out of control, Strabane knows this now – a man who likes always to be in charge, particularly of the women in his life.

No one knew he was with Lydia when she died. As far as anyone could tell, she walked out one evening and decided to fling herself from the edge of the gorge, unable any longer to bear her grief.

A reasonable explanation. And no one cared to dispute it. Least of all Owen.

It's always been so easy to cover his tracks.

Until now.

What The Birds Can Tell Us

Callum wakes without a sore head this morning, although he barely notices as he sips his coffee. There is something troubling him, nibbling at the edges of his mind. It's early and he takes his cup out into the yard, sits down on the bench, and feels the warmth of the sun on his face.

He's still so glad he lives here and not in some housing estate. His ex-wife always aspired to own a house like Mrs Robertson's and she has finally arrived at what she wanted, the pinnacle of her desires, washed up in a cul-de-sac exactly like the one he visited last night.

Callum knows where he would rather be.

He lifts his head as he notices a vehicle pass by the gap in the hedgerow. Nathan on his way to his long shift in the castle gardens. Now that would be a job to envy. Looking after those acres, mowing the lawns, deadheading the roses, overseeing the forest estate. Although Callum knows he would rather not have someone like Strabane to answer to. It seems to work for Nathan, though. He spends his time fluttering about, sitting on upturned plant pots. He's come across him before, just sitting in the glen, gazing at the burn, thinking of nothing.

He checks his phone again.

No callers.

It's still early, but he decides to ring Laura, wishing he'd called her late last night. He doesn't know why, some residual worry. When it goes straight to voicemail he feels an unnamed dread begin to form in the pit of his stomach, especially when he hears her cheerful voice, saying, *I'm not available to take your call right now, but please leave a message after the YOU-KNOW-WHAT and I'll get back to you.* The light upward beat at the end of her words, the playful tone.

He hangs up. Calls again and leaves a message this time. 'Laura, can you call me? It's important.' Then adds as an afterthought, 'It's about Strabane.'

He sits for a while, finishing his coffee, but is seized with restlessness. He climbs into the van, turns the key in the ignition and drives out towards the castle, passing Joan's place on the way. He thinks about stopping and filling Joan in. He has to speak to her at some point soon, but decides it can wait for now, whereas he needs to get hold of Laura. Let her know what Brodie told him about Strabane, just to alert her, so that she knows what kind of person she might be dealing with.

He passes the gamekeeper's cottage, devoid of life, and on up the drive to the castle, over the cattle grid and into the estate gardens. Glossy rhododendron bushes mass at the side of the vast driveway, partly screening the gardens from view, together with the sheltering walls, but he sees Nathan parked up beside the sheds and outbuildings, waves to him.

What strikes him first is that Laura's camper van isn't here.

Winding his window down, he greets Nathan, who nods. 'I was hoping to see Laura. Is she about?'

Nathan looks at him. 'She was, yesterday. She was here last night. Haven't seen her this morning.'

Nathan studies Callum's face. 'Gone off to her dig site maybe?' he suggests.

Callum nods. 'I'll check there. Oh, and you haven't seen Strabane around, have you?'

'Not so far.'

'Thanks.'

He does a three point turn and drives back the way he

came, then, just past the gamekeeper's cottage, he takes the road that forks right and winds up into the forested woods of Kilbroch towards Gallows Hill.

The landscape falls away to his left, lovely as ever, with the hills and mountains topping the blue sky in the distance, green sweeping land as far as the eye can see, with a soft morning mist caught between the trees.

He hears the red kites circling above the woods.

He pulls up in the lay-by below Gallows Hill. No sign of Laura's camper van, so he tries her phone again. And once again, it goes straight to voicemail. He stands still, surrounded by trees, and listens to the eerie cry of the birds.

As he does so, a feeling of desolation sweeps through him.

Glentye

When Joan wakes at her usual time, she knows the house is empty. She can sense it. She doesn't panic though. Ruthie will return in her own good time.

She stares out the window while she waits for the kettle to boil, scatters loose leaf tea in her pot and tops it with the boiling water, a morning ritual she swears by. She decides to carry her tray outside into the garden. Nothing eases her mind more than the playful movements of the birds in the nearby hedgerow and their intermittent song.

She is still sitting here, in her own moment of morning peace, when Ruthie returns. They don't speak, but her granddaughter quietly sits down near Joan, who pours her a cup in silence. She knows that the last thing Ruthie needs right now is a bombardment of words – words that don't really mean anything, senseless chatter that fills the air and leads nowhere.

She does lean over, however, and lightly touches the back of her granddaughter's hand. Ruthie looks down at her paint-stained knuckles, the nails rimmed with soil. Nothing is said.

They just sit quietly together.

They are still sitting there when Callum turns up.

'Can I talk to you for a second?'

'Of course.' She indicates a chair, but he hesitates and she picks up on his gesture. He doesn't want to talk in front of Ruthie, she gathers that much. So she stands and walks with him towards her greenhouse. 'Have I shown you how well my tomatoes have been doing lately?'

He walks with her around the corner of the house and

Ruthie follows them with her eyes, silent as ever, until they are out of sight.

'There have been some developments I need to tell you about, Joan, and I just... I didn't want Ruthie to hear.'

'Understandable. So tell me.'

'I went to visit a couple of Robbie's old school pals last night in Dunbrochan.'

'Any luck?'

'One had moved away and his mother was less than helpful. The other, Pete Brodie, had one or two things to say about Strabane.'

'Oh?

'And that's the difficult bit.'

'Go on.'

'Well, the boys used to camp up there when they were teenagers and Pete reckons they witnessed some strange goings-on at the castle. He claims that Strabane was involved in shady parties involving underage girls.'

Joan's eyes widen in disbelief.

'There's more. You're not going to like this bit.' He pauses. 'Pete said that Lydia was having an affair with Strabane, and that Robbie knew about it.'

Joan stares ahead of her in silence and Callum waits for the shock to register.

'But... I don't understand.'

He waits, in silence.

'Why would she do that?'

'She was human, I guess.'

'But why him?'

She glances back at the house, checking for Ruthie. 'And you're saying Robbie knew about this?'

He nods. 'Of course, all this could be hearsay. It's just the testimony of a teenage boy, who never came forward at the time. And who knows if he's remembering correctly, or if he made it all up? But he reckons that they all knew, that lots of people knew.'

'I didn't!' Joan responds shortly.

'No.'

'You think Lydia knew? About the parties?'

'I think she may have found out. Who knows. Maybe through Robbie? Maybe he told her what he'd seen.'

Joan stares at him. 'But, Owen...?'

'What does this mean about Owen?' Callum shakes his head. 'I have no idea at this stage. I don't even know how to verify the facts.'

'Other than ask Pete Brodie to stand as a witness.'

'Could be tricky. He didn't seem inclined to want to step forward. After all, he's kept quiet about it all these years. I'm the only one he's told so far.'

'D'you think he could be persuaded to share what he knows with the police?'

Callum looks uncertain. 'It's hard to say. Maybe.'

'D'you think he's telling the truth?' she asks.

'Who?'

'Pete Brodie.'

'I've no reason to doubt it.'

'Why didn't the boys say anything at the time?'

He shrugs. 'They were teenage boys. I guess they didn't think anyone would listen to them. It would be their word against his.'

A sudden rage travels through Joan's body and she says in a low growl, 'I never did trust that man. We have to tell the police.'

Callum sighs. 'Easier said than done. Strabane is a powerful man. We need proof first.'

'What proof do we need? We have a witness.'

'And I can hear the defence lawyer in court already, saying that memory is an unreliable thing, blah blah...'

'But we have to do something, Callum! Robbie saw what he saw and no one believed him.'

The old look of pain on her face has returned and he can feel her desperation. 'We don't know that, Joan. We don't know who Robbie told.'

Joan glances over his shoulder and sees Ruthie walking towards the house.

'Leave it with me,' he tells her. 'I'll get to the bottom of it. I'll speak to Dan.'

'Be careful, Callum. Strabane is well-connected. Men like him are untouchable.'

'There's something else too. I can't find Laura.'

'What d'you mean?'

'I've checked with Nathan and she was there last night, but she hasn't turned up this morning. Her van is missing.'

Joan struggles with her fears for a moment, then adds, 'She's a free agent. She'll be off in that van of hers somewhere. She'll turn up, you'll see.'

Callum sweeps a hand across his jaw. 'I hope you're right.'

Joan thinks fleetingly of her son-in-law, Owen. She thinks of his taciturn nature, his difficult silence, the way he never made a move to defend himself.

'Did we get it wrong, Callum? Did the police get it wrong?'

Callum remains quiet.

'A man like that,' she goes on, referring to Strabane, 'gets away with anything. He'll have connections. His sort always do.'

327

Friends in High Places

It is with some trepidation that Callum drives back to the castle. When he parks his van near Nathan's old car and walks across the forecourt, Strabane sees him coming.

He seems in a jovial mood, sitting out on the terrace above the gardens, reading his newspaper. 'Callum!' he calls, and waves.

Callum knows that this man has never greeted him with such open warmth before, so why now?

'What can I do for you?' and he actually pulls out a chair, inviting Callum to sit.

Callum hesitates. The last thing he wants to do now is sit down on that chair, with this man. 'I was looking for Laura. D'you know where she is?'

'Oh…' Strabane's face falls in an exaggerated display of sympathy. 'You just missed her, I'm afraid.'

'Really?'

'She left. Early this morning. Said she had some things to tie up.'

'Bit sudden!'

Strabane looks convincingly vague and mild-mannered. 'I don't know. She had some issue with the research funding, said she needed to head back to Edinburgh pronto. Such a shame.'

Callum waits. 'And?'

'And what?' Strabane adds, countering Callum's question with a hint of ice.

'And that's it?'

Strabane smirks to himself. 'I must admit, I was beginning to suspect you carried a bit of a candle for the archaeologist,' he jokes. 'And maybe I was right.'

'She's not answering her phone,' Callum says.

Strabane shrugs. 'She obviously has a busy life elsewhere.'

'Have you any idea what time she left?'

Strabane lets his gaze rest on Callum for a second or two longer than is necessary. 'I couldn't say. Early, I'd guess.'

'So you didn't speak to her before she left?'

'Are you questioning me?'

'No, I'm just curious to work out how you knew about her problem with funding if she didn't speak to you about it first, and tell you when she was leaving.'

Strabane pauses, lays down his newspaper and fixes his gaze on Callum. 'You enjoy living in your cottage, do you?'

'What do you mean?'

Strabane leans forward in his chair. 'I think you know what I mean.'

Callum takes a step back. 'If you've hurt her in any way, you'll spend the rest of your life regretting it.'

'It wouldn't be a very good move to threaten me, Callum.'

Callum stares at him. 'You were doing so well up until that point. But you've just let your guard slip.'

Strabane struggles to keep his temper under control. He is completely unused to being spoken to in that manner, particularly by someone who has a lease on his land, but once again his complacency slides back into place. 'Have you any idea who you're dealing with?'

'Friends in high places, you mean?' A hot flame of anger rises in Callum's gut, and before he can stop himself, he adds, 'I've heard about your parties. Long time ago, was it? Well, not long enough. Men like you get away with murder…'

In the distance, Nathan lifts his head to listen, observing them both through shrewd eyes.

'You'll pay for this,' Strabane whispers. 'How many

years have you been at Glenwhilk now? Well, maybe your days there are numbered.'

Despite himself Callum feels a lurch in his stomach. Pushing one of the chairs so that its metal legs scrape on the flags, he sweeps a quick glance across the windows of the castle. So many darkened window panes hiding who knows what secrets, and without a search warrant or permission to intrude, he can do nothing.

He knows he needs to contact Dan. Without a word, he walks away to his van and with Nathan watching him, he accelerates down the drive, his tyres spitting gravel.

After he has left, Nathan stands still and eyes his employer across the space that separates them. Strabane glances at him once, without saying anything, then slowly rises and makes his way inside.

History Lies in Layers

As Callum drives away all he can think about is Laura. Where is she, and why did she leave so suddenly?

The cattle grid rattles the inside of the van, a brief shaking which he has become wonderfully familiar with, then he's driving past the empty gamekeeper's cottage. There is an air of haunting menace about the place, as if it bears the scars of tragedy.

Joan once told him that a sister and two brothers lived there long ago and were some of the last victims to be accused and tried as witches in the area. They were executed on Gallows Hill, hung from the branches of the great oak, their bodies left for days to dangle in the wind. He shudders as he thinks of this. Probably three siblings who were known to be strange, with learning difficulties maybe, so they were targeted and scapegoated to satisfy a local lust for blood.

Then his thoughts turn to Owen and his family. Now the place is scarred by another terrible event, within living memory this time.

He needs to contact Dan, and quickly. Pulling over, he dials Dan's number.

'You again?' the voice on the other end says cheerfully.

I haven't got time for this, Callum thinks, but doesn't say. 'Dan, there's something I need you to help me with.'

A listening silence on the other end of the line.

'Laura is missing and I've found out some disturbing information about Strabane.'

'Laura? The archaeologist?'

'Yes.'

'Wait a minute. What do you mean? Missing?'

'I mean she parked her van up at Strabane's place last night and this morning it's not there. He claims she left in a hurry.'

He can hear an exhalation of breath. 'Callum, what are you talking about, man?'

'I'm saying you need to file a missing person's report on her and…'

'We don't know she's missing yet.'

'We do. I do.'

'How?'

Of course he can't answer that, and he realises he's running out of steam, failing to sound at all convincing. 'You need to get the police to question Strabane,' he tries.

'Why, exactly?'

'I spoke to a couple of school pals of Robbie's. One of them, Pete Brodie, still lives in Dunbrochan. He claims to have witnessed strange parties up at the castle, including what looked like the trafficking of young girls.'

'And how long ago was this?'

Callum sighs, clamping down on his frustration. 'Around the time of Robbie's disappearance.'

'So, twelve years ago then?'

Callum's silence corroborates this. He can't be bothered to respond.

'Not exactly recent, is it?'

'That's not the point.'

'And why didn't your Pete Brodie come forward with this information at the time?'

'I can't tell you that. They were teenage boys. Probably thought no one would believe them.'

Silence. He tries again. 'You asked me to help you, Dan. So I did. I made some inquiries, as you said. I dug the dirt, and now you don't want it.'

'Listen,' Dan says. 'If I go to my superiors with an accusation like this, based on the historic hearsay of two

332

teenage boys, twelve years ago, which was never reported at the time...'

Callum is scraping a hand through his hair, listening. He can see where this is heading, and he understands.

'...against a man like Strabane, for Chrissake?' Dan adds. 'They'll never believe me.'

'And what about Laura?'

'If she chooses not to answer her phone or be in touch, sudden as it may seem, why is that of any concern of yours?'

Callum sighs.

'Did she have any family you can contact?' Dan asks then, a trace of sympathy buried in his voice. 'Just to verify where she might be?'

'There's a twin brother, but I don't know how to contact him.'

'Leave it with me, for now. But listen, Callum, she's probably fine. You're jumping to conclusions, man. I'll see what I can find out.'

As Callum hangs up, he does not feel particularly reassured.

Lottie

After Callum has left, Strabane pushes open the storm door into the great hallway of the castle. Calm shadows drape the walls and for a moment he can't see a thing as his eyes, still dazzled by the sun, adjust to the darkness. Then he notices a stationary figure on the staircase, standing there, watching him and he gasps before recognizing his youngest daughter. She's regarding him with a strange and quizzical stare.

'Lottie?'

She doesn't answer him. She just regards him coldly.

Strabane is a man with things on his mind and he dismisses her with a cursory wave, frowning. 'Whatever it is,' he says 'I haven't got time for it right now.'

Women! He much prefers the wild birds he feeds, the bees that he tends, none of whom answer back, but have the rare ability to simply exist, to be useful as well as decorative, without causing any disharmony in his life.

Women, on the other hand, are forever breaking out of the fixed frame he tries to put them in. He doesn't understand it. He gives them everything money can buy, a life of protected privilege. Neither of his daughters understand what the real world can be like. They have absolutely no idea what lies out there, beyond the world of Kilbroch.

Flashbacks of former arguments come crashing into his consciousness. Lottie yelling at him, and him yelling back, 'You have no idea! You stupid girl!'

Stupid girls, both of them, who don't understand when they're fortunate. Just like that stupid woman before them – their mother – and the other one. The one who betrayed him.

He crashes through the house, taking refuge in his study, slamming the door behind him.

His daughter, Lottie, watches him go. At sixteen, she wants to leave home, get away from all of this. She knows that Sophie has turned down a place at university, and when Lottie asked why, she just said, 'I can't leave you here alone.'

'I won't be alone. I have Daddy.'

Sophie had winced at the affectionate epithet, Daddy, which seemed so incongruous, given what their father actually was.

She moves through the interior of this castle, their home, with its portraits and its history, and stops in front of one painting in particular. It's of their mother, painted a long time ago when she was a young woman, at a time before Lottie knew her. In fact, Lottie cannot remember her at all, except as a vague memory of someone ailing and ill, lying in bed, pale, inert, barely able to communicate. Her father was always the one who figured large, who parented them, who made life tick and move forward in his own peculiar way, with his love of order and control.

Staring at the portrait of her dead mother, Lottie tries to see herself in those features and she can, just as she can see her sister Sophie, in the line of the nose and across the wide brow, but she cannot for the life of her see the woman she remembers as her mother. A woman faded and worn out and on the verge of extinction. It is as if she was obliterated, rubbed out like a bad sketch. And although people say you cannot miss what you never had, Lottie grieves for the mother she never knew, the mother who became ill when her daughters were young children, who lay in an upstairs room and was never able to participate in the important moments of their lives. She was simply too ill.

And in all those years, their father had cared for their mother so kindly, so attentively, so selflessly it seemed.

Hiring a nurse to tend to her, to deal with the mess and the inconvenience so that he and his daughters would be spared from the worst of it. As she moves through the interior of the castle with its weight of history, it occurs to her that she feels trapped, like an insect caught in amber.

Restraint

'Try not to worry,' Joan reassures him, as he paces back and forth in her kitchen.

He turns and looks at her, exasperation writ large on his face. 'Try not to worry?'

'I know it's hard, but we don't know that anything has happened to her. It might be as Dan says, that she's simply tootled off somewhere…'

'Tootled off!'

'Okay, I know that sounds like I'm not taking it seriously.'

'Just a bit.'

'You're right,' Joan says, 'Damn it, how do we get in touch with her twin brother? Ask him if he's heard from her?'

'Dan told me to leave it with him,' Callum says.

'And you believe him? Since when has that man given us any reason to have faith in him?'

As he turns away he notices Ruthie watching him from the hallway.

He speaks her name softly, an acknowledgement.

She responds with a faint smile and a nod. The girl who watches everything but gives nothing away. He suddenly has the overpowering suspicion that she might in fact know where Laura is, what has happened to her, but that's absurd. Why would she know any more than the rest of them?

She's in that gorge often, wandering the fields and hills, moving through Kells Wood like a deer, like a girl transformed into a wild creature. Maybe she saw something?

He suddenly has the overwhelming urge to grab her by the shoulders and shake her, to shake some sense into her.

'You didn't see anything, Ruthie? On your travels?'

She stares at him for a long moment, then gently shakes her head.

Joan watches him clench his hands in frustration and gives him a warning glance. She knows the limits of her granddaughter's patience, knows how far she can be pushed.

He stares at Ruth, certain, suddenly, that she knows more than she ever admits. Perhaps, after all, she is the key to it all. Perhaps she alone can unlock the whole mystery.

With that thought he longs to break through her wall of silence, but he feels a hand on his arm. Glances down. Joan's paint-stained fingers are clutching his sleeve, the gentlest of restraining touches. His old friend understands, she has always understood everything. It's why she has been his closest friend for the past five years.

He moved here, to the tied cottage at Kilbroch, a few years after Joan lost her grandson and her daughter. You couldn't really call it a village – a few scattered farmhouses and tied cottages along the road to Kilbroch, a lonely chapel, and an old castle. It didn't amount to much in terms of habitable buildings, but there was a strong sense of place here and Callum had felt it immediately. It was a place with its own history, which you could feel in the mixed woodland as you walked between the trees, hearing the red kites, the snap of a branch, glimpsing the ghost of a deer vanishing between the tall stands of birch.

Joan had educated him in a lot of that history. She had sensed in him a man who needed a friend, and she had supplied that friendship unconditionally, without prying, without making judgements.

So when she touches his arm as a warning not to push Ruthie too far, he listens to her advice. Sound advice, given without words.

He heads for the door, head down, desperate, beyond words.

'Where are you going?' Joan calls after him.

'To work.'

She shrugs and watches him go. When she turns back, Ruthie is still standing there, watching her. Joan sighs, lets out a quiet breath, feeling the burden of all she has been left with.

Clearing

As the van rattles and bumps its way along the dirt track, he feels the silence of the trees begin to crowd around him.

It's been a while since he turned his attention to clearing a patch of woodland – Strabane's woodland. He can't afford to alienate Strabane any more than Owen could afford to alienate him. Strabane is the man with the power around here, the power to make lives and to break them.

Callum opens the back of his van, pulls on a pair of thick leather gauntlets that protect his hands and wrists and drags his tools out of the back. He dumps them on the ground at his feet and takes a cursory glance around the area, assessing what can be achieved here, what can be taken.

It takes his mind off the problem of Laura. Maybe everyone is right, and she simply chose to absent herself from them all, with good reason. Perhaps she didn't like the feeling that she was getting too involved, too drawn into their lives. Perhaps that was it?

A few fallen birches lie in the clearing, great branches and boughs which he can saw down to size to throw in the back of the van. You can burn birch straight away, it doesn't need to be seasoned, but it doesn't fetch as much money.

He steps his way over a fallen tree, courtesy of the last storm to rip through Kilbroch. Without the storms, where would he be?

He bends down, leans on the fallen trunk, tests its weight. Lots of branches stretching away from the main trunk, ripe for harvesting.

He picks up his buzz saw, pulls down his visor, feels the kick-back as he switches it on and begins to slice. Like

340

cutting into a cake, the buzz saw makes light work of the branches, severing them at the trunk, and what was once a tangle of fallen limbs eventually becomes a neatly stacked pile.

He feels the tension in his back and neck, lifts the visor and wipes the sweat from his brow. It's basic work, manual labour, but it's honest, and while he does it, he's a free man. Up to a point.

It's only after he's been working for upwards of an hour, trying to silence the thoughts in his mind, that he realises there's a second set of tracks indented in the dried up mud around his vehicle. A second set which leads away, deeper into the trees. He stares, frowning, bends low to touch them, then begins to follow them off into the nearby woods.

There's a track here, through the deeper pine plantation. There are always tracks, suitable for a quad bike or a buggy, a small tractor maybe, bumping over the rough uneven ground. He stares along the dark corridor of pine, keeps walking, and several yards inside comes across the sight of metal glinting through a network of branches.

Feeling his pulse rate quickening, he steps closer, pulls aside a branch to reveal what lies hidden. He already knows what he will find. A metal panel, painted sky-blue, a silver bumper with round headlamps.

Laura's camper van.

The breath leaves his body and he staggers back, then tears aside more of the branches until he is able to yank open the door, half-afraid of what he might find inside.

Wreckage

Seconds turn to minutes as he searches all around the van, a moment of sliding horror as he notices a drop of blood on one of the sofa cushions.

He scrambles back out into the relative fresh air of the clearing, stands gasping and trying to breathe, quickly takes the mobile from his pocket and dials Dan's number.

No answer. He knows what he should do. He should call the police instantly. Instead, he rings Joan.

'Callum?'

'I've found her van!'

'What?'

'Laura's camper van. It's hidden in the woods.'

He hears a gasp at the other end, and pictures Joan standing there in her hallway or her kitchen, her hand covering her mouth, trying to stifle the shock.

Both of them immediately understand what this means.

'Call the police,' she commands him.

'It's him. Strabane.'

'Don't do anything rash,' she begs him, but he barely listens.

Crashing through the trees, leaving the tools where they lie, he leaps into the front of his van and is off, tearing over the rough track and bursting out of the clearing onto the Kilbroch road. He doesn't even consider the thought of oncoming traffic, as he rounds the bends at speed, each turning obscured by its banks of wild gorse and woodland either side.

He knows exactly where he is heading, and fast. And

not even Joan's words of wisdom – to avoid doing anything rash – can stop him in his tracks.

The road is narrow and full of blind bends but it's a road Callum drives almost every day, to the remotest part of the hills where he clears abandoned woodland and fills his van with it. But just now it seems to stretch before him, limitless, unending.

He roars past Gallows Hill, past the cottages and turns left at the junction, changing gear for the hill, speeds past the gamekeeper's cottage, under the trees and over the cattle grid. He knows he ought to take a minute, gather himself, but he doesn't care.

Nathan, the gardener, has heard him coming and stands outside on the drive, shovel in hand, as he roars onto the forecourt, spitting gravel.

The windows of the castle gape, black as ever, hiding their secrets, but no one can avoid hearing Callum's arrival this time.

Nathan watches in silence as Callum strides to the storm doors, pushes them open and bursts straight into the flagged entrance porch, where muddied boots and wellies, walking sticks and umbrellas clutter the shelves and hooks either side. He tries the door but it's locked so he rings the huge bell, then bangs the glass with the flat of his hand, watches through the glass panel as a shadowy figure emerges. He can see Strabane saunter into the light, annoyingly nonchalant.

He frowns when he sees Callum, and opens the door with, 'Well, well, well. If it isn't yourself again.'

'Where is she?' he cries. 'What have you done with her?'

Strabane glances over his shoulder. There's no one else visible inside the massive vestibule or on the spiralling staircase, but he ushers Callum outside and closes the door behind him.

Callum is not in the mood to be ushered anywhere.

They stand outside, observed by Nathan, and Callum confronts him.

'I found her van in the woods!' He's practically shouting and Strabane backs away from him, alarmed, shaking his head.

'Calm down, man.'

'I'll calm down when you tell us where she is, what you've done with her.'

Their noisy exchange is stopped in its tracks as another vehicle comes tearing up the driveway, its tyres creating a roar on the gravel, and Dan leaps out, holding out a hand in an attempt to restrain Callum.

Callum stares at him.

'Joan called me,' he explains.

Strabane observes them both with a look of derision. 'I appreciate the visit, but if you gentlemen will excuse me, I have a lot to do this afternoon, so...'

He is the epitome of gentlemanly calm which infuriates Callum even further.

'Mr Strabane, I think we need to have a little chat,' Dan begins.

Strabane eyes him suspiciously. 'You are?'

'I found her van in the woods!' Callum says. 'I can show you. He's lying through his teeth. He said Laura left here to go back to Edinburgh.'

Strabane narrows his eyes. 'I know nothing about her van or where it might be. She was a free spirit, as I'm sure you both recall.'

'Was?' Callum says. 'What do you mean – was?'

Strabane shrugs. 'Don't you think you might be over-reacting just a tad?'

'You're lying and you know it. We have witnesses to some of your past behaviour, hosting parties here involving underage girls.'

Strabane sighs. Despite the circumstances, he's still not

unduly alarmed, although he ought to be. 'Okay, so I had a few parties,' he says, holding his hands up. 'Long time ago.'

'Twelve years, to be exact,' Callum cuts in. 'Round about the time Robbie went missing.'

Strabane glares at him and half-turns towards the windows of the castle, a small gesture of body language revealing his concern at being overheard by his daughters.

Dan takes a step forward, and begins, 'Mr Strabane, where is Laura?'

'I have no idea.'

'If you don't tell us, I shall have no alternative but to take you into custody for questioning. Do you understand?'

'Questioning? About what?'

'On suspicion of the murder of Laura Pettigrew and Robbie MacBride.'

'What? This is ridiculous.'

Dan turns and begins to radio in to his boss.

'I didn't murder Robbie MacBride,' Strabane bursts out suddenly.

His protest falls on deaf ears as Dan makes a move to detain Strabane.

'She's not dead, okay?'

'What do you mean?' Dan says.

Callum, listening, feels a surge of hope.

'I mean what I say. If you bothered to do your job properly.'

'Where is she?' Callum says, standing so close to Strabane he can feel his damp breath on his face, tainted by a slight whiff of expensive whisky.

Strabane sneers at him. 'She's in the basement. Stupid bloody woman wouldn't keep her mouth shut. I didn't kill her. She's down there, all in one piece, I assure you. I might be lots of things, but I'm not an axe murderer.'

Callum barges past him while Dan ensures Strabane is secure.

'You'll regret this. I have connections.'

'So I gather,' Dan says. 'Maybe some of them can act as witnesses?'

The Basement

When Callum makes his way back into the castle, he finds one of Strabane's daughters standing on the staircase, staring at him.

'What's going on?' she asks him.

Callum shakes his head. 'I need you to show me the entrance to the basement.'

'The basement? But why?' She peers past him through the storm doors, trying to take in what is happening to her father outside.

'Daddy?' she screams, but she knows inside herself what is going on. All those suspicions, those buried fears that she never wanted to acknowledge or believe.

'Just do it. Please.'

She moves along a dark corridor which leads off the main vestibule and points to a discreet wooden doorway, tucked away in the shadows. Callum steps forward, turns the handle, and it opens with a creak to reveal a flight of uneven stone steps going down into the foundations of the castle. Sophie doesn't follow him as he makes his way down them, using his mobile as a torch, and for a terrible second it occurs to him that she could shut him in, trap him down here.

Below is a vast cellar-like room, filled with an earthy smell. Wide, cobwebbed shelves containing bottles and crates, stacked up and abandoned in the darkness, seem to stretch for miles, a library or archive of bottles. He shines his light into the corners, calling her name.

Nothing. No sign of Laura and his panic begins to mount. What if Strabane was lying to buy himself more time? What if she isn't down here at all? He wonders for a moment how Dan is faring out in the courtyard.

Eventually the light from his phone encounters an archway and he ducks his head low. The air is damp and he has the feeling the gorge lies just beyond the earth here.

There's a sound coming from the corner, near the ground. He holds his phone high and its circle of radiance picks out a shape, hunched up, bound and gagged in the darkness.

'Laura?' He bends, tears the tape from her mouth.

She takes a deep gulp of air and cries, 'The bastard!' as if that word has been waiting to explode from her for a long time.

'And that's the thanks I get?' he offers, as he cuts the tape from around her wrists and ankles.

'I thought I wasn't going to get out of here alive.'

'It's okay. You're okay now,' and he leads her back past the long dusty shelves for what seems like an eternity. Laura massages her wrists and stumbles in the darkness against the bottom step, holding onto Callum's hand, following him back up into the light.

He's relieved to see daylight pouring down the uneven stairs. They climb slowly up the steps and out into the cold marble interior of the hallway, Laura still swallowing down her panic and relief.

It was truly terrifying to be entombed down there in the darkness, not knowing what her fate might be, if she'd simply be left there to die, but her anger and rage at Strabane overtakes any sense of fear.

They walk out into the courtyard where Strabane is standing beside Dan, quietly handcuffed. The sneer of outrage and superiority is still in place, but he's looking a little less sure of himself now.

Laura runs a cursory glance over him and then speaks to Callum as if Strabane isn't even present. She can't bear to look at him. 'I found his four-by-four in one of

348

the outhouses, buried under a tarpaulin. I went in there to borrow a light. And there it was, a dent on the front bumper. It was him who rammed me off the road that night.'

Callum looks at him – the man he has paid rent to for the past five years, who owns most of the land they all live on, for miles around. 'You knew Robbie was buried there, on Gallows Hill.'

Strabane doesn't reply, at first, then blurts, 'I didn't kill him, if that's what you're thinking.'

'We'll let others be the judge of that.'

He turns to Callum with a contemptuous sneer. 'And maybe, just maybe, you'll not like the answer.'

Dan, glaring at Strabane, mutters, 'I don't believe you. And neither, I suspect, will the courts.'

Strabane laughs. 'We shall see.'

Homecoming

Owen finds the key in its usual place. Only he and Ruthie knew it was kept here, under a stone in the boundary wall of the garden. He stands in the cold shadows of the front porch, hidden from the road, and twists it in the lock. It's the door they never use, but always keep a key hidden just in case.

It's a strange homecoming.

He pushes the door open, stands in the hallway, listening to the silence. Ghosts rush before him, disappearing into the shadows. Despite his release, his heart is as heavy as it ever was. None of it will bring his wife and son back. Loss fills the air he breathes.

They've declared him innocent, but he knows he is far from innocent. The secrets he bears are secrets which no man should bear alone, although he has done so for all these years.

He walks through the flagged hallway, past the grandfather clock that no longer ticks because he chose to stop winding it twelve years ago when time stood still for him and his depleted little family. He pauses. He senses an unseen presence on the staircase landing behind him, turns, but there's no one there. He remembers his daughter standing there as a child, listening, while her parents argued. He and Lydia.

They always had a hard time getting along. There were problems, same as in any marriage. All he'd ever done was strive to keep his daughter safe, to protect her from the worst of it.

'How can you protect her?' Lydia had cried.

'She doesn't remember!'

'How do you know?'

'We did what we thought was right, Lydia.'

'Burying him, you mean. Like a dog? He was our own,' she wept. He can hear her voice still. The agony in it. 'Our son!'

'Nothing can bring him back.'

'But what if she needs help?'

'Who can help her? She has forgotten. She's wiped it clean.'

'But what if she remembers?'

He'd thought it was the right thing to do at the time. When he realised Ruthie could no longer recall the trauma of what happened that day, he thought he could protect her.

He remembers now that he used to have conversations with his friend, Callum, about that very subject. Telling the truth doesn't pay. That's what they'd both agreed. After all, Callum had told the truth on a witness stand at a public inquiry and it ruined his career. Ruined his life, you could say. So, as the years sped on, Owen had felt no qualms at withholding the truth, even if it pained him to bear the burden of such unimaginable guilt.

He has struggled with it every day of his life and will continue to struggle. He is paying the price. He lives with it every day. Every day is a penance.

'How can we?' Lydia had sobbed. 'Our own son.'

'But at least we will know where he lies. And Ruthie will be safe.'

'You call that safe?'

He walks through into the kitchen, switches on the overhead light. Brightness fills the empty room, with its ghosts, its terrible memories which he will share with no one. He will carry his secret to the grave, for his daughter's sake.

Guilt has driven him several times to almost confess, but there is one thing that keeps him from doing so.

Ruthie.

She's not here at the moment. She's staying with her grandmother. Lydia's mother, Joan. He wonders how that will pan out.

As he walks into the glass lean-to at the end of the kitchen, he finds the ghost of his dead wife Lydia standing in the corner of the room, looking at him.

'How could you?' she asks him.

And he answers her in the way he has answered her for the past twelve years, without fail.

'I did it for Ruthie.'

Sleeping Dogs

Callum stands in the doorway of his cottage, nursing a cup of coffee, and gazes out at the scene before him. Laura has parked her camper van in the yard outside his workshop and she's serving hot drinks to a small group gathered nearby on stools and chairs. Covid is still with them and the habit of gathering outside remains. It's become commonplace to prefer the outdoors. There's no need for blankets as the hot August weather continues, leaving a shimmering golden haze over the sloping fields.

Callum feels as near contented as he has felt in a long while, looking out at his friends. Joan is sitting beside her granddaughter, listening to something the young woman is saying and there is even a tentative peace between her and Owen. For Owen is with them now. He has been released and suspicion has been lifted from him.

All seems peaceful, the ghosts of the past finally laid to rest.

The police have arrested George Strabane and he remains in custody for now. Pete Brodie has said he is prepared to come forward and testify to what he witnessed when he was a boy, the parties at the house and the underage girls who were brought into the castle under cover of darkness. He remembers those nights, standing beside his friend in the tangle of rhododendron bushes, watching the cars in the driveway, recognising one or two faces of the guests from the TV. Important men who would not want the world to know what they were up to. Pete knows that Strabane was angry with Robbie and his mother because they'd found out what had been going on up at the castle. He remembers Robbie telling him that, the night before he disappeared.

'We all thought he ran away,' Pete will testify sadly. 'I wouldn't have blamed him if he had.'

'Hey, Callum!' Laura calls, 'Come and join us.'

He nods and smiles, steps down from his kitchen and ambles towards the others. Woodsmoke drifts on the air from a small fire which Owen tends.

Callum rests a hand on his friend's shoulder as he passes, glad to see him. It was Laura's idea to have a barbecue. She's been spending the past few days parked up near Callum's house while she finishes the dig. Her Bronze Age people remain elusive, but she's getting closer. She's found the outer wall and an inner wall of the structure where they lived, which has given this hamlet its name, and she has identified several small fragments belonging to objects left behind in the clay. The people of the past may have vanished, but they have left their mark just the same, for those who know how to look.

There's a feeling of warmth and camaraderie, and Callum knows that, whatever happens now, he has a connection with these people. They're connected by what they've all been through, the things they know, and the things they withhold.

'Cheers,' Laura smiles and touches her tin mug against Callum's own.

'What are you putting in that coffee?' he jokes.

'Nothing you need worry about.'

'Why the air of celebration?' Owen adds.

'Well, you're free, aren't you?' Joan says unexpectedly.

'Exactly,' Laura choruses. 'Cheers to that.'

Joan smiles, and rests a conciliatory hand on her son-in-law's arm.

'So, how long have you got left?' Callum asks Laura quietly.

'I'm leaving on Thursday.'

He nods, holding his tin mug, and prods the fire.

'I think Joan will miss you,' he adds.

Laura smiles. 'But not you?'

'Well, that as well,' he admits.

'It's been a strange summer.'

'It has that.'

Joan's voice breaks into the moment of quiet that envelopes them. 'George Strabane! I never did like that man,' she adds, staring into the flames with eyes that have suffered and seen too much.

'I wonder what will happen to the castle now, if he's found guilty?' Laura says.

'If?' This from Joan, a word loaded with anger. Then she adds, 'I imagine his daughters will be left to deal with it. I'm sure it won't be any hardship.'

At that point Ruthie lifts her head and gazes straight at her father. No one else notices, except Callum. And he wonders at that. He wonders what else they do not know, what stones have been left unturned, what secrets kept and truths withheld.

The phrase 'sleeping dogs' rises in his mind, but he keeps silent. No point in disturbing the dead.

October 10th 2010

Owen and Lydia were alone in the house that day. The woods outside were peaceful, bathed in a lightly glimmering mist. They'd been arguing again. Not so much violently, but with a quiet, passive aggression. She slammed the kettle onto the stove with a deliberate clatter, as if to make a point.

He merely looked at her, and went out.

With his gun.

The kids were at school still. They weren't due back for another hour.

He made his way slowly down to the paddock, looked across at the layer upon layer of hills and soft woodland, beech and birch, oak and larch. All crimson and gold.

A pheasant exploded from the undergrowth with a wild clatter and others followed, flying low across the hillside, right within his aim.

He lifted his rifle and held it there against his shoulder, following their flight. He thought of Strabane, the way the bastard had even taken his marriage, his wife.

But in the end he lowered the gun and spared them to live another day. After all, it wasn't his job to cull them. His purpose was merely to harvest them for the season, so that Strabane and his cronies, his invited guests, could blow them out of the air for sport.

His anger was like a rod of steel inside him as he stood there in the lower paddock, leaning against the gate. All of this land and none of it his, yet it flowed in his blood. It belonged to him. No one else could claim that connection with the forests and woodland the way he did – except perhaps Ruthie. He knew it inside out, since he was a boy.

And right now, nothing could be more delightful than this peaceful Perthshire wood. Wispy grey smoke mingled with a lilac mist and drifted through the soft mellow shadings of trees.

Eventually, he abandoned his post by the gate and left his anger there too. He trudged his way back up to the house, leaving his rifle in the front porch, and found his wife in the kitchen.

He took her in his arms, and kissed her.

A few miles away, the sound of children's laughter could be heard drifting along the narrow road to Kilbroch as Robbie and his little sister made their way home from school. The bus always dropped them at the end of the lane and they had a two mile hike, giggling and teasing one another along the way.

Happy sounds.

By the time the chimneys and jumbled rooftops of their house came into view through the treetops, both were tired and silly with hunger.

From an upstairs window Owen and Lydia could hear them coming, calling to each other, playing. Robbie ran on ahead, and Ruthie followed him.

They slammed the glass door but no one answered. To the children, it seemed like there was no one at home. Their father's gun was still propped in the porch where he'd left it.

They were used to rifles lying about the place. There was a rule. One essential rule. You broke the barrel, emptied it of bullets and stored the ammunition separately. It was a rule they always observed up at the castle and here at the gamekeeper's cottage too. Their father never left a rifle loaded.

Robbie – who had a flair for dramatics – picked up the rifle. He pretended to fire it at Ruthie, then rehearsed a perfect slow motion death scene, arms akimbo, body jerking with the impact of the bullets raining down on him as he fell backwards onto the couch.

'I got me an Injun!' he shrieked, leaping up again, resurrected.

'Come on, Ruthie!'

He handed her the rifle.

'Blow me away!'

And she did.

There was silence afterwards.

A terrible silence fell across the acres of Kells Wood, across Gallows Hill, and for mile upon mile into the future.

That silence will follow Ruthie for the rest of her life.

But Kells Wood remains unperturbed, for it can hold silences and secrets that last a thousand years.